Queerly Beloved

Queerly Beloved

A NOVEL

Susie Dumond

THE DIAL PRESS | NEW YORK

Queerly Beloved is a work of fiction. Names, characters, places, and incidents are the products of the author's imagination or are used fictitiously. Any resemblance to actual events, locales, or persons, living or dead, is entirely coincidental.

A Dial Press Trade Paperback Original

Published in the United States by The Dial Press, an imprint of Random House, a division of Penguin Random House LLC, New York.

LIBRARY OF CONGRESS CATALOGING-IN-PUBLICATION DATA
Names: Dumond, Susie, author.
Title: Queerly beloved: a novel / Susie Dumond.
Description: First edition. | New York: The Dial Press [2022] |
Identifiers: LCCN 2021033742 (print) | LCCN 2021033743 (ebook) |
ISBN 9780593243978 (trade paperback; acid-free paper) |
ISBN 9780593243985 (ebook)
Subjects: LCGFT: Novels. | Lesbian fiction.
Classification: LCC PS3604.U494 Q84 2022 (print) |
LCC PS3604.U494 (ebook) | DDC 813/.6—dc23
LC record available at https://lccn.loc.gov/2021033742
LC ebook record available at https://lccn.loc.gov/2021033743

Printed in the United States of America on acid-free paper

randomhousebooks.com

2 4 6 8 9 7 5 3 1

First Edition

Book design by Susan Turner

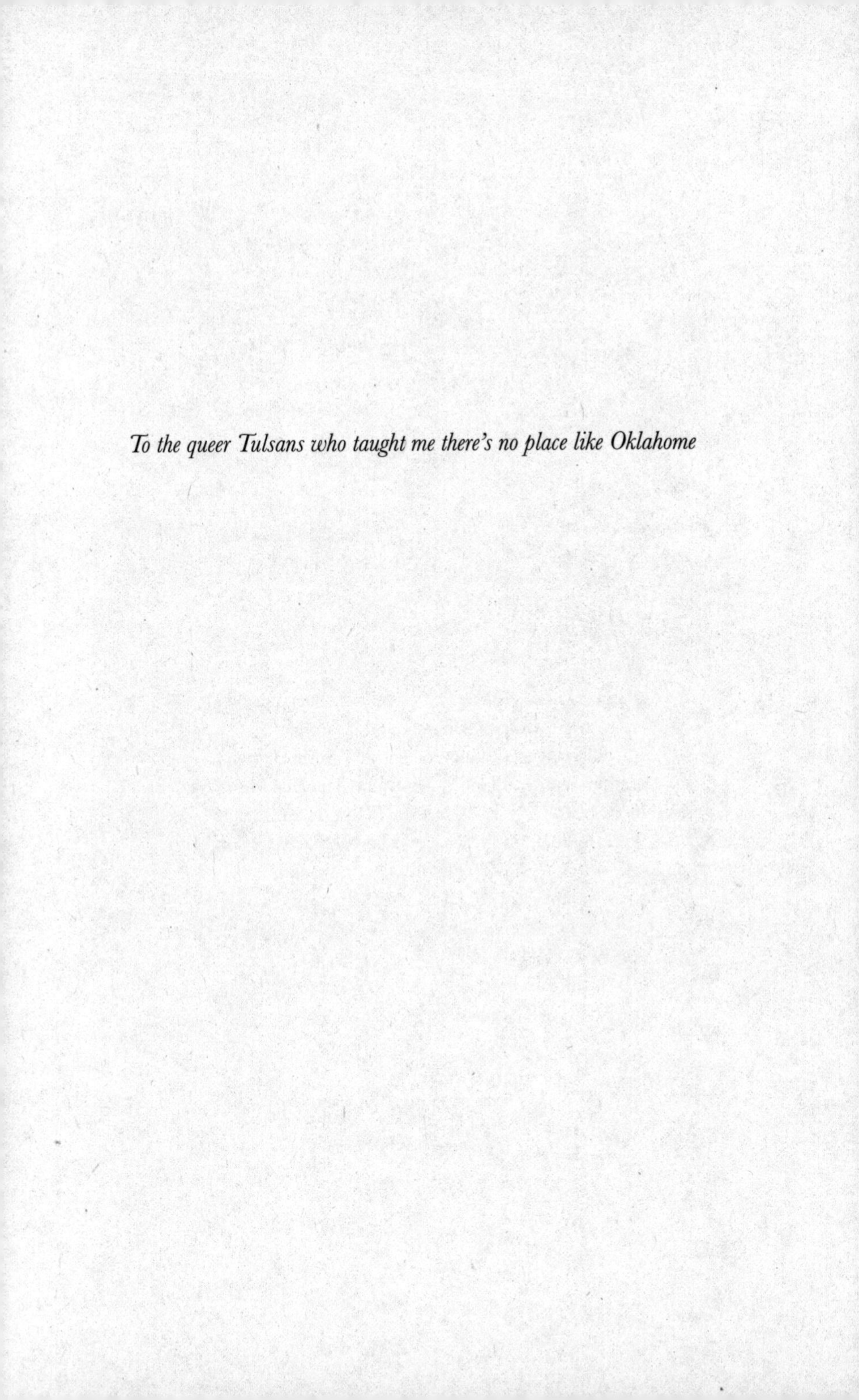

To the queer Tulsans who taught me there's no place like Oklahome

Queerly Beloved

1

Amy breathed a hefty sigh of relief, briefly dropping the customer-is-always-right smile she'd had pasted on her face for the past eight hours. The digital clock on the bakery wall had finally hit noon, marking the end of her shift at Daily Bread, which meant she was only a five-minute drive from collapsing into the worn flannel sheets on her bed.

Her fourth cup of coffee had hardly made a dent in her exhaustion. Even the cool November air rushing through the door as customers entered and exited couldn't keep her alert. She'd been at Daily Bread since 4:00 A.M. with the rest of the kitchen shift, but unlike her fellow bakers, Amy hadn't gone to bed early the night before. She'd hardly had a moment to shower between her start time at the bakery and her closing shift at Ruby Red's. And that shower had been crucial. The smell inside Daily Bread was Amy's favorite in the world: a combination of freshly baked bread, warm vanilla, caramelized sugar, and a touch of cinnamon. She usually arrived home with the scent absorbed deep into her clothes and hair. But Amy couldn't rely on the bakery's thick, sweet air to cover up the equally strong odor of beer and cigarette smoke that lingered whenever she left Ruby Red's. She didn't love the idea of her co-workers judging her for being out late at a bar (which, here, they definitely would). But the main reason she needed to wash away any lingering smell was to make sure they never had a reason to wonder where exactly Amy had been.

When a co-worker appeared to take over Amy's position at the cash register, she gratefully stepped aside and returned to the kitchen to consult her pre-clock-out checklist. Amy headed toward the chalkboard that hung on one of the only wall spaces not covered by cabinets, above the time clock and several framed pictures of the bakery owner's family. There were posed photos of a perfectly coiffed husband, wife, teenage son, teenage daughter, and golden retriever—always forcibly reminding Amy of what she'd find if she googled "stock family photo"—and a few candid shots of the kids playing various sports. Next to her name on the chalkboard, Amy found a note reminding her to frost and rebox a couple of cupcake orders before she left for the day. She sighed and wiped a sheen of sweat from her forehead with the crook of her elbow. At least it was a fun and relatively easy task. She could practically frost cupcakes in her sleep—something she'd often claimed but might now have to prove, since she was all but sleepwalking after back-to-back shifts.

Amy located the two boxes of cupcakes assigned to her tucked among the shelves of unfinished special orders for birthdays, baptisms, baby showers, and Bible studies. Daily Bread was beloved among Tulsa's Christians and especially among members of Tulsa's biggest megachurch, where the bakery owner was a deacon. He was also a successful businessman and city council member known for loudly and publicly endorsing far-right political candidates, and for his favorite catchphrase, "Jesus would have open carried."

The store manager, Donna Young, was his wife. In true Oklahoma tradition, Donna was just as tough as her husband, but her meticulously applied layers of red lipstick and hairspray and her "bless your heart"–isms often caused people to underestimate her. A former employee with a particular gift for sourdough had been shown the door after some good-natured ribbing about Donna's Methodist church choir placing third at a regional choir competition. All it had taken was one joke, one snide comment, and she had been out of a job. Amy, who loved a little friendly teasing, trod carefully around Donna after that.

So maybe Daily Bread didn't have a float in Tulsa's tiny annual Pride parade, but it was undeniably the best bakery in town. Everyone with a sweet tooth or a love of fresh pastries knew that Daily Bread was the place to go, and they were exactly the clientele Amy wanted to woo with her culinary magic, especially if she hoped to attract them to her own bakery someday.

Amy filled a piping bag with raspberry buttercream frosting and got to work. The bag felt like a natural extension of her arm as she swirled pink dollops atop the naked cupcakes. Ever since childhood, Amy had turned to baking when things got tough. She was fairly convinced baked goods could tell if she wasn't giving them her full attention, so having a whisk and spatula in hand always seemed to clear her worried mind. Her mother's cramped kitchen had had no room for bullies or money troubles or existential dread. And as an added bonus, it's hard to hate someone who is always handing out homemade goodies. So over the years, Amy had concocted a recipe for just about every problem she'd encountered. Bad grade on a test? Peanut butter cookies. Messy breakup? Chocolate lava cake. Cousin telling you you're going to hell for being gay? Lemon meringue pie. Total terror about figuring out what to do with your life? Well, that called for getting a job at Tulsa's best bakery.

Amy had learned a ton about baking *and* business during her first year and a half in the kitchen at Daily Bread. Donna let her experiment with new recipes once she grew to trust Amy's work. And a steady flow of customers meant better tips than she'd get at any other bakery in town—even better than at the various server jobs she'd worked before she started at Daily Bread. That's why Amy was willing to hide her personal religious beliefs (or lack thereof) to hold down her job there.

With the first order of cupcakes completed, Amy swapped the raspberry frosting for a piping bag of chocolate ganache and moved to the next box. Sometimes she felt guilty for staying closeted at the bakery, both because she was pretending to be someone she wasn't and because she was allowing her colleagues' homophobia to go unchecked. She felt worse for helping the Young family make more money, some of which they probably donated to harmful anti-LGBTQ organizations and politicians. But a paycheck was a paycheck, and technically, with one of Ruby Red's best bartenders on their payroll, the Young family was financially contributing to Tulsa's queer community, even if they didn't know it. Amy's friends joked that she was the lesbian Robin Hood, stealing from the homophobes to pay the queers (mostly just herself). But she could assuage some of her guilt by knowing she was getting the best bakery training and experience Tulsa had to offer. Amy had lived her whole twenty-five years in Oklahoma. Like any queer person living in a red state (even if it *was* 2013), she knew how to pick her battles—especially after the battle scars she'd gained along the way.

After frosting the second order of cupcakes, Amy topped

them with chocolate-covered espresso beans and taped up the box. She placed the two shiny yellow boxes on a rack of special orders and then untied her apron, stifling a huge yawn. Finally, she was cleared for clock out. But just as she prepared to punch her time card, Amy heard the panicked voice of her co-worker Leanne calling her name. Well, her Daily Bread name.

"Amelia! Thank God you're still here." Leanne burst through the swinging kitchen doors, gripping her cellphone in one hand. Amelia was Amy's official name, but she had never really gone by it except on legal documents. When she'd filled out her application, she'd put her full name on the form, and she'd never bothered to correct her Daily Bread colleagues when they started calling her Amelia. Besides, responding to a different name served as a reminder that she was playing the role of a straight, churchgoing young woman.

Small droplets of sweat glistened around Leanne's auburn hairline. "I just got a call from Connor's school. He vomited in class, and apparently he's running a fever. I'm sorry it's such late notice, but any chance you can stay until six? Someone has to pick him up, but Dave is in a deposition and I can't get a hold of my mom. It would be a lifesaver if you could cover for me."

Internally, Amy screamed. She'd hardly sat down since walking into Ruby Red's eighteen hours earlier. Taking over Leanne's job at the cash register for the afternoon would mean working twenty-four hours straight. Amy's aching feet and back begged her to say no.

But what excuse could she give? "Sorry, I was up all night slinging drinks at that lesbian bar a block away that you probably have no idea exists"? And although she was exhausted, Amy knew the holidays would soon come barreling through her bank account. She also genuinely liked Leanne. Of all her bakery coworkers, Leanne was the closest in age to Amy and the one she could most easily imagine herself hanging out with outside of the kitchen. "Imagine" being the key word—Leanne could only ever know Amelia, not Amy.

But the real reason Amy decided to say yes was simply that she was terrible at saying no. No matter how desperately she needed sleep or food that wasn't a protein bar scarfed down between demanding customers, she couldn't say no to someone who needed her help. Amy was the kind of person who always came through in a pinch, even if that meant it was her getting pinched in the end.

"Of course, Leanne," she said. "No problem."

Leanne's relief was immediate. "Bless you. I owe you one!"

"Don't worry about it. I've got you. Tell Connor I hope he feels better soon!"

Leanne disappeared through the front door with a quick wave. After only a brief moment of self-pity, Amy returned to the kitchen to start a fresh pot of coffee. She would need it.

Thankfully, the rest of the day went by in a blur. Friday was one of the busiest days of the week for the bakery, as customers treated themselves for making it to the weekend. Things only began to wind down fifteen minutes before closing time. The flow of customers trickled to a manageable pace, and the end of Amy's interminable workday was finally in sight. Most of the Daily Bread employees had clocked out after the rush; Amy was tasked with putting away the remaining baked goods and locking up.

She was taking stock of inventory when she heard the loud laughter of her two best friends outside the store. She could identify Joel's merry shrieks and Damian's hearty guffaws from a mile away. Amy had met Joel during freshman orientation at the

University of Tulsa. After being paired up on a campus scavenger hunt, they'd become inseparable, always giggling and scheming and charming their way out of trouble. But now that Damian was in the picture, Amy had forgotten what it was like to be only a duo. Her initial skepticism, due to Joel's history of dating boys who weren't good enough for him, had faded once she got to know Damian. His calm nature and steady presence grounded Joel, and Joel's creativity and high energy kept Damian on his toes. Their perfect dynamic could have made Amy feel like a third wheel, but she was never happier than when she was hanging out with them.

As they came through the bakery door, she saw their demeanors change. They grew quieter and kept a notable distance from each other. Amy peeked through the swinging kitchen door and saw that her only remaining co-worker was washing dishes. "You're good. Donna already left," she said quietly, already sliding the glass door open on the cupcake display. "I thought you were both at Damian's boot camp in the park today, not coming to use me for my employee discount. How did you even know I was working?"

"Hard to miss ol' hell on wheels out there in the parking lot." Joel nodded toward Amy's dilapidated Toyota Corolla rotting away in front of the building, an ancient metal beast with chipping paint and a cracked windshield, made even more frightening by the array of strange noises it emitted whenever she turned it on.

"And boot camp was a success," Damian added. "We already sweat, showered, and beautified ourselves, and now it's time to eat the calories we burned. Please tell me you have Funfetti." He bent to examine the cupcakes of the day. Amy noticed a college student slow her exit from the bakery, straightening her posture and smoothing her hair while looking Damian up and down. With his perfectly sculpted physique, rich brown skin, and short beard carefully maintained to emphasize his chiseled jawline, Damian had someone checking him out in just about every room he entered. Ever humble and grounded, he never seemed to notice when strangers were trying to catch his attention.

"One Funfetti, extra sprinkles." Amy plucked a cupcake from the middle of the tray and set it on a glass plate. "Joel?"

"Chocolate peanut butter?" Joel asked, swiping a finger of frosting from Damian's Funfetti cupcake.

"Sorry, we're out," Amy said.

Joel rolled his eyes and gave a dramatic sigh. "This is worse than when Miley Cyrus and Liam Hemsworth broke up. How am I supposed to go on?" He leaned toward the display, caressing the glass in front of the sign marking the empty peanut butter cupcake tray. "I totally get how she felt writing 'Wrecking Ball' now. 'Don't you ever say I just walked away. I will always want you—'" Joel whisper-sang to the glass before Amy cut him off.

"Cookies and cream?"

Joel immediately dropped the ballad and held out a hand for the cupcake. "Oh, yummy." Like his boyfriend, Joel was distractingly handsome. He had that boy-next-door charm with a stunningly bright smile and hair so perfectly coiffed that it begged comparison to a Ken doll's. Having two hot best friends sometimes made Amy feel like the considerably less hot sidekick, but she could mostly convince herself that their beauty was contagious. Joel and Damian looked like they belonged in a department store catalog, at least one of the ones that weren't too afraid to piss off conservative protestors. But unlike Damian, Joel was perfectly aware of his charms and very lucky that his boyfriend didn't mind his habit of flirting with strangers for special treatment. Joel's flirtatious behavior often doubled his tips when he was bartending alongside Amy at Ruby Red's.

"You're on call tonight, right?" Joel asked. "I'm opening in an hour. Any chance there will be leftover cookies?"

Amy glanced at the mostly empty display. "Still about a half dozen now, so I'd say you're probably in luck. I'm in dire need of some sleep, but I can drop off cookies on my way home." Seeing her best friends had provided a rise in Amy's energy level, but she knew it wouldn't last long. She rang up the two cupcakes and plugged in her employee discount code. "That'll be four-fifty, babe."

Amy took Joel's money and waved goodbye. She'd already started counting out the till when she heard Damian say something at the door and looked up.

"Um . . . yes? Funfetti," he'd said in a guarded voice as the door swung shut. Amy could see him and Joel on the sidewalk talking to someone she didn't recognize who seemed to be on the way in. Damian and Joel looked tense at first, but then Amy heard Joel's laugh, muffled through the closed door. He gestured to the cupcakes, up and down Cherry Street in front of them, and through the window toward Amy. The stranger turned their head toward Amy, who quickly looked down and busied herself with the register. A peal of muffled laughter sounded again from the other side of the bakery window, and by the time Amy looked back up, Damian and Joel were walking away, arm in arm.

The door opened, causing the bell above it to tinkle. When the stranger stepped inside, Amy quickly realized two things: first, that she'd never seen this person before and, second, that theirs was a face she would never forget.

The customer shot Amy a lopsided grin as they approached the counter and bent down to examine the remaining pastries, hazel eyes sparkling through long, dark lashes. One hand rose to smooth the short, carefully coifed hair from their forehead. In a forest-green sweater and perfectly fitted jeans, the stranger was devastatingly attractive. And queer. It wasn't just the short, intentionally choppy hair; there was something about the way they walked, the tension in their shoulders. The customer placed a hand against the counter and looked over Amy's head at the chalkboard menu. Amy glanced at the messenger bag slung across the stranger's torso and saw a small button with the words "she/her" pinned to the strap. *Definitely queer, right?*

Amy was instantly intrigued. Although it wasn't fair to say *all* the queer people in Tulsa knew one another, it wasn't far from the truth. But this person in front of her was unfamiliar. That meant either she was an enthusiastic straight ally who had made surprising hair and fashion decisions for conservative Oklahoma, or she was Amy's lesbian dream girl from out of town, floating in on cinnamon-scented air. Or maybe Amy was so sleep-deprived that she was having some kind of gay hallucination. Where was this person from? Where was she going? What did her laugh sound like? Was she one of those people who hated cilantro?

Amy almost knocked over a tray of quiches in an attempt to wipe off her apron, suddenly hyperaware of how worn-out she must look. Compared to the stranger's fresh, clean appearance, Amy's frizzy hair and flour-dusted dress felt embarrassingly messy. And thanks to the full pot of coffee rushing through her veins, she could feel her eye twitching slightly. She brushed a hand across her cheek, which felt unusually warm. Was she blushing? Amy sometimes wished she could pull off a flawless, stunningly attractive look, but she was forever cursed to be "cute." With her big brown eyes, huggable curves, and deep dimples, she was definitely more of a girl next door than a hot lesbian you'd happily ruin your life for. She gave the customer her best dimple-on-one-side smile.

"Hi! Welcome to Daily Bread. It's your first time here. . . . I mean, sorry, is it your first time here?" Amy said.

The woman's eyes swept from the pastry display to Amy's face, and she laughed, answering one of Amy's million questions. It was a wonderful laugh: melodious, warm. Amy already wanted to hear it again. "Yes, it's my first time. What gave me away?"

"I just didn't think I'd seen you here before, is all." Amy kicked herself internally. Why was she always so awkward around cute queer girls? "Are you, um, from out of town?"

"Just moved here, actually. I'm Charley. She/her pronouns." She tapped the button pinned to her bag. "Thought you might want to know my name since you seem to keep track of your customers."

Amy smiled, embarrassed but pleased and delighted to hear someone share their pronouns in Daily Bread of all places. Plus, was that flirtation in Charley's tone? Or just politeness? Amy did a quick scan of the room to verify that there weren't any other employees in earshot, then replied, "I'm Amy, she/her. Welcome to Tulsa! It's a pretty great place once you get to know it." She'd never introduced herself this way inside the bakery, but maybe because of adrenaline or lack of sleep, she felt daring.

And maybe she hoped she'd get to know this Charley more than the average customer. Amy wondered what had gotten into her. She'd hardly even considered dating someone since a messy breakup with Autumn, her notoriously unfaithful ex, almost a year ago, despite Damian and Joel's constant cajoling to get back on the metaphorical horse.

The door from the kitchen swung open as the last remaining other employee came to collect her portion of the tips from behind the counter, and Amy's magical bubble seemed to burst. Amy and Charley weren't alone; Amy was still on the clock at a Christian bakery, where she was straight, goody-two-shoes Amelia, not gay, flirtatious Amy. Amy gave her co-worker a tight smile as she returned to the kitchen to gather her things. "What can I get you?" Amy asked Charley in a more businesslike tone.

Charley browsed the remaining items in the display case. Amy was suddenly self-conscious about the limited selection after a full day of customers. "I'll take that last croissant," Charley said. "And a coffee, if you have any."

"For here or to go?" With only a few minutes to close, Amy normally would have packaged the order to go without a question. But she hoped Charley would stay, even just a little longer.

Charley looked at a small table by the front window. "For here, thanks."

Amy filled the order and took Charley's money, then watched as she settled at the table and pulled a book out of her messenger bag. *Just when I thought she couldn't do anything to make me like her more,* Amy thought. There was something so attractive about reading in public, something so intimate. After a moment, she remembered that it's weird to stare at strangers as they eat croissants and read books. Begrudgingly, she returned to her closing tasks.

Just as Charley finished her croissant, the last baker reappeared from the kitchen, swinging her coat on. "I need to run to choir practice, but everything in the kitchen is cleaned and shut down. You can lock up, right, Amelia?"

"Yep, I've got it!" Amy replied a little too enthusiastically, but the other baker hardly noticed as she was already halfway out the door and humming scales to warm up. Amy glanced at Charley to see if she'd noticed that her co-worker called her Amelia, but Charley seemed engrossed in her book.

The bell above the bakery door chimed as Amy's co-worker said "Have a good night!" over her shoulder.

Charley looked up. "Oh, I'm sorry. Are you closing? I can go—"

"No, stay. I'm still wrapping some things up, so it's no trouble." Amy left her position behind the counter and used flipping the "Open" sign as an excuse to wander closer to Charley. She tried to subtly look at what Charley was reading and couldn't hold back her excitement when she recognized the title. "Oh, is that David Sedaris?"

"Yes, his newest."

Amy's eyes lit up. Of course, lots of straight people enjoyed his writing, but any hint of queerness was a win. "I love him! My mom and I listen to his Christmas story on NPR every year. That impression he does of . . . Who is it? The jazz singer . . ."

"Billie Holiday!"

"Yes!" Amy laughed just thinking about it. "So good."

"One time in college, I was reading *Me Talk Pretty One Day* in the library and got kicked out because I couldn't stop laughing out loud."

"You're making that up," Amy teased.

"I'm not," Charley said, trying and failing to hold back a grin. "I'm a terrible liar. I get all sweaty and talk too much. I just tell the truth instead. See? I'm doing it right now!"

Amy was charmed, easily returning Charley's smile with one of her own only to feel it faltering a moment later. Being closeted at work and hiding relationships from her family had turned Amy into quite the accomplished liar. Sometimes she put so much energy into being whoever she thought the people around her wanted her to be that she couldn't tell if there was any true "Amy" underneath it all.

Feeling suddenly ashamed, Amy wondered if she should try wearing her heart a little more on her sleeve, at least while they were the only two people in the building. "Be right back," she said, and walked behind the counter to move the last two blueberry muffins from the display case onto two small plates. Amy approached Charley's table again before she could talk herself out of it. "These will go in the trash unless someone eats them now. Do you like blueberries?"

Charley looked up from tucking her book into her messenger bag. "Are you sure? I don't want to keep you here late."

"Consider it a welcome-to-Tulsa gift. But I can put them in a to-go box for you if you're in a hurry."

"Well, since there are two, would you like to join me?" Charley used the toe of her boot to push the empty chair across from her toward Amy. "I'd love to pick your brain about the city."

Amy pulled her apron over her head, slung it across the back of the chair, and sat down heavily across from Charley, her swollen feet tingling with relief. "You can pick my brain about anything you'd like." Was she really being so bold as to flirt with a stranger? Here, of all places? She leaned back and pinched off a bite of the muffin in front of her. "So, where did you move from?"

"Austin." Charley grabbed the second muffin and moved it to the plate that had held her croissant. "Grew up in Houston, but I've been in Austin since college. Have you been?"

"No, but I want to visit! I hear it's the coolest place in Texas. Is that true?"

"I love it! Sad to leave, but it was time to move on for . . . a variety of personal and professional reasons."

Amy nodded, holding herself back from prying into the vague response. "Well, good news for you—Tulsa is apparently positioning itself to become the Austin of Oklahoma. At least that's what the city council hopes. There's a lot of new investment into the arts scene, cool outdoor spaces, making the city more walkable. Maybe I can show you around sometime and you can tell me how Tulsa compares." Amy focused on her muffin, surprised—and a little thrilled—by her own audacity.

"If you show me around Tulsa, maybe one day I can return the favor and show you around Austin," Charley said.

Amy tried to mask her delight under a layer of flirtatious

cool, but she could feel her dimples deepen. "I'd like that. So what brought you to Tulsa?"

Charley described her new job at an oil company, where she had been hired to focus on environmental impact and sustainability. Her passion for her job was evident from the excitement on her face and how quickly she dove into a slew of acronyms and industry terms Amy didn't recognize, despite having grown up in an oil town. Amy did her best to pay attention but was somewhat distracted by Charley's firm and measured gestures while she talked, the quieter laugh that punctuated her sentences, and the devastating way her collarbone peeked out from her V-necked sweater. She'd never found a scientific lecture so sexy. Amy was biting her lip and imagining running her fingers across that collarbone when Charley stopped midsentence. "Sorry, I'm boring you, aren't I? Engineer problems. I get caught up talking about my work."

Amy shook the daydream from her head. "No, not at all! It sounds really interesting." Despite her distraction, it *did* sound interesting—and also a little intimidating. Amy had gotten her degree in theater three years earlier, and her knowledge of costume design and various dialects felt worlds away from the scientific terms Charley was casually dropping. She had no idea what kind of question about sustainable engineering would sound smartest but ventured a guess based on what she'd most recently seen making headlines in Oklahoma: a strange rise in the state's seismic activity, likely related to oil and gas practices. "So will your new job be involved in researching the earthquakes and fracking?"

Charley's eyes instantly lit up, showing Amy that she'd guessed right. "Absolutely! It's the reason I'm most excited to work in Oklahoma. But despite everyone pointing at fracking as the cause, early research shows it probably has more to do with wastewater disposal. It's going to be a huge focus for me. I'll travel to a lot of the fracking sites around the state and track info on seismic activity and hopefully get oil companies on board to change their wastewater practices. It's a huge job, but if I do it right, I feel like I can actually make a difference, you know?"

"That's incredible." Amy racked her brain for an intelligent follow-up question but instead found only bone-deep exhaustion and a caffeine headache. She fiddled with the paper wrapper on her muffin to buy time. "So what do you think of Tulsa so far? Is it what you expected?"

"I haven't had much time to explore it yet, between unpacking and my first week at the new job. I only stopped by here on my way home from work because I couldn't look at any more boxes." She paused to take a bite of the muffin in front of her. "This is delicious, by the way. Thank you."

There was a brief lull in their conversation as they both chewed, during which the silence of the empty bakery seemed to remind them both that it was now past closing time. Finishing her muffin, Charley pushed back her chair and stood to go. Amy felt a rush of unexpected panic at the thought of Charley walking away. Amy didn't know for certain if Charley was interested in women, but they'd definitely been flirting, right? Charley, the dapper engineer hoping to change the world, with her refreshing honesty and that crooked smile, could certainly have her pick of queer women in Tulsa. But Amy, with her long hair, cartoonishly cute face, floral dresses, and practice of hiding her queerness at work, was used to being read as straight. Charley had seemed open to Amy's offer to show her around town, but maybe she wasn't ready to ask out a potentially straight woman. If Amy wanted a shot with Charley, maybe she needed to be the one to make a move.

"Are you serious about a tour? As a lifelong Tulsan, I think

I'd make a pretty good tour guide." Amy took a breath, hoping she sounded more casual than she felt. "I can, uh, show you the cool queer spots in town too, if that's something you'd like. What are you doing tomorrow around noon?"

Charley paused while reaching for her bag, arching an eyebrow. "Are you asking me on a date?"

Amy's heart raced. "Yeah, I think I am. Are you going to say yes?"

"Yeah, I think I am," Charley echoed before furrowing her brow. "Shit, I've got a work thing on Saturday until five. How about that night?"

"I'm going to a family wedding tomorrow evening." Amy made a sour face at the unfortunate timing.

"Yeah, weddings are the worst," Charley said, misinterpreting Amy's expression. "I'm booked on Sunday too. Are you a morning person, by chance?"

"Um, sure?" Amy wasn't really sure what her natural circadian rhythm was anymore, as she mostly worked whenever she could get on the schedule at either of her jobs and crashed into sleep anytime she had a break. Early shifts at the bakery and late shifts at the bar meant she saw her fair share of sunrises. Did that make her a morning person?

"How about a breakfast date? Monday morning, say around six?"

Amy did a quick calculation while Charley stood waiting for an answer. Amy was scheduled to close Ruby Red's on Sunday night, meaning she'd be off around 3:00 A.M., giving her a few hours to make herself presentable. And she had Monday mornings off from Daily Bread, so she could catch up on sleep after the date. Maybe Charley was onto something with this breakfast date idea. "Yeah. Yeah, six A.M. on Monday works." Then she remembered the hacking cough sound her car made on chilly mornings.

She couldn't imagine anything less attractive for Charley than hearing her car drive up or, worse, being inside it. "Any chance you'd want to pick me up? I live just a couple blocks from here."

"Wow, asking me on a date and then asking me to drive. Bold move, baker."

Amy blushed. "Is it working?"

"It is." Charley pulled a pen from her messenger bag and scribbled her number on a napkin, then swung the bag over her shoulder. "Text me your address, and I'll see you Monday morning, bright and early." With a wink that left Amy breathless, she was gone.

2

The next afternoon, Amy sat next to her mother in the old, cushionless back pew of Sheridan Valley Baptist Church, holding a blissfully attentive expression on her face as her cousin Christina's wedding ceremony came to a close.

As children, Amy and Christina had spent countless hours playing "wedding." The two girls would wrap the day's bride (usually Christina, as she was a crucial three months older and therefore in charge) in whatever white materials they could find: old clothes, sheets, towels, even toilet paper if they were desperate. The bride would parade down the hallway, a look of gracious tranquility on her face, as the cousin playing maid of honor hummed a rendition of Wagner's "Bridal Chorus." The groom, usually played by an old family dog, would wag his tail patiently as the cousins improvised wedding vows and dramatic objections from imagined attendees. They lost track of time picturing what they thought would be the most important day of their lives, when they would start their own future families. Christina always spent far too long describing the potential groom for Amy's taste, and Amy would annoy Christina by obsessing over how the officiant would wax poetic about the meaning of love. But no matter where their imaginations took them, each wedding was full of laughter, excitement, and the lofty promise of "till death do us part."

Which is why, as she watched Christina and her new husband begin to return down the aisle, Amy was surprised to find herself disappointed. Sure, they'd grown apart since their childhoods. The cousins had stayed close through the beginning of high school, doing homework side by side in each other's kitchens even though Christina attended Tulsa's most prestigious private high school and Amy went to public school. But after Amy came out during junior year, making plans with Christina had become nearly impossible, and Amy had distracted herself with her high school drama club. By the time they graduated from their respective colleges, they barely spoke, only seeing each other at extended family events, and Amy hardly felt like she knew Christina at all.

But still, this day felt nothing like the weddings they'd dreamed up as children. Christina had been a rambunctious kid, their playtime together full of adventure and mischief. Now Amy wished she could have seen more of her childhood friend in the ceremony. Christina's had felt so generic that it could have been any bride and groom standing at the altar. Amy wasn't sure what it was that made a wedding feel authentic, but whatever it was, she hadn't seen it from the back pew. Would the ceremony have felt different if Amy really had grown up to be the maid of honor she'd always promised Christina she would one day be? Or *had* it been authentically Christina, and Amy just didn't know what that meant anymore?

Amy smiled at Christina and her bridesmaids as they passed her and her mother's pew. With a squint up at the now-empty altar, Amy could picture things differently. Sunflowers, Christina's favorite, instead of roses. A dress with more sparkle and personality. A speech from the pastor that highlighted Christina's sense of humor and optimism. *Maybe a dog ring bearer,* Amy thought with a smile. But to be fair, given that she had been to twenty-two weddings, and all of them had been traditional Southern Baptist events, everything glamorous and enchanting Amy knew about weddings came from fairy tales and rom-coms. And everything she knew about Christina was from before either of them were old enough to drive.

Amy's mother gave her a pat on the knee and a knowing look as they stood to follow the crowd shuffling toward the church's dining hall for the reception. Through a window, Amy caught a glimpse of the bridal party laughing and posing for the photographer in front of the church. In some alternate universe, Amy might have been laughing with them.

When she arrived in the dining hall, Amy was unsurprised to find her nameplate at a table in the back corner of the room, far from the family tables where her mom was assigned to sit. Ever since Amy came out, her place in family gatherings had moved farther and farther away from the action. The worst part was always being seated alone. If only she could bring a date, she'd have someone to keep her company and distract her from the million tiny heartbreaks the Fariner family threw at her. But Amy had yet to be offered a plus-one to any extended family events. In some ways it was fun to imagine whispering and giggling alongside some stunning woman among the outraged guests. In other ways, not so much.

"You 'kay, hon?" her mom asked under her breath before they parted. Amy gave her a tight nod, pushing down the heavy feeling in her chest. She'd survived many family weddings with her mother's support. After the reception, they'd decompress together, turning the snide remarks and snubs into jokes to laugh away the lingering pain. For the moment, all she could do was smile through it alone.

But then came the part of the wedding she could really get behind: the food. In a wise move, Christina and her new husband had paid the kind old ladies who usually cooked for church events to whip up a wedding feast of Christina's favorite dishes. It finally felt like something true to Christina and the toilet-paper-wedding days of yore—and was exactly the comfort food Amy needed to gracefully ignore the glances reserved for the family's black sheep. Amy happily made her way to the back of the line for the buffet of Oklahoma's most important food groups: barbecue, fried chicken, cornbread, and gravy.

A tap on her shoulder distracted Amy from hungrily eyeing a serving platter of fried okra. "Oh, hi, Aunt Sheila! The wedding was lovely," Amy said, smiling politely, surprised that with so many guests to entertain, Christina's mother had chosen to approach her.

A glimmer of sweat was forming at the edges of Aunt Sheila's blond football helmet of a bob, sprayed within an inch of its life to make it stay put throughout her responsibilities as mother of the bride. "Amy, thank heavens I caught you. Can you come with me? We have a bit of an emergency."

Before Amy could nod, she felt the tips of her aunt Sheila's acrylics gripping her upper arm and pulling her from the buffet line. Her barbecue dreams promptly disappeared. Amy was about the last person she would expect her family to look to during a church wedding emergency. "What's the situation, exactly?" Amy jogged to keep up as her aunt wove through the crowd.

"The wedding cakes were delivered during the ceremony," Aunt Sheila said in an undertone, turning her head in Amy's direction even as she sped up. "We ordered a peacock groom's cake for Tom. They've been his favorite animal since he studied abroad in Sri Lanka during college, you know."

"Sure." Amy had not known this about Tom. In fact, she wasn't entirely sure she knew how his last name was spelled.

"And I promise you I said it completely clearly on the phone. The woman said, 'Oh yes, we do those all the time. Birthday parties, bachelorette parties, you name it.'" Sheila pushed through a set of swinging doors into the church kitchen. "I thought, *Wow, I guess peacocks are a pretty popular bird.*"

They stepped into the industrial light of the kitchen, the smell of hot oil lingering in the air. A group of aproned women stood around a table across the room, their whispers coming to a halt as Sheila and Amy entered.

"Anyway," Sheila went on, "there must have been some kind of miscommunication." The women parted as Amy and her aunt Sheila approached, revealing a three-tier white wedding cake and a large closed cake box beside it. "Instead, we got this . . . this . . . Well, you'll have to look for yourself."

Amy swallowed before lifting the corner of the lid, then threw a hand over her mouth, stunned—and trying to stifle the laugh threatening to spill over.

Sheila cleared her throat. "When I said '*pea*cock,' I guess they only heard . . . Oh, I can't say it in church."

"I can't look, it's so vulgar," one of the church ladies said as she fanned herself with a paper plate.

Sheila sighed. "Please, Amy. Can you do something? Anything? I'm worried the bridal cake won't be enough to serve everyone, and we can't present this monstrosity. Granny would have a heart attack. Again."

Amy closed the lid and pinched her lips together, barely suppressing a giggle. Maybe she wasn't Christina's maid of honor, but at least now she had a concrete way to participate in this wedding. Professional bakers didn't get called on in emergencies all that often. Amy imagined a flight-attendant voice over an intercom: *Are there any bakers on the plane? We have an emergency.*

"How long until cake is served?" Amy asked, standing straighter.

"An hour, maybe an hour and a half if we do toasts first," Sheila said.

"I've got this, Aunt Sheila. Don't worry about it. Just buy me as much time as you can, and I'll figure something out."

Sheila's shoulders dropped as she sighed with relief. "Thank you, Amy. I'm so glad you're here."

That was something she hadn't heard from a member of her extended family in a long time. As much as she didn't want to care, Amy felt a small burst of warmth. Sometimes being needed didn't feel so different from being loved.

Amy jumped into action the moment the kitchen doors swung shut behind her aunt. She tasked the church ladies with finding an apron, a stand mixer, ingredients for buttercream frosting, and a piping bag before she turned back to the cake box. After tying her unruly hair in a knot on top of her head, she opened the box again.

Although she would never tell her aunt Sheila, Amy had a fair amount of experience making dick cakes, mostly for friends' birthday parties or gag gifts. In fact, she had more experience with the pastry versions of dicks than with real-life models and, as such, usually went for a more cartoonish decoration style. She had to agree with the scandalized church ladies that the hairy balls and veins on this one were a bit much. Amy pulled out her phone and snapped a picture of the cake, already making a mental list of the people in her life who would appreciate the visual supplement to what was shaping up to be a very memorable story.

She turned to find one of the church ladies behind her, sliding an industrial-sized bag of powdered sugar onto the table. Amy blushed as she tucked her phone into her pocket. “Sorry, just trying to, um, get photographic perspective before I redesign.”

The woman slid her bifocals down her nose. “Is that what the kids these days call a dick pic?”

A quick laugh escaped Amy’s lips. “Yes, ma’am, I think you’re correct.”

With a glance over her shoulder, the woman turned conspiratorially to Amy. “If we didn’t need to serve such a big crowd, I might have snuck that cake home with me. I think my bridge club would appreciate it much more than these prudish old cows.”

Amy raised an eyebrow, surprised to find such an entertaining ally amid the Sheridan Valley Baptist Church kitchen crew. “It’s quite the work of art,” Amy said. “But unfortunately, I think I have to do some revising.”

“What’s the plan?”

“Well, I’ll start by taking off all the frosting I can. This, um, peachy color is no good for a peacock.” Amy pulled a spatula from a nearby counter and began scraping frosting from the cake. “There’s not enough time to do a very detailed bird, but with the right colors, I think I can get close enough. The shape is the tricky part. I’d need something with a little more structure to make the plumage erect.”

Catching her own mistake, Amy turned to the woman, aghast. The church lady’s blue-tinted hair trembled with her effort to keep in a laugh. Unable to hold back once their eyes met, the two burst out in giggles.

"Beatrice, please don't tell me you're making dirty jokes in the Lord's house again!" one of the other women chided from across the kitchen.

"Worry about yourself, Louise!" Beatrice shouted. "We need butter and milk stat!"

With the help of the church ladies, a bowl of buttercream, and an armful of rice cereal bars, Amy managed a reasonable approximation of a peacock in under an hour. It wasn't as detailed as she would have preferred, but considering what she'd had to work with, it was pretty impressive—and certainly less phallic if you weren't looking too closely. Once she washed up and returned to the reception, she tracked down Aunt Sheila and gave her a subtle thumbs-up from across the dining hall. Sheila visibly relaxed before returning to her conversation with the pastor's wife. Resolving the cake dilemma had left Amy feeling lighter than before. It wasn't the role in Christina's wedding she'd pictured for herself, but it was nice to feel like she'd contributed to Christina's special day in some way.

Although the buffet was picked over by the time she arrived, Amy was still able to pile her plate with plenty of food. If there was one thing Oklahoma cooks got right, it was always making more than enough food to go around. She'd just settled down at her place in the back and finished introducing herself to the rest of the table when her uncle Terry stood to begin toasts. Amy raised her glass of sparkling water, wishing that it could somehow magically transform into champagne. A nice drink would have been lovely after the stressful rush to repair the groom's cake. But she'd had enough experience with Southern Baptist weddings to know the drill.

Amy stuffed the last few bites of potato salad into her mouth as the toasts concluded. She could see her mom laughing with some of her aunts and uncles at a table at the front of the room. She looked away, deciding to make her own fun no matter where she was seated. Years in the hospitality industry had made Amy a master of small talk. She could break the ice with anyone, whether a cute queer customer at the bakery or Christina's wedding guests.

Amy turned to the two strangers to her right and dug in her brain for the names they'd provided when she first sat down. "Regi and Jared, right? I'm Amy, Christina's cousin. How do you know the couple?"

Jared swallowed a mouthful of baked beans. "I'm Tom's co-worker."

"And I'm his plus-one." Regi smiled warmly. "Nice to meet you."

Jared looked across the table to the other guests, who were deep in conversation about the University of Oklahoma versus the Oklahoma State University football team. He leaned across Regi and lowered his voice. "So, uh, when do the real drinks come out?"

Amy gave Jared a sympathetic smile. "You haven't been to a Southern Baptist wedding before, have you?"

"Um, I guess not. My family's weddings are mostly Jewish."

"And my family's nondenominational," Regi added.

"Well, not all Baptist weddings are this"—Amy looked for a nice way to describe her family's weddings—"strict, I guess I'd say? I try to focus on the food. It's always the best part."

"I'm always down for some epic barbecue." Regi nodded down at her nearly empty plate.

Jared glanced at their tablemates, who were still intensely debating the merits of the two football teams' new recruits, then whispered to Amy, "You know, we have something a little more festive to toast with, if we'd like to offer a private cheers to the newlyweds. Is there somewhere we could maybe listen to a few tunes and celebrate?" He pulled open the side of his suit jacket, revealing a silver flask peeking out of the top of an inner pocket.

In response, Amy reached under her chair and pulled a thick Bible from her sizable purse. She lifted the cover and angled it so that Regi and Jared could see the flask hidden within the carved-out book. "I think we're on the same page."

Amy quickly closed the cover, slid it back into her purse, and threw the bag over her shoulder. She usually reserved her backup drinks and hidden church spot for when she and her mom needed a break from family. But seeing Teresa deep in conversation across the room, she knew her mom wouldn't mind. "Follow my lead."

A few minutes later, Amy was leading the way up a flight of stairs to a Sunday school room she'd visited as a child, Regi and Jared close behind. She dug in a toy cupboard and emerged with three plastic teacups covered in purple and pink butterflies, which she scrubbed in a small sink while her new friends explored the room.

Once they were clean, Amy filled each teacup with a generous slosh from her flask and handed two of them to Jared and Regi. "To Christina and Tim—"

"Tom," Jared corrected.

"Tom! Yes, sorry. To Christina and Tom: May their lives together be filled with joy and merriment and their love be as crispy fresh as that fried chicken."

"Hear, hear!" cheered Regi as they clinked their cups—well, it was really more of a thunk than a clink, the cups being plastic—and tossed back the vodka. Amy shuddered as she felt the burn of the cheap liquor.

Settling themselves as best as they could on a set of child-sized plastic chairs, they chatted for a while about Jared's work with Tom at an oil company and Regi's job as a museum curator before the conversation inevitably turned to Amy's profession.

"I'm, um, in the service industry. I work at a bakery, and I bartend on the side." It was nothing to be ashamed of—something she had to tell herself every time she felt her face turn red as she shared it with a new acquaintance. She actually really enjoyed both of her jobs. But she hated the glazed eyes that often met her in response, the way some people would immediately start searching for someone more interesting, someone with more power and influence to chat up. Luckily, her two new friends seemed interested.

"That's awesome! Which bakery?" asked Regi, readjusting her skirt while balancing on her tiny chair. "We did a cake tasting at, like, every bakery in town while we were picking someone to make our wedding cake. We're getting married two weeks from today."

"Congratulations!" Amy said. "Wedding cakes are one of my favorite things to make. More work but so satisfying. I work at Daily Bread, the one on Cherry Street."

Jared's eyes lit up. "No way! That's the bakery we chose to make our cakes! The raspberry mint cake blew my mind."

Now it was Amy's turn to light up. "I actually created that recipe," she said, trying to temper her pride with the right amount of humility.

"Seriously?" Jared said. "No fucking way! That cake—"

"Jared! We're in a church!" Regi said. "Speaking of which, with that fancy Bible flask trick, I wouldn't have pegged you for working at such a conservative bakery. There's been Christian pop music playing, like, every time I've been in there."

"I prefer to call it 'the Holy Spirits,' thank you. And yeah, I never expected to know every MercyMe song ever written, but you learn to tune it out after a while. Speaking of cakes," Amy said, leaning in, "can I show y'all something? And it's probably best if this information isn't shared with the rest of the wedding guests."

"What happens in the Sunday school room stays in the Sunday school room," Regi said reverently.

Amy explained the whole caketastrophe and showed them the premakeover photo. Tears of laughter rolled down Regi's face as Jared begged Amy to text the photo to him.

"I can't wait to see the finished product," Regi said. "I have no idea how you managed to make that look like a peacock."

"I think I did about as well as I could given the limited time and resources, but at the end of the day, it's a penis cake with feathers."

Jared refilled their teacups from his flask. Amy was glad for this invitation to stay upstairs a bit longer. She knew they'd need to get back downstairs soon, but Christina and Tom had been in the middle of their sizable visiting line when they'd sneaked away, so she figured they had no reason to rush. Plus, she was having a good time. "So tell me more about your wedding." An easy conversation starter but also a topic Amy genuinely enjoyed. Joel and Damian were the only friends of hers who knew about her love of rom-coms and *Say Yes to the Dress*. If the rest of her queer friends found out about her love of weddings, she would be sure to lose some hip-lesbian-bartender street cred.

Regi chatted amiably about their location (a new art studio), colors (raspberry and navy), and flowers (calla lilies and Queen Anne's lace). By the time she described her plans to have an artist painting during the reception, Amy was beginning to feel a little warm and fuzzy, thanks to the combination of wedding talk, new friends, and her and Jared's flasks. "Can I tell y'all a secret?" Amy looked behind her theatrically before whispering, "I *love* weddings. I know, I know! It's not cool or trendy or whatever to like weddings. I'm supposed to be like, *Blech, weddings, so sappy and expensive.* But seeing two people making a big, scary promise to love each other forever, no matter what? In front of all of their families and friends? In this world, where people change and everything goes wrong all the time? That's brave as hell, and I love to see it."

"Good weddings can be fun, but bad weddings are so bad," Regi said. "No offense to Christina and Tom! But before we met you, this wedding probably would have fallen solidly in the bad-wedding column for me."

Jared gulped the last of the liquid from his plastic teacup. "The actual wedding part is usually a snoozefest, but I love a good reception. A DJ and a dance floor could have turned this reception around for sure."

Amy agreed but couldn't help thinking about how bizarre this situation was. Her younger self never would have believed that she would spend her closest cousin's wedding hiding in some Sunday school room, laughing with a couple of strangers about how bland the wedding was. Maybe it felt special to Christina—Amy sincerely hoped so, but couldn't be sure. The truth was that she and her cousin didn't really know each other anymore. Amy had thought she'd come to terms with that years ago, so she was surprised to find that she was nearly on the verge of tears.

She needed a pep talk, and she was not afraid to give one to herself. "You know what?" Amy tucked a loose curl behind her ear, only for it to immediately bounce back to where it had been before. "It's a real loss for Christina that she asked all of my other cousins to be her bridesmaids instead of me, just because I'm—" She barely caught herself before spilling the lesbian beans. Regi and Jared seemed cool, and as a Black woman and a white man in a relationship in Oklahoma, they probably knew what it was like to have strangers judge them unfairly. But coming out in this setting felt all wrong. "Because I don't go to their church," Amy said. "But you know what? She needed someone with a good eye to fix those wonky centerpieces, and her dress was laced up all wrong in the back. I'm sure I would have noticed that the groom's cake was wrong hours ahead of time, not during the reception." Amy was on a roll, emphasizing each point with her empty teacup and finding, partially thanks to the memory of that ridiculous cake, that she now felt more like laughing than crying. Regi nodded encouragingly and Amy went on. "I'm awesome at crafting and Pinterest and all of that shit. I do my best work under pressure. I live for the wedding drama—and there's *always* wedding drama."

"Plus, you have an emergency Bible and know all the best church speakeasies," Jared added gallantly.

"Exactly! It was Christina's loss for sure." Amy eyed the wall clock above the door. "Anyway, we should probably head back downstairs."

As Amy made to stand, Regi leaned forward and placed a hand on her knee, her eyes alight. "This is going to sound weird, but what size dress do you wear?"

Amy self-consciously hugged her arms around the curve of her stomach. "A twelve. Why?"

"Oh my God. Oh my God!" Regi bounced out of the tiny, awkward chair and began pacing around the room. "This is going to sound strange, but my friend Andrea was supposed to be my bridesmaid, and she just got this incredible new job in Dubayy and had to move before the wedding. We were just going to deal with having more groomsmen than bridesmaids, but I actually could use some help from someone crafty on the big day, and we already have her dress, and it's a size twelve, and it just seems like fate! Could you . . . Would you be my bridesmaid?"

It did sound strange to Amy. "That sounds super fun, but you can't mean it. It's your special day! You don't want some stranger around in all the pictures."

"I'm a little tipsy, but I swear the offer will still stand when I'm sober!" Regi said. "Like, what are the chances? You just said how much you love weddings and what a great bridesmaid you would be, and here I am with an extra size-twelve bridesmaid dress and bouquet. God forbid we have some—what did you call it?—some caketastrophe. And yeah, we just met, but you're cool. Right, Jared?"

Jared considered the two women in front of him. "It's going to be an awesome party. There will be a DJ and no secret partying in kids' church rooms or wherever we are. And we're getting catering from Regi's cousin's mac and cheese food truck."

"Oh my God, Cheesy Noods? I love them!" Amy was no stranger to the gourmet vendor's smoked Gouda and mushroom mac, and she *had* eaten it in front of *Four Weddings* too many times to count.

"I know this seems impulsive, but I have good instincts about people. Just come have a good time! Have a free meal!" Regi gave Amy a pleading look.

"Well, you *are* speaking my language," Amy said with a cautious smile. "Fun wedding, free food, and impulsive, high-stakes, last-minute plans." A swooping feeling in her stomach reminded Amy of her most recent impulsive plan—her date with Charley, only a day and a half away. She was on a roll when it came to meeting cool strangers.

"Plus," Regi added, "you'd be paired with Jared's friend Ross, who is super cute *and* single, if you're looking."

Amy chuckled, the image of Charley still in her head. "No, that's okay."

"Fine, then you could bring your own plus-one!"

Partly to change the subject, Amy said, "The thing is, I usually work at the bar on Saturday nights. It would be tough to pass on the tips, and I already had to call out for tonight." Amy was embarrassed to admit that giving up a second bar shift in one month would make it difficult to make rent, but it was simply her reality.

"How much do you make in a shift? Two hundred bucks?" Jared asked. Amy hesitated, thinking that $200 would be amazing for one night at Ruby Red's. "We were planning to pay for Andrea's hotel room, but since she's not coming, we've got two hundred fifty dollars back in the budget. What if we just give you that to make up for what you would have made bartending?"

Amy felt torn. She hated saying no to anyone, especially people she liked and especially when she might actually be able to help. Plus, the spontaneous part of her loved the idea of a totally random challenge. But she'd never heard of anyone doing something like this before. Didn't it seem too good to be true? And honestly, Regi and Jared barely knew her. It might be fun to hang out with her rather than sit through a stiff reception, but what if they realized she wasn't so interesting in the light of day, compared to their closest friends and family? Also, $250 seemed like a lot of money for something she might have done just for the free Cheesy Noods. Then again, it was *a lot* of money, money she could definitely use. Should she negotiate them down? Amy's instincts all seemed to be in conflict.

She looked at Regi's earnest face and took a deep breath. "That's ridiculously generous of you," Amy started. "But—"

Before she could finish, Regi grabbed Amy's hands and gave her a pointedly sober look. "It would be worth two hundred fifty dollars to my sanity if you would help me fix wonky centerpieces and check to see if my dress is laced correctly and make sure we don't have to serve my grandparents a penis cake. Honestly. Please?"

Amy's desire to please—both Regi *and* her bank account—

won out. “All right, I’m in. Yes, I’ll be your bridesmaid!” Regi squealed in delight as she grabbed Amy’s phone and typed in her number.

“So it’s settled!” Jared cheered. “Can we go eat the dick cake now?”

3

Amy woke up the next morning in a good mood. Sunday shifts at Daily Bread were easily her favorite. The bakery opened late to allow employees to attend church services, time Amy instead spent catching up on sleep, although she usually arrived in her Sunday best. It didn't hurt to pretend she'd spent her morning in a pew. This Sunday, Amy also thought she'd clean up in case a certain charming new-in-town lesbian dropped by. While imitation church clothes weren't her first choice for seducing Charley, Amy knew exactly how well they accentuated her curves.

Plus, she was excited to visit her unofficial family before her shift started. After Christina's wedding, she'd made a birthday cake to drop off with her uncle Max on her way to the bakery. Although Max wasn't technically her uncle, he and his husband, Greg, had played a much bigger role in her childhood than any of her real uncles and aunts. They were her mother's lifelong friends, her Joel and Damian, and they'd always come through for Teresa when she needed an extra hand or moral support.

Teresa had met Greg as a classmate in grad school, a time when she had learned for herself how cold the Fariner family could turn when you made a life choice they deemed inappropriate. Her decision to pursue a PhD in education and become a professor had been at odds with the family's expectations for her to become a stay-at-home wife and mother. Greg and his partner, Max, both intimately familiar with being ostracized by family for following your heart, took Teresa under their wings. A few years later, Teresa got pregnant and, knowing Amy's father would never be in the picture, took on the Herculean task of single parenthood. While Teresa's family was scandalized, Max and Greg were supportive from day one, stepping up to make sure Amy and Teresa never felt alone. During Amy's childhood, Max and Greg were at every birthday and Christmas and kindergarten play. Max, a professional hairstylist, gave Amy and Teresa a lifetime of free haircuts. He and Greg even helped fund Amy's college education.

And as Amy got older, they became the mentors who showed her what it meant to be queer and out in the Bible Belt. She had been in high school, working behind the scenes of a community theater production of *Little Shop of Horrors,* when she fell for the college-aged lesbian stage manager. Nothing really happened beyond a make-out session at the cast party, but it was enough for Amy to realize she was gay. Her first call was to Max and Greg, who celebrated with her and gave her tips for coming out to Teresa. Later, they taught her the hard truths about how to get by as a queer person in Tulsa, like watching your surroundings, avoiding PDA in public, and changing your partner's pronouns in uncertain situations. They educated her about how she had it easier as a cisgender white woman and taught her to use that privilege to protect her friends who didn't have the same advantages. But they also showed her the best parts of being queer: the amazing people, the cool hangouts, and above all, the freeing power of living authentically.

While she was dropping off the German chocolate cake, Max's favorite, the couple convinced Amy to stay for a cup of coffee and a chat. Max caught Amy up on the construction of his new salon, and Amy shared the story of the peacock cake, which proved to be a hit. All in all, the brief visit was certainly worth being a few minutes late to the bakery.

But as Amy entered the kitchen to clock in, conversation ceased. All eyes turned to her before everyone quickly returned to their tasks—exactly the way people act when the subject of their discussion comes in unexpectedly. How late *was* she? Amy checked the clock, but it was only three minutes past eleven.

"Hi, everyone! How's it going?" she said, deciding to go for cheerful nonchalance. She was greeted with a few mumbled responses. Amy wasn't the most popular employee at Daily Bread, as most of the bakers attended the same church and were friends outside of the kitchen. But this cold response was unusual. Amy felt a sense of unease as she pulled an apron over her pink dress and picked up the list of cakes to be made by the end of the day. Had she forgotten to do something when she closed the bakery on Friday? She'd been distracted, sure, but closing was easy. She couldn't think of anything she'd done incorrectly. Maybe it didn't have anything to do with her. Was Donna in a bad mood? The door to her office was closed, but a crack of light from under the door showed that she must be inside. Had someone been fired?

Amy gathered the ingredients for a pumpkin spice cake and got to work, trying to shake off the eerie silence in the kitchen. Just as the batter came together, the door to the manager's office opened. Donna stepped into the kitchen, arms akimbo beside her shoulder pads and mauve pencil skirt.

"Good morning, ladies!" she said. "God has blessed us with another beautiful day." The bounce in her step and thoroughly teased hair suggested she was in a particularly pleasant mood. Amy took this as a positive sign; maybe she'd misread the room. Donna strode around the bakery, criticized the muffin display, demanded that someone rewrite the daily specials on the chalkboard behind the register in a more feminine cursive, and then came to a stop over Amy's shoulder. "Amelia dear, can I see you for a moment please?"

Her stomach suddenly felt as if she had swallowed a barbell. Donna had never asked her to her office before. Amy felt as if she were being called out of class to go to the principal's office.

"I'm almost finished with this batter," she said. "Should I get it in the oven first?"

"No, someone else can handle that. Leanne! Can you see to this cake please?" Donna strode to her office door and held it open, turning back to Amy. "Come on in."

The few steps it took to reach Donna's office felt like miles. Once they were both inside, Donna shut the door firmly behind them. "Have a seat."

Amy perched on the edge of the wooden chair across from Donna's desk and fidgeted with the hem of her vintage floral dress. "Hi, Donna. How are you today?"

"Oh, just peachy." Donna straightened a pile of papers on her desk. "How long have you worked here, Amelia?"

"Almost two years, ma'am." Was she getting a raise? Amy wondered wildly. Maybe everyone was behaving strangely because they were jealous?

Donna plucked a pair of scissors from the pen drawer of her desk and spun the handle around one polished finger. "Two years, wow. Time flies!" She chuckled. "And in that time, I really thought we'd gotten to know you."

Amy's first reaction was irritation. It was laughable for Donna to act as if she knew anything about "Amelia." *You think you've really gotten to know me even though you've never asked me a single question about myself?* Amy thought. *Even though you probably don't know my last name off the top of your head?*

But her next reaction was a familiar panic. Ever since her first day at the bakery, she'd worried about getting outed. She constantly assessed the expressions of her co-workers, over-analyzing every frown to see if they were on her trail. Worst-case scenarios played out in her head daily, reminding her to dot her heterosexual *i*'s. She racked her brain, trying to think of what could have potentially tipped Donna off. On Friday, Amy had made sure that everyone else had left before her conversation with Charley veered from casual customer banter to flirtatious territory, and the bakery didn't have cameras inside. Had someone seen her leaving or arriving at Ruby Red's? The bar was only a block away, so she always parked behind the building, even outside of the bakery's regular hours. If one of her co-workers had seen her drive behind the building, what was the likelihood they knew it housed a lesbian bar? She'd taken every precaution, but a sense of foreboding hung heavy in the room.

"What's your relationship like with our Lord and Savior, Jesus Christ?" Donna said.

Amy's stomach twisted. So this was it, the moment she'd dreaded since she'd first delivered her résumé to Donna's desk. Somehow Donna had found her out. Any remaining doubts—or hopes—she harbored were quickly extinguished with Donna's next words.

Donna laid the scissors on her desk and leaned in. "It's come to my attention that you're not leading a godly life, Amelia."

Amy sat silently, her heart pounding in her throat.

"As you know," Donna continued, "my husband and I do our best to live our lives as the Lord wants us to, and we expect the same of our employees. And as the Bible tells us, homosexuality is a mortal sin in the eyes of the Lord. We cannot and will not tolerate it at Daily Bread."

Amy's first thought was to lie, to defend herself, to deny. But there was a difference between omitting discussion of her love life, dressing up on Sundays, intentionally keeping her life outside of work as vague as possible, making sure her friends knew to call her Amelia if they ever came in, and *actually* saying she wasn't gay. Or at least that *felt* different. In the time it took for her to breathe in and out, Amy felt humiliated, guilty, ashamed that she felt guilty, guilty that she felt ashamed, and then the first spark of anger. Anger was definitely preferable to humiliation. This was so unfair. Yes, she'd chosen to remain closeted at the bakery, but she would never have been able to work there otherwise, to get this degree of training along with a reasonable paycheck. Nobody should have to hide who they are to learn how to make pâte à choux and be able to pay rent at the same time. Even though this was a scene she'd feared for the past two years, it still felt like a shock now that it was actually happening. And why *was* it happening? Which of her co-workers had betrayed her?

Amy looked at Donna's smug, self-righteous face and fought the urge to ask how she'd found out. It didn't matter at the end of the day, but mostly, she didn't want to give Donna another opportunity to deny her something. "Are you firing me because I'm gay?" Amy asked. She knew the answer was yes. It wasn't even illegal. She just wanted to hear Donna admit it, hoping it would give her some of the same feeling of self-righteousness Donna felt in this moment. If she had to walk out of the bakery after this horrible indignity, she preferred to do it knowing she'd made Donna spell out her own prejudice.

"No, dear." Donna shook her head, feigning dismay. "I'm firing you because you have a clear disregard for the family values of this bakery, and we cannot financially or spiritually support your sinful lifestyle."

To her horror, Amy felt tears fill her eyes. Crying when angry was a terrible reflex of hers, and she hated that it was happening now, of all times. Amy bit her tongue and looked away for a moment to collect herself. Her gaze landed on yet another family photo before shifting up to a decorative poster over Donna's shoulder that read, in huge pastel cursive, "Love thy neighbor as thyself." The irony was not lost on Amy.

Even though she knew Donna was being cruel, and she *knew* it was prejudiced to fire someone over their sexuality, there was something about Donna's self-possession and air of authority that, for a moment, made Amy feel not only as if she'd done something wrong but as if she *were* something wrong. She had always been a good student in school and a reliable employee at all of her jobs and had always been mortified on the rare occasions when she hadn't met expectations. Even now, some deeply ingrained instinct to please told her to apologize, to beg Donna to reconsider, not because it was what Amy wanted to do, but because that was the kind of reaction she suspected Donna thought would be most appropriate. But the more honest part of herself, the part responsible for her angry tears, was so damn tired. Tired of baking her heart out while simultaneously keeping her heart walled up. Tired of inventing some of Daily Bread's bestselling baked goods while spending every moment afraid of this exact situation.

She was *good* at this job. Maybe even great. And if Donna

couldn't see that through her own bigotry, then she didn't deserve Amy as an employee.

Before she could lose her nerve, she stood. Donna looked momentarily taken aback by the hostile screech of Amy's chair sliding against the tile floor. Amy took advantage of the moment to speak. "I've been a great employee for you. I work hard. I've come up with some of your most popular new recipes. I'm always on time. The customers love me. So yeah, I'm gay. But you might want to take a closer look at your own little trite Jesus-isms. Gay people, queer people, trans people—we're all people too. *We're* the neighbors Jesus told you to love. We have feelings and families and dreams. You're the one making yourself miserable because you can't handle us being happy with ourselves. And you might be able to fire us, but you can't get rid of us. No matter what you do, we'll always be here. We're your hairdressers, your siblings, your mail carriers, your children, even your pastors." Amy paused for breath, her chest heaving. She was pretty sure that last part wasn't true for Donna's church, but she figured pointing out that there was queerness within Christian circles too would get under Donna's skin.

Before Amy could think of what else to say, Donna stood too. Her composure had cracked; the self-righteous calm was gone, replaced by fury and something else less definable. Was it fear?

"How dare you?" Donna's face was bright red, even through her thick foundation and powder. She seemed nearly beyond words in her righteous indignation. "You don't . . . This just confirms everything I . . . You people are sick, spewing this nonsense. Get out. Now."

Amy didn't need asking twice. With the pull of a string, she lifted her apron above her head and threw it across Donna's desk before leaving the office and slamming the door behind her.

Amy felt as if she physically collided with the hustle and

bustle of the kitchen and all its familiar smells. It was jarring to see business as usual, to realize that the rest of the world hadn't shattered as Amy felt hers just had. All of Amy's co-workers turned to her at once with widened eyes, the door slam seeming to reverberate around the room, before each looked away again to busy themselves with their various tasks. In that moment, Amy realized two things: that they all knew what had happened—she hadn't exactly kept her voice down—and that none of them were going to do anything about it. All of these people, who each presumably contained at least an ounce of human kindness, were going to stand by and watch this happen without coming to her defense. Or even, at the very least, asking if she was okay. She looked desperately toward Leanne, but she stared intently into her stand mixer. Amy stood there for a long moment, thinking of all the times she had defended these women to her friends when they called them fake, hypocritical, closed-minded. Just two days before, she'd worked twenty-four hours straight to cover for Leanne when she needed help. Was it worth it now? Then again, she realized, maybe they were just doing what Amy had done for the past two years: hiding their true feelings about the situation in order to protect their jobs.

Amy threw back her shoulders and walked with all the confidence she could muster to gather her coat from the far end of the kitchen. Then, without a word, she pushed through the swinging kitchen doors into the front of the bakery, unlocked the front door, and burst into the parking lot with a jagged intake of fresh air. As soon as she climbed into her car, the tears began in earnest, sliding down her cheeks in hot streaks. At least she'd parked facing the street instead of the bakery's interior. She turned her key in the ignition only to hear a mighty whine, the engine refusing to turn over. Amy desperately turned the key again, begging the old car to start. After a mechanical groan, the noises stopped completely, and the lights on the dash blinked out. "Shit shit shit," Amy murmured. "Cherry on top of a perfect day." With her last remaining courage, she wiped her eyes, stepped out of the car, and without once looking back at Daily Bread, set off toward her apartment on foot.

4

A few hours later, Amy was cocooned in a blanket, watching her sixth episode in a row of *Say Yes to the Dress* through swollen and teary eyes. Her cat, Truffle, stared judgmentally from the other end of the couch. Adopting Truffle, a beautiful long-haired tortoiseshell with bright yellow eyes, had been Amy's version of a breakup haircut.

"You should be used to watching me wallow by now," Amy said bitterly in the cat's direction. Truffle blinked once in response. "This is way worse than a cheating ex!"

Truffle yawned.

Amy heard a knock on the door, signaling the arrival of Joel, the only person she'd managed to text with her bad news before melting into the sofa. She groaned, more as a greeting than as a protest. A minute later, Joel had let himself in with his copy of her apartment key and dropped a large paper bag on the coffee table in front of her. "Oh, babe. You look rough."

"My outsides match my insides," she mumbled, scooting over to make room on the couch. Joel sat down and pulled the end of the blanket over his legs. Truffle immediately curled into a ball on his lap.

Joel muted the TV and wove his fingers into the cat's fur. "Okay, we have two hours before I have to be at the bar. Tell me everything."

Amy launched into a blow by blow, giving him every awful detail she could remember. Joel was the perfect audience, gasping and yelling at all the right places. Damian was the best friend you went to when you had a problem that needed to be solved, but Joel was the best friend who let you cry and scream and wallow in your feelings for as long as you needed.

As soon as Amy was done, Joel jumped in. "I can't believe that awful woman. They can't do this to you! It must be illegal. It's discrimination!"

Amy shrugged dejectedly. "It's not," she said. "Freedom of religion, you know."

"Yeah, but when do we get freedom from other people's religion? This is garbage."

Amy agreed, but she had run out of rage three episodes ago. Since applying for the job at Daily Bread, she'd understood the risk. She had known she was giving up safety and a certain amount of pride in exchange for new baking skills and generous tips. In a way, it was a relief to not have a huge gay secret hanging over her head. But losing her biweekly bakery paycheck? That was something new hanging over her head.

She gestured to the brown bag on the coffee table. "What did you bring? Please tell me it's full of cash. My bank account is crying right now."

"Next best thing. Crab rangoon and pad thai." He unloaded boxes from their favorite Thai restaurant, along with two cartons of Ben & Jerry's ice cream. "I think this occasion calls for two pints."

Amy gratefully agreed. Emerging from her blanket nest, she collected plates and silverware from her tiny kitchen and spooned their food onto dishes. Joel unmuted the show, and they ate while critiquing the onscreen bride, who adamantly refused to try on a ball gown while reiterating her desire to look like a princess.

Once the episode reached its happy conclusion—the bride chose a ball gown, obviously—Joel slurped the last noodles from his dish, and Amy dug a spoon into the first Ben & Jerry's pint, her mind wandering to her financial quandary. She could only pick up so many extra shifts at Ruby Red's. Even if she could get a job at another bakery without a recommendation from Donna, there was no way she would make as much as she had at Daily Bread. But with her broken-down car still stranded in the bakery parking lot, rent due at the end of the month, and an empty refrigerator, she didn't exactly have time to be picky.

"I'm screwed," she told Joel. "And I'm dreading telling my mom. She'll want to help, and that's just out of the question. She still has so much medical debt to pay off." Teresa's breast cancer diagnosis two years prior had shaken Amy's little family to the core. The doctors had caught the cancer early, and now Teresa was gratefully cancer-free, but the medical debt lingered on. Teresa refused Max and Greg's offers to help, saying they'd already spent too much on Amy's college fund. But Amy hadn't let her mother fight to pay off her bills alone. Now Amy went on, her voice sounding higher than usual. "Not to mention, how am I going to keep up my payments for Mom's debt? You know it took me months to convince her to even accept a little help. I can't stop contributing now."

"You'll be able to help her again." Joel wrapped a comforting arm around Amy's shoulders. "You might just have to take a little hiatus. We'll figure something out."

"Thank God I said yes to Regi and Jared's offer. Their wedding isn't for another couple weeks, but that two fifty will be a godsend."

"Whose what?" Joel said. Amy, who had forgotten she hadn't told him about it, quickly filled Joel in on the serendipitous offer and, of course, the peacock cake. "First of all, obsessed with you making a quick two fifty," Joel said. "Second, I'll go ahead and set this snapshot as your contact photo in my phone. . . . Done. And third, I'm sure Damian and I can spot you some of your rent this month if it comes to—"

"No," Amy cut him off. He opened his mouth to protest, but she hurried on. "I love you, and thank you, but I . . ." She paused. "I think I just need a minute before I can even accept that that's something I might have to consider." Amy needed to remember she still had options. If worse came to worst, she could find a cheaper place with a roommate or move into her mom's one-bedroom rental. That thought was depressing. As much as she loved her mother, it was only in the past couple of years that Amy had felt like she was really starting to come into her own. With it having been just the two of them for so long, they were extremely close. But she loved building her own life, being her own person in her own space. She didn't want to give up on that yet.

Then she remembered the very thing she'd thought she couldn't forget: her date with Charley. Amy buried her face in her hands. "Oh no, I can't do it."

"Can't do what?" Joel asked.

"I was supposed to go on a date tomorrow." Amy's voice was muffled by her fingers.

"A *what*? Why am I just hearing about this now?"

"I'm sorry, I was a little too busy flirting to put you on speakerphone while I asked her out."

"*You* asked *her* out?" Joel bounced around on the couch until he was facing Amy, his legs crossed and a mischievous twinkle in his eye. "Who's the lucky girl?"

"Her name is Charley. She came into Daily Bread on Friday." Despite the sense of doom and gloom that came with saying the bakery's name out loud, she couldn't deny the spark of excitement in her chest as she thought about Charley.

"Oh my God, stop. Is she the one who came in as Damian and I were leaving? The one who was asking us what she should order like we were cupcake connoisseurs?" Joel whipped out his phone with a squeal. "He totally owes me ten dollars. I *knew* it!"

"I told you two to stop betting on my romantic life. And anyway, there's no way I can go on a date in"—Amy looked at her watch—"fifteen hours. I'm a wreck."

"Fifteen hours?" Joel squinted while counting in his head. "What is that, three A.M.? Babe, I know it's been a long time since you've dated, but that sounds more like a booty call."

"Cool it with the math before you hurt yourself." Amy quickly explained her morning date plan with Charley, and Joel cringed only a little at the early start time. "But whatever," she said, shaking her head. "There's no way I can go now. I'm a giant ball of emotions and puffy red eyes and crab rangoon and cat hair. Charley is super put together. Meanwhile, I have never been less impressive. I just won't text her, and maybe she'll forget I exist. She'll be the one that got away. At least that's still romantic." Amy glanced at Joel, not wanting to go on the date but also not wanting him to agree with her. Luckily, Joel was not so easily convinced that one of his most beloved friends was unimpressive.

"Absolutely not," he said with an air of finality. "You're a goddamn catch every day of the week, Amy Fariner. Even on your worst day, you're the cutest, most supportive and loving person I know. You can't let Donna Young dull your shine. Plus, what if Charley's the one? What if you're calling off your fairy tale before it even starts? And even if she's not the one, you've got to get back on the horse sometime. You are going on that date if I have to chaperone you myself." Joel grabbed Amy's phone from the coffee table and typed in her pass code. "How do you spell 'Charley'? I'm not seeing her in your contacts."

"Oh, her number is on a napkin in . . . Shit." Amy buried her head in her hands again. "My car."

Thankfully, Amy and Joel had performed many shenanigans during their friendship, and they knew their roles well. With good looks, a loud voice, and charm, Joel was the distractor. Meanwhile, Amy found she could get away with just about anything with enough confidence and her innocent dimples. Throughout their friendship, the approach had helped them sneak into movies, fancy VIP events, and even a bat mitzvah where Carly Rae Jepsen had performed live.

After Amy spent a half hour pulling herself together, they set off on their mission. Joel drove a few blocks east and pulled up next to Amy's defunct car. She slouched so far down in the passenger seat that she almost smothered herself in her own breasts. Seeing Daily Bread's painted sign through Joel's windshield felt like rubbing coarse sea salt in a fresh wound. After a determined nod, Joel got out of the car and strode toward the bakery. Peeking above the dashboard, she saw him promptly knock over a table full of cake design binders upon entry, causing an immediate flurry of activity. Amy could hear his loud apologies. That was her cue.

She slipped from his SUV into her own car, where a quick rummage through the glove compartment turned up the wrinkled napkin with the ten magical digits she sought. Amy traced the numbers with her index finger, admiring the angular scrawl of Charley's handwriting. Their moment together at the café table felt so close yet so far. She noticed a blueberry stain at the corner of the napkin and thought of Charley's crooked smile, melodic laugh, and attentive gaze. It was only when Amy made eye contact with Joel through the bakery window that she realized she'd dreamily brought the blueberry-stained corner halfway to her lips. His eyebrows furrowed as he jerked his head toward his car, a clear sign for Amy to shake a leg. Seeing Donna, Leanne, and her other former co-workers bustling around Joel to clean up his mess startled her. How were they still wearing the same clothes from when she'd been fired? Was it really the same day?

Amy ducked into Joel's car right as he emerged from the bakery shouting apologies over his shoulder. They made a quick escape to Ruby Red's, arriving just before the start of Joel's shift. Amy's shift wasn't scheduled to start for a few more hours, but Joel offered to work together and split tips until she formally clocked in. The bar was just over a block down Cherry Street from Daily Bread, its interior magic disguised by its nondescript, windowless brown brick exterior. The only indication that the one-story building housed anything at all was a dimly lit sign in front with the bar's logo, "R.R.," in red block letters next to an illustration of one of Judy Garland's sparkling red slippers from *The Wizard of Oz*.

At its most basic level, Ruby Red's was the definition of a dive bar: dark and dank, filled with a permanent haze of cigarette smoke. An old wooden bar ran down the left wall, with a combination of rickety tables, mismatched chairs, and ripped leather booths filling the main space. A large TV and old-school jukebox provided entertainment in the front, pool tables and darts drew patrons toward the back, and a small covered patio accessible through the back door offered privacy from passersby. Two dingy single bathrooms filled one of the back corners, each covered in graffiti listing who loved whom and who hated whom, with names crossed out and replaced multiple times.

But the thing that separated Ruby Red's from your average dive bar was the decorations. The owner was a reclusive older lesbian who lost more money on the bar than she made from it but kept it open out of sentimentality. Like many queers old and new, she was obsessed with *The Wizard of Oz* and dreamed of being able to escape the dreary plains for a world of rainbows, music, and beautiful witches. She'd decorated the bar with an eclectic mix of *Wizard of Oz* memorabilia: some traditional, like old movie posters and Dorothy dolls, and some more obscure, like a Glinda the Good Witch bong and a life-size Toto doll made of actual dog hair. The final effect was somewhere between migraine inducing and deeply horrifying, but after you hung around for a while, it felt like home. At least, that's what the bar's group of faithful regulars would say.

Upon arrival, Amy and Joel performed their opening duties, the bar's traditional Sunday afternoon HGTV playing in the background, then flipped on the light that illuminated the "R.R." sign outside, unlocked the front door, and finally sat down side by side to formulate a text to Charley. Amy typed a draft and showed it to Joel.

Hey Charley. This is Amy. Looking forward to tomorrow. My address is 1414 S. Quincy Ave.

"Too boring. We need you to sound interesting, but also relatable. Familiar yet mysterious. Funny, but not too funny. That can be intimidating. Let me try." Joel grabbed Amy's phone and started typing.

The front door creaked open, a beam of sunlight cutting through the grimy old bar. "Damian!" Amy jumped up, a wide grin on her face. "I thought you were doing personal training sessions all afternoon. Gin and tonic?"

"Yes, please, and a big glass of water." Damian greeted Joel with a sweaty kiss before claiming the barstool next to him. "My last two clients canceled, and I wanted to see how you were doing." He took Amy's hand and squeezed it. "Did Joel bring you crab rangoon? And Ben and Jerry's? I told him there's no healing without ice cream."

Of course Damian was the one who had made sure Joel showed up with edible reinforcements. Having a shoulder to cry on was nice, but Damian knew that actions (and sweets) were even better. "He did good," Amy said. "Thanks for looking out for my heart and my stomach."

Joel cut in, pushing Amy's phone in front of Damian's face. "Damie, read this text. Are you seduced?"

Damian squinted at the screen. "Why are there so many ellipses? And so many winky faces?"

"They're flirtatious!" Joel said.

"I think I need some context here," Damian said.

Before Amy could fill Damian in, two other regulars showed up: Jae, a genderqueer DJ whose sneaker game always put the rest of the bar to shame, and Tala, a photographer and token straight friend of Ruby Red's. Amy poured their drinks while telling them about getting fired. After hundreds of nights spent together at the bar, they had become like family, and she knew their solidarity would be a balm to her injured feelings. Zee, the third bartender at Ruby Red's, and her partner, Arnelle, arrived halfway through the story, forcing Amy to start over. Despite the pain of rehashing her firing, they made the perfect audience: Arnelle, full of sympathetic looks and tears, balanced by no-nonsense Zee's furrowed brow and observant questions. The whole group expressed the outrage and condolences Amy needed after her long day.

Once they'd all properly bashed Donna and Daily Bread, Joel tapped Amy's phone. "That's not Amy's only update," he said. "And her other news is *much* more fun."

Happy to change the subject, Amy caught everyone up on her upcoming date with Charley. Everyone cheered before circling around her phone to weigh in on the text. They'd all witnessed the disaster of Amy's last relationship unfold. In fact, most of Ruby Red's customer base had been privy to her two-year on-again, off-again relationship with Autumn, Tulsa's resident lesbian heartbreaker.

Autumn had a history with pretty much every queer woman in Tulsa, but her relationship with Amy had been her longest. They had first met at Ruby Red's, of course, shortly after Amy started working behind the bar. Autumn hosted the bar's biweekly trivia night. Her rakish charm and Amy's cute naïveté had sparked instant chemistry that soon turned into a real connection. Queer Tulsa watched with bated breath, wondering if Amy would finally be the one to tame playgirl Autumn. But Autumn's flirtations quickly shifted from Amy to a series of other people who caught her eye. Instead of dumping Autumn, Amy blamed herself for not fulfilling her girlfriend's needs. So began a cycle of Autumn cheating, the two of them fighting, then Amy trying a new outfit or haircut or sex toy in increasingly desperate attempts to keep Autumn's attention. After two years of drama, Autumn finally cheated on her one too many times, and Amy called it quits. The breakup was much harder on Amy than on

Autumn, who had a new girlfriend by the end of the week. Luckily, the core group around Amy today had chosen her side and been there for her through the past year of tears, regret, anger, and, eventually, healing.

Needless to say, Amy's friends were thrilled to hear she was putting herself back out there and eager to see her find a more peaceful partnership. As customers trickled in, Amy and Joel settled into their natural rhythm, mixing and pouring drinks side by side. The group of friends passed around her phone, arguing over the flirtatiousness of a semicolon in a first text. The daylight from the open back door had nearly disappeared by the time they reached a consensus and returned the phone to Amy.

Hey there, it's your favorite baker, Amy! Get a good night's rest because we're going to take Tulsa by storm. See you at 6 AM tomorrow at 1414 S. Quincy Ave ;)

Amy looked up at the six smiles awaiting her response. The text *did* sound like her, actually—a version of herself that felt confident and sexy, at least. Still, she hesitated. "Can I even call myself a baker anymore?"

Joel gathered Amy into a hug. "Of course you can! You're a baker because you bake, not because some old homophobe pays you." He poked a finger into Amy's sternum. "The baker was in here all along, babe."

"And you know we'll all eat your cookies anytime," Jae said.

"Is that a euphemism?" Tala asked, earning her an elbow in the side from Damian and a much-needed laugh from Amy.

"All right, all right," Amy said. "But is the winky emoticon strictly necessary?"

The group yelled "Yes!" as if they'd been prepared for her emoticon-specific pushback.

"Fine! I'm pressing Send. There, I did it." Amy tucked her phone under the bar. As grateful as she was for her friends' support, she knew the best way to make it through the night was to put her horrible day at the bakery and her nerves about Charley out of mind. Thankfully, the bar was quickly filling with customers eager to get a drink in hand before trivia started.

Amy was muddling mint and lime for a mojito when the voices in the bar seemed to hush momentarily and she heard a familiar voice at the door. She looked up. With her artfully messy jet-black hair tucked under a snapback hat, her fashionably androgynous style, and her relaxed smirk, Autumn may have been queer Tulsa's most notorious heartbreaker, but she was also great for business. Once she'd started hosting Sunday trivia nights, the lesbians had come out in droves. Everyone wanted to see what lucky (or unlucky) girl Autumn was flirting with at the moment, even those who'd already had their hearts broken by her. In fact, Amy counted three women at the bar who she knew had dallied with Autumn—one before, one after, and one during her relationship with Amy. She'd tried to hold a grudge against the people Autumn had cheated with, but Amy had learned fast that if she couldn't be friends with Autumn's ex-lovers, she wouldn't have many queer friends. And besides, Autumn was the only person who had promised fidelity to Amy. The cheating had been Autumn's fault and Autumn's fault alone.

The first time Amy saw Autumn after the breakup, she had thoroughly embarrassed herself by screaming and crying in front of the late-night trivia crew. It had started to get easier around the six-month mark, thanks to a combination of time, rom-com marathons with Joel, home improvement projects with Damian, picking up a ton of extra shifts at the bar and the bakery, and her adoption of Truffle, which reminded her she still had the capacity to love. Autumn made herself scarce outside of trivia nights for a while, a gesture Amy recognized as a peace offering, as there were only so many places in Tulsa a queer person could go on dates without stares and homophobic comments. It was only recently that Autumn and Amy had reached a kind of unspoken truce, making things at Ruby Red's more amicable for everyone.

"Ames, hey, it's good to see you," Autumn said in her gravelly voice. Amy saw that Autumn had come with a date, who slid onto the barstool next to her, a lovestruck expression giving away her guileless infatuation. "You playing this week?"

"Nah, I can't beat the customers at trivia every week. It's bad for business," Amy said in a brave attempt at humor. While she usually did all right on the food and pop-culture categories, trivia definitely wasn't Amy's forte. She poured a whiskey and coke, Autumn's usual, and slid it across the bar before turning to her new date, who was examining Ruby Red's weathered booths, dusty light fixtures, and antique flying monkeys mounted above the bar with unembarrassed excitement. Autumn dated too broadly to have a specific type, but Amy had to admit she saw a bit of herself in the girl—or at least the version of herself that had first fallen for Autumn. The girl didn't look much like Amy—she was slender with shiny dark hair pulled into a flawless ballerina bun—but the attitude was definitely there. Cute, perky, with youthful enthusiasm. Her polka-dot dress even looked like something Amy would have worn to the bakery.

"ID?" Amy asked.

"Oh yeah, one sec." The girl dug through her bag and fumbled for her wallet, which she flipped open to reveal a driver's license.

"Look at that, you just turned twenty-one last week. Happy late birthday"—Amy squinted at the name on the card—"McKenzie. A Scorpio. Fun," Amy said, hoping Autumn would catch the sarcasm. Amy may have decided to be the bigger person, but that didn't mean she couldn't be a little petty. Although a couple years older than Amy, Autumn had always had a thing for barely legals or newly out queers, mostly because they were less likely to know about her reputation. "What can I get for you, McKenzie?"

"I would like an amaretto sour, please." It sounded as if she had rehearsed how to order a cocktail, her lean against the bar a little too stiff, and she looked delighted to be legally purchasing a drink. As much as she wanted to hate McKenzie for being younger, skinnier, and cuter than her and able to catch Autumn's attention, Amy had to admit McKenzie's earnest warmth and lack of self-consciousness was endearing.

Amy made the syrupy-sweet drink and placed it in front of McKenzie. "One amaretto sour. A sweet drink for a sweet girl, right?" Amy winked, more to pester Autumn than to seduce McKenzie.

Just then, Joel returned with a bin full of dirty drinkware. "Why, look what the cat dragged in. Autumn Webber, as I live and breathe. Only half an hour late this week!" He dropped the bin by the dishwasher and dried his hands on a nearby towel. "Who is this cute young thing?"

McKenzie blushed as she presented her hand. "McKenzie Gwon. This is my first time here."

"You don't say!" Joel grabbed and kissed her hand with a campy curtsy. "Joel Garrison. Charmed. Brave of you to bring a newbie, Autumn, with all these thirsty lesbians desperate to double up for cuffing season. I'd watch her closely if I were you."

McKenzie giggled, pleased with what she'd interpreted as a compliment, while Autumn shot Joel a warning look. Barely suppressing an eye roll, Amy accepted Autumn's card and opened her tab.

Leaning into Autumn, McKenzie said, "The bartenders are super nice. You must come here a lot." Dammit, how could Amy stay bitter toward someone so delightful?

Autumn made eye contact with Amy while carefully holding in a laugh. "I guess so. Why don't you come with me while I set up trivia?"

The group of regulars watched Autumn and McKenzie walk away. Once they were out of hearing range, Jae said, "Eventually she'll run out of people in town to date, right? She must be through at least seventy-five percent of queer Tulsa at this point."

"Well, the young ones keep coming out and providing fresh meat," Tala said. "Look at Shirley Temple over there. I'm pretty sure she was literally born yesterday. And when Autumn's done with the young queers, she'll just convert the straight women. To be honest, if she caught me at the right level of drunk, I would probably hook up with her too."

Jae bumped their shoulder against Tala. "Hey, don't say that too loud, or she'll appear out of nowhere to seduce you. She's like a lesbian vampire. She can smell your attraction, and she's out for blood."

Tala snorted. "There *is* something about her, you know? She's got to be good in bed. Was she?" Tala had directed her question at Amy, but murmurs of agreement arose from not only her but also Zee, Arnelle, and Jae. Tala looked shocked. "Damn. Really? All of you?"

"It was just one time," Jae said.

Arnelle shrugged. "I was new to town. I didn't know any better."

Everyone looked at Zee, the most down-to-earth butch among them. "Things were different in high school, okay?"

The group laughed as Autumn's voice came over the speakers to announce the beginning of trivia. As everyone else looked toward Autumn, Amy turned to her phone, where she was delighted to see a new message from Charley.

Hey Amy! Looking forward to breakfast
with the cutest Tulsa tour guide ;)

A huge grin filled Amy's face. She had to admit, her friends had been right about the winky emoticon. In fact, she thought, maybe she should use them more often.

5

After locking Ruby Red's doors at close to three in the morning, Amy turned down Joel's offer for a ride and set off on foot for her apartment a few blocks away. Although she didn't consider herself a morning person, there was something she loved about those quiet hours after shutting down the bar when it felt like the rest of the world was asleep. No cars rushing down Cherry Street, no customers demanding her attention, no ringing phones. Just her and the flickering streetlights. She reveled in the chilly early morning silence.

A hot shower eased Amy's aching back and washed away some of the previous day's trauma. Even if she hadn't slept since her disastrous shift at the bakery, freshly shampooed hair felt a little like a new start. But an hour of trying on outfit after outfit brought back some of the anxiety she thought she'd washed down the drain. Should she wear a feminine dress, like she'd been wearing at the bakery when she met Charley? Or something gayer, like flannel and ripped black jeans? She picked apart each outfit in the mirror, trying to guess what kind of girl Charley might like. Soft femme? Tomboy? Artfully androgynous? She tried an outfit that spoke to all of those things—floral skirt, Tegan and Sara T-shirt, leather jacket, Converse—and flinched at her reflection. She was all over the place. Something simple would have to work until she figured out Charley's type.

After deciding on a loose-fitting plum sweater and dark wash jeans, Amy did her best to conceal the puffy skin under her eyes and control her frizzy cloud of hair. She was examining herself in the mirror, considering changing clothes again, when her front door buzzed, announcing Charley's arrival. "Ready as I'll ever be, I suppose," Amy mumbled. Truffle gave her an affirming chirp.

With Truffle's approval, Amy locked up and jogged down a flight of stairs to open the small brick apartment building's front door. It was still pitch black outside, but Charley was lit dramatically by the building's motion-sensor lights.

"Wow," Amy said. "You look great." Charley was even more devastatingly dapper than Amy remembered. Not a strand of her short brown hair was out of place. Her cheeks were rosy from the cool November air, matching the red cashmere scarf draped around her neck over a brown herringbone tweed suit. Amy's fingers twitched, eager to touch the lush material. She'd never been on a date with a woman in a suit before. It made it seem like Charley really cared about the date, about impressing Amy, but it also made her feel underdressed in her jeans. Would it be weird to change clothes again? *Yes, definitely weird,* Amy decided.

"Thanks!" Charley's voice cracked. She paused to clear her throat. "Good morning. Shall we start our tour?"

Amy followed Charley to her spacious SUV and settled in, delighted by the electrically heated passenger seat. Charley buckled in and turned to her. "Where to?"

Amy had spent her walk home from the bar obsessing over the perfect intro to Tulsa. Although some would call it flyover country, Amy knew Tulsa was something special, not to be missed among its rural surroundings. Besides its rich history as "the Oil Capital of the World," it also had unique art deco architecture, a surprisingly robust arts scene, amazing food, and if Amy said so herself, the best queer community in the plains. She was hoping that if she played her tour guide role well, she could make Charley love the city too. "Have you seen the Golden Driller?"

Charley's brow wrinkled. "The what now?"

"Perfect," Amy said, pleased. "It's best when it's dark outside, and we've got some time before sunrise. Take a right up there, and keep going straight for a couple miles. You're going to love this."

"How was that family wedding, by the way?" Charley asked as she pulled onto the road.

"Oh, you know. Long and boring."

"Sounds exactly like a wedding," Charley said.

"Totally," Amy said, deciding in the moment to follow Charley's lead. "But the food was good."

As Charley drove, Amy narrated the ride. "Fifteenth Street, which you're on now, is also known as Cherry Street. It's my personal favorite part of town. Great restaurants and boutiques, good nightlife spots, and an amazing farmers market during the warmer months. If we went in the other direction, we'd pass Ruby Red's, which is basically the queer center of the city."

"That seems like somewhere I should know about," Charley said. "What is it?"

"It's the best queer bar in Tulsa," Amy explained. "I actually bartend there. Tulsa has a surprising number of queer bars. There's the main gay club downtown, Rampage; then there's a leather bar, a bar for the older crowd, and a bar with lots of go-go dancers and drag performances, most of which are primarily for gay men. There's a pretty run-down lesbian bar across town too, but Ruby Red's is the best of them all. It started in the nineties as a lesbian bar, but now it's more like an any-kind-of-queer-welcome bar. You should definitely come by some time. We have tons of events. Themed costume nights, karaoke, cookie decorating, trivia . . ." Amy tried to reel herself in, not wanting to talk about anything to do with her ex on a first date.

"Cool. I'm guessing you spend a lot of time around here?" Charley looked over her shoulder to check her blind spot before changing lanes. Amy took it as a good sign that Charley was asking questions about her life instead of just the tour.

"Oh yeah. I chose to live here because both of my jobs are on Cherry Street . . . or, well . . ." It didn't seem like it would be good for the first-date vibe to tell Charley she'd just gotten fired. Amy suddenly felt self-conscious. She was a part-time bartender with an ancient, busted car, being driven around in an SUV that had been bought within the last decade by a successful engineer. She thought she probably shouldn't go too far into personal details if she wanted to keep this date on track. "It's a great place to live," Amy finished awkwardly. Hoping to pivot out of these dangerous waters, she changed tactics. "Where's your new place?"

They chatted for a moment about Charley's rental house a few miles north in a residential midtown neighborhood full of lovely midcentury homes. Amy could picture Charley's house based on the location. At least two bedrooms, she guessed, probably with a spacious yard and two-car garage, all to herself. It sounded like quite a luxury to Amy, but then she remembered Charley had moved from Austin. Tulsa housing costs must have seemed delightfully low in comparison to what they were in the trendy Texas city. Amy interrupted the talk of Charley's new neighborhood to direct the car into the state fairgrounds, a bit east of downtown. Charley gasped as a towering concrete statue came into view, dramatically lit from below. "What the . . ."

Amy laughed. "Ah, to lay eyes on the Golden Driller for the first time. I envy you. Park over here." She was pleased to have offered something impressive enough to make Charley respond like that—although she had some more intimate ideas to make her gasp again. This being only a first date, and it being just after 6:00 A.M. at that, Amy decided to save those for later.

Within minutes, they were standing at the enormous feet of a seventy-five-foot-tall oil worker, one hand placed on a decorative oil derrick, a concrete hard hat atop his head, all painted a bold mustard yellow. They stared in silence for a moment, Charley looking at the statue, Amy looking at Charley.

"Take your time. It's a lot to take in. The tallest freestanding statue in the country, in fact," Amy said in her best tour guide voice. "Besides the massive state fair each fall, these fairgrounds host a bunch of random events and competitions. Livestock auctions, car and gun shows, and my personal favorite, the Oklahoma Sugar Arts Show, to name a few. This guy was originally built as part of some petroleum exposition, but they decided to keep him around permanently."

Charley squinted at the statue and tilted her head. "I have some . . . er, anatomical questions."

"Ah yes. The Ken-doll crotch." Amy looked up at the Golden Driller's tightly fitted pants and notably flat groin. "Rumor has it he used to have quite the package that was later altered due to public backlash."

A surprised laugh escaped Charley's lips. "I can imagine the country's largest penis might have been a bit shocking."

"I like to think of it as a tribute to LGBTQ Oklahoma. Our very own genderqueer statue! But I'd say that's more of a niche interpretation. I can take your picture with it, if you want. If I angle it just right, I can make it look like he's resting his arm on your head."

"Oh, that's all right," Charley said, waving away the offer.

"But you moved here to work in the oil industry! And it's a classic Tulsa picture, like our own version of holding up the Leaning Tower of Pisa. Don't you need a shot with the Golden Driller for your scrapbook?"

"I don't have a scrapbook."

"You might someday."

That garnered a smile from Charley, who whipped out her phone and waved Amy closer. "Come here, let's make it a selfie." Charley looped an arm over Amy's shoulders, and they both smiled at the camera. With Charley that close, Amy got a whiff of what smelled like sandalwood and a dash of citrus. The smell was so warm and inviting, she never wanted Charley to move. Charley captured a shot of their two smiling faces with the Golden Driller statue looming in the distance, and then Amy took one on her phone, both of them beaming. Amy lowered her phone. Charley stepped away and cleared her throat. Was she blushing?

"If that was your first stop, I'm not sure how you're going to top it," Charley said. "Literally."

"Very punny. I like it. And don't worry, I've got more where this came from."

"Does this tour include breakfast? We could swing by Daily Bread. I would love another blueberry muffin."

Amy felt her heart jump into her throat. "I have a better idea," she said in a voice she hoped came across as nonchalant. "Let's get back on the road."

Amy directed Charley through Riverside, an area along the Arkansas River with running trails and parks, and down Peoria Avenue, past historic mansions and the sprawling rose garden at Woodward Park. Amy had once planned a picnic at the rose garden with Autumn, who had shown up over an hour late with a questionable excuse, which had led to a huge fight. It had kind of ruined the beautiful location for Amy. But looking at Charley, who had shown up right on time and seemed completely enthralled by whatever Amy had planned, she thought she might be ready to visit the garden again when the roses bloomed in the spring.

Next, Amy directed Charley to Mornings by Brookside, a quirky diner that specialized in decadent breakfast platters and, for the Monday-through-Friday rush, delicious breakfast sandwiches. It was a favorite place for Joel and Damian to carbo-load after early-morning workout classes. Amy usually skipped the workouts but joined them for the pancakes. Today, with much left to see, Amy ordered breakfast sandwiches to go—two egg Florentines on Parmesan bagels; Charley had decided to get one too at Amy's recommendation. Charley insisted on picking up the bill, a small price to pay for such a personalized city tour, she insisted. Amy had never before felt so pampered by a seven-dollar breakfast sandwich.

The sun peeked above the horizon as they made their way down Peoria Avenue on foot, most of the stores still dark and locked. The conversation turned personal as Charley discussed her family and hometown. Although she had also grown up in a red state, Charley's childhood in Houston sounded totally different from Amy's in Tulsa. She was the middle child of five, two older brothers and two younger sisters, and had followed her father's footsteps into the oil and gas industry. Charley seemed to embrace her role as the cool aunt, showing Amy pictures on her phone of enough nieces and nephews to leave her head spinning with names and ages. Seeing Charley light up as she described her family melted Amy like butter on a hot roll. It was so damn *cute* in a completely different way from how she talked about her job, and she had none of the awkward tension in describing her family that Amy was used to from her queer Oklahoma friends. Although Charley didn't say it outright, Amy could tell that Charley's family loved her for exactly who she was. It explained a lot about how Charley could be so queer and confident and unflinchingly honest in a place like Tulsa.

Realizing she'd hardly touched her breakfast sandwich, Charley asked Amy to tell her about her family while she ate. Amy explained her close relationship with her mom and how growing up with it being just the two of them had meant they'd both had to fill many roles for each other beyond mother and daughter. She also talked about Max and Greg, the only people in her childhood who felt like the kind of loving, supportive family Charley had so enthusiastically described. Briefly, she considered mentioning Christina, who had been a prominent figure in her childhood after all, but decided against it. The conversation was so uplifting, and they were connecting so well. Why bring it down with a sad ending?

Their walk ended back at the Mornings by Brookside parking lot. Amy saw Charley check her watch and remembered that for Charley, the day was just beginning. "Do you have to go?" Amy hoped Charley couldn't hear the disappointment in her voice.

"Thankfully, I have another half hour." Charley beamed at Amy, looking genuinely happy to keep their date going.

Amy blushed, equally grateful for more time together. "Are you ready for the last stop on our tour? It's only a short drive away."

They drove toward downtown, Amy pointing out the hallmarks of Tulsa's art deco architecture along the way. She caught Charley watching her out of the corner of her eye. With all the beautiful old buildings around, Amy was pleased to find that Charley seemed to want to look at her even more.

Charley executed a perfect parallel parking job in the Arts District, something Amy found surprisingly sexy. Amy led them on foot across the Guthrie Green, a beautiful park right in the middle of downtown. "This way." Amy almost reached for Charley's hand to lead her south but stopped herself, covering the move with a this-direction gesture. She felt hyperaware of Charley's hand, which was swinging by her side, only inches from her own, and wished she had the nerve to reach out and grab it. As much as Amy wished she could ignore the nine-to-fivers driving by them on the way to work, the voices of Max and Greg echoed in her head, telling her to play it safe in public.

They walked for a few minutes without speaking, Amy focusing on the palpable energy between their swinging hands, before they reached a large pedestrian bridge crossing a set of railroad tracks below. Although located right in the middle of downtown, it was set apart from the busy roads and office buildings, more for strolling than for actually connecting anything of import. The bridge was completely empty of other people at that time in the morning. "We're almost there," Amy said, leading the way onto the bridge.

At the midway point, where a small concrete circle was surrounded by concentric rings of bricks extending eight feet across, Amy stopped and turned to Charley, who wore a bemused smile. "What is it?" Charley asked.

"Welcome to the Center of the Universe," Amy said with a grand gesture at the underwhelming brick pattern.

Charley tilted her head in confusion. "Is that a metaphor?"

"No, it's literally called the Center of the Universe. Here." Amy finally grabbed Charley's hands, emboldened by the desire to show her one of the worst-kept secrets in Tulsa, and pulled her to the center of the concrete circle. She leaned toward Charley's ear and whispered, "Say something." She then stepped back past the edge of the brick circle and waited.

"What am I supposed to say? Wait. Whoa," Charley said, or at least that's what Amy gathered between the distorted sound of Charley's voice and reading her lips. Charley looked around, her eyebrows raised in confusion. "Hello!" she mouthed, jumping as Amy imagined the sound of Charley's voice echoing around her. *Hello! Hello!*

Amy laughed and gestured for Charley to step out of the circle. "What was that?" Charley asked, her eyes wide with confusion.

"They call it an 'acoustic anomaly,'" Amy said. "If you stand in the middle of the circle, everything you say is amplified and echoes. But here's the weirdest part." She took Charley's place at the center of the circle and began to speak. "Hey, Charley." *Charley. Charley.*

"What?" Charley yelled from outside of the circle. Amy knew Charley could only hear a quiet, muffled sound.

"You're cute," Amy said. *Cute. Cute.*

Amy stepped back out of the circle. "When you're at the Center of the Universe, you can hear every sound you make amplified. But if you're outside the circle, the sounds are quieter and impossible to understand."

"How does it work?" Charley asked. Amy could see her engineering brain already beginning to analyze the phenomenon as she looked around at the railroad tracks below them and the downtown buildings that might reflect the sound.

"No one knows."

Charley raised her eyebrows in suspicion. "Really? *No one* knows?"

Amy held up a hand. "Shhh, no one knows! It's all part of the great mystery of the Center of the Universe."

Charley looked from the brick pattern on the bridge to Amy. "You can hear the other person if you're both in the circle, right?" Amy nodded. Charley grabbed her hand to pull them both to the center. They turned to face each other, their bodies only inches apart. Charley took a breath. "I like you." *Like you. Like you.*

The words seemed to echo not only around them but all the way through Amy's chest. She shifted even closer to Charley. "I like you too." *You too. You too.* Although she'd whispered, the sound reverberated clearly in time with her beating heart.

Charley reached out and tucked a loose curl behind Amy's ear. The golden morning sun behind Charley's shoulders bathed her in an otherworldly glow. "Can I kiss you? Here, in the Center of the Universe?" *Universe? Universe?*

"Yes." Their lips met before the echo of Amy's consent reached an end, and the kiss felt every bit as earthshaking as the acoustic anomaly of their voices echoing. It held a softness that hardly accounted for the fireworks in Amy's chest, tingling out to her fingertips. Charley's hand pressed against Amy's lower back. Amy wove her fingers into the back of Charley's short hair, both of them holding each other with a gentleness that only seemed to supercharge the explosive current of energy just under the surface of their skin.

Finally, Charley pulled back, the early-morning sun illuminating the tender look on her face. "I've wanted to do that since the first moment I saw you." *Saw you. Saw you.*

Suddenly, the sound of a phone alarm, amplified in the reverberation, jolted them apart, shattering the intimacy of the moment. Charley stepped out of the circle and fumbled with her phone to silence it. "That's my alarm to get ready for work." Her voice was flat and quiet.

Amy stepped out behind her and ran a hand along her lower back where Charley's fingers had been only seconds before. "Right, of course." She was quite suddenly aware of all the morning commuters walking just beyond the ends of the bridge, perfectly capable of having witnessed their kiss, even though the Center of the Universe lent a sense of privacy.

Then, to Amy's surprise, as they began walking back in the direction of Charley's car, Charley grabbed her hand. Charley's hand was warm and smooth with long, slender fingers. It was a perfect fit. Amy, a little dazed by the abrupt end to their magical kiss, thought of how impossible it had felt to reach out for Charley's hand just minutes before. Now, with their fingers intertwined, an undeniable chemistry thrumming between them, Amy hardly cared who saw. *Hardly,* she thought as she surreptitiously scanned the sidewalks ahead of them.

"Please tell me we can do this again," Charley said. "Soon."

Amy's heart leapt. "Of course," she said. "There's so much more I want to show you."

After a short drive, which Charley somehow managed while holding Amy's hand the whole time, the date came to its inevitable end. Amy waved goodbye from her apartment building's stoop as Charley's car joined the morning rush down Cherry Street.

6

Amy spent the next few days working shifts at Ruby Red's, scouring the internet for open positions at local bakeries and restaurants, and feeling sorry for herself. She wasn't sure just how much money Charley made at her oil industry job, but her fancy car and tailored suits didn't look cheap. She probably wouldn't be too pleased to find out she'd been on a date with an underemployed, flour-coated ragamuffin struggling to make ends meet, even if that ragamuffin had been fired unfairly. Amy wasn't sure when she'd started envisioning herself as a Charles Dickens character, but it certainly made her moping and overreliance on ramen feel more noble.

At first, Amy was determined to find a new job before she reached out to Charley for a second date. After a week went by, Amy decided she would settle for an interview. But as the days passed without any interest from prospective employers, the memory of that perfect kiss fading from her lips, Amy worried her second-date window was closing. Beyond a brief thank-you text and promises they'd exchanged to see each other again soon, Charley had been silent since their early-morning date. And as Joel kept reminding Amy, if she didn't act fast, their tenuous connection could fade away entirely, and some other Tulsa lesbian would be quick to pick up her slack. Besides, Regi and Jared's wedding was only days away. That counted as a job, right?

So, exactly eight days after their first date—not that she was counting—Amy allowed herself to dream up a cheap, yet charming, date idea: a homemade dinner at her apartment. She could make a more impressive meal on a budget than she could get at a restaurant, and she hoped Charley would be wooed by the magic she could make in the kitchen, which would give Amy a much-needed confidence boost. Plus, Amy definitely wanted a repeat of the Center of the Universe kiss and knew she'd feel more comfortable with a bit more privacy.

Now that she had a great idea, she needed to figure out timing. Charley worked during the day and was available only on weekday evenings and weekends. The upcoming Friday and Saturday were the first nights Amy had off from Ruby Red's that week, and she'd taken off Saturday for Regi and Jared's wedding. After that, she wasn't off work until the Wednesday before Thanksgiving, and she didn't want to wait that long, especially since she might get called in last minute. Having her date with Charley the night before the wedding wasn't ideal, as she hoped the date might last into the night, and she wanted to be at her best for Regi and Jared's wedding. But Friday seemed like the best bet unless she wanted to wait a full two weeks from their first date before seeing Charley again, so she decided to make it work. When she texted Charley the invitation, she responded enthusiastically, along with a brief apology for being so silent while inundated with her new job.

When Friday finally arrived, Amy spent hours creating the perfect meal, only remembering to prepare herself about thirty minutes before Charley arrived. She rushed to shave her legs and put on enough makeup to look effortlessly beautiful while occasionally running back to stir a large pot on the stove. With no time to fret over what outfit Charley would find most attractive, she threw on one of her simpler dresses, a maroon swing dress with long sleeves, pulling it over her head and smoothing her hair just as the door buzzed. Amy answered it with a dimpled, out-of-breath smile. She paused to take Charley in: her short hair styled up and out of her face, a perfectly crooked smile on her face, her camel coat open to reveal a striped button-down and well-fitted navy pants. Amy hadn't realized just how much she'd missed that grin until she saw it again, along with that sense of quiet confidence, that grounded Charley energy that made Amy want to forget all the messiness in her life.

"Are you going to invite me in, or should I make myself comfortable out here?" Charley said, her smile growing wider.

Amy jumped to the side and gestured Charley in the door. "Hi! Welcome. Sorry, you're just . . . I'm really happy to see you."

Charley shrugged off her coat and kissed Amy on the cheek. "I'm happy to see you too. And who is this?"

Truffle, infinitely curious about any new visitors to the apartment, was already circling Charley's feet with her bottlebrush tail high in the air. "Oh, that's Truffle. She has to check you out before she can decide to let you stay."

A vibrating purr emanated from the fluffy creature as Charley scratched behind her ears. "Seems like she's pretty hard to win over."

"Well, I've been giving her the scoop on you, trying to get you on her good side."

Charley ran her hands down Truffle's back as the cat chirped. "I'll do my best to live up to her expectations."

Amy took Charley's coat and hung it on a hook by the door. "Anyway, make yourself at home. Dinner is almost ready. I just need to wrap up a few things."

"It smells amazing in here." Charley followed Amy into the small kitchen, looking around at the counters crowded with cooking and baking tools. Amy threw a fresh apron over her head and stirred a pot of marinara sauce, then dropped tangles of pasta from the floured counter into a pot of boiling water. Charley's eyes widened. "Wait, is that homemade?"

"Mm-hmm," Amy said as she separated the pasta in the pot.

"I thought you said this was a low-key dinner," Charley said with a laugh that suggested a touch of jitteriness. Maybe Amy wasn't the only one nervous about the intimate nature of their second date.

"It's just pasta and marinara sauce. Oh, and garlic bread!" Amy opened the oven, which released a fragrant burst of steam, and pulled out a tray of herbed, toasted bread.

Charley moved closer to investigate the steaming loaf of bread. "Is this from Daily Bread?"

Amy winced, but Charley didn't seem to notice. Amy turned back to the bubbling pots on the stove. "Well, that's where I learned the recipe."

"You're telling me you made bread *and* pasta from scratch? Let me guess, the marinara is homemade too." Amy nodded. Charley wrapped an arm around Amy's aproned waist and dropped a soft, sweet kiss on her cheek, a gesture that made the whole kitchen scene feel to her like a glimpse into what she hoped could be their loving, domestic future. "When you said pasta, I was picturing something out of a box. I should have known that a casual dinner date with a baker would be spectacular. What can I do to help? I may not be a good cook, but I'm great at washing dishes."

"Please, you're my guest! No dishes until at least date four," Amy said, her cheek burning in the place where Charley's lips had been. "Would you like a glass of wine while I finish up dinner? I have . . ." Amy reached to the top of the fridge and pulled down an eight-dollar bottle she'd picked up earlier that day. It wasn't as nice as she would have preferred to serve, but at least it wasn't Two-Buck Chuck. "Merlot?"

Charley grimaced. "Oh, no thanks. I'm good," she said, waving the bottle away. Amy kicked herself internally, embarrassed. She knew Charley was probably used to higher quality wine but hoped she wouldn't take the cheap wine as a reflection of how Amy felt about her. At least the food was worthy of Charley, Amy thought as she returned to the stove.

Once dinner was served on Amy's small kitchen table, she had to admit that she'd outdone herself. The ambiance was just right: a couple candles in the living room, her small rosemary planter on the table for decoration, and the entire apartment practically sparkling, thanks to Damian's help cleaning up (while Joel watched *Orange Is the New Black* on the couch). As for the meal, it had turned out perfectly. The pasta was fresh and precisely al dente, and Charley described the rich, garlicky flavor of the marinara as "life changing." But Amy saved the true masterpiece for last: a creamy, rich, coffee-infused tiramisu. She'd sweated at the cost of the authentic mascarpone cheese, but it was worth it when she saw the look of bliss on Charley's face upon her first taste. Feeding someone the perfect meal made from scratch was absolutely Amy's love language.

Once their dessert plates were emptied, Charley wiped her mouth and leaned back in her seat. "Amy. That meal. There are no words that can describe how amazing it was, so I'll just say thank you."

"Oh, no problem," Amy looked shyly at the napkin in her lap.

"Are you kidding? Making a meal like that definitely wasn't 'no problem.' "

Amy blushed, delighted by Charley's recognition of the work she'd put into it but also worried she'd perhaps come across as trying too hard. At least Charley seemed into it, if that was the case. "All right then, *you're welcome.*" Amy brushed the crumbs from her lap and stood. "Here, let me bus these."

"I don't care if it's only date two. I'm helping." Charley rose and grabbed her own dishes. Amy agreed to let Charley dry the dishes after she washed them. She found that she enjoyed having a small task to share, their hips gently bumping together as they passed plates.

After they were out of dishes to clean, they stood in the kitchen for an awkward moment, neither sure where the night would take them next. The sexual tension was palpable, but now that there was nothing left to cook or clean, Amy felt a little unsure of herself. She rubbed a hand across the back of her neck. "Do you, uh, want to hang out on the couch? Keep talking?"

"Yeah, yeah, sounds good," Charley said quickly, pivoting to the living room. They settled down on the couch, where Truffle curled up to Charley's side. Amy stretched her arm across the back cushion. She could feel their bodies opening toward each other, the air between them growing electrically charged. But the conflicting urges to take it slow and to press skin against skin seemed to keep both of them from knowing what to do next.

Charley tried to break the silence first. "So how old is Truffle?"

Amy relaxed slightly, happy for an easy conversation starter. "She was about two and a half when I adopted her, so over three now?"

"Ah, still young and sprightly." Charley scratched Truffle

behind the ears. "I've always wanted a cat, but I'm away on work trips too much."

"I'd wanted a cat for a long time, but my ex was allergic. Truffle was definitely the silver lining of the breakup." As she said the word "breakup," Amy realized she'd waded into dangerous territory. "Sorry, exes are bad date conversation," she said with a tense laugh.

Charley laughed more genuinely, seeing Amy's discomfort. "Don't worry about it. Tulsa is the silver lining of my breakup. I get it."

Amy's curiosity was piqued. She briefly considered asking about Charley's ex but knew it was a bad road to go down if she was hoping to turn up the heat later. With both of them feeling the weight of their exes in the room, Amy tried another direction. "But at least you got a really cool job out of the move too. Right? Are you still enjoying it?"

Now it was Charley's turn to look pleased to have something to grab onto in the conversation. She crossed her right ankle over her left knee and tucked an arm behind her head. "Oh yeah, I'm loving it! The other people on my team are just as passionate about sustainability in the industry as I am, which can be hard to find. I'm so glad I get to do something I care about so much. You must feel that way about baking too. From what I've eaten, you've clearly got the magic touch."

Shit, Amy thought. She'd somehow changed lanes from exes to an even worse topic. Nothing would kill the mood faster than an unjust, homophobic firing. She decided on the spot to tiptoe around the subject, discussing baking without referring to Daily Bread. "It's definitely satisfying to do something I know I'm pretty good at, you know? And baking is so fulfilling for all of the senses. You see it turn from dough into something beautiful. You have these great smells; you feel every ingredient, taste the finished product, and some of it even makes noise. Like, there's this particular crackling sound bread makes fresh out of the oven as it releases all of the steam. It's almost like it sings to you." For a moment, all of Amy's senses remembered what it was like to pull a beautifully browned loaf of sourdough from the giant ovens at Daily Bread, the hot burst of steam in her face, the sound it made when she knocked on the bottom to make sure it was ready. Suddenly, she realized her eyes were tingling with the threat of tears. *Shit, change the subject fast, anything that won't make you cry.* "Um, what's that on your arm?"

Charley rolled her sleeve a little higher, above her elbow, to show the bottom of a tattoo that wrapped around her biceps, her gaze fixed on the place where Amy had pointed. Amy couldn't tell whether Charley had missed her rush of emotions or had noticed and was gracefully allowing Amy a moment to collect herself. "I have a half sleeve. I got it for myself as a graduation present, back when I didn't realize how stuffy office culture could be. It's fine, though, since I mostly wear suits to work."

Amy was intrigued. Pointing out the slightest edge of ink on Charley's arm was a pitiful excuse for a conversation starter. She hadn't even fully realized it was a tattoo when she asked, but now she was grateful for a chance to see what art Charley had chosen to permanently display on her body and for a chance to get a little closer. She scooted toward Charley and traced the black lines forking and twisting around a geometric pattern. "Is it . . . rivers? A map?"

Charley licked her lips, the tension between them more noticeable than ever with Amy's fingers lightly caressing Charley's arm. "I can show you, but I, um . . . would have to take my shirt off. Is that okay?"

"Yeah, totally," Amy said, her voice noticeably higher than usual.

Charley unbuttoned the top half of her shirt without breaking eye contact with Amy, then reached behind her head and pulled it off by the back of the neck, the gray tank top underneath briefly sliding up her torso. The threat of tears completely gone, Amy felt her body grow warmer. Charley angled her left arm toward Amy, reminding her why she'd taken the shirt off. With the full tattoo visible, Amy could see that it was an intricate tree with branches that reached toward Charley's shoulder, in all black ink, devoid of leaves as if depicted in winter. But below the tree, on the lower half of Charley's upper arm, was so much more: deep, twisting roots drawn into a geometric pattern of triangles that grew smaller and denser as they reached Charley's elbow. Amy couldn't help but also notice that Charley's arms and shoulders were surprisingly toned; she'd been able to tell that Charley was fit beneath her suits and sweaters, but seeing the shape of her muscles under her bare skin was different.

"It's a bur oak," Charley said. "As a bit of a geology nerd, I'm more into root systems than the green leafy part. Roots do all kinds of interesting things that you'd often never guess from looking. I like bur oaks because their root systems are mirror reflections of what you see above the ground. So those huge centuries-old oak trees down in Texas, we look at them and see this breathtaking enormous tree, so tall we can't really see the top. But underneath us, it stretches just as far toward the center of the earth." Charley pointed at the triangles forming the ground around the roots. "And these represent the soil layers and how much more complex the earth grows with water and minerals and . . . Sorry, like I said, geology nerd," Charley finished, perhaps interpreting Amy's silence as boredom.

Amy moved even closer, tracing her way from the tree's uppermost branch to its deepest root. "It's stunning." She'd never really thought about tree roots beyond the gnarled bits that peeked up through the soil or cracked the sidewalk. The showier bits of trees, like the colorful leaves and blooming flowers, usually grabbed her attention. But Charley was right; the part of the tree you couldn't see held so much more power and majesty. Amy was surprised that Charley had something so artistic, so beautifully full of meaning, beneath her buttoned-up exterior. But then again, hadn't Charley been her full passionately nerdy, earth-loving self from the beginning? She'd been showing Amy her roots all along.

Goosebumps rose across Charley's arm as Amy's finger lightly brushed her skin. "Do you have any tattoos?" Charley asked, her voice unsteady.

"Nothing as beautiful or deep as yours." Amy turned away from Charley and reached an arm behind her to tug the neck of her dress down toward her bra strap. "I got this one right when I turned eighteen. Can you see it?"

Charley reached out to pull the stretchy material of Amy's dress far enough down her shoulder to display the tattoo. It was a pink cupcake, cartoonishly drawn, with a swirl of frosting and sprinkles. Beneath it was a whisk and spatula crossing each other in an X. "An homage to a skull and crossbones?" Charley asked.

"Exactly! And then . . ." Amy turned back toward Charley and pulled up the hem of her dress, displaying a tattoo of a rainbow atop two fluffy white clouds on the side of her right thigh just below her hip. "My best friend Joel and I got matching tattoos on a whim after a Pride parade one year, but his is on his butt cheek. Cheesy, I know."

"I like them." Charley ran a fingertip across the arc of the rainbow on Amy's thigh. God, Amy wanted to kiss her. "I have one more, but it's on my calf. I don't think I can show you with my pants on, and that seems like a pretty unfair distribution of clothing," Charley said.

Amy felt the air around them shift, and it wasn't just the

candles flickering. Emboldened by the amount of skin they'd already shown, she leaned in so their faces were only inches apart. "So help me take off this dress. For fairness's sake."

Closing the remaining distance between them, Charley reached for the hem of Amy's dress and leaned in for a kiss. Having both held back for so much of the evening, they were quick to wrap themselves around each other now. Amy's hands tangled into Charley's short hair. Charley's hand traveled under Amy's dress, past her specially selected lacy underwear, to grab the bare skin at her waist. Their lips separated briefly as Charley pulled the dress over Amy's head. Feeling the cool air against her hot skin, Amy reached for Charley's waistband and unbuttoned her navy slacks. Charley lifted herself from the couch enough to slide down the tight pants, her lips still hot on Amy's.

Remembering the supposed purpose for taking off Charley's pants, Amy pulled back. "Where's your other tattoo?" she asked, out of breath.

Charley looked like the biggest heartthrob Amy had ever seen, with her tousled hair, flushed cheeks, gray tank top, and black bikini-cut underwear. She shifted to one hip, lifting her leg up toward Amy to show a watercolor-style geode tattoo on her outer calf. It was a beautiful combination of hard and soft, the craggy lines of the geode colored with touches of blues and greens. "Like I said, geology nerd."

Finding the art on Charley's body—and everything it told Amy about her—completely irresistible, Amy leaned down to kiss the drawing on Charley's calf. Within moments, they were back kissing at full speed. Amy tugged Charley's tank top over her head. Their mostly naked bodies met as they lay down full length across the couch. But as Amy's arm slid under Charley's bra strap, Charley pulled back. "It's really late. Should I . . ."

"Please stay." Amy's entire body was pulling her toward

Charley. Saying it out loud felt bold, but nothing mattered to Amy as much as feeling Charley's perfectly tattooed skin against hers.

Charley hesitated. "Are you sure? This is our second date. Are we moving too fast?" She seemed like she was physically holding herself back from Amy, like taking a moment was a challenge but worth the effort.

Amy brushed a thumb across Charley's lower lip. "Ever since the Center of the Universe, I've been thinking about that kiss and waiting to see you again. I'm not ready for this date to be over. But if you want to hit Pause for tonight, I respect that." She forced herself to sit back a little as she spoke, trying to give Charley the space to make her own decision.

Charley's gaze traveled from Amy's eyes to her full lips, down past her collarbone, to where her chest rose and fell with each breath. Charley leaned in, then whispered, "I'm hitting Play."

With Charley's eyes on her and permission to launch, Amy suddenly became aware of her mostly naked body. She couldn't help but feel self-conscious, even in her nicest bra and panty set. At least her breasts looked good, pushed up by the lacy lavender bra. Maybe that would distract from the pouch of her stomach, and her soft upper arms, and her rounded thighs. She was so used to being called "cute" that she'd learned to use it in her favor; "sexy" was somewhat outside of her comfort zone. With Autumn, she'd managed to pull it off with a little feigned confidence. But this moment with Charley felt too vulnerable, too real for her to pretend.

Amy stood from the couch, hoping straighter posture would be more flattering. But seeing Charley's sleek, muscular body, Amy knew no position would make her look as good. "Um, should we . . . ? The bedroom . . ."

Charley followed Amy through the short hallway to her

bedroom and climbed onto the bed. Amy caught herself staring, frozen as she watched Charley's nearly perfect body arrange itself on her comforter. To hide her blushing cheeks, the physical evidence of her self-consciousness, Amy dug into her closet. She needed something that would distract Charley from her physical shortcomings.

"What are you doing in there?" Charley asked over the sound of Amy's rustling.

"Just looking for . . . Here it is!" She emerged with a green plastic tub, attempting to subtly wipe away a fine layer of dust as she removed the top. These hadn't been in Amy's plan for the evening, but she desperately wanted her first time with Charley to go well and felt like she needed reinforcements. "Pick your pleasure."

Charley peered over the edge of the bin at a pile of sex toys, most in their original packaging. She looked confused. "Oh."

"I must admit that I, uh, haven't had a lot of practice with most of these." Most of Amy's supply came from her desperate attempts to keep Autumn's attention during the final weeks of their relationship. Unfortunately, things had taken a downturn before they had a chance to give them a try, and Amy, reeling from the breakup, had shoved them to the back of her closet.

Amy shook herself from the memory. Now was not the time to think about her ex. She reached into the bin and pulled out a strap-on harness, her attempts at orienting it in her hands making it look more like a cat's cradle. "I can try this on, unless you want to? It goes with . . . this dildo, I think. Or maybe it was . . . Shit." Her rummaging set off some device deep in the bin, causing the whole thing to vibrate. By the time she located and turned off the correct vibrator, Amy's bed was strewn with toys and loose batteries. All of her confidence had evaporated. She wanted to look like she knew what she was doing, but she felt so out of practice.

Charley eyed the array uncomfortably, but her eyes softened as she took in Amy's anxious face. "What if we just took it slow? Got to know each other without this stuff?"

"Yeah, of course!" Amy swept the pile of sex toys into the plastic bin, her hands shaking. "Whatever you want."

Charley grabbed Amy's hips and pulled her toward the bed. "It's whatever *you* want too, you know." She pressed her mouth to Amy's, biting her bottom lip gently before kissing her way down Amy's sternum. "Do you want this?"

"Yes," Amy breathed. With Charley's lips against her skin, Charley's hands caressing the parts of her body that made her most self-conscious, she was surprised to find that she *actually* felt sexy. Not cute, not like she was pretending to feel sexy, but genuinely sexy. And it felt amazing.

Charley slid a hand under the lacy band of Amy's bra, her thumb positioned to unclasp it. "And this?"

Amy nodded. She felt cool air across her chest as the bra fell to the floor. A gasp escaped her lips as Charley's fingers grazed the curve of her breasts. "What if I . . ." Amy's voice trailed off as she reached around Charley's back and unclasped her black jersey bra.

Slowly, the two explored each other's bodies, discovering sensitive spots and the fiery responses they triggered. As their pulses and breaths and desires rose and fell, rose and fell, the box of toys lay completely forgotten on the floor.

Amy awoke the next morning to a sunrise that seemed extra bright, feeling a bit sore in her neck, arms, and back from the physical exertion of the previous night. But despite her soreness, the intimate admiration Charley had shown for her body the night before made her feel better in her own skin than she ever had before. With Autumn's constant desire for new toys, new experiences, and new bodies, Amy had never felt like enough. But cuddled next to Charley and remembering their profound connection the night before, Amy thought that maybe her body had everything she needed. She watched Charley's naked sleeping form rise and fall with each breath beneath her sheets for a moment, then pulled herself away from the bed, wanting to be in top form for Regi and Jared's wedding. Trying to move quietly, Amy dressed, brushed her teeth, and put on a bit of makeup in an attempt at a natural-yet-unnatural morning glow. She returned to bed a few minutes later with two mugs of fresh coffee. After placing one mug on her bedside table, she used a finger to trace the uppermost branches of Charley's oak tree tattoo.

"Good morning, sunshine," Amy said as Charley began to stir.

Charley's eyes squinted open as she slowly processed where she was. "Mmm, g'morning." She pushed herself up to a sitting position and stretched her arms. Eyeing the coffee, she let out a groggy grunt that seemed to mean "For me?"

Amy handed her the mug with a nod. "I'm going to throw together some breakfast. How do you like your eggs?"

Amy loved making breakfast. Whenever she stayed too late at Joel and Damian's and slept over on their couch, she had a full breakfast on the table by the time they woke up. Sometimes she thought her best friends tricked her into losing track of time on purpose just for the omelets. She used to dream of lazy, romantic breakfasts with Autumn, but she had always turned her down, only ever wanting coffee and a protein bar. Now, even with a long wedding day ahead, she couldn't bear the thought of Charley leaving yet.

Charley squinted at the clock on the bedside table. "I, uh . . . Yeah, I guess I can stay for a quick breakfast. Um, scrambled?"

Amy reflexively checked the clock as well. It wasn't even eight o'clock yet, and it was a Saturday. Why was Charley in a hurry to leave? Did she feel bad about imposing? Or had her experience last night not been the dream it had been for Amy? Did Charley regret their time together? Amy tried to look casual and carefree as her mind raced with more and more dire possibilities. "Are you sure? You don't have to stay." She hoped her voice didn't sound desperate.

"Yes," Charley said more firmly, smiling up at Amy. "Sorry. I just—no. I mean yes. That sounds great."

Amy moved to the kitchen to start breakfast. After getting dressed, Charley appeared in the kitchen door, absorbed in her phone. Minutes passed with only the sound of Amy whisking eggs or flipping hash browns on the stove. She felt distinctly awkward, like the tender mood of last night had disappeared with the sun rising.

"Not much of a morning person, are you?" Amy said after a while.

"Sorry." Charley tucked her phone away. "Work emails. I'm just used to a morning routine." Amy carried two plates laden with eggs, toast, and hash browns to the kitchen table. "But this looks amazing. Thank you."

"No problem!" Amy said in what she hoped was a cheerful voice. "And anyway, sometimes changing up your routine can be good, right?" Charley smiled, then reached across the table and put a hand on Amy's cheek. Amy's skin burned, and she knew she was blushing. As they tucked in to their eggs, an idea occurred to her. "Hey, speaking of, what are you doing tonight?"

"Not sure yet," Charley said through a bite of toast.

"Any chance you want to be my plus-one to a wedding?" She'd just remembered that Regi had offered to let her bring a date, and though she'd nearly forgotten since she hadn't been planning to use the offer, given that she'd have to focus on working, this morning, she could picture it so easily: Charley in one of her fantastic suits, Amy all dressed up, dancing the night away at Regi and Jared's actually *fun* wedding reception. Her first ever wedding that wasn't in a Baptist church. She hadn't come out to Regi and Jared yet, but maybe, with Charley next to her, it wouldn't be so hard. Just imagining it made her stomach do a somersault. "Free dinner, drinks, music, dancing. Could be a good time." Amy's voice trailed off as she realized Charley had frozen, a forkful of hash browns halfway to her mouth.

"Tonight? That's, um, not a lot of notice."

"Oh, no, of course. I totally—just a last-minute—I thought you probably wouldn't," Amy said, stumbling over her words in her effort to backpedal. "No, I mean, no problem. I'm sorry, I shouldn't have asked. It's a lot to throw at you."

Charley's phone dinged with an incoming text. "Shit, that's my boss," Charley mumbled. She shoveled the last of her eggs into her mouth. "Actually, I have a lot to get done today. I should go."

Amy's heart sank. She had definitely freaked Charley out with the wedding invite. She cursed herself for never being able to play it cool. But then, as she remembered how weird Charley had been about staying for breakfast, an even worse thought occurred to her. Was Charley simply not interested anymore? Or had Amy done something last night that had turned her off? It had been a long time since she'd dated someone, much less had sex. She cringed inwardly as she remembered the sex toy box. But after that mishap, she'd thought they'd really connected. Was she a little rusty? She was pretty sure that both of their multiple orgasms had been a good sign, but Charley's weirdness this morning cast everything in a new light. Charley didn't seem like the kind of person who was just looking for a one-night stand.

But with a sinking feeling in her stomach, Amy had to wonder: Was she getting herself into another Autumn situation? Was Charley just another player? Now that she'd slept with Amy, was Charley off to the next conquest?

She watched in an increasingly panicked silence as Charley collected her things from around the apartment and put on her coat. Her thoughts spiraling, Amy realized that she still hadn't told Charley about getting fired from Daily Bread or even that she was getting paid for the wedding tonight. Should she tell her now? Could some honest vulnerability make a difference at this point? But if Charley was about to break Amy's heart, it didn't feel worth embarrassing herself by telling the story of her getting fired. No, maybe she'd already shared too much of herself with Charley too soon.

After scratching Truffle behind the ears, Charley turned to Amy, who stood like a statue next to the table. "Thanks for dinner and breakfast and . . . you know, everything in between," Charley said.

"See you soon?" Amy asked, wondering if her words sounded as desperate as they felt.

"Yeah, for sure. We'll talk soon." Charley leaned in for a sweet but too-short kiss. "Have fun at the wedding."

And before Amy could finish saying goodbye, Charley was gone.

7

Joel pulled his car up to the art studio where Regi and Jared's wedding would take place and turned on his hazard lights.

"What exactly did she say again?" Joel asked as Amy gathered her bag of makeup and hair supplies.

Before saying goodbye to Jared and Regi at Christina's wedding, Amy had offered to pick the cakes up from Daily Bread on the way downtown, partially to make things easier for Regi and partially because she was feeling a little guilty about accepting $250 for going to a wedding. She'd figured any extra favors would relieve her discomfort. And since she'd designed the cakes and their watercolor-inspired frosting decoration herself, she'd felt a certain obligation to see they made it safely to the art gallery. But that was before the shit hit the fan. Luckily, Joel had been kind enough to go inside Daily Bread and pick up the cakes while Amy yet again slunk down in the passenger seat, hoping not to make eye contact with any of her former co-workers.

"She said she had a lot to get done today and she should go," Amy said in a flat voice.

"Maybe the wedding thing was a little too much too soon. Or maybe she hates weddings! She seemed into the sex, right?"

"Definitely. I am positive I was not the only one having a good time." Amy sighed. "But this morning was *so weird*. Maybe I misread what was happening. I feel like such an idiot. I just . . . I haven't liked someone like this since . . ." She didn't want to say Autumn's name, but it hung in the space between them.

Joel was silent for a moment. "I don't know what to tell you. But if she tried your tiramisu, she won't be able to stay away for long."

"Is that a euphemism?"

Joel's loud laugh made Amy feel a little better. "Yes, but also literally. That shit is delicious."

"Thanks for the ride and for the pep talk, babe, but I better get inside."

"Anytime. And listen: Don't spend too much time stressing about Charley or about the job hunt. Just enjoy this wedding, and make that sweet bridesmaid cash. We'll figure out all of your problems later."

"You make it sound so easy." She took a deep breath, trying to let it all go. She didn't want to bring her drama to Regi's day. Even though they hardly knew each other, she wanted Regi's memories of her wedding day to be perfect. Trying to make things run smoothly was the least she could do, not just for the $250, but because she genuinely liked Regi and Jared. Plus, this was her first chance to attend a wedding of someone her age outside of her conservative family, and she was excited to finally see that wedding movie magic come to life. Amy glanced at the enormous cake boxes in the back seat of Joel's car. "Can you give me a hand with these before you go? Just to get them inside the door."

Amy and Joel got the cakes from the car to a table in the entryway of the gallery before hugging goodbye. As Joel's car pulled away, Amy pulled out her phone to text Regi.

Hey, I'm here! Can you send someone to help carry the cakes?

Great, Kim and Denise are on their way down!

As she waited for the two other bridesmaids, she reviewed her backstory in her head. Amy and Regi had agreed that it was weird to tell everyone they'd met only two weeks before. But with all of Regi's closest friends and family around, they would need to explain why none of them had met Amy before and why she hadn't shown up to any of the wedding showers, bachelorette parties, and other wedding-adjacent events the couple had held in the previous weeks. They'd agreed on a half truth: that Amy was an old elementary school friend who had moved away in third grade and was filling in last minute for the bridesmaid who'd moved to Dubayy. Amy realized that her high school and college theater experience would finally come in handy today for the improv she would have to do, as would the hair and makeup supplies she had gathered from her old costume box. She'd never really been the star of the show but had spent plenty of time in the chorus, creating elaborate backstories for her unnamed roles. Even better for wedding purposes, she thought, was her experience on costume crew and stage-managing behind the scenes. Her ability to solve problems and keep things moving onstage had definitely translated well to the service industry. And what was a wedding if not a theatrical production?

Amy spotted two women walking through the gallery who had to be Kim and Denise. One had curlers in her blond hair, and both were wearing monogrammed silk bathrobes over T-shirts and leggings. Amy waved them toward her and the tall cakes in the entryway. The one with curlers reached her first. "Amy? Hi! Oh my God, it's so nice to finally meet you. I've heard Regi talk about you for years!" Amy smiled but inwardly rolled her eyes. She knew it was just the kind of thing people said to each other to be nice, but Kim clearly didn't know how obvious a lie it was. "I'm Kim, Regi's sorority sister. But practically real sisters! I'm a hugger," she added unnecessarily as she wrapped her arms around Amy's tense shoulders. Amy's nose was filled with the scent of hairspray and expensive perfume as she lightly patted Kim's silk-clad back.

Kim released her, and the other bridesmaid presented a French manicured hand. "Denise. Regi's college roommate. Good to meet you." After Kim's over-the-top greeting, Denise's calm voice and demeanor put Amy more at ease.

"Really nice to meet you both," Amy said. "Do you know where the kitchen is? I think we can drop these off with the caterer."

Denise nodded. Amy directed Kim and Denise to each take an end of the tall, unwieldy box containing the three-tier wedding cake, while Amy balanced the smaller groom's cake and her hair and makeup bag. As they made their way back to the kitchen, Kim launched into a monologue about what jewelry would look best for the ceremony, considering the neckline and color of the dresses, her planned hairstyle, and the precise shade of her smoky eye. "I would wear these gorgeous pearl earrings that I inherited from my grandmother, but I'm saving them for my wedding in April. I definitely can't ruin them by wearing them now when they'll be in all my wedding pictures in a few months! That would be super embarrassing, right?"

"Yeah, embarrassing," Denise said dryly. Amy barely bit back a laugh, navigating around a large glass art piece as they entered the largest part of the gallery.

The ceremony space was draped with raspberry and navy fabric, and a couple of event staff were setting out chairs at reception tables. Amy was impressed by the way Regi's decorations highlighted the beautiful artwork hanging in the gallery, rather than upstaging it. Amy knew Regi was into art, but her choice of the space and the decorations within it showed she had great taste, and the final look—or at least the in-progress look, as things were still coming together—seemed to really fit the couple. It was young and fresh, classy but not too formal. And Jared and Regi's sense of humor was present in the way the art met the decorations, like in the large painting of a man making a supplicating gesture hung above the bar so he appeared to be offering drinks to wedding guests.

After dropping the cakes off with the caterers, Amy followed the other two bridesmaids up a flight of stairs. They led her to a small room that was arranged for the day as a makeshift bridal lounge, full of folding chairs, curling irons, makeup mirrors, and hanging dresses. Amy, Kim, and Denise joined Regi and four more bridesmaids, who waved in greeting as they bustled around the room. Across the room, a hairstylist, a photographer, and a woman Amy guessed was Regi's mother were reviewing the wedding program.

Regi waved from the far side of the room, where another stylist was applying a thick layer of eye shadow. "Amy, hi! I'm so glad you're here!" She gestured for Amy to come over. Amy stepped over piles of high heels and boxes of bouquets and grabbed Regi's outstretched hand.

"Regi, you're glowing! You look beautiful." This was mostly true, although the glow was a bit diminished by the stress apparent in Regi's eyes. "The cakes are with the caterers, and the space looks great. What can I do to help?"

"Actually, it would be a big help if you could take the boutonnieres to the groomsmen's room across the hall. And maybe you could check on the florist downstairs? The delivery guy seems pretty clueless. I don't even know if he knows which side of the floral arrangement is up."

Amy gave Regi's hand a reassuring squeeze. "Of course. Don't stress. I'm on it."

Regi's face relaxed. "You're a lifesaver."

Amy's smile mirrored the relief in Regi's. Amy had been nervous that she wouldn't have much to do, wouldn't be able to prove that paying her to be a bridesmaid was worth it. Plus, staying busy would help keep thoughts of Charley at bay. She found the long, thin box of boutonnieres and stepped into the hall, where she followed the sound of male voices to the room holding the groom and his half of the wedding party.

Entering the groom's lounge was like being transported to a wholly different universe. The bride's room had been bustling with nervous energy, full of chatter and debates over hairstyles, every surface covered with beauty products. Regi was like a queen bee, the others circling around her and vying for her attention. Jared's room felt more like a sports bar. The groomsmen were half-dressed in their suit pants and T-shirts, sipping beers while watching a University of Oklahoma football game. Were they really preparing for the same event? "Amy!" Jared rose from his seat on a couch. "Good to see you! Can I get you a beer?"

"Sorry, I'm here on official bridesmaid business to deliver

these boutonnieres. I'm pretty sure taking a beer from you would count as fraternizing with the enemy. But congrats, really. Can I get y'all anything from downstairs? I'm heading down to check on the flowers."

"No, we're good." As Amy reached the door to leave, she heard Jared call out, "Oh, wait! Hey, there are only half of our boutonnieres in here. There should be four more. Was there another box?"

"Let me check. I'll be right back," Amy replied with the same voice she used as a bartender when checking the back for extra beers. She could totally handle this bridesmaid thing.

Amy crossed spheres again to the bride's room and hunted for another box. Finding none, she returned to Regi's makeup station. "Have you seen the other box of boutonnieres?"

"What do you mean? That's the only one they brought." Regi's voice grew steadily faster and higher pitched. "Please don't tell me they didn't bring them."

"Never mind!" Amy quickly backtracked. "I'm sure I saw them downstairs. Don't worry about a thing!" The moment she exited the room, Amy's reassuring smile turned to a grimace. She shouldn't have tried to bring Regi into this when she was already in a whirlwind of stress.

But Amy could handle this. What was she there for if not to track down a few missing flowers? She ran downstairs, hoping to catch the florist. Amid the hustle and bustle of chair and table setup, she asked one of the venue workers if the florist was around. "Oh, no, that guy dropped the flowers and ran. He left everything over there." He pointed to a stack of boxes and vases near the door.

Digging through the pile of flowers, Amy quickly realized there were no additional boutonnieres. She refused to panic, determined to reduce Regi's worries, not add to them. This was a solvable problem, she reminded herself. First step: Call the florist.

"We dropped off the full order. I checked," said a defensive voice on the other end of the line.

"But there should be eight boutonnieres, not four. Are you sure there isn't an extra box in the back of the truck?"

While waiting for the florist to double-check, Amy felt a tap on her shoulder and turned to find one of the caterers. "We've had, um, a bit of a mishap with the cake."

Amy looked across the room to see two other caterers barely holding the cake together as the top tier tilted dangerously to the side. "Shit! Hold it, I'm coming! Don't move!" Another caketastrophe? Well, at least she was more prepared to handle this than the flower debacle. She threw her phone down on a table, ran to the kitchen and scrubbed her hands, then grabbed a butter knife and wad of paper towels. "Do you have plastic straws? I need four plastic straws now," she said to one of the caterers as she rushed to perform emergency surgery on the cake. "Actually, make it eight."

As she wedged her hand between the middle and top layers, she heard a small voice coming from her phone. "Someone hit Speaker on that phone, please!" Amy said.

Now at full volume, the florist said, "I just double-checked the order and we're real sorry; we missed the other four boutonnieres. We'll comp them on your final bill."

"Comping won't help us now! We have a wedding in an hour and only enough boutonnieres for half of the groomsmen. How quickly can you get them here?" Amy said, projecting toward her phone, hoping the florist could hear her on the other end, as she trimmed straws with one hand and inserted them into the cake to stabilize it.

"Sorry, ma'am, but we don't have any more lily boutonnieres."

Amy glanced over her shoulder at the vases by the front door of the gallery. "Do you have succulents that match the ones in the arrangements here?"

The florist sighed. "I'll have to check."

"Succulents or even roses, something that goes with the color scheme? Something you can get in our hands in forty-five minutes or less?" Her questions were met with silence. Luckily, thanks to her job at the bar, this wasn't her first time handling an unhelpful vendor. "What's your name?"

After a pause, the florist said, "Uh, Kendall?"

"Look, Kendall, if you can make this happen for me, there's a very complimentary Yelp review in your future. Hell, I'll call your boss and tell them you deserve a promotion."

There was another pause on the other end of the line. "I think I can make something work."

"And in forty-five minutes? Faster is even better!"

"I have another delivery in an hour. I'll drop it off before then."

"That's what I like to hear! Thank you, Kendall!" Amy mouthed to one of the caterers to end the call just as she finally stabilized the top tier of the cake. The frosting was smeared from the near collapse, but thanks to the watercolor style decoration, it wasn't too far gone to save. With the butter knife and paper towels, Amy was able to smooth out the bumps and clean up the mess. Then she turned the more affected side of the cake toward the wall. "Good as new," she said as she wiped her hands.

The caterers gawked.

"Cakes are kind of my thing," Amy said. "Nice work, everyone. Is everything else good to go?"

In a way, Amy felt more at home among the paid wedding crew than in the bridal suite. Working behind the scenes to make the customer happy was definitely in her wheelhouse. Sitting around getting her hair done and small-talking with the other bridesmaids? That was a little harder to pull off, especially while lying about her relationship to Regi.

Amy spent the next fifteen minutes directing the setting up of the flowers and table centerpieces and testing the sound system with the DJ, then turned to see Kim standing on the stairs, her head cocked. "Wow," Kim said. "I was wondering where you've been, but I see you've had your hands full. Get back upstairs! Everyone else is already dressed."

Amy returned to the bridal room and navigated through a cloud of hairspray to find Regi. "The boutonnieres are taken care of, downstairs looks beautiful, and I think I saw guests starting to arrive and park outside," Amy reported. "Anything else I can help with before I get ready?"

"That's such a relief," Regi said. Thank goodness she didn't know how close it had come to a sticky situation with the cake. "You better start on your hair and makeup. We have stylists here, but they're pretty busy with the other girls. Do you feel comfortable doing your own?"

Amy looked over to see Kim talking to a stylist about what shade of blush worked best for her complexion. She assured Regi that she could handle herself.

It didn't take long for Amy to apply makeup and pin her curls back from her face in a simple but flattering updo. For the first time since she'd arrived, she didn't have anything to do, and she itched for a task. She scanned the room, looking for anything that might need tidying up, and noticed the flower girl in a battle with her mother over her frilly pink dress. As her mother, who Amy had gathered was Regi's sister, tried to slip the dress over the girl's head, she flew into a full-blown tantrum. "*I don't wanna!*" she screeched, throwing herself on the floor.

Amy hurried over and kneeled down next to the little girl. She didn't have a ton of experience with kids, so she decided to utilize the same tactic she used with drunk bar patrons: distraction. "Hi. I'm Amy. What's your name?"

Amy's quiet, pleasant tone and smiling face threw the girl off. She stilled on the floor, tears still present on her face but no longer flowing. "Onae." Amy looked up at the girl's mother, already in her own bridesmaid dress, who appeared grateful for the help. Getting down on the floor to deal with an upset child without messing up her dress and hair seemed like it would have been quite a challenge. She nodded her approval for Amy to continue.

"Hi, Onae," Amy said. "I was just about to put on my dress, and I could use a helper. I heard you're really smart and kind, so I thought you might be able to help me."

Onae sat up thoughtfully. "I like to help. My teacher Ms. Sanderson gives us stickers when we help."

"That's so cool! I love stickers. And maybe if you help me with my dress, I can help you with your dress. What do you think?"

"I hate that dress," Onae said with a sour face. "I hate pink and I hate dresses."

Amy checked to make sure Regi wasn't paying attention and was glad to see her pouring and passing out glasses of champagne with Denise across the room as the photographer snapped pictures. "I'm not a fan of pink either, and my dress looks a lot like yours," Amy said in an undertone. "See?" She gestured to her dress, hanging on a rack nearby. Although not awful, it was obviously a bridesmaid dress—a dark pink, one-shouldered chiffon dress with a big fabric flower at the waist. Definitely not something that could be worn again without looking as if you'd stepped out of a David's Bridal catalog. "But to me, it's more than just some pink dress. It's my spy outfit," she improvised.

Onae's eyes widened. She whispered, "You're a spy?" Her mother looked amused and curious where this was headed.

"Well, I'm not always a spy, but I'm going to be one today. Sometimes people come to weddings like this one and they want to make things go wrong. They want to make people sad or throw things off from what your aunt Regi and uncle Jared have planned. And I'm going to be a secret spy to make sure Regi and Jared have a really great day. Do you want them to have a great day?" Onae nodded enthusiastically. "So I'm going to wear my pink dress so I look just like every other bridesmaid, but really, I'm a spy making sure everything goes right and no one snuck into the wedding to ruin it."

She had Onae's undivided attention.

"You know, now that you know my secret, I could use some help in there. If you wear a pink dress too, maybe you can be a spy with me. If you wear your dress and drop the flower petals just like your mom taught you"—she looked to Onae's mom, who nodded discreetly—"everyone will think you're just a flower girl, but you can pay attention to the guests to make sure everyone is happy and here to celebrate Regi and Jared and not here to mess things up. What do you say?"

Onae jumped up, suddenly serious and focused. "I accept my mission," she said with a slight lisp.

Amy raised an eyebrow. It seemed like Onae was well versed with spy protocol for someone just out of diapers. "All right then, you're hired. But you can't tell anyone that you're a spy. You have to make them think that you're the perfect flower girl. Can you do that?"

Onae nodded confidently. "Hand me my spy costume."

"Please," Onae's mom said with a wink toward Amy.

"Hand me my spy costume, *please,*" Onae corrected herself.

Her mother breathed a sigh of relief and pulled the frilly

flower girl dress over Onae's head. Where once she had screamed and fought, Onae was now all business. She smoothed the skirt of her dress with her tiny hands and picked up the flower girl basket, then looked Amy up and down. "You better put on your spy costume too. We got a lotta work to do."

Amy nodded. "Right you are. How about I get dressed while you start gathering intelligence on the other bridesmaids?"

Onae leaned in toward Amy's ear and whispered, "I've had a bad feeling about that one all morning." The girl nodded toward Kim, whom Amy was surprised to find looking right at them. At least she was out of hearing distance.

Amy looked up to see that Onae's mom was turned away, chatting with the photographer. "Me too," Amy whispered back. "Let me know what you learn. And remember: If anyone asks, you're just a flower girl, right?"

Onae lifted her chin confidently and held out her hand for a shake. "You got it, boss."

Amy took Onae's tiny hand in her own and gave it a firm shake. With a big grin and a flounce of her skirt, Onae skipped off toward the other bridesmaids.

Onae's mom turned back toward Amy, looking more relaxed. "Thank you," she said. "I've had it with fighting her about this. She's always been a bit of a tomboy, but she loves her aunt Regi. I'm Rachel, by the way. Regi's sister and matron of honor." She extended her hand and Amy grabbed it.

"I'm Amy, Regi's . . ." She paused for a moment. If Rachel was Regi's sister, she might see right past her elementary school lie.

"Don't worry about it. Regi told me everything. We're happy to have you," Rachel whispered. "And sorry about Onae. She's . . . willful, you might say."

"Onae's obviously a great kid. Everyone gets stressed during weddings; I'm happy to help. Hey, since I missed the rehearsal dinner last night, would you mind catching me up on anything I should know before we hit the aisle?"

Rachel filled Amy in on the order of the ceremony, finishing just as someone knocked at the door. Amy rushed over to find the florist, who looked to be in their teens, with box in hand. "Excuse me, are you the wedding coordinator?" they asked.

"Close enough." Amy opened the box to find four succulent boutonnieres. "Yes! Thank you very much. You're just in time."

The florist lingered for a moment. "And that positive review you mentioned . . ."

"You've got it, Kendall. Just as soon as they say, 'I do.'"

"Um, my name is actually Tyler. I just thought you were asking because you were gonna talk to the manager. Like, in a bad way." The teenager shrugged in apology.

Amy snorted. "All right, *Tyler,* I'll tell your manager you did a great job."

After Tyler left, Amy sneaked over to the groom's dressing room and presented him with the new boutonnieres.

"Oh, thanks. I totally forgot." Jared accepted the box and opened it. "Are these different from the others?"

"Mismatched boutonnieres are all the rage these days," Amy improvised. "Just make sure they're staggered. Lily, then succulent, then lily, then succulent."

Amy rushed back to the bridal prep room, pulled off her T-shirt, then slid the chiffon dress over her head and zipped it up the side. She and Rachel tied the silk ribbons on the backs of each other's dresses. They grabbed champagne glasses just in time to join the other bridesmaids in watching Regi's mother zip and button the back of Regi's wedding gown, a strapless mermaid dress with an embellished belt. After securing and smoothing the dress, the stylist and Regi's mother stood on each side of Regi to pin the veil into her natural corkscrew curls.

Regi turned around, the look completed. Amy felt tears prickling in her eyes. She couldn't help it: Regi looked so beautiful and so happy. She and Jared seemed genuinely in love and good for each other. Suddenly, the strange situation became more real. Amy was about to stand in front of Regi's and Jared's whole families and pretend she had any right to be there. She was going to play a major role in the wedding of an almost complete stranger, when she wasn't even invited to do the same for her own family members. Thinking of Christina's wedding stung for a moment, but she pushed the memory away. This was Regi and Jared's day, not hers, and she was going to do everything she could to make it perfect.

8

Although preparing for the ceremony had been hectic, the real challenge for Amy lay in the reception. The ceremony itself was short and sweet. Amy's duties were minimal: walk, stand, smile, hold a bouquet. She teared up during the "I dos," seeing Jared's face so full of love and hearing Regi's voice break with emotion. Regi and Jared's promises to love and care for each other for the rest of their lives sparked something in Amy that really did feel like magic. And given the tears and laughter and smiles in the audience, she knew she wasn't the only one who felt it. There was even some comic relief when Jared attempted to break the ceremonial wineglass and missed not once but twice before managing to stomp on the right spot with the right amount of force—a truly human moment that only made everything feel more perfect.

The only hitch was Ross, the groomsman Amy had been paired with. He'd pregamed for the ceremony a little too enthusiastically and paraded down the aisle smelling like straight liquor. At least she was able to keep him steady as they walked to the reception area before she deposited him at the bridal party table and put a glass of water in front of him. She wasn't sure how much of a chance he'd have to sober up, though, with the drinks flowing and music bumping.

All in all, Amy was having a great experience at her first non-Baptist wedding. The Cheesy Noods buffet was a hit, and once everyone had eaten their fill, Regi and Jared ceremoniously cut the cake. Amy felt a rush of pride as the guests oohed and aahed at the beautiful dessert, which, she was glad to see, showed no signs of having recently been a near disaster. A few minutes later, a caterer delivered slices of the cake to the guests, and as Amy lifted her fork to her mouth, the scent of raspberry and mint transported her momentarily to the Daily Bread kitchen, where she'd painstakingly tested and perfected the blend of flavors. She took a tiny bite and was annoyed to find it tasted just as good as when she made it. If she had a do-over, she would alter the instructions or leave a secret ingredient out of them, something to make it difficult to nail the cake without her.

Amy's seat was in between Kim and Ross, who seemed to be in a competition for being the least appealing person to sit next to at a wedding reception. Ross had already staggered off to the bar again, his water glass untouched, and Kim was mid-monologue. "I've already booked a live band for my wedding," she was saying. "Having a DJ is fine for some people, I guess, but you just can't compete with a live band! It's like the food truck thing. This mac and cheese is good, but isn't a seated dinner with four courses a little more elevated? I love soul food, but it's just not as formal as other cuisines, you know?"

Amy grunted noncommittally. Calling Kim on her casual racism at the dinner table didn't seem like the most helpful thing

Amy could do as a bridesmaid. She tried to remind herself that Kim had to have *some* redeeming qualities if Regi liked her.

"Not to mention Jared's suit," Kim went on. "Floral? In November? Everyone is going to look back at those wedding pictures and be like, *Why did Regi marry that . . . you know . . . ?*" Kim made a limp-wristed gesture while pursing her lips and raising an eyebrow. Amy bit back a retort, excusing herself and heading to the bar. After all that time working at Daily Bread, she was somewhat inured to casual homophobic comments like this. "Somewhat" being the key word. If she weren't being paid to be there—and if she didn't genuinely like Regi—she would have given Kim a piece of her mind. *Wouldn't I?* Amy suddenly wondered, navigating the crowds of celebrants. Outside the safe bubble of Ruby Red's and her friends, Amy was either closeted at the bakery or biting her tongue at events with her extended family. When was the last time she'd felt comfortable or brave enough to tell someone their comments were wrong or hurtful? Maybe that was why she'd blown up at Donna, she realized. She'd been holding it all in for too long.

At the bar, Amy squeezed in next to a silver-haired woman, who extended her hand, her eyes crinkling in a smile. "I'm Regi's aunt Patrice. And you are?"

Amy took her hand, smiling back. "Amy. An old friend of Regi's from elementary school."

"Kendall-Whittier Elementary?" she asked, her eyes lighting up. Amy nodded. Amy had actually attended an elementary school across town from Kendall-Whittier, but she figured it was close enough. "That's wonderful!" Patrice said. "I was the Kendall-Whittier school secretary for over twenty years. What years were you there?"

"Um," Amy said. The bartender nodded her way, and Amy ordered a vodka tonic. "Feels like a hundred years ago!" she said, turning back to Patrice.

"If you were there with Regi, we must have been there at the same time. I'm sure I look a little older than I did back then." Patrice clasped Amy's upper arm. "Wait, are you Amanda Fuller? Tim and Paula's girl?"

"Oh, um, no. Different Amy. Excuse me, bridesmaid's duty calls! Nice to meet you!" She accepted her vodka tonic from the bartender and dashed away as quickly as she could in three-inch heels.

Halfway across the room, she felt a tug on the back of her dress and turned to find Onae. The flower girl looked surreptitiously around her before gesturing for Amy to lean closer. Amy squatted next to her and whispered, "Have you learned anything from your spying?"

Onae nodded urgently. "That man over there with glasses?" She pointed to a guest at a nearby table. "He says he's not eating any cake, and I think that's weird. Do you think it's poisoned?"

Amy held back a laugh and made as serious an expression as she could muster. "I also don't trust anyone who doesn't eat cake. But I actually helped make this one, so I'm pretty sure it's not poisoned."

Onae visibly relaxed. "Good, because I really want to eat it." She tilted her head and examined Amy. "Do most spies know how to make cake?"

"Only the best ones."

Amy returned to her seat just as the toasts began: the best man went first, followed by Regi's sister and father. The groom then made a move to stand and thank the collected guests, but he was interrupted by a slurred statement from Amy's right. "I've got a toast!"

Ross pushed his chair back and stumbled to the center of the room, his tie askew. "I've got a toast for my buddy here, Jared, and his girl, Regi." Jared eyed Ross warily, then ceded the floor and sat back down. "They got married! Did y'all know? They tied the fuckin' knot!" A few guests laughed nervously. Amy saw Rachel reach to cover Onae's young ears. "Marriage is bitchin', but shout out to the single ladies! Who's single? Anyone?"

As Ross continued to ramble, Amy glanced at Regi, who looked pained. Amy saw her whisper something to Jared, who shook his head and shrugged. Regi's eyes darted around the room, taking in her guests' surprised, wary expressions. Amy wished she could do something, but what? She wasn't even sure it was her place.

It was Kim's whisper in her ear that changed her mind. "No offense to Regi, obvi, but a sloppy, drunken toast is *so* on brand for this wedding." Amy stood so abruptly that Kim let out a surprised little squeak. She strode as confidently as she could to where Ross was standing at the front of the room and placed a hand on his shoulder just in time to interrupt his stream-of-consciousness monologue about how single and available he was.

"That's right, Ross, we're all here to celebrate Regi and Jared's love, aren't we?" Amy said, projecting over him. He looked confused, as if for a moment he'd forgotten how he ended up in front of the crowd. "And we're here to toast to a long, happy life for these two wonderful people. Regi and Jared reminded me a while back that toasts have a great power to bring people together, to offer a moment for reflection, and to bolster our spirits." She turned to the couple and winked. "Now please, join us in raising a glass to Regi and Jared. May this be the first of many joyous married moments."

"To Regi and Jared. You're married!" Ross slurred as Amy pulled him back to their table. *Good enough.*

The best man appeared behind Ross. "Thanks for handling that," he said to Amy. "I'll take over for a while." He clapped a firm hand on Ross's shoulder. "Hey, buddy, let's go to the bathroom and clean up a little. Maybe splash some cold water on your face." Amy could see that this wasn't the first time he had stepped in to deal with a rowdy, drunk frat brother. She sat back down, glad to have Ross off her hands, as the two guys headed off toward the restrooms.

Denise and Kim looked at Amy with equal measures of admiration and sympathy.

"Nice work up there," Kim said. "It was like a train wreck. I wanted to look away but I couldn't."

Denise nodded in agreement. "That could have been so much worse. You really turned it around. I wish I had the nerve to jump in like that."

Amy smiled and nodded her thanks. Between Ross, the missing boutonnieres, and the narrowly avoided cake collapse, she was starting to feel like she'd actually earned that $250. She'd always thought she'd make a great bridesmaid; it felt good to find out she'd been right.

Kim was midway through a criticism of the tablecloths' thread count when they were interrupted by the DJ announcing the newlyweds' first dance. The bridal party arranged themselves around the dance floor as Jared led Regi into the center of the space, the opening notes of "At Last" filling the room. Because there had been no dancing at any of her Southern Baptist relatives' weddings, this tradition was fairly novel to Amy, and she couldn't help but find it a little strange. Watching this quiet, sentimental moment felt intrusive, almost voyeuristic. Were Regi and Jared uncomfortable? Amy could never imagine dancing like that with a partner, their bodies pressed together, whispering into each other's ears, with so many eyes on them. She hadn't even had the nerve to hold Charley's hand while walking to the Center of the Universe with hardly anyone nearby.

When the song ended, other couples began to drift onto the

floor. Amy retreated to the sidelines, watching wistfully, and now that she had nothing left to do to make sure the wedding went smoothly, the thoughts of Charley she'd been suppressing all day came rushing back. The wonderful night. The awkward morning. What had happened? Would there be a next time? Would they ever have a chance to dance together? Would Amy ever feel comfortable dancing with a woman in a crowd of strangers?

Amy headed back toward her table, suddenly aware that she looked every bit the cliché sad, single bridesmaid. When she sat down, she realized that the silver lining of Ross being drunk was that he hadn't even noticed his slice of cake. Amy slid it onto her plate and dug in. For something to do, she scanned the room and confirmed what she'd already suspected: no visibly queer couples. It wasn't as if she expected to see other queer folks at a straight Oklahoma wedding, but it would have been a pleasant surprise. Could she really be Regi and Jared's only gay friend? She realized that, despite how much she now knew about the couple, they hardly knew her at all.

Amy hated the idea that "coming out" was a once-and-done event, that you're either out or you're not. Every time she made a new acquaintance or engaged in small talk with a stranger, she had to decide if, when, and how she would come out to them. And in this case, the timing just hadn't yet lined up for her to bring up her sexuality with Regi and Jared. Which raised an even more awkward coming out question: What would happen if she waited too long to come out to them? Would it feel like a betrayal of trust when she eventually did? As if she'd been waiting to decide if they deserved the truth from her? And of course, the longer she waited to tell them, the more she grew to like them, the more hurtful it would be if it went poorly.

Amy put her fork down, realizing this reasoning also applied to her holding back from telling Charley about getting fired from

Daily Bread. Wasn't it rational, though, to play it a little safe and get to know someone first, instead of always oversharing? She knew that the "perfect time" to say or do something rarely existed, but she also knew there were absolutely *wrong* times and places to share deep truths. Couldn't there be an unintimidating middle ground? She hated the way not coming out right away made her feel like she was hiding something, like she had to "come clean," the implication being that she had something negative to confess. She didn't think it was shame that was holding her back from coming out to Regi and Jared; it was just timing. Maybe the situation with Charley was different. She *did* feel ashamed about getting fired, even knowing it reflected more poorly on Donna than it did on her.

As she continued to watch the crowd, Amy learned that the first dance couldn't hold a candle to the awkwardness of the father/bride and mother/groom dances. Who had decided it was normal or, worse, *expected* that you slow dance with your own parents? She realized she might be alone in finding the ritual odd, after looking around the room and seeing so many affectionate, adoring faces. It was her first time seeing the tradition in real life, instead of in the movies where it was carefully directed and edited to be sentimental and sweet instead of weird.

Amy certainly didn't want to pull a Kim and spend the whole wedding analyzing it for how she would have done it differently. But at the same time, it was hard not to picture herself in Regi's shoes. How would any of this work at queer weddings? She had a sudden vision of her and her mother dancing at her lesbian wedding in some alternate universe. Would it be a reversal of the straight tradition, so it was both brides with their mothers? Maybe she would dance with Max or Greg. Or both. Could three people slow dance together?

When the reception reached its end a couple hours later,

Amy and the other bridesmaids handed out sparklers to the guests, and everyone lined up outside the venue for a send-off. The couple promenaded through the colorful sparks, waving goodbye. The joyful looks on their faces at the end of a beautiful evening, along with the champagne, made Amy feel warm and amiable. Sure, she'd only swept in at the last minute to help out, but she knew all of her crisis management and running between vendors had been worth it. Maybe the whole paid-bridesmaid gig wasn't so weird after all. In fact, Amy had kind of enjoyed it.

After the send-off, the bridesmaids trailed back inside to clean up their dressing room. Once everything was in order, Amy waved goodbye to a drowsy Onae, hugged Rachel, and headed for the door.

"Wait up!" called a voice from behind her. Amy turned to see Kim jogging after her, now in athleisure wear with her pink bridesmaid dress flung over her shoulder. "Hey, can I steal you for a second?"

Amy looked at her phone, wishing a call from Damian would pop up. "My friend is picking me up any minute."

"I'll be quick." Kim gestured for Amy to follow her to an empty hall of the gallery. She looked around and lowered her voice. "Regi told me what you did for her."

"Sorry?"

"That she, you know, paid you."

"Oh." Amy felt her face turn red.

"And, well, one of my sorority sisters was supposed to be my bridesmaid, but now she's pregnant and the dresses I have picked out will look awful on her. I can't have her ruining all of my pictures like that, right?"

"Um, sure."

Kim flipped her hair over her shoulder. "So anyway, I was wondering if you were free on April nineteenth. Although it would be great if you could be around for the other stuff too. You know, dress fittings, bridal showers, bachelorette party, the works. For consistency."

Amy blanched. "This was kind of a one-time thing."

Kim waved a manicured hand. "I'd make it worth your while. How does twenty dollars an hour sound? For all the events?"

Twice her hourly rate at the bakery. Definitely more than she made in tips at the bar. But Amy had the distinct feeling that Kim would be a very different bride than Regi and that her expectations would be quite different as well.

But then she thought of her desperate job search. And her car, still broken down in the Daily Bread parking lot. And her monthly contribution to paying off her mother's medical debt. And the vet bill she was paying off in installments from Truffle's last checkup. And the gas bill getting more expensive as the weather turned colder.

"I, um, would need half of the ceremony charge up front," Amy said. "Is that possible?"

"That can certainly be arranged! Check your calendar and get back to me. Here, take my card." Kim pressed a business card into Amy's hand just as her phone buzzed with an incoming call from Damian.

"Sorry, my ride's here. But I'll be in touch."

"It would be a huge help. I saw what you did today. It was really impressive. Anyway, ta-ta! Talk soon!"

Amy mirrored Kim's finger-wiggling wave, then tried not to break into a run as she escaped to the sanctuary of Damian's car.

9

Amy spent Sunday recuperating from the physical and emotional exertion of Regi and Jared's wedding, with the occasional dalliance into moping, as she typically spent Sundays working at Daily Bread. Much of the day was lost drafting texts to Charley that she never mustered up the courage to send. And although she was on call at Ruby Red's, business never picked up enough for her to be needed. So the next morning, she was relieved to have a reason to get out of her apartment and start the day off on a different note.

After Amy graduated from college and moved out of her mom's place, she and her mother had established a routine of meeting at Teresa's house for brunch every other Monday, when both were typically off work. It was their opportunity to catch up and talk through any problems weighing on them in a more intimate way than they could on their phone calls, which were frequent but brief, usually sneaked in between Amy's shifts at work and Teresa's teaching schedule.

Over the years, they'd agonized (and later laughed) about countless things during these brunches: the huge fight Amy and Joel had gotten into over whether Lady Gaga's meat dress was a publicity stunt or genuinely groundbreaking art back in 2010 when Joel was moderating a Little Monsters Facebook group; Amy's fears about whether she'd lose Joel's friendship once he started to fall in love with Damian; the petition by Teresa's students to move her from an adjunct professor position to tenure track in the University of Tulsa's education department, which almost got her fired; and Amy's decision to apply for a job at Daily Bread, even though it meant she'd have to stay closeted. It was during a Monday brunch partway through her cancer treatment that Teresa had broken down crying, confessing for the first time how frightened she was. Amy had known Teresa was scared, of course. She stayed up many nights herself worrying about worst-case scenarios. But what stuck with her was gratitude that her mother trusted her enough to let go of her normally sunny disposition, even just for an hour. Amy knew all too well that her mother's instinct was to put other people's needs and feelings above her own; it was a habit she'd passed down to her daughter.

Amy's phone buzzed with a text from her mom, a five-minute warning of her arrival to pick Amy up. As she rushed around the apartment to finish getting dressed, she thought about how lucky she was to have such a close relationship with her mother. Sure, they'd had their fair share of arguments, especially when they shared a one-bedroom rental a few blocks from the University of Tulsa campus during Amy's high school and college years, but that had mostly been because they had no room to breathe. It had also been a little tense while Amy was a student at the university where her mom taught, even as they tried to stay out of each other's business. Luckily, things got much better when Amy saved up enough to get her apartment just off Cherry Street after graduation.

Despite their rough patches in the past, Amy knew having her mom's full support was a blessing. The majority of her queer friends would describe their relationships with their parents as somewhere on the spectrum from rocky to downright nonexistent. Damian's fell closer to "rocky." His family loved him but also thought he was going to hell, and their constant evangelizing and microaggressions meant he made the journey to visit his tiny hometown in Southwest Oklahoma only every few years. Joel's relationship with his family fell firmly into the "nonexistent" category. His parents had kicked him out after they caught him kissing a boy at sixteen. He'd moved in with his more accepting grandmother, but once she passed away in 2009, his ties to family were officially severed. Not only did Amy have the good fortune of having Teresa as a mother, but she even got to share her with her friends when they were in need of some maternal care.

Amy gave Truffle a goodbye scratch beneath the chin and locked her apartment door, then headed down the stairs to find Teresa's car waiting at the curb. Amy hopped in, hugging her mother across the console. They spent the short drive chatting through general updates—Regi and Jared's wedding, Teresa's upcoming finals season—as Amy worked herself up to telling her mom about Daily Bread. She knew her mom wouldn't be upset with her; it was more that she hated bringing her mother stressful news. These last few years had been so difficult for her, and Amy never wanted to add to the burden.

Amy was greeted at her mother's front door by the slobbery kisses of Papaya the pit bull. Her mom had fostered Papaya when she was undergoing treatment, then formalized the adoption when she went into remission; that was actually where Amy had gotten the idea to adopt Truffle in the wake of her breakup with Autumn.

As Teresa and Amy prepared breakfast, Amy finally shared the story of getting fired. Her mom wrapped her in a hug, then comforted her over bacon, eggs, and waffles while Papaya laid her head on Amy's feet beneath the table in an act of empathy or an attempt to sneak some bacon. In either case, it made Amy feel better.

Once they were done eating, Teresa placed her hand on top of Amy's on the table. "You know I'll help you however I can. Right?"

Amy's stomach twisted. "I know, Mom," Amy said. "I'm fine, though. I have some savings, and I'm going to pick up extra shifts at Ruby Red's." The savings part was a lie, but Amy couldn't bear to take any of Teresa's meager adjunct professor earnings. "I've got some things in mind, anyway. I'll figure it out."

Her mother sighed. "I just hate that Donna said those things to you. It makes me sick to my stomach."

Amy sipped her orange juice, eyeing her mother. "Can I ask you something?"

Teresa nodded.

Amy drew shapes with her fork in the leftover syrup pooled on her plate. "You consider yourself a Christian, right? But your family and the church were pretty terrible to you. For having me, and not getting married, and choosing a career over being a housewife."

Amy's mother nodded again.

"So how do you reconcile your Christianity with the way people have used Christianity against you?" Amy heard the slightly accusatory note in her voice and backed up. "I know there are Christians who don't believe queerness is a sin and think we deserve the same rights as everyone else. But I just don't understand how people like you can attach themselves to an institution that has also caused so much harm."

Teresa was silent as she gathered the dirty dishes from the table and began scrubbing them in the sink. Amy waited. She knew it was easier for her mother to talk about difficult topics when her hands were occupied.

"Well," she began, "I believe that what many people are taught about God doesn't come from God. It comes from other people. And even with the best motives, people can get God really wrong."

"Okay," Amy said. "But aren't you still mad at those people? For not being more open-minded? For using their idea of God to justify their bad behavior?"

Teresa wiped her hands on a dish towel and turned on the coffee maker. "Maybe I'm an optimist, but when I see people behaving badly, I try to think of what good they're trying to achieve. Like when I got pregnant with you, my parents said terrible things to me, like that I would be a terrible mother and couldn't possibly raise a child without a husband. But the point wasn't to make me feel ashamed. It was to push me to live what they pictured as the one and only path to a happy, normal life. To get me back on the track that they thought God wanted. Because in their home, and their neighborhood, and their church, that's all they'd seen."

Teresa took a couple mugs out of the cupboard, then leaned back against the counter, facing Amy.

"But what if the 'good' Donna thinks she's pushing me towards is being straight?" Amy said. "Doesn't that make you angry? People making assumptions about God based on their own lives? People telling you how to live like they know what God wants? I can't even hold hands with"—Amy caught herself before saying Charley's name; she didn't want to tell her mom about Charley until she figured out if the relationship was more than a one-night stand—"with another woman without worrying some stranger will feel the need to tell me I'm going to hell. Max and Greg have been together longer than I've been alive, and they still tell strangers they're cousins."

Teresa poured the coffee and returned to the kitchen table, pushing one mug toward Amy. "Yes," she said, her voice passionate. "It makes me so mad I could spit." She was clutching her mug so tightly that her knuckles had turned white, and in the brief pause after she'd spoken, Amy felt like she saw a lifetime of pain and rage flash across her mother's face. When Teresa looked up, though, her voice was warm again. "Good intentions don't excuse bad behavior. But letting that anger fester doesn't fix anything; it just poisons you. So I try to remember my parents wanted me to be happy, secure, and safe. I try to believe that everyone is doing the best they can—and that some people's 'best' has been shaped all their lives by mistaken ideas about God and goodness."

This all sounded nice enough, but Amy wondered, not for the first time in her life, what the fine line was between peacemaking and people-pleasing. She considered her mom's words, trying to think of Donna as an imperfect person just like her, whose "best" happened to include firing someone she thought of as a sinner. For a second, Amy felt some sympathy for her former boss, but then her anger returned. Had Donna ever considered that maybe Amy was doing *her* best? Why was the burden on Amy to do all the mental gymnastics?

Amy grabbed the creamer from the fridge and returned to her seat. In a more upbeat voice, she said, "While you're doling out life advice, want to give me some feedback on a new money-making scheme?"

"Absolutely!" Amy could tell her mom knew she was changing the subject on purpose, and she appreciated her mom's willingness to go with it.

"You know how Regi and Jared paid me to be a bridesmaid? Well, one of her bridesmaids found out about the whole thing and asked me to do the same thing for her. So I was thinking, maybe there's a market for that kind of service." She'd only thought of it the day before, and it felt bold to say it out loud for the first time.

Teresa leaned back in her seat. "A professional bridesmaid. Now, that's an idea."

"Whoa now, I don't know about professional. I've only done it once."

"With a second gig scheduled! It worked out twice, without you advertising or looking for the opportunities at all, right? They just fell in your lap. Think about what you could do if you really tried."

"Sure. But what I'm struggling with is: How many people would really be willing to pay a bridesmaid when they have friends and family that would do it for free?"

"Why did Regi and the other woman do it?" her mom asked. "Someone had to drop out, or there's a big fight in the bridal party, or the bride lives away from her friends and needs someone in town to help, or she needs help with the crafty stuff. . . . I could go on."

"The other problem is how to find people. So far it's just been word of mouth. Unless I just stand around at bridal salons with fliers?"

"Sounds like you have your next step: marketing." Amy was relieved to hear her mom defend her idea. She hadn't had much time to think it through, but the more they talked, the more reasonable it started to seem. Teresa reached down to pet Papaya, who had perked up in response to the new, excited tone of the conversation. "Right, Papaya? Don't you want your sister to try something new and see what happens?"

Papaya wagged her tail in response, a string of drool hanging dangerously close to Teresa's leg.

"Maybe," Amy said.

"That's the spirit, honey." Teresa clinked her coffee mug against Amy's. "To moving on to better things."

Her mom was talking about her career, but Amy immediately thought of Charley. Was Amy moving on in her love life too? She really wanted Charley to be her better thing. But that was a topic for another day. Amy smiled hopefully at her mom over her mug. "To better things."

10

That afternoon, Amy sat at the coffee table in front of her laptop and a glass of red wine. She typed a few more words of her draft Craigslist post, then stood up to pace. Truffle looked on, bored, from her perch in the living room window. The more Amy tried *not* to sound like a catfisher posing online as a bridesmaid for hire, the creepier the ad got. She'd actually typed out "I'm not a catfisher posing online as a bridesmaid for hire" before deleting it. "I can't do this," she told Truffle. "This is so embarrassing. What was I thinking?" Sure, Regi and Jared's wedding had had its fair share of minicrises that she'd handled well, but maybe that was just beginner's luck. A fluke.

Although she had only four words to show for the past hour ("Looking for a bridesmaid?" which felt dicey enough on its own), Amy decided to take a break. When she clicked away from Craigslist and opened Netflix, her recommended movies popped up: *The Big Wedding* starring Katherine Heigl and Robert De Niro, *Save the Date* starring Alison Brie and Lizzy Caplan, and *Bachelorette* starring Kirsten Dunst and Isla Fisher. Even Netflix was telling her to stay on task. *Well, I might as well lean in*, she thought. She rose from the couch, walked over to her DVD collection, and dropped an old favorite into her DVD player: *My Best Friend's Wedding*. It was a comfort movie for Amy, one she frequently played in the background while baking, although she found Julianne's last-resort marriage pact set for age twenty-eight more and more stressful to contemplate as she approached her late twenties herself.

As the opening credits played over a group of retro bridesmaids singing "Wishing and Hoping," Amy pulled her computer onto her lap and stared at the blinking cursor. She was sure that for Regi and Jared, their wedding had felt exactly like the kind of life-changing, best-day-of-your-life events Amy knew by heart from all her favorite movies. She could still see the love on their faces during the vows, feel the warmth and joy of their family and friends as they danced the night away, and picture a future for them filled with true partnership, no matter what flower and cake mishaps came their way. That was the kind of wedding Amy wanted to have someday, one that felt authentic and special. Based on the fact that she hadn't heard a peep from Charley since their date three days before, Amy thought with a cringe, being a bride definitely wasn't in the cards for her anytime soon.

She decided to swap her wine for coffee, resettling on the couch a few minutes later with a steaming mug. What would she want to know if she were getting married and considering hiring a bridesmaid? Besides wanting to know it wasn't a scam, she'd probably want to know that the person had some experience.

There it was: a starting point. Okay, she'd only been a bridesmaid once so far. But wasn't being a bridesmaid something like her customer service work at the bakery or the bar? At the end of the day, it came down to problem-solving, getting things done, and managing emotions. Plus, attending those twenty-two Southern Baptist weddings had to count for something. She set down her coffee and picked up her laptop up again, starting to type just as, on the TV screen, Kimmy asked Julianne to be her maid of honor. The terrified look on Julia Roberts's face in the speeding, swerving convertible perfectly matched Amy's nerves as she wrote.

Besides having customer service experience, Amy looked the part. Cute but not beautiful enough to draw attention away from the bride. A little curvy but still a pretty standard dress size. And if there was any skill Amy had mastered, it was being whoever she needed to be to get the job done. She could play the chaste, cheerful, goody-two-shoes Amelia at Daily Bread. She could play the quiet but helpful cousin who always brings good food to holidays with her extended family. Why couldn't she play the perky, competent, supportive bridesmaid?

As she started to type in earnest, she realized she was trying to sell this idea not only to brides in need but also to herself. And she was starting to believe that if she could do this, *really* do this, it had amazing potential. She'd be her own boss, get to pick and choose her clients, and make better money than she could dream of at Ruby Red's. Plus, she'd be building something, creating a business all her own.

A small voice in Amy's head wondered if she was getting herself into another Daily Bread situation—pretending she was straight to participate in the very straight wedding industry, much like she'd pretended she was a Christian to work at a very Christian bakery. Of course, just because she hadn't come out to Regi didn't mean she would always be closeted while working as a bridesmaid. In some cases, the fact that she was a lesbian might come up naturally. And who said you had to come out to everyone you met at work? Anyway, right then she really needed to focus on making enough money to get her car fixed and pay December rent.

Fifteen minutes later, Amy sat back and read through her draft, but while she was definitely getting somewhere, it still wasn't quite right. As she looked at her description, she wondered how what she was offering was any different from a wedding planner. Well, a wedding planner for whom you had to buy a dress. She took a walk around the small apartment, thinking, then paused for a moment to watch Cameron Diaz's hilariously bad karaoke scene. If only Amy's own shortcomings could be so endearing.

Returning to her ad draft completely out of ideas, Amy knew it was time to call in reinforcements. And she knew just the person: Damian. Not only was he reliably helpful, but he would know how this whole self-promotion/freelance thing was supposed to work. After all, he had advertised his personal training sessions and group workout classes on Craigslist and local message boards for years, with a lot of success.

Damian answered Amy's call after one ring. "I think it's fantastic!" he said once Amy explained her idea. Then he shifted to pep-talk mode; she must have sounded just as doubtful and anxious as she felt. "If anyone can pull it off, it's you. Weddings can be exhausting, but if you can survive them, you can really cash in on that big wedding industry money. You're smart and levelheaded, great in a crisis, helpful. Plus you're like a social chameleon. You had the pious act down pat at Daily Bread. You gave me major Sunday school vibes whenever I came in. That's one of the most important queer superpowers."

"What is?" Amy asked.

"The ability to read a room and know what needs to happen

and who you need to be in one second flat," he said, not unkindly. Amy knew he was right. That kind of code-switching was second nature to her and all of her friends by necessity. *Or am I just a good liar?* she wondered.

"Thanks, Damian," Amy said. She was relieved to hear him responding so positively to this whole idea. "Social chameleon—do you think I can put that on my résumé?"

Amy emailed over her draft advertisement. Damian paused for a moment to read through it. "You're on the right track, but you need a more confident tone. It reads like you're nervous, like you think it's a silly thing to do."

"But I do think it's a silly thing to do!"

"Sure, but you've got to be one hundred percent confident in your services in an ad like this. The people looking to hire you are going to be stressed out of their minds already. One of their bridesmaids canceled last minute, or they've got no one they can count on to support them in a crisis, or whatever the case may be. They're not going to feel reassured by 'customer service experience' and 'pleasant demeanor.'" Amy heard the sound of typing in the background.

"More confidence, got it. Does it sound too much like an ad for a wedding planner? I would be in way over my head if that's what people thought they were signing up for," Amy said.

There was silence over the phone line as Damian read through the advertisement again. "Let's emphasize the bridesmaid part a little more. You're there for the *bride*, right? To be whatever kind of support she needs, not to plan and run an event."

"Exactly!" Then another thought occurred to Amy. "Do you think it's bad timing to post this right before Thanksgiving? Should I wait until next week?"

"I think it's great timing," Damian said. "Holidays make

everyone feel desperate. Also, I think you need to include a picture of yourself since you'll be in all their wedding photos. Don't worry, it's not weird. I include one in my ads too."

Amy thought for a moment. "Regi, the bride from that first wedding I was in, sent me a pretty cute picture of me at her reception. Would that work?"

"Sounds perfect!" Amy heard more typing on Damian's end of the call. "And you need to charge more. You're barely asking more than minimum wage, and what you're offering is worth way more than that. Going through all of that wedding hell? They should pay you at least double. I made some edits and just sent it back to you."

"Thank you so much, Damian. You're the best." The email came through a moment later, and Amy opened the attachment and reviewed his changes. "Hey, do you think I'm an idiot for doing this? Do you think it could actually work?"

"Of course you're not an idiot. It's brilliant. You're going to be the best damn professional bridesmaid anyone has ever seen." Amy could hear a smile in Damian's voice. "I'll buy drinks after you get your first gig from this ad. And then when you're rich from all that sweet bridesmaid cash, you can buy."

Amy agreed and thanked him again for his advice. After hanging up, she read through the advertisement once more:

Looking for Someone to Support You on Your Special Day?

> Your wedding day should be about you and your groom, not about drama, stress, and last-minute tasks. That's why you need an experienced bridesmaid to balance out your wedding party. I'm Amy, a professional bridesmaid located in Tulsa, Oklahoma, and I want to help make your wedding day perfect. Your friends and relatives love you, but

they don't always know how to help when it counts. I'm a drama-free alternative, with the skills to execute DIY projects, manage difficult guests and family members, and handle last-minute complications. While wedding planners are focused on the overall event, I'm focused on *you*, immersing myself in your bridal party to be an advocate and problem-solver whenever you need one. If you need someone on your side of the altar to have your back, look no further.

Experienced in: DIY crafting, flower arranging, sewing / dress repair, baking, hair and makeup styling, sorting out last-minute crises, deescalating interpersonal conflict, and anticipating whatever you, the bride, might need in the moment

Travel area: Oklahoma, Arkansas, Missouri, northern Texas

Dress size: 12

Pricing:
Flat fee for wedding & reception: $300
Rehearsal dinner: $50
Bridal shower: $50
Bachelorette party: $50
Wedding dress shopping: $15/hr.
Décor creation/assistance: $20/hr.
Other needs: priced upon discussion

Let me help make your wedding day dreams come true!

Feeling somewhere between brave and reckless, she pasted the text into the Craigslist form. "Well, here goes nothing," she said to Truffle, then clicked Post.

When Amy woke up the next morning, she found three responses to her ad already in her inbox. The first was from someone who needed a last-minute fill-in for a wedding in two weeks. That meant a down payment would be in her pocket before rent was due! The next request was for a winter wonderland wedding in a barn in December, and the third email inquired about her services for a black-tie wedding at a historic hotel in Oklahoma City in January.

She turned to Truffle, who was grooming her paws at the foot of her bed. "What do you think, Truffle? Are we really doing this?" The cat lifted her head and blinked her yellow eyes. "I'm taking that as a yes." Amy pressed Reply and began to type a short response to the first bride. "Shit, what do I do now? A written agreement? A contract?"

A quick Google search produced a variety of contract templates. She found one designed for wedding photographers and made some edits to reflect her bridesmaid responsibilities. Pleased with her work, she sent it off to all three brides, hoping it wouldn't have to withstand legal review. And by the time she sent the last response, an email had appeared in her inbox from a fourth bride, this one planning a May wedding in Muskogee. Amy squealed in delight. Four responses in less than twenty-four hours was more than she'd dared to imagine just the night before. And with the contract template now in hand, Amy located Kim's business card in her makeup bag, where she'd left it after Regi and Jared's wedding. Even if Kim was unlikely to be her favorite bride, fulfilling Kim's high expectations would be valuable experience, and after all, it was her offer that had sparked the business idea for Amy in the first place. She sent an email to Kim with a contract, compensating for her lack of enthusiasm with an excess of exclamation points.

Amy settled back into her pillows, feeling accomplished. With renewed confidence and fewer financial worries than for the past two weeks, Amy's mind turned to Charley. Yes, their Friday-night date had ended on a strange note, but there were a hundred possible reasons. It was quite possible that Amy had given off a cold or intense vibe considering how stressed and defeated she'd felt since getting fired. Maybe Charley was just as nervous about reaching out as Amy was. And considering how brave she'd been already this morning, she figured she might as well try to carry that bravery over from her professional life to her love life. Before she could change her mind, she sent a text to Charley.

Happy Tuesday! As your official Tulsa tour guide, it's crucial that I show you one of the best Tulsa attractions before it gets too wintery outside. Are you free this week?

She tried to busy herself with making a grocery list for the Thanksgiving dishes she was planning but kept checking her phone obsessively. After a half hour that felt much longer to Amy, Charley's reply came through.

Hi tour guide! Work has been nuts trying to get things squared away before Thanksgiving, but I'm off early tomorrow.
Any chance that would work for you?

A wave of relief washed over Amy, and she laughed, thinking of how anxious she'd been since Saturday morning. Why did she always jump to the worst conclusion?

Can't wait. Bring a jacket!

11

From the moment Charley and Amy laid eyes on each other the next day, all of Amy's doubts about Charley's interest disappeared. After opening the passenger door of her car for Amy, Charley greeted her with a kiss that warmed her all the way down to the toes.

As Amy directed them south of downtown, Charley peered into the back seat, where Amy had stored a small soft-sided cooler. "What's in there?"

"Eyes on the road, nosey."

Charley smirked as she turned back toward the windshield. "All right, but the suspense is killing me."

They chatted for a few minutes about their respective holiday plans as Charley drove down Cherry Street. Charley would set out for Houston early the next morning and spend her Thanksgiving break spoiling her nieces and nephews with gifts. Amy described her annual Thanksgiving tradition of cooking with her mom, eating dinner with their extended family, and then wrapping up the day with her chosen family at Ruby Red's.

When the conversation hit a lull, Amy turned on the car's audio and was rewarded by the warbling tones of "The Story." She leaned back into her seat, delighted.

"Do you know Brandi Carlile?" Charley asked.

"Duh! They'd take away my lesbian card if I didn't. Plus there's a woman who sings this song at Ruby Red's karaoke night every single Wednesday."

Charley laughed. "The same song every time?"

"Every time! At least she does it justice." Amy looked coyly over at Charley. "Much better than I could do." Amy began to belt out the lyrics with what she hoped was a charming level of enthusiasm, if not skill, and Charley waited only a beat to join in. Neither was destined for musical greatness, but that didn't stop them from singing through the rest of "The Story" and the next two songs on the album as well, although they were both a little fuzzier on the lyrics of those ones.

The sing-along lasted until Amy directed Charley into the parking lot of a stately 1920s villa. "Welcome to the Philbrook Museum," she said. "This used to be the home of some old oil baron, but he donated it to Tulsa to become an art museum back in, like, the 1930s." Once Charley had parked, Amy led them toward the front doors, the cooler strapped over her shoulder. "It's a beautiful home, but the art is also pretty amazing. They have all kinds of stuff, a lot of Native American art, contemporary works, some Italian Renaissance stuff to match the architecture."

They entered the stately rotunda, and Amy watched, completely enamored, as Charley took in its beauty, her mouth hanging slightly open. As Amy began their tour through the exhibits, Charley stopped at nearly each one to read the plaques, occasionally sharing an interesting fact with Amy. Amy had been to the Philbrook countless times, but she wasn't much of a plaque reader. She preferred wandering the halls and letting the art speak to her however it wanted. But today Amy spent more time enjoying Charley's reactions than she did appreciating the art.

After a short while, Amy pulled Charley into her favorite room of the museum and pointed out the thick frosted-glass flooring. With no plaque to help her, Charley tilted her head curiously at the odd design choice. "What is it?"

"When the house was built in the 1920s, the oil baron wanted to throw some wild parties, so he had the architect design this dance floor of glass with colored lights installed underneath. When the seventies came around, everyone realized that it's basically a disco floor, just very ahead of its time. They still light it up sometimes for special events."

Charley leaned closer to the floor, inspecting the thick glass. "So you're saying the Philbrook invented disco."

"Basically."

The museum was quieter than usual since it was the day before Thanksgiving. They were the only people in the ballroom. Amy grabbed Charley's hand and led her into the center of the dance floor. She placed her hands on Charley's hips and began dancing to an imaginary beat. "Picture it," Amy said, "a Roaring Twenties house party, champagne flowing like the oil that paid for this house, lights of all colors shining up through the glass dance floor." Charley stood stiffly for only a moment before giving in to Amy's dance, wrapping her arms around Amy's shoulders and moving her hips in time with Amy's. Amy stepped back from Charley to do the Charleston.

Charley smiled and pulled Amy back to her, their faces only inches apart. "I would have liked dancing with you then. You would be the most charming flapper, with those dimples and a curly bob, and I would be one of those chic twenties lesbians in a top hat and tails, my hair all slicked back."

Amy smiled wide, loving the image of the two of them at a Gatsbyesque Philbrook party. But then she heard voices coming down the hallway and the fantasy evaporated. She stepped back from Charley just as a woman and two middle-school-aged children wandered into the room, the kids bickering about what to buy from the museum gift shop. Amy smiled apologetically at Charley before wandering back toward the art displayed on the walls around the glass dance floor. It suddenly felt silly to imagine dancing publicly with Charley almost a century earlier when she didn't even have the nerve to show Charley public affection in 2013.

They returned to their winding route through the rest of the museum, Amy trying to focus on soaking up the quiet moments with Charley, the two of them occasionally brushing shoulders or whispering commentary as they examined the museum's collection.

Once they returned to the rotunda, Amy turned to Charley. "Ready for the big finish?"

"Didn't we see everything?"

"Certainly not!" Amy led Charley through the back door of the museum onto an intricate terrace decorated with stone arches and sculptures. As they approached the balustrade overlooking the gardens, Amy held back to watch Charley take in the museum's formally designed gardens. A geometric pattern of triangular shrubs and trimmed grass created mesmerizing paths downhill with foliage that grew more wild and colorful the farther it got from the terrace. The paths eventually reached a mirror pond, perfectly placed to reflect the villa on its surface, surrounded by flowers and bushes in shades of orange, yellow, and deep red. The garden fanned out on both sides of the building, with walking paths, sculptures, and a colorful landscape as far as the eye could see.

Amy stepped up to Charley's side. "It's unbelievable in the spring, when everything blooms all at once. But I like it most in fall, with all the colorful leaves falling and the flowers getting their last look of the year. Plus, it's less crowded."

Charley eyes moved from the manicured lawns to the colorful late-blooming flowers and the perfectly reflective pond that doubled the impact. "The museum was great; don't get me wrong. But this . . . This is stunning."

Amy adjusted the cooler on her shoulder, grabbed Charley's hand, and led her down a ramp onto the lawn. After wandering the gardens, they sat down at a table under an iron arch, and Amy unloaded the contents of the cooler: a couple of cheeses, a homemade baguette, and raspberry macarons.

"Why have I never dated a baker before?" Charley said, impressed. Amy beamed.

As they tucked in to the food, Amy said, "Okay. If you were a cheese, what kind of cheese would you be and why?"

Charley laughed, the same rich, clear laugh Amy had fallen for when they first met. "What do you mean?"

"It's the questions game!" Amy said. "My mom and I used to play it on road trips or just to pass the time. You ask each other questions, the more ridiculous, the better, and have to take each answer seriously. I introduced my friends Joel and Damian to it, and now we play it with all the regulars at Ruby Red's. Look, I could ask you if you're an ENFJ or an ISTP or whatever, but I promise this is more interesting."

"All right, I'll play," Charley said. "My favorite is feta."

"I didn't ask your favorite. I asked which one you *are*."

Charley furrowed her brow. "If it's my favorite, isn't that what I would be?"

"Not necessarily. A feta person would be a little dry, salty, maybe not great at holding everything together, since it's so crumbly. A strong personality that's great in certain situations but not always the most reliable. I don't see you as a crumbly cheese. Are you more of a soft cheese or firm cheese person?"

"Can I get an example?"

"I'm mozzarella. Definitely a softy. Adaptable, blends well with different flavor profiles. Great at holding things together in heated situations. That's what makes it a great pizza cheese."

"Oh, I see." Charley paused for a moment, looking out at the reflecting pond. "Well then, I think I'm Manchego. Firmer, reliable, a little peppery, can melt well under the right circumstances." She winked at Amy. "And my dad's family is from Spain, so regionally appropriate."

Amy nodded, impressed. She reached out and laced her fingers through Charley's, letting their hands rest on the table.

"My turn. What's your favorite thing to bake?" Charley asked.

"Tough one. Bread and pastries have their merits, but cakes are closest to my heart. Cupcakes are probably my favorite, though. They're the first thing I learned to bake from scratch, and they're just so cute and cheerful, you know?"

"That suits you. And explains that tattoo on your back." Charley reached her other arm behind her head, basking in the November sun and immediately looking like a lesbian model. "Your turn."

The combination of Charley's pose and the memory of the last time she'd seen Amy's tattoo brought heat rushing to Amy's cheeks. Amy pulled a favorite question from her brain while trying to collect herself. "What's your mundane superpower? Like, something you're really, really good at but is kind of boring or random."

Charley was silent for a moment, biting her lips in thought. "I think I need another example."

"Okay, but next time you ask for an example, I'm counting that as your question." Amy squeezed Charley's fingers a bit tighter to show she was teasing. "My mundane superpower is always figuring out the secret ingredient. Like, when your great-aunt won't tell anyone what makes her sweet potato casserole so good, I taste it and immediately know it's maple syrup or marjoram or whatever."

"Really? What's the secret ingredient in KFC's fried chicken then?" Charley asked.

"It's a bunch of different herbs and spices and they're all secret, right? But if I were to guess the wild card, I think it's powdered ginger. Gives it that zesty sweetness. And celery salt for that bright, earthy flavor."

"Huh. All right, I guess my mundane superpower is following bad directions. The ones like 'Take a left at the big tree. Drive for a while till the road curves. Turn right when you see the old barn.' Comes in handy when visiting oil drilling sites for sure, but I probably picked it up because my mom is really into antiquing and used to drag us along as kids to the most out-of-the-way shops."

"That's a good one."

"My turn," Charley said, getting into the rhythm of the game. "Favorite holiday. And in the spirit of fairness, I'll tell you mine first: Fourth of July. But not for patriotic reasons, just because I like barbecue and fireworks. Especially the really big ones or the ones with cool effects."

Amy nodded in approval. "Mine's Thanksgiving. Any holiday centered around food is a holiday I can get behind. The part with my extended family is a little boring, but the cooking with my mom and the after-party at Ruby Red's make up for it. It's like Christmas but without all the stress of buying presents and lying to children."

Just then, the doors to the museum opened, and a big group of visitors entered the garden, their voices spilling down the pathway to the pond. Amy instinctively pulled her hand away from Charley's but regretted it at once. There was no reason to be afraid of being seen with Charley in public, she tried to reason with herself, especially now that the damage of being fired was done.

"Is everything okay?" Charley asked, looking concerned.

"Yes," Amy said firmly and, gathering her courage, scooted her chair closer to Charley's and reached an arm around her lower back. Charley pulled her closer and kissed her temple. It felt nice having her arm around Charley in the fresh air of the garden, even if Amy couldn't stop thinking about the eyes of the other museumgoers. Charley seemed like she hadn't noticed them; she was so completely herself regardless of who else was around. Amy wished she had that confidence, that fearlessness. "All right, my turn. Are you out at work?"

Charley eyed her curiously. "The woman with a men's haircut who always wears men's suits? No point in trying to keep it a secret. I haven't passed for straight since Y2K."

"And your co-workers are, like, cool with that?" Amy tried to sound nonchalant.

"Yeah, pretty much. I think they see me as one of the guys, which is problematic but better than the alternative. And they're kind of inclusive in their own way. Why do you ask?"

"Women make up, what, less than a quarter of oil and gas workers? I just thought that might make for a tough work culture," Amy said, realizing too late that Charley might ask her the same question and wanting to deflect.

Charley lifted an eyebrow. "Have you been researching the industry or something?"

Amy could feel her cheeks grow red. "Just a little. I mean, I've lived in Tulsa my whole life, and it seems like I should know at least a little about—"

"Oh wow, I was joking but you actually did," Charley said, turning her body toward Amy and resting her chin on her hand. "You went and googled 'oil and gas careers' so you could talk to me about it."

There was no escaping the embarrassment at this point. "Actually, I googled 'interesting facts about oil and gas industry,' thank you very much. It's fine; I'm appropriately humiliated now. I'll just disappear into the earth and never bother you again."

"I went with 'best baking tips,'" Charley said, holding Amy's gaze.

Amy paused her nervous fidgeting, glowing in the intensity of Charley's focus. She felt a twinge of guilt for not yet coming clean about Daily Bread, but how could she ruin this moment? She tried to remember what Joel had said about her being a baker even if she didn't work at the bakery anymore. "You did?"

"Well, I googled 'how to make homemade pasta' first but got overwhelmed too quickly. When it started talking about how the dough should feel velvety, it totally lost me."

They both laughed, Amy's embarrassment and guilt dissolving in their shared pleasure. "It's more of a smooth elasticity than a velvety feeling. You'd know it if you felt it."

"I doubt that." Charley leaned her forehead against Amy's. "Thanks for another perfect tour stop. But I was thinking—I know one place in Tulsa you haven't seen that I can show you."

Amy raised her eyebrows. "Is that so?"

Charley grinned, a mischievous glint in her eye. "My place."

"Did you just use a pickup line on me?" Amy laughed, pulling back and swatting Charley's leg.

"I don't know. Is it working?" They shared a private smile,

clearly both thinking about Amy saying those same words when she'd first asked Charley out.

Amy grasped the lapels of Charley's shirt, tugging her closer until their faces were only inches apart. "It absolutely is."

An hour later, Charley cried out, her body tensing all over and then collapsing against the tangled sheets. As she caught her breath, Amy emerged from between Charley's legs, leaving a trail of kisses along her inner thigh.

With a stretch, Amy pulled herself up the bed and curled into Charley's side. They enjoyed a quiet moment of bliss as Charley's breathing slowed to match Amy's. But once Charley began kissing her, running her fingers along the curve of Amy's bare breast, Amy checked her watch.

"Wow, only six P.M. It's so dark outside. I could have sworn it was later." She sat up on the edge of Charley's bed and rolled her neck. Amy had been nervous that Charley's home would be intimidatingly expensive, based on her nice car and custom suits. But the modest two-bedroom home was anything but ostentatious; decorated in a spare yet stylish manner, it was clean, organized, and thoughtfully designed. Even though Charley had just moved in, Amy could see that having an orderly and calming home base mattered to her.

"Where are you going? It's your turn." Charley tucked a hand into the waistband of Amy's underwear, then wrapped an arm around her waist to pull her back.

Heat rose to Amy's cheeks. "I should probably head out soon. I have an eight o'clock shift at the bar."

"We can have a lot of fun in two hours." Charley's fingers crept down the inside of Amy's panties, almost reaching their goal before Amy pulled away.

"I'm, um, I'm on my period." She'd said it so many times over the past decade. Why did it still feel so awkward?

Charley sat up and pushed Amy's mess of curls away from her face. "That's okay. I can still make you feel good, on your terms."

Amy scrunched her nose. She wouldn't have minded if Charley were on her period; after all, Amy had never thought twice about having sex with other partners while they were menstruating. But even though she knew there was no reason to feel weird, that any period-related shame she felt was thanks to misogyny rather than anything logical, Amy just felt too self-conscious.

"I'm not scared of a period. I get them too, you know." Charley squeezed Amy's hand, which felt like Charley being sweet and encouraging while intentionally giving Amy a little space. "I won't go down on you if you don't want me to, but we can lay down a towel and try something else. Or take a shower together."

Amy was touched by Charley's understanding. Autumn had always made herself scarce while Amy was on her period. In retrospect, Amy guessed that had had less to do with any period-related uneasiness Autumn might have felt and more with the fact that, knowing Amy's shyness about this, Autumn had found it easy to use that week to visit other paramours without raising Amy's suspicions. But she definitely couldn't blame Autumn for the shame society had taught her to associate with menstruation. For the thousandth time in her life, Amy wished that knowing she shouldn't feel shame about something, *wanting* not to feel shame, were enough to make it all evaporate. That she could wish herself into having a cooler, more confident personality. The truth was that though Charley's offer was tempting, she wasn't ready to be that vulnerable. Not yet.

"I'd rather not," Amy said. "I'm sorry. And really, I should go."

Charley gave Amy's hand one last squeeze and sat back. "No need to apologize. I'm glad you told me how you feel. Do you want anything before you go? Coffee? Dinner?"

"Could I bother you for a ride home?" The words came out more abrupt than Amy had meant them to, and she cringed. "Thanks, though. I don't need anything."

"Of course," Charley said. They dressed in silence, an invisible distance seeming to grow between them.

Once Amy had gathered her things and Charley had locked up, Amy buckled into the car and attempted to break the tension. "So, you leave for Houston in the morning?"

"Yep. Still have to pack too."

"And when do you come back?" Amy asked.

Charley turned right without direction, and Amy felt an unexpected rush of pleasure as she realized that Charley already seemed to know the route to her apartment by memory. "Well, I actually fly straight from Houston to a conference in South Dakota, then back into Oklahoma City for a work dinner in Norman. So I'll be back . . . next Wednesday morning?"

Amy swallowed, trying not to look too disappointed. "Wow, big week! I wish you could come to the late-night Thanksgiving at Ruby Red's."

"I wish I could be there too." Charley reached across the console to grab Amy's hand. "Is Daily Bread open on Thanksgiving morning? Are you working? Maybe I could drop by on my way out of town."

Amy's shoulders stiffened. She couldn't answer the question without lying. Gathering her courage, she decided she might as well rip off the Band-Aid. "I've been meaning to mention that Daily Bread and I . . . parted ways."

"You're serious? When?"

"Not too long ago." In truth, it had been almost three weeks, but Amy knew it would sound dramatic, not to mention highlight her lies of omission, if she said *The day before our first date.*

Charley's head tilted to the side. "I can't believe you quit. I dropped by a few times before work hoping to run into you and just figured you worked afternoons."

"You did?" Amy said distractedly. Quit was a generous interpretation—one that Amy wasn't ready to correct. The firing was still too raw. She couldn't talk about it yet without crying, and she didn't want to ruin the end of their date again. "Sorry, I should have told you."

"Why did you leave?"

"Irreconcilable differences."

Charley glanced over while Amy stared fixedly ahead at the road. After a moment, Charley seemed to decide to let it go. "So what's next, then?"

Amy paused, remembering what Charley had said when they first met: *"Weddings are the worst."* Amy wasn't sure her barely existent bridesmaid business would sound all that impressive, especially compared to Charley's fancy job. No, she needed to get her shit together a little more before she was ready to share that, make sure it was actually going to work. "I'm still figuring things out. Might try something new."

"No more baking?"

Charley's disappointment was palpable. Amy chewed on a cuticle. "Not sure if it's in the cards." They turned onto Amy's street. "I can still bake for fun! I love it too much to quit entirely. I just . . . want to see what else is out there is all."

Charley was silent as she parked in front of Amy's building.

"Are you upset?" Amy asked.

"No, no. Just surprised, I guess. You seemed like you really liked working there. And you were so good at it."

"I did. And I was." If the period fiasco had left Amy feeling ashamed, this topic made her feel about two inches tall. "It's a long story, and I've got a closing shift ahead of me, and you've got a big trip ahead of you." She rallied the most confident smile she could before planting a goodbye kiss on Charley's lips. "Safe travels, Charley. See you when you get back?"

Charley kissed Amy back longer. "See you when I get back."

"I can't believe you made a toast at a wedding for people you don't even know," Joel said a few hours later over the sounds of clinking glasses and loud voices at Ruby Red's. The Wednesday night before Thanksgiving was always busy and not just with the regulars who were looking forward to a few days off. There were also plenty of queer folks who had grown up in Tulsa, moved away, and come back to visit family for the holidays. Joel's night off hadn't kept him and Damian from stopping by, and with Zee pouring drinks at the other end of the bar, the full bartending team was together for the first time in a while. It felt like the holiday had started early.

"Hey, I was just trying to earn my keep, okay?" Amy yelled from beneath the bar, where she was unloading a tray of clean pint glasses. She was trying not to obsess over whether or not the second date in a row with an awkward ending would lead to another period of silence between her and Charley, and catching Joel up on Regi and Jared's wedding was the perfect distraction. She'd had a chance to fill Damian in when he picked her up after the reception, but Joel made such a good audience that Amy had been waiting to tell him all the details in person.

"And I can't believe you got *paid* to do it! Have y'all seen Amy's Craigslist post? Professional bridesmaids are going to be all the rage before we know it!" Damian said.

"Oh my God, I want in!" Joel yelled. "I look amazing in halter tops."

"Joel's onto something," Damian said. "Gay best friends are very in right now."

Amy laughed and emerged from below the bar, having finished unloading the pint glasses. As Joel and Damian debated who would be the better maid of honor, she heard a familiar voice on the television and reached for the remote to turn up the volume. Heads turned toward the TV as *The Rachel Maddow Show* logo filled the screen. The program had slowly gained popularity since it premiered in 2008, but Amy remembered the first time Rachel Maddow had caught her eye as a guest on another MSNBC show. Amy had been cooling down at Max and Greg's house one Saturday morning after helping Max replant his flower beds for spring. Amy wasn't big on talk shows, but she hadn't been able to look away from Rachel Maddow. Seeing a lesbian on TV outside of *The L Word* and *The Ellen DeGeneres Show* felt like such a treat at the time. And now that Amy thought about it, it was quite possible that her "type" was heavily influenced by all the evenings she'd tuned in to *TRMS* at home or the bar. A good suit, great haircut, intense gaze, on a woman who was supersmart, bordering on nerdy? Irresistible.

Rachel Maddow adjusted a pile of papers on the desk in front of her as she welcomed the viewers back. Joel and Damian groaned, and Amy shot them a dirty look, turning the volume up a few more notches.

"Come on, Amy. Just because you have a crush on Rachel Maddow doesn't mean you can make everyone watch with you," Joel said with a dramatic eye roll.

"This isn't just for me, Joel," Amy said, using the remote to gesture toward the screen, where Rachel was talking about which states had passed same-sex marriage legislation and which were likely to do so next. "First of all, marriage equality is something we should all be paying attention to. And second, look around.

I'm not the only fan." She gestured to the roomful of queer people staring reverently at the screen, including Zee, who had completely forgotten the inventory sheet that was slipping from her hand. "She has universal lesbian appeal. And a fair amount of straight and genderqueer appeal."

Damian turned toward the pool tables at the back of the bar and shouted, "Jae! What are your thoughts on Rachel Maddow?"

"I would die for her," Jae called back instantaneously. "Why? Is she on?" They dropped their pool cue and pulled a barstool closer to the television.

Amy gave Damian her best I-told-you-so look and turned back to watch Rachel Maddow ask one of her guests a question about the Defense of Marriage Act. Joel pushed his empty mojito glass away from him. "Fine, but it sucks to listen to pundits debate your rights like you're some kind of imaginary creature instead of a real person."

"Hey, it's not like I'm making you watch Fox News or something. Rachel's been with her partner since the nineties. It's real for her too," Amy said.

"Don't talk about her partner in front of me, Amy," Jae said. "Let me have my fantasies."

"Sorry, dear," Amy said. "I'm sure Rachel only has eyes for you."

Joel sighed. "It's super depressing to hear about all of these states passing gay marriage when you know Oklahoma's never going to do it. Mary Fallin would rather die than let us heathens destroy our state's moral fiber." Amy had initially harbored hopes that, as the first woman governor of Oklahoma, Mary Fallin would prove at least the tiniest bit progressive. But in addition to her staunch opposition to LGBTQ rights, Fallin had spent her first two years in office fighting legal battles with the Choctaw Nation and Chickasaw Nation over water rights, refusing to comply with federal climate change regulations, and pushing for more lethal injections of inmates. She was recognized by Tulsa's queer community as a kind of supervillain.

Jae took a chug of their beer. "Hawaii just passed same-sex marriage. I say we all move there. They need DJs and bartenders and physical trainers too, right?"

Amy smiled at the idea of their lovable little Oklahoma bar in Maui. She pictured a tornado lifting Ruby Red's up and dropping it in some liberal, welcoming town.

Damian shook his head vehemently. "That's just what the homophobes want—to scare us off to somewhere else so they can keep their backwards beliefs intact. We can try to convince Oklahoma politicians to stop passing anti-LGBTQ laws, but they'd rather us move away too. But who would be the little baby gays' role models? Leaving is the easy thing to do. Somebody has to stay in the Bible Belt to drag the haters kicking and screaming into the future. And moving away is a kind of privilege, you know? Not everyone has the resources to do it. Being gay in Oklahoma, *staying* gay in Oklahoma, is a radical act." He took a chug of his cider, eyeing some of the queer former Tulsans. "So basically, we're all badasses."

Joel pulled Damian in for a kiss. "You're a badass."

Damian grinned. "Thanks, hon. You're a badass too."

Jae set their empty beer bottle on the counter. "Everyone's situation is different, though," they pointed out. "Sometimes folks have got to get out if they want to survive, especially queer people of color and people who don't stick to the gender binary, like yours truly."

Tala, who had wandered up during the conversation, jumped in. "Wait, Jae, are you moving?"

"No, but I'd be lying if I said I hadn't thought about it," Jae said. "It's hard out here for a gender nonconforming babe, and I don't even have family tying me here. But it's not like anywhere would be easy for me, so I might as well make my home among you weirdos." Jae draped an arm around the back of Damian's chair.

"We're *your* weirdos, Jae. And you're ours," Amy said, sliding a fresh beer across the bar.

Jae lifted the beer in a toast. "To being badass weirdos."

12

Amy's mother picked her up early on Thanksgiving morning. By noon, they were already hours into food preparation, Papaya wandering between them, hoping to catch a misplaced ingredient. Being in the kitchen with her mother was a welcome restorative for Amy, who, aside from cooking dinner once for Charley, had hardly picked up a whisk since her last shift at Daily Bread.

Despite Teresa and Amy's unofficial status as Fariner family black sheep, they were invited to Thanksgiving every year. Amy suspected there were two reasons for this: their relatives' conflict-averse nature and, more important, Amy and Teresa's cooking. As the oldest girl in a Southern Baptist family with six children, Teresa had been taught at a young age how to feed a crowd—an especially important skill for young women in the Bible Belt, who were raised to believe that the way to a man's heart was through his stomach and that there was nothing more important than obtaining a man's heart. Teresa had happily taken to cooking, her abilities quickly eclipsing those of her sisters and eventually her own mother. It was a skill—and passion—Amy was happy to have inherited from Teresa. In her younger years, Amy had served as sous-chef to her mother, at first just collecting ingredients or stirring, later chopping vegetables or weaving together lattice piecrusts. By the time she graduated high school, Amy had reached a level of expertise in the kitchen far beyond her years. But it wasn't until after college that Amy, waiting tables and wondering if her degree in theater had been a mistake, realized that baking could potentially be a career for her.

Amy and her mother worked in a contented silence, comfortable in their familiar rhythm. As she loaded the dishwasher, Amy thought absentmindedly about the day ahead, realizing she couldn't remember a time when Thanksgiving hadn't had an undercurrent of competition or a time when she and her mother hadn't been striving to win. The Fariner family declared blue-ribbon dishes each Thanksgiving, a process that had been informal in Amy's childhood but had grown into a complicated blind voting system with winners for best featured meat, best vegetable side, best bread, and best dessert. Amy and Teresa always took home a win in at least one category but strove to sweep them all—with the exception of the meat category, an honorary award that always went to the hosting family's turkey. Each Thanksgiving was another chance to outdo their creations from the previous year, and as Amy's cousins grew up and learned their way around their own kitchens, the competition only grew stiffer. While everyone enjoyed the friendly rivalry, Amy knew it meant something else for her and her mom: a chance to prove their worth, to show that they belonged at the Thanksgiving table, even if they didn't always feel welcomed with open arms.

As always, they had an entry in every category except for

meat. Their rental homes had always been too small for them to host, so they never had the occasion to show their turkey-cooking prowess. This year, Teresa had prepared her signature pumpkin cheesecake the previous day, allowing ample time for it to set in the refrigerator. But despite the incredibly light texture, complex flavor, and handmade whipped cream of the dish, they knew they couldn't count on their old standard to take the prize this year. The previous year, Amy's cousin Laurel had elevated the competition with a lemon meringue pie, and her aunt Elaine had surprised everyone with an elegant Black Forest cake. And since everyone had enjoyed Teresa's cheesecake in the past, it no longer had the element of surprise it once had. So Amy had made a second dessert to improve their odds: a three-tier cranberry and orange cake, which she was in the process of decorating with sugared cranberries. Teresa was finishing off their vegetable dish, a pan of roasted carrots, butternut squash, and turnips with an apple cider glaze. Their entry for the bread category, which historically had been an easy win for Amy and Teresa, was a tray of herbed Parmesan biscuits.

"Another five minutes on the biscuits, and we'll be ready to load the car, I think," Teresa said, peeking into the oven. "When you're done with the cake, I've got a box ready for it on the dining room table."

Amy swept stray frosting and bits of sugar from the edge of the cake plate with a damp napkin before carrying it to the dining room table. Her mother's house in midtown was only a twenty-minute drive from the suburban home where Amy's aunt and uncle were hosting this year's celebration, but she had learned from years of experience that a poorly protected cake on a bumpy road could only lead to tragedy.

As Amy loaded the cake into the box, she thought suddenly of the Thanksgiving two years prior, when her mom was first diagnosed with breast cancer. Amy had channeled all of her emotions into making sure their dishes still upstaged the rest of the family's. Even though Teresa, sick and weak from radiation, was able only to smile encouragement in Amy's direction, they'd managed to win the bread and dessert categories that year.

This Thanksgiving, Amy and Teresa were celebrating the second annual cancer screening that had come back clear, only days earlier. Maybe eventually a clear cancer screening would seem mundane, but for now, it still felt like a gift.

After she finished packaging up the cake, Amy returned to her mother's side. "So what's my excuse this year when Granny and Papa ask when I'm getting married?"

Her mom considered the question for a moment while she arranged the roasted vegetables on a serving platter. "Focusing on your career?"

"I used that one last year. And Granny gave me that terrible lecture on my biological clock and geriatric pregnancies, remember?"

Teresa frowned. "Haven't met any nice boys?"

Amy chuckled. "I haven't met any nice *straight* boys, that's for sure. But what if she tries to set me up with one of the guys at her church? I can't handle that again." While the news that Amy was gay had gotten to the rest of her extended family through the family gossip mill, everyone was afraid telling the two oldest and most religious family members that Amy was gay might lead to a heart attack.

"Well then, I'm out of ideas," Teresa said.

Amy took the biscuits from the oven and began transferring them to a cooling rack. "When did they give up on trying to find a nice husband for you?"

Teresa paused, holding a dripping spatula aloft as she thought. "I guess about the time I told them I was pregnant with you. You could try getting pregnant?"

"Very funny, mom." In all of Amy's years, she'd never known her mother to have a boyfriend. Occasionally she'd had a lurking suspicion that Teresa was on a date, like one night in middle school when she'd said she was going to Max and Greg's, but when Amy had called their house with a homework question, she'd found out her mother wasn't there and hadn't made plans to visit. But every time Amy tried to ask her mom about her love life, she deflected, saying that she didn't need a man in her life to be fulfilled. Eyeing Teresa curiously across the kitchen, Amy wondered if it was worth trying again. "So, who do you hang out with these days?"

"Same people I always hang out with: you, Max, Greg, and my students," Teresa said. "Why do you ask?"

"Sure you don't have any new *special* friends?" she probed.

Teresa whipped around, the spatula in her hand flinging droplets of cider glaze across the counter. "I know what you're doing, Amelia Fariner, and if I had a special someone I wanted to talk about, you'd be the first to know." Amy pressed her lips together in chastened silence as Teresa turned back to the vegetable dish. "What about *you*? Any girlfriends I should know about?"

"If I had a girlfriend I wanted to talk about, you'd be the first to know," Amy said, unable to resist. Amy was typically a little more forthcoming about her love life than her mother was. But she wasn't ready to get her hopes up about Charley just yet. After all, they hadn't put any labels on whatever they were doing. She wasn't even sure if they were exclusive. More than that, though, she was being cautious because she wanted to avoid another Autumn situation.

Teresa had been enamored with Autumn. This was partly because Autumn was so charming and likable and partly because Amy, who had wanted more than anything for her mom to love the person she was in love with, had always highlighted Autumn's most endearing qualities and stories that cast her in the best possible light. As the relationship deteriorated, Amy hadn't wanted to tell her mom what was going on, not just because Teresa was in the throes of chemo and radiation, but also in case things improved between her and Autumn. Even more, Amy had known that if she told her mom about the cheating, Teresa would be outraged and heartbroken on Amy's behalf. She didn't want to be responsible for upsetting her mother right as she was finally getting better. Amy already felt ashamed enough of what she saw as her failure to persuade Autumn to stay faithful.

Over a year later, Amy knew her mom was still holding out hope that she and Autumn would get back together. Telling her about Charley might finally convince Teresa that the Autumn phase was over. But what if either Amy or her mom got too attached and then things didn't work out again? For the time being, Amy decided as they finished loading the car, she'd keep Charley to herself.

Later that evening, their stomachs full to bursting, Amy and her mom drove toward Ruby Red's, rehashing the day's results. Teresa and Amy had almost managed a sweep this year. The biscuits and glazed vegetables won their respective categories, but when it came to dessert, they'd accidentally split the vote between Amy's three-tier cake and Teresa's classic cheesecake, clearing the way for Aunt Sheila's caramel cake to take the gold. Teresa and Amy agreed that it wouldn't be Thanksgiving without their traditional cheesecake, but next time, they should make it without putting it on the official ballot.

All in all, the dinner had been pleasant enough. Amy had had a polite, though stiff, conversation with Christina about her honeymoon. She managed to respond to her grandparents' questions about finding a husband with awkward laughter and shrugs. And the rest of the family was too busy chasing around small children to spend much time dropping hints to Amy about her lapsed church attendance. All things considered, the extended family's avoidance of Amy's queerness (or "phase" as they called it) was an improvement over the days when they would invite eligible young Christian bachelors to family events to introduce to her.

Pulling up in front of the bar, Teresa put her flashers on before getting out and rooting around in a large cooler in the trunk. "I made an extra cheesecake for your party tonight," she said, coming around to the passenger side and pressing a chilled box into Amy's arms. "I have to keep my patron saint of Ruby Red's title somehow."

Amy (and her mom's cheesecake) received a warm greeting from the small crowd already gathered around the bar's makeshift dining room table, composed of small tables pulled alongside a large plastic folding table. The bar was covered in casserole dishes and Tupperware, while one of the large booths served as the dessert buffet. Amy pushed aside a plate of brownies to make room for the cheesecake and then went behind the bar to locate a bottle of tequila that had been tucked away beneath the register. The reclusive bar owner rarely made an appearance at Ruby Red's but always left a full bottle of Patrón before special occasions for a round on the house. Joel and Damian joined Amy as she counted heads and began to rim the appropriate number of shot glasses with salt.

"Sooooo," Joel prompted.

"What?" Amy asked, looking up.

"We let you get away with distracting us last night," Damian said. "Not that we didn't fully enjoy talking about all of your wedding shenanigans."

"But," Joel continued, "Charley? Hello? We've barely heard

anything about her since your fancy *Lady and the Tramp* spaghetti-date-turned-sleepover. How are things going? Are you madly in love? Are you u-hauling? I need the deets!"

Amy beamed at her friends' rapt faces. Maybe it was because it was her favorite day of the year, but the memory of her last date with Charley didn't feel as cringeworthy as it had the day before. She filled them in on everything except her period-sex weirdness, which she definitely did not feel like revisiting right then. When she was done, Joel slapped his palms on the bar, nearly toppling the shot glasses.

"I knew it!" he squealed. "I *knew* it. She's the one."

"That's a leap, babe," Damian said, but he was smiling too.

Amy rolled her eyes but was secretly pleased. "We're still getting to know each other."

"Still," Damian said. "We haven't heard you talk about someone this way in . . . well, in a while. This is good."

"I do really like her," Amy admitted.

"Is that tequila?" Jae shouted from across the room.

"Coming right up!" Amy called back.

"When's date number four?" Joel asked.

"Sometime next week hopefully. She's out of town until Wednesday." Amy began filling the shot glasses.

"That's fine," Joel said in a tone that suggested Wednesday was farther away than he would have preferred, "as long as you promise to tell us all the details without making us beg."

"I think the only one begging is going to be Char—" Damian began before Joel cut him off with a delighted squeal.

After the three of them distributed shots and lime wedges to everyone in the bar, Amy offered a toast. "Some of us survived difficult family interactions today. Some of us weren't welcomed home at all." She gave small nods toward Jae, Arnelle, and Joel. "And some of us are lucky to have loving and supportive families but we still want to celebrate with our friends. Here's to all of you beautiful people, my queer family, for surviving another Thanksgiving. Cheers to queers!" The group clinked glasses and threw back the shots.

Still full from her family dinner, Amy relieved Joel and Zee from their duties behind the bar so they could load up their Styrofoam plates and join the table. After refilling wine and beer glasses and mixing up a pitcher of sangria, Amy sat down for a while as well, laughing along to stories others shared about Thanksgivings past. It didn't take long for Teresa's pumpkin cheesecake to disappear, and Amy made a mental note of the rave reviews to share them with her mother later.

Halfway through the late dinner, a few cheers arose as a familiar face entered the bar. Autumn greeted the room and filled up a plate before tapping a knife against an empty glass. The room quieted in anticipation of the tradition Autumn led at each Ruby Red's Thanksgiving.

"Friends, loved ones, chosen family—"

"Past girlfriends, exes, scorned lovers," Zee murmured with a smirk.

"I hope you're all having a lovely time," Autumn said. "I'm here with my annual reminder that as much as we love to spend this celebratory meal together, it marks a holiday with a history of violence and oppression and genocide. We are standing on stolen land. As a member of the Muscogee (Creek) Nation, I know that this is a day with a complicated legacy of gratitude and mourning. I'd like us to all take a moment of silence in memory of the indigenous people who once stood where we stand."

In the quiet that followed, Amy was reminded of what had first drawn her to Autumn: her clarity of mind, her passion, her way of speaking right to the heart. And remembering why she'd fallen so hard for Autumn gave Amy a little unexpected compassion for herself. Autumn may have broken her heart a few times over, but she was also a sweetheart. Amy realized, looking at Autumn's bowed head, that she no longer thought of their relationship with regret. It was brave to try and love someone. Brave for both of them.

Autumn raised her head. "All right, thank you all. I put a bucket over there for donations to the Native American Rights Fund. Now hug your neighbor, and let's finish eating so we can dance!" Autumn clapped, and conversation around the table resumed.

Once everyone was sufficiently stuffed and thankful, Joel and Amy pushed the tables apart to clear the floor for dancing, and Jae got to work as DJ.

Bars in Oklahoma couldn't legally serve alcohol past 2:00 A.M., but closing time came and went without a last call, Amy, Joel, and Zee hoping no one would have the heart to break up a holiday party. The hours of eating, drinking, and dancing slowly wore the group down, though, and by three in the morning, the crowd had dwindled to only a handful of stragglers. Amy sent Joel and Zee home around half past three when they both looked so tired they could drop, waving away their protests. She figured shutting down was the least she could do since she had arrived late and missed setting up and opening the bar.

Amy was corking open wine bottles behind the counter, her back to the room, when she heard Autumn say, "Sit down and have a drink with me." Amy turned, startled to find that she and Autumn were the only two people left in the building.

"Autumn, it's four A.M.," Amy said, checking the Tin Man's ticking heart clock on the wall. She remembered all too well a time when that wouldn't have made any difference to her, when being alone with Autumn in Ruby Red's was all she wanted. But that was before. "I have to close up."

"You've been cleaning and shutting things down for an hour. And I saw that pitcher of sangria you put away. You know it won't taste as good tomorrow. We'd be doing it a favor."

Amy knew Autumn's argument about the sangria was bullshit, as it would only get better overnight. Even so, she hesitated. Part of her wanted to decline just for the feeling of saying no to Autumn. But truthfully, she wouldn't mind having a little time to set things right with her. They hadn't quite nailed the landing in the dismount from breakup to friendship, and that was something Amy genuinely wanted between them. It had been a year, and they couldn't avoid each other in Tulsa's tight-knit queer community. Besides, Amy had Charley now. Sort of.

"Come on, Ames," Autumn said. "It's been such a nice night. I just want to spend a minute with you before I go home."

Won over, Amy pulled out two glasses and the sangria pitcher. "Fine. But only if you let me beat you at a game of Bullshit."

Autumn laughed fondly. "No way I'm letting you win. You've got to earn it. But you're at an advantage, because I think I've had a little more to drink than you."

Amy came out from behind the bar and set the sangria pitcher and glasses on the table of a booth, then slid onto one of the benches. Autumn handed Amy a deck of cards from a shelf near the pool tables, then attached her phone to the bar's audio system and began playing "Give Me One Reason" by Tracy Chapman. It was an old favorite of theirs from road trips they'd taken together.

Not sure what to make of the song choice, Amy shuffled and dealt, and Autumn sat down across from her. After a few rousing games of Bullshit (most of which Amy won after all, even though she was almost thwarted by a couple of cards missing from the old deck), Amy glanced at the clock across the bar. "Oh shit. It's five in the morning." She grimaced. "Normally I'd be making croissants at a Friday morning bakery shift."

"Closed for the holiday?"

Amy leaned back in the booth, comforted by the familiarity of the ripped fake leather. "You haven't heard? I thought Joel would have told everyone in town by now. He was so mad about it. The jig was up. Someone outed me and I got fired."

Autumn's jaw dropped. "You're kidding."

"I wish I was."

"That old bitch. I'm so sorry, Ames. You were their best baker! Well, their mistake. I hope they go out of business without you."

It felt surprisingly good to hear those words from Autumn. She had tasted a countless number of Amy's best creations during the two years they were together. Not that Amy needed Autumn's approval, she reminded herself. "Thanks, Autumn. But I'm sure they'll do fine without me."

Autumn leaned into the table, looking seriously into Amy's eyes. "You deserve better than that place. You shouldn't have to hide who you are to bake. Hell, you should open your own bakery. It would take over the town."

"I . . . Well, I've thought about it. Maybe someday." Compared to her awkward conversation with Charley, telling Autumn about getting fired had been easy. Maybe it was because Autumn already had the backstory, and Amy didn't have to worry about first impressions. Or maybe it was because she was too exhausted to overthink it. "Anyway, I really should go home. I'm wiped." Amy pulled herself from the booth and added the glasses and pitcher to the dishwasher. A few minutes later, ready to lock up, she slipped on her coat and grabbed two giant trash bags to take to the dumpster.

"Let me help you with that." Autumn took one of the trash bags from Amy's hands and held open the back door of the bar. After lobbing the bags into the giant dumpster behind the building, Amy locked the back door, and Autumn followed her around the building as she went to lock the front. It was a once-familiar routine for them.

When Amy turned around, Autumn was only inches away, ruffling her dark hair, something Amy knew to be a nervous habit. "Tonight was really nice," Autumn said.

"It was. A perfect Ruby Red's family night." Amy put her hands in her pockets, shivering slightly as the cold air cut through her coat. The sun hadn't yet begun to rise, and the street around them was silent and empty, giving the early morning a dreamlike quality.

"I've missed you," Autumn said.

Amy felt a tightening in her chest, not excitement, but a certain surprise and apprehension. She could act like she thought Autumn meant she missed her as a friend. Maybe she did. "Autumn, I . . ."

Before she could finish her thought, Autumn grabbed her by the hips and kissed her. With Autumn's warm body against her own, the familiar feeling of Autumn's lips, Amy felt . . . nothing.

And after two years of on-again, off-again drama, followed by a year of pain and longing, it was the most wonderful nothing Amy had ever experienced. She gently pushed Autumn away, unable to prevent a smile of relief from breaking across her face.

Autumn returned her smile, misunderstanding. "Oh, Ames—"

"Autumn," Amy cut her off gently. "It's over."

"But you kissed me." Autumn's beautiful brown eyes looked scared. Not so long ago, Amy would have done anything to take that look off her face.

"*You* kissed *me*. And everything we used to have—I don't feel it anymore. I've moved on. And you have too."

"Come on, Ames. It's us. It's always been us." Autumn grasped the hem of Amy's shirt, a wrinkle appearing on her forehead.

"I've been seeing someone else, and it's good, Autumn." Well, Amy thought, at least it had the potential to be good. "I'm happy. And you! You have . . . What's her name, McKenzie?"

Autumn shook her head. "It's over with McKenzie. All the fun you and I had together tonight? It reminded me of the good times. We have something."

Amy took Autumn's hands from their place on her shirt and squeezed them. "I care about you. Deeply. I always will. But we're not right for each other romantically. You know it. I know it."

Autumn stepped back, the rejection Amy knew she so rarely faced seeming to finally hit her. "So what was tonight? What have we been doing? Talking and reminiscing . . ."

"Friends," Amy offered. "We were being friends."

Autumn thought it over. "You're sure we can't have one more night together? To say goodbye?"

Amy laughed, then said gently but firmly, "I'm sure."

Autumn shrugged, the hurt fading from her eyes as a hint of her charm and humor returned. "All right. Friends. I'll give it a try."

And as the first morning light cracked over the horizon, Amy and Autumn said their goodbyes and walked in separate directions down Cherry Street.

13

Guess who's back in town! Plans tonight?

Welcome back! I'm working at Ruby Red's. Want to drop by? Xmas karaoke and cookie decorating, if that's your thing.

Sounds like fun!

By the time Amy made it to Ruby Red's on foot with her arms full of cookies the Wednesday after Thanksgiving, Damian and Joel were already finished setting up the karaoke machine and had turned their attention to convincing the dusty old DVD player to play *The Judy Garland Show Holiday Special.*

"Babe! You look hot!" Joel called from the far end of the bar. "Why so fancy?"

Amy straightened her blazer self-consciously. Maybe the time she'd spent styling her hair to the side and applying makeup had been a bad idea. But if there was anywhere she felt totally safe flirting with her crush, it was Ruby Red's. "Charley's coming. Does it look like I'm trying too hard?"

Joel screamed and Damian covered his ears, grimacing. "I finally get to meet her! It really is Christmas!"

"It's December fourth," Damian corrected.

"Close enough!" Joel said. "And no, Amy, you're gorgeous. Stunning. Perfection. Never change."

"It's too much," Amy said.

"It's really not. And I can't wait to meet her." Damian greeted Amy with a hug. "Can I help you set up the cookie station?"

Wednesday evenings at the bar were often slow. Over the years, Amy and Joel had experimented with special events and themes to bring in more business. After some of their ideas more than doubled profits on weeknights, the absentee bar owner had granted them carte blanche for themed events and access to the bar's social media accounts to advertise.

Baked goods were a frequent feature of Joel and Amy's event ideas. Amy had worked out an agreement with the owner to charge groceries to Ruby Red's and add her hours spent baking to her time sheet. Amy wasn't sure if baked goods made in her own kitchen could be legally sold at Ruby Red's, so she'd worked around the risk by charging customers for decorating materials and throwing in the cookies for free. Amy had spent the afternoon baking sugar cookies and organizing her schedule of upcoming bridesmaid obligations, leaving hardly any time for her to worry about introducing Charley to her friends. Hardly.

While prepping the cookie station, Amy tried to lay the groundwork for a good first meeting between Charley, Joel, and

Damian. She asked them to avoid talking about Daily Bread and her new bridesmaid business, which they cautiously agreed to do once Amy promised she was working up to telling Charley. "And Joel, please no embarrassing stories, especially the one about the glitter cannons at the Kesha concert."

Joel pouted. "But it's my favorite! How come I'm the only one who doesn't get to tell embarrassing stories?"

"Because my other friends know better," Amy said. "Right, Damian?"

Damian nodded proudly and stuck his tongue out at Joel.

Zee arrived early for her shift to help Joel, Damian, and Amy dig a couple of boxes of holiday decorations out of a back closet. By the time the bar opened, the dive looked marginally more festive. Ruby Red's was already what most would call "overdecorated," and the Christmas décor strung atop of the *Wizard of Oz* memorabilia made for quite a mash-up. In most cases, the multicolored lights, tinsel, and fake snow covered the Ozian pieces, but some were incorporated, like the life-size Toto, which wore a jauntily crooked Santa hat.

"So, any more responses to your Craigslist post?" Damian asked as he settled himself on a barstool.

"Actually, yes." Amy organized a row of sprinkles and colored frostings on a tray for Zee to bring over to the cookie station. "A lot more than I expected. I have a wedding booked for this upcoming weekend, a couple more later this month, and several requests for the spring."

Damian congratulated Amy, looking impressed. "I know it's only been a week, but have you thought about setting up a website? It might make the whole thing look a little more legitimate. Maybe you could even get a testimonial from that woman whose wedding you were in. I built my own freelancing website. I can help you create one and show you how to use it."

Amy gratefully accepted the offer. She felt a bit strange making a website when she had just made the leap into professional bridesmaiding, but what could it hurt? If she was going to give this business idea a try, she might as well go all in.

The karaoke system made a high-pitched squeal, and Damian ran to fix it. Joel took Damian's place on the barstool while Amy began mixing cocktails for a group who'd claimed one of the booths. "It's good you're getting all of this practice because I fully expect you to be my maid of honor when Damian and I get married. You might be a hot commodity by then. Should I ask you now so that I can be on the list before you start charging your friends? Pencil me in for whenever gay marriage is legal in Oklahoma, so, like, 2090."

"Will people even still have bridesmaids in 2090? Or pencils?" Amy said. "Anyway, I thought you both hated weddings."

"Straight weddings," Joel said. "Gay weddings are a totally different thing."

Amy paused midpour, a cocktail glass in one hand and a shaker in the other. "Will you two really get married, you think?"

Joel looked toward Damian, who was crawling under a table to adjust the speaker. "Yeah, I think we will. We've been together for almost three years now. I know that's not the longest time, but I can't really picture life without him. I would propose today if I could."

Amy smiled at the surprisingly intimate confession. "What's stopping you?"

"Oh, I don't know, Oklahoma law?"

"Maybe that's stopping you from the marriage part, but no one can stop you putting a ring on it, can they?" Amy said.

"I guess you're right," Joel said, sounding unconvinced. "It seems like getting engaged would feel fake, though, since I can't actually follow through with the wedding part." He looked dejected. The mood was a stark contrast to his usual bubbly personality.

Amy set down the glass and shaker and grabbed Joel's hand across the bar. "What better way to stick it to the homophobes than being loudly and openly in love? Committing to each other? Showing them they can't control your relationship?" As she spoke, Amy felt a twinge of guilt, knowing "sticking it to the homophobes" was something she could rarely bring herself to do. Maybe if she had someone she wanted to marry, as Joel did, she'd feel a little braver.

"Maybe." Joel looked back toward Damian, who emerged from behind the speaker and gave the bartenders a thumbs-up. "Nice work, hon!"

As customers began to arrive, Joel settled himself at the karaoke table, Zee kept the drinks flowing, and Amy split her attention between the cookie station and filling drink orders. Before long, holiday spirit was thick in the air. Customers donned ugly sweaters, frosted cookies, and belted along to karaoke Christmas tunes.

Every time a cold burst of air from the open door signaled a new arrival, Amy looked up hoping to find Charley. But another familiar face found its way into the bar first. It took Amy a moment to place her, but when she approached the bar and dug in her enormous purse for her wallet, Amy realized who it was. "McKenzie, right? Welcome back. Amaretto sour?"

"Wow, I can't believe you remember my name!" McKenzie unwound a long purple scarf from her neck. "You must be, like, literally the nicest bartender ever. Can I actually get three peppermint spritzers?" A couple of McKenzie's friends headed to the back to grab a booth.

Amy grabbed three glasses and filled them with ice. "I tend to remember repeat customers." *And new members of the Autumn's*

Exes Club, she added mentally. "Autumn not coming in tonight?" Amy felt guilty toying with the poor kid but was too curious to pass up an opportunity to find out what had happened with the breakup. And besides, if McKenzie was going to stick around at Ruby Red's, she'd have to learn to run in the same circles as her ex.

McKenzie attempted a carefree chuckle that came out more like a tearful hiccup. "God, I hope not."

"Trouble in paradise?" Amy said, ladling peppermint spritzers from a large punch bowl into the glasses.

"She's a liar and a cheater," McKenzie said bitterly. "I can't believe I trusted her."

"Tell me about it," Amy muttered.

"You too?"

Amy placed a candy cane garnish in each glass and slid them across the bar. "Yeah, a while back. I'm sorry I didn't warn you when you were here before."

McKenzie glanced back toward her friends' table. "Has she slept with, like, every lesbian in Tulsa?"

"And every bisexual and pansexual woman in Tulsa, a handful of gender nonconforming people, and a pretty impressive number of straight women who felt like experimenting," Amy said honestly but not unsympathetically. It wasn't McKenzie's fault she had fallen victim to Autumn. "Don't worry about it. Everyone is an idiot when it comes to Autumn. She's got that charm that helps you ignore what you don't want to see, you know? And she really is a good person under all of that playboy persona. It helps to remember that."

"Yeah, I know." McKenzie stirred a glass with the candy cane garnish. "Part of me just wishes I could go back to Sunday, before I found out."

"Sunday?" Amy repeated.

"Yeah, I walked in on her having sex with my best friend. My best friend! Can you believe it?" She snorted. "You probably can."

Sunday. Three days after Thanksgiving, when Autumn had kissed her. Even though the kiss hadn't been Amy's fault, she felt a rush of guilt and renewed anger at Autumn, whom she'd defended only seconds before.

McKenzie straightened as she gathered the three cocktail glasses. "But I decided there are only so many queer bars in town, and I'm not giving this one up just because Autumn introduced me to it. I won't give her the satisfaction."

"Good for you!" Amy felt a sudden protective instinct for the young queer woman. "You're always welcome at Ruby Red's. And let me know if Autumn ever bothers you while you're here. Us spurned lovers have to stick together."

McKenzie beamed. "I knew I liked it here."

Watching McKenzie find her place at Ruby Red's was sentimental for Amy, who could clearly remember her first visit to the bar on her twenty-first birthday. She'd heard about it from a few upperclassmen in college. It was one of the rare queer spots in town she hadn't learned about from Max and Greg. When the clock struck midnight, she and Joel had celebrated the official start of her birthday by going to Ruby Red's for Amy's first legal drink. Upon seeing the dingy booths, worn pool tables, and old *Wizard of Oz* movie posters tacked to the walls, Amy had known it was a place she could someday call home. Mostly it was the room full of queer Tulsans, spending time with friends and lovers in a place they knew welcomed them with open arms, that made Amy feel warm and fuzzy inside on that first visit. If only there had been somewhere else for her to find that community before she could legally drink. It seemed cruel to see McKenzie only now discovering a whole new world where she fit in. But it was that love of Ruby Red's that kept Amy's spirit up for her entire shift, through jazzy renditions of "I Saw Mommy Kissing Santa Claus" and spilled sprinkles and sticky peppermint spritzer glasses, as she kept watching the front door that Charley never walked through.

14

Amy resisted texting Charley at first. Feeling the sting of rejection, she wanted to tell Charley off, demand to be treated with respect, or at least tell Charley she was hurt by being stood up. But from what Amy knew of Charley, no-showing seemed out of character. Hadn't she always been reliably prompt before? Maybe Charley had had a family emergency. Maybe she'd gotten into a car accident! Maybe she was in the hospital, too injured to reach out. Amy tried to figure out how to send a message that would hit the right tone without saying, *Are you near death in the hospital, or do you hate me?* Finally, she settled on something simple:

Is everything okay?

Amy didn't have much time to obsess over Charley's silence, though, because the first wedding she'd booked through Craigslist was scheduled for the upcoming Saturday, and the rehearsal dinner was only a night away. That afternoon, Amy met the bride, Corinne, for coffee to discuss what to expect from the wedding. She learned that it would be quite a different beast from Regi and Jared's. Standing no more than five foot two with a fashionably asymmetrical bob and a peplum dress, Corinne was a big ball of energy in a tiny package. A middle school history teacher, Corinne was used to putting her foot down to settle student drama, but as she told Amy, handling drama in her own family was much more challenging. Amy would be filling the dress of Corinne's sister-in-law, who had backed out after a screaming match with Corinne's mother while planning the bridal shower.

"I'm worried my wedding may lead to the end of my brother's marriage," Corinne said as she massaged her temples, the pear-shaped diamond in her engagement ring gleaming. "I wouldn't blame her. My family can be, well, difficult. I just hope she doesn't tell Joseph to run before it's too late and he's married into the chaos."

"I totally get having complicated family dynamics," Amy said reassuringly. She wondered if this was a good moment to bring up being gay, just to put it out in the open, but decided they should focus on the wedding at hand. "And the good news is I'm coming in with no preexisting drama. I'm totally on your side, and I'll have your back. Now, what should I watch out for?"

Amy's tangible tasks for the wedding day would mainly be setting up and taking down decorations with the rest of the bridal party and keeping an eye on the crystal cake plate, which was a family heirloom, but Corinne also asked Amy to watch out for any signs of danger-to-come from family members in attendance. "They're—how do I say this?—not exactly afraid of conflict. They have a lot of strong opinions and take too much personally, but things really get messy when anyone feels like they or their mother is being disrespected. I could really use one level-headed person on my side to keep things from coming to blows. My cousin Shawn's wedding literally ended with a fistfight over the garter toss."

The wedding itself would take place at First Presbyterian Church, a downtown church with Gothic-spired towers and beautiful stained-glass windows. The reception would follow at the Mayo Hotel, a lush art deco building originally opened in the 1920s. But while the wedding and reception were to be held in two of Tulsa's nicest historic buildings, the Friday night rehearsal dinner was going to be at a much more casual sports bar and grill best known for its honey pepper bacon burger.

The following night, Amy felt glad Corinne had asked her to attend the rehearsal dinner, as it gave her a chance to see the family dynamics in person. Corinne's family was indeed a boisterous bunch; Amy could hardly keep up as they talked over one another, debating everything from the seating arrangements to the consistency of the queso. Amy found the noisy group entertaining but also saw how things could escalate quickly, especially when Corinne's grandpa's story about a family fishing trip devolved into a heated argument about which lake they'd visited before he could even reach the punch line. Meanwhile, the groom's family had a wide-eyed look of terror about them as they stuck firmly to their own tables, heads leaned together to hear one another over the ruckus.

As this was her first real wedding event since making her Craigslist advertisement, Amy had spent plenty of time plotting out a detailed backstory—she was a friend Corinne had made online in a teachers' chat room—and thinking through how to divert the conversation if people asked too many questions. But seated at a long table of Corinne's family and friends, she found that she could hardly fit a word in edgewise. In fact, there were two to three people talking over one another at pretty much all times, except for a few brief moments after the food arrived.

Feeling guilty for cashing in on the free meal without doing anything but smiling and nodding, Amy did her best to mingle once everyone had finished eating. The casual bar setting was familiar to her, and she had plenty of experience deescalating fights fueled by a few too many beers. She watched for aggressive body language and raised voices, then slid herself into the conversations where she saw them and changed the subject. "Wow, what a nice tie! Hi, I'm Corinne's friend Amy. I don't think we've met" was a standard entry. She'd fully exhausted her stock of noncontroversial discussion topics by the time things were winding down, and once the event was over, she was grateful for the peace and quiet of the three-mile walk home. Although she would have been more grateful for a working car.

The next day, the wedding ceremony went off mostly perfectly, minus a late start due to an argument between Corinne and her sisters over how the wraparound bridesmaid dresses should be tied. The more formal setting seemed to put Corinne's family on best, or at least *better,* behavior. Amy laughed along with the crowd when the pastor joked that "I do" might be the only words the groom would be able to squeeze in with all of Corinne's family in attendance. She teared up unexpectedly when she spotted the bride's parents, whom Amy had last seen yelling about the prices on the wine list at the rehearsal dinner, holding hands and smiling proudly during the vows. There it was again: that spark of wedding magic. Amy could get used to the light, hopeful feeling tucked under her ribs.

But this time, there was another feeling vying for her attention: a sour taste of envy in the back of her throat at the knowledge that her kind of love wasn't allowed. Maybe it was the fact that they were at such a breathtakingly beautiful historic church that made her think about it, or maybe it was Rachel Maddow's show the previous week, but it was something that hadn't occurred to Amy at Regi and Jared's art gallery wedding, and it took a bit of the joy out of the moment. She did her best to bury her discomfort, remembering that she hadn't said anything to Corinne or her family about being queer. Maybe they would be totally accepting of it if she gave them the chance. But anyway, why was she thinking about herself on Corinne's special day?

At the Mayo Hotel an hour later, the bridal party took the elevator to the ballroom on the sixteenth floor and made a big entrance, dancing their way into the space as they were introduced by the lead singer of the band onstage. Amy spent a fair amount of time gawking at the crystal chandeliers, glittering terrazzo floors, and beautiful views of downtown Tulsa, and the rest of the time popping into tense conversations with a big smile and peaceful energy. The reception was a bit chaotic—Amy hadn't realized that toasts could be so interactive—but the bride and groom seemed pleased by the time their limo arrived for the send-off. Corinne briefly grabbed Amy's hand before departing, thanking her for all of her work setting up the space and keeping things light among her family. Amy wished Corinne and her new husband, Joseph, all the best, feeling a little like she hadn't done enough to earn her fee but relieved to see that Corinne seemed happy with her work.

Once the taillights of the newlyweds' car disappeared into the night, guests returned to the ballroom upstairs to gather their things and make their exits. Amy pulled out a list the bride had left behind with a few tasks the bridal party was meant to complete before leaving. As hotel employees began to remove tables and chairs, the bridesmaids and groomsmen gathered around her. With the wedding coordinator gone and the bride well on her way to the honeymoon, it looked like Amy was in charge.

"All right, everyone. Let's get two volunteers on collecting centerpieces, three on breaking down the photo wall over there, two checking under tables and in restrooms for any forgotten items, and the rest loading gifts onto that dolly for the courier to pick up tomorrow."

Their tasks assigned, everyone dispersed, and Amy joined the group transferring gifts from the display table to a large two-level dolly. Since she'd spent much of the rehearsal dinner and wedding focused on Corinne and her rowdiest family members, Amy had hardly spoken to her fellow members of the bridal party. Now that most of them were several drinks deep and visibly exhausted by the hours of wedding festivities, it was an awkward time for get-to-know-you conversations.

"It was a beautiful wedding, wasn't it?" Amy said, in an attempt at casual chatter, to a bridesmaid named Alayna who was loading the dolly alongside her. Corinne's cousin, Amy was fairly sure. Or maybe her stepsister? Or was that the bridesmaid with the long blond waves?

Alayna shrugged. "Corinne seemed happy. But it's been a long day. These heels are killing me." She hobbled toward a table near the gifts, wincing with each step until she finally collapsed into a chair. "I can't believe we set all this stuff up this morning and have to take it all down now. Couldn't they have hired someone for this?" Amy focused intentionally on the gift pile, as if trying to decide which one to take next. They had indeed hired someone for this: her.

A groomsman grunted in agreement as he shifted the weight of a large box with a bow on top. "I wouldn't have bought a gift if I'd realized I'd be giving free manual labor too."

"Oh, it's not that much to do. I bet with all of us here, we'll be done in no time!" Amy said with forced cheer. With the music gone, the bar disassembled, and the glow of the evening fading, spirits were falling fast. She was just as drained as the rest of the bridal party, but at least she had the promise of the remaining balance of her bridesmaid fee to keep her going. The check was already in her bag, and Amy could hardly wait to deposit it first thing Monday morning and finally get her car repaired.

Alayna eyed her with skepticism. "Annie, right? How do you know Corinne?" Amy had the impression that this was the bridesmaid's half-hearted attempt to distract from the fact that she'd stopped helping.

"It's Amy, actually. We met online in a teachers' chat room and hit it off." Amy stacked two light boxes on top of each other in her arms.

"Teacher Creatures?" Alayna asked, suddenly perking up.

"Yep, that's the one!" Amy said, remembering Corinne's suggestion for her cover.

Alayna leaned back in her chair, tilting her head curiously across the table. "I could have sworn I knew everyone in Teacher Creatures. I'm so sorry I didn't recognize you! What's your username?"

Shit. Why hadn't Corinne warned her there was another teacher that might catch her in the lie? Amy readjusted the packages in her arm, thinking. At their initial meeting, she'd asked Corinne what cover story would be best, and Corinne had said she didn't think it was necessary. But Amy had pushed, saying she didn't want questions about her relationship to the bride to distract from Corinne's big day, so when she'd offered up the teachers' forum, Amy had run with it. At Regi's wedding, it had been easy to disappear toward the dance floor when her aunt started asking too many questions about her elementary school friendship claim. Amy knew she could come up with some way to deflect Alayna's question, but this late in the game, maybe she should just come clean. It might even lead to another client connection, like with Kim.

Amy lowered her voice conspiratorially, leaning across the table toward Alayna. "Honestly, I'm not in Teacher Creatures. Corinne actually hired me for the wedding. I'm a professional bridesmaid." The words were thrilling in her mouth. She was really doing this! Only a few weeks ago, being a paid bridesmaid would have sounded absurd to her, but here she was with two weddings under her belt.

Amy gave Alayna a shy smile that she did not return. "Wait, Corinne paid you?" Alayna said, sounding incredulous.

"Well, yes, as a last-minute substitute for her sister-in—"

"Liz! Danny! Did y'all hear that? This woman is a *professional bridesmaid*." The same words that had just given Amy a feeling of pride sounded embarrassing in Alayna's disdainful voice. Amy cringed as heads turned to look in their direction.

"Professional as in she's getting paid to be here?" called a voice from across the room.

"Yep," Alayna replied. "While the rest of us are doing all this shit for free, *Amy* here is turning a buck."

Great, now she remembers my name, Amy thought.

"Oh, Corinne and Joe are rich enough to pay for fake friends but not rich enough to pay for a cleanup crew?" one of the other bridesmaids said. "That's messed up."

Amy blushed. "No, no, that's not what happened. I'm just—"

A man behind Amy, the groom's brother if she remembered correctly, spoke over her in retort to the bridesmaid who'd just spoken. "Maybe if Corinne's family members were actually helpful, she wouldn't have had to hire anyone."

A hush fell across the ballroom as everyone seemed to freeze in place. A man a few steps in front of Amy, who Amy was fairly sure was Corinne's stepbrother Danny, glared around her at the groom's brother, a huge gift box in his arms. "What did you say?"

Although the groom's family had previously been far more subdued, it seemed his brother was out of patience. "I said, maybe if y'all weren't constantly pestering each other and starting drama and yelling, Corinne wouldn't have had to pay someone to actually get things done. Right, Amy?"

Amy, fully aware that she was both metaphorically and literally in the middle of this, began slowly shifting away from the two men.

Danny set the gift on the floor and began rolling up his sleeves. "Oh, you got shit to say about my family? Better say it with your fists."

"What the hell, man?" the groom's brother said. "Can you people chill for one second? If you'd just fucking do what Corinne—"

He didn't have a chance to finish, as Danny went flying toward him, making full-body contact and knocking them both to the ground. Their limbs tangled together as one man tried to punch and the other tried to push him away, sending them both rolling across the floor. The rest of the room exploded in shouts. Amy couldn't tell whether the other members of the bridal party were yelling at them to stop or cheering them on.

As the two men rolled closer to the table full of floral arrangements, Amy's eyes widened. The crystal cake plate Corinne had pointed out as a family heirloom was tucked among the vases. "Stop!" Amy cried out.

"You *dare* talk about *my* family, you wimpy piece of . . ." Danny yelled while trying and failing to land a punch.

The groom's brother seemed to be gaining the upper hand as he flipped Danny around and pinned him to the ground. "Wimpy? Oh, it's on now."

As Danny fought back, they knocked a chair into the table of floral arrangements. Amy saw the cake plate slide closer to the edge. Noticing that the other family members were more interested in watching the fight than stopping it, she knew she had to act quickly. She didn't have the strength to pull them apart, and throwing herself between them seemed like a bad option. If she couldn't stop the fight, she could at least minimize the damage. Dropping her boxes, Amy ran to the table and slid it away as quickly and carefully as she could, gaining a couple feet of distance from the brawl. But with more space, the men continued to roll closer to Amy. As the groom's brother staggered to his feet inches from the table and Danny followed suit, gearing up for another punch, Amy grabbed the heirloom cake plate and sprinted in the other direction. Just as she made her getaway, she heard a huge crash and turned to see that the groom's brother had fallen into the table from the force of Danny's blow, causing several vases to slide off the edge and smash onto the floor.

The sound of breaking glass distracted the men for a moment, long enough for two other groomsmen to jump into action and pull them apart. Neither Danny nor the groom's brother seemed seriously injured, though they were a little disheveled, with one man's shirtsleeve ripped nearly off and the other nursing a swollen lip. As the tension in the room cooled, Amy hugged the cake plate to her chest, relieved that she'd saved it just in time.

One of the bridesmaids led the groom's brother out of the reception hall to look for ice for his lip, while another groomsman offered Danny a cigarette and took him outside. Unsure of how to proceed, the remaining bridal party members looked around at one another. One of the groomsmen broke the silence. "All right, I'm out. Going to the hotel bar if anyone wants to join me."

A couple other members of the bridal party followed him

toward the door. "Whoa, wait," Amy said. "There's still a lot on Corinne's list, and now we have to clean up that broken glass."

"Well, good thing *someone's* getting paid to do it," the groomsman said without turning around. A couple of bridesmaids laughed before they followed the groomsman out of the room.

"Wait! We can get this done quickly if we work together!" Amy called desperately to their receding backs. Recognizing a lost cause, she turned back to the remaining members of the bridal party, who looked at her in silence. They were all friends or family of the groom. "All right, well, at least we've gotten a good start. I think we can knock out the rest of this in about half an hour. What do you think?"

A groomsman cleared his throat. "No offense or anything, but since you're the professional here . . ." He looked askance at the others. "I don't think we can really be that much help, so . . ." He took a few steps in the direction of the exit.

"Come on," Amy coaxed. "We just need to get these gifts and centerpieces loaded up, take down the rest of the pictures, and clean up those broken vases. It won't take long."

But the group was already gathering their things and heading for the door. "Nice to meet you!" one person called out meekly.

Two exhausting hours later, with everything marked off Corinne's postwedding list and the damage from the fight cleaned up, Amy limped on blistered feet out of the hotel ballroom. She was sweaty, cursing her heavy bags of makeup by the time she found the concierge to ask for a cab.

"They'll have a car here in thirty minutes," the concierge said after hanging up the phone.

"Thirty minutes?" Amy protested.

"Welcome to Tulsa, ma'am. There are only about a dozen taxis in the whole city," the concierge said.

"Yeah, I know. I live here," Amy said with a sigh.

"If you want, you can have a drink at the bar, and I'll come find you when your car arrives." The concierge looked Amy up and down, taking in her mussed hair, wrinkled bridesmaid gown, and heavy bags. "Here, have a drink ticket. On the house."

Although she wasn't particularly interested in a drink, Amy was grateful for the opportunity to sit down. She traded in the drink ticket for a ginger ale and collapsed onto a barstool as a roar of laughter sounded from the other side of the room. It looked like Corinne's family had gotten a second wind. Amy half expected them to start another fight after what she'd just seen. But instead, they seemed to be in good spirits. A few were dancing. Others were circled around a table, their arms slung over one another's chairs. Luckily, they seemed to be having too much fun to notice Amy. As she sipped her ginger ale and stretched her feet, she watched Corinne's family members poke fun at one another, bicker over song choices at the jukebox, and rehash their favorite moments of the wedding.

The family's rambunctious, argumentative style had kept Amy on her toes all day. Every tiff had seemed like a spark that could set the whole event aflame. But watching them now, she realized that their passion was backed by a lot of love. With her own extended family, Amy was used to avoiding any topics that could lead to disagreement. The Fariner family was nothing if not polite, even if there was judgment and resentment simmering beneath the surface. But Corinne's family wasn't afraid of conflict. And from where Amy was sitting, it seemed like their tendency to share their big emotions and protect one another made their bonds even stronger.

15

By the time her cab arrived, Amy had to admit that Corinne's family had grown on her, even if she was still a tad bitter about cleaning up by herself. The Fariner passive-aggressive streak didn't seem to have done her many favors. It was something to consider, but on the ride home, all she could think about was crawling into bed and resting her aching muscles. After paying the driver, she dug around in her purse for her keys to the building, fantasizing about how good it was going to feel to kick off her heels and trade her dress for pajamas. But then she heard a voice calling her name. A very familiar voice.

"Amy!" She turned to see Charley walking toward her on the sidewalk in the glow of the streetlights. "You're . . . very dressed up for bartending."

Amy looked down at her wrinkled bridesmaid dress and ran a hand self-consciously along her now frizzy and disheveled updo. "Long story. What are you doing here? It's almost three in the morning." Despite her overwhelming exhaustion, Amy couldn't deny that seeing Charley gave her a thrill.

But she was also surprised and more than a little confused. It had been over a week since they'd last seen each other, they'd hardly spoken while Charley was away beyond sharing a few texts of food pictures on Thanksgiving, and then Charley had stood her up at Ruby Red's. Amy hadn't forgotten her friends' pitying looks once they'd realized Charley wasn't going to show. And Charley had never responded to her text two days before asking if she was okay. The lack of communication had Amy ready to give up on the whole thing. But as Charley reached her, pressing her hand lightly against Amy's lower back as she leaned in to kiss Amy on the cheek, Amy suddenly wanted to forget all that other stuff, at least for one night.

Charley pulled back. "Can I come in?"

Amy's body screamed yes, but she forced herself to hesitate. "Now?" she said. It came out more coldly than she'd expected. "Of all the times to talk?"

Charley scratched the back of her head, a look of embarrassment crossing her face. "I'm, uh, sorry I never responded to your text. And that I didn't show up Wednesday night. I want to explain."

A dozen instincts waged a quick battle in Amy's head. Part of her, still angry about being stood up, wanted to tell Charley to leave. Another, more familiar voice in her head told her to brush her feelings under the rug, pretend she was easygoing and hardly even noticed Charley's absence, and be the fun, chill girl she so desperately wanted to be. And part of her just wanted to sleep. But with Corinne's family still fresh in her mind, the way they wore their hearts on their sleeves and seemed to be closer for it, she decided to take a page out of their book. Amy put her keys in the door. "Fine. Come on in. But no judging me for putting on pajamas."

By the time Amy was out of her bridesmaid dress, into a pair of flannel pants and a Tulsa State Fair T-shirt, and wiping off her makeup, Charley was sitting on the couch, Truffle purring happily on her lap. Amy sat at the farthest end of the couch from them and hugged her arms around her knees. "So. That explaining you promised. You can start with why you were hanging around on my street at almost three A.M."

"Oh, right, that." Charley rubbed the back of her neck sheepishly. "Well, it's actually related to why I didn't make it to your bar the other night. Work has been totally nuts lately. I got back from that conference in South Dakota, and then everyone at my office was freaking out about this crude oil spill in a lake by the Panhandle. I had to leave the dinner in Norman early to drive out to Woodward and meet with the Environmental Quality department and the Wildlife Conservation folks, test the soil nearby, then everyone was worried about water quality in the Fort Supply Reservoir, and I had to stay a couple more days. . . . Anyway, it's been a hell of a week. I just got back this evening and dropped by your place to see if we could grab dinner. When I buzzed your apartment and didn't get a response, I figured you were at the bar, but I didn't want to show up while you were working, so I came back a little later figuring you'd be home after the bar closed."

Amy fiddled with a loose string at the hem of her shirt. If she wanted to stick to her normal no-problem-just-happy-to-be-here persona, that was an easy out. She knew Charley cared deeply about her job, and this sounded like a pretty good reason why she hadn't shown up Wednesday night. But it still didn't sit right with Amy, and what purpose had hiding her feelings ever served? She'd tried brushing her feelings under the rug with Autumn, and look how that had turned out.

"I get that you had a lot going on, but were you really so

busy that you couldn't even text me?" Amy paused, checking the petulance in her voice. She didn't want to end up rolling around in a fistfight on the ground, but she did want to be able to tell people when she was upset with them. "It hurt when you no-showed. But it hurt worse when I didn't hear from you afterwards. I didn't know if you'd gotten into some terrible accident or were just blowing me off. Are you sure there wasn't more to it than just being busy at work?"

Charley exhaled slowly. "Well, my job really is a huge thing for me. It's why I moved here, and I'm still trying to prove myself, you know? I want my bosses to know that I can handle difficult situations. I have to work twice as hard to get the same respect as the men." She swallowed. "But another reason I didn't come to the bar is because . . . Well, because I don't drink."

"Oh!" Amy's eyes widened. "Why didn't you just tell me?"

Charley wove her fingers into Truffle's long fur. "I don't know. It's just awkward, right? I'm the sober lesbian who fell for a bartender. I kept thinking there was no way it could work out, and I kept liking you more and more, and then it felt like I had missed my window to tell you without it being weird, you know?"

Amy did know. She rubbed her forehead, thinking about how she hadn't exactly been fully honest with Charley about Daily Bread. "Is it, like, a temptation thing? Shit, sorry, that's so personal. I shouldn't have asked."

"I'm not an alcoholic, if that's what you mean. I just hate the way drinking makes me feel. I like to feel like I'm in control, and drinking brings too many unknowns." Charley looked up at Amy. "Not that I judge people who drink. Shit, this is all coming out wrong. This is why it's so awkward to tell people."

Amy scooted closer to Charley and put a hand on her knee. "It's not awkward, and it's not weird! My uncles Max and Greg, my mom's friends I told you about—they both stopped drinking when I was in high school. Max felt like it was hurting him more than helping him, and Greg quit in solidarity. It's a decision they made together, and they're happier and healthier for it, I think. Although it's a lot harder to find queer-friendly spaces that aren't bars, which sucks. They still go sometimes but not much."

As Amy spoke, Charley seemed to relax. "Yeah, I still went to gay bars in Austin sometimes when I just wanted to dance or hang out with friends. But I usually only stay for a little while. I don't love seeing people get sloppy as the night goes on."

"I totally get that," Amy said, thinking of all the patrons she'd had to basically drag out of Ruby Red's at last call. "So you've just never really drank?"

"Yeah, pretty much. My oldest brother, Ben, he, uh . . ." Charley paused, seemingly to decide if she was oversharing. Amy smiled encouragingly. "Well, he's an alcoholic. He partied too hard in high school. It seemed like my parents were always having to smooth over whatever bad situations he'd gotten himself into, paying to fix whatever thing he'd broken at a friend's house. I think they figured it was just teenage rebellion. But then it got worse in college. His grades were shit because he was always partying. He even had to retake a couple of classes. Then he was driving home from a frat party one night in junior year and drove straight onto the quad before crashing into some benches." Charley shook her head. "Thank God the worst that happened was that he ruined a few flower beds. But campus police saw the whole thing. He got expelled, and his drinking only got worse. Turned our whole family upside down for a while."

"I can't imagine how hard that must have been." Amy squeezed Charley's knee. Charley's vulnerability had melted away any of Amy's lingering frustrations. Corinne's family really was onto something.

"Yeah, it was a rough few years. But Ben's sober now. I was

sixteen when all of that went down, so I was the one who ended up driving him to and from AA meetings and work and everything since his license was taken away after the quad incident. Seeing all of that, how painful it was for my parents to watch him struggle, how hard it was for Ben to get sober . . . it really makes drinking look a lot less appealing. I drank a couple of times in college just to see what it was like. I found out that I like the person I am when I'm sober and I don't like the person I am when I drink. So that's that."

Amy nodded, taking in Charley's story. "This probably sounds stupid, but from what you've said about your family before, it just sounded like this big happy, loving, supportive family with no problems. I had no idea y'all went through something like that."

"It is a big happy, loving, supportive family," Charley said. "But that doesn't mean it's rainbows and sunshine all the time, you know? We've all had our rough times, Ben's maybe rougher than most, and we stick together through them. That's what family does."

That wasn't what the Fariner family did, based on Amy's and her mother's experience. But it did sound a bit like her friends at Ruby Red's, who had stood firmly by her side during her mom's cancer, when she broke up with Autumn, and when she was fired.

"Anyway, thanks for letting me get all that off of my chest," Charley said. "I'm really sorry, Amy."

"No, thank you for telling me. When I didn't hear from you, I thought you just wanted to end this," Amy said, feeling the lightest she had since before the cookie-decorating party at the bar now that the air had been cleared between them.

"Definitely not. I shouldn't have let my awkwardness stop me from telling you what was going on with me." Charley brushed one of Amy's curls behind her ear. "But hey, I would love to see

Ruby Red's. Just because I don't drink doesn't mean I can't hang out at a bar. I just didn't want you to find out when I only ordered Diet Cokes."

"So you don't drink, and you're dating a bartender. It sounds like the setup for a joke."

Charley held Amy's gaze and placed a warm hand against her neck, running a thumb along her jawline. "If we want this to work, it will, right?"

Amy leaned in and kissed Charley, wrapping an arm around her waist. Their torsos pressed together as the warmth between them ignited into full-blown flames, and they moved apart only to pull pieces of clothing, one after another, from each other's bodies, until they were lying naked on the couch, skin against skin. Amy held herself above Charley with one arm as the movement of their fingers grew more urgent, their pulses rising. For once, Amy wasn't thinking about stretch marks or unfamiliar sex toys or her analysis of Charley's every expression. She followed what her body wanted, and it led her and Charley to the same place at the same time, gasping into each other as they came. Even as Amy collapsed on top of Charley, she was too elated to fret about whether she was crushing Charley's smaller frame.

After catching their breath, they moved to Amy's bedroom, meaning to fall asleep but instead getting swept up in the feel of their naked bodies together between the cool sheets and going for a second round. Amy even felt brave enough to introduce a fingertip vibrator into the mix. While the toys she'd lugged out that first night had intimidated her, the simplicity of this one fit seamlessly into what they were doing, and before long, both of them were seeing stars. As Charley lay prostrate, breathing heavily, Amy slid out of the bed on shaky legs to get them a snack. Wrapped in blankets, they shared an impromptu cheese plate of odds and ends from Amy's refrigerator.

Charley composed a perfect bite of cracker, Monterey Jack, and blueberry jam and paused before lifting it to her mouth. "So are you going to explain the fancy dress?"

Amy eyed the abandoned bridesmaid dress still strewn across the floor. "In short, it's a new job."

"That was fast. What's the new gig?"

Amy furrowed her eyebrows. "Don't laugh. You promise?" Charley nodded. "Professional bridesmaid. I get paid to . . . Stop laughing!"

Charley's failed attempt at controlling a laugh shook her entire body. "Sorry! Professional bridesmaid. Not funny."

"Yes. I get paid to be a bridesmaid, and do whatever the bride needs, and help with bridal showers, and . . ." A giggle escaped Amy's lips. "Okay, it's kind of funny. But I'm good at it!"

"I thought you hated weddings."

"I never said I hate weddings." Amy was briefly confused before remembering that, in an effort to play it cool, she hadn't contradicted Charley's saying weddings were "the worst" the day they'd first met. "Anyway, it's not so different from working at the bakery or the bar. I smile and laugh at people's jokes and make sure they get enough food and drink. And when things go wrong, I run interference."

"Huh. I guess that makes sense. Is this, like, a thing that people do? I've never heard of it."

"I haven't either. To be honest, I'm kind of making it up as I go along. But I've already done two weddings and have six more lined up over the next few months." Even though she was downplaying it a little, Amy felt proud of the work she'd done. She'd started a whole business from scratch, and it actually seemed like it was working. And to Amy's delight, Charley seemed impressed, asking questions about Amy's clients and how her first two weddings had gone as they snacked. Telling Charley about all of the crises she'd averted at Regi's wedding reminded Amy how good it felt to save the day. And though Corinne's wedding hadn't felt like a total success, Charley pointed out that Amy had single-handedly managed to finish the postwedding tasks *and* saved a family heirloom from certain doom.

Charley popped a grape into her mouth. "So that wedding you invited me to last month. That was a bridesmaid job?"

"Yeah, that first one I told you about."

Charley smacked her open palm against her forehead. "You just wanted moral support on your first day on the job. I thought you were inviting me to some big family wedding as your significant other."

"I realized afterwards that inviting you to a wedding on date two was a little premature. Your face looked like I'd just invited you to an appointment with my gynecologist." A chuckle rumbled up from Amy's stomach as she remembered that awkward morning, and it turned into a full-body laughing fit. Charley couldn't help but join in, and they both roared until tears rolled down their cheeks. And by the time each had caught her breath, the gap of misunderstanding between them had grown a bit smaller. Maybe Charley was right, Amy thought. Maybe all it would take was both of them wanting this to work.

16

The combination of getting her bridesmaid business off the ground and reconnecting with Charley gave Amy a new sense of confidence going into the next week. First thing Monday morning, she deposited her payment from Corinne's wedding and hired a tow truck to bring her poor, bedraggled car from the Daily Bread parking lot to a nearby repair shop. The car hadn't been towed away to some mystery lot during the month it had taken Amy to save up the money for repairs, and for that, she was a tiny bit grateful to Donna. While she waited, she texted her mom, who was thrilled by the car development, and rescheduled their regular brunch to the following week. A couple hours later, with a new set of spark plugs installed, the car groaned back to life. Finally, Amy felt like she was getting things together, like she'd mixed all the ingredients into the batter and just needed time to let it bake.

She went over to Joel and Damian's that afternoon before

her shared shift with Joel at Ruby Red's. Damian helped her build her website—nothing fancy but enough to make her feel a bit more legitimate—while Joel pestered her for the latest Charley update.

She spent Tuesday posting new ads on Craigslist that linked to her website and reaching out to a few local blogs about advertising opportunities, as well as responding to emails from brides who'd previously signed contracts. Coordinating her schedule proved an important lesson for Amy. She'd been quick to accept any offer that came her way when she first posted two weeks ago, but there was more demand than she'd anticipated, and between bartending shifts, weddings, and all the other bridal events, things were starting to get sticky. In fact, she'd accidentally booked three back-to-back bridal events for the coming Saturday. It was too late to cancel any of them, but she was fairly sure she could make it work. Given how often she'd pulled double and triple shifts running from the bar to the bakery and back, the hectic schedule felt a bit familiar. Amy had always been bad at saying no, and her precarious financial situation made her hesitant to turn down any paid gig. But as new inquiries rolled in, Amy thought she should probably start turning some offers down in order to better balance her brides. The idea of having more business than she could handle was a delightful treat. For once, Amy felt just as busy with and excited by her career as Charley seemed, something that made Amy feel more on equal footing with her as they texted flirtatiously throughout the week.

When Saturday rolled around, Amy mentally prepared for a bridesmaid marathon. She had a wedding gown shopping appointment in the morning, followed by a wedding shower luncheon and finally a bridal party dance class all the way in Oklahoma City. And before any of that began, she had baking to do. Amy's second bride of the day had paid her to make four dozen cupcakes for the shower, themed to match the wedding venue at ONEOK Field, home of the Tulsa Drillers.

After scrubbing the frosting from her hands, Amy threw on a ruffled teal dress and low wedges carefully selected to fit all of the day's events. She packed the cupcakes into a cooler, which she put in her car along with a duffel bag she'd put together earlier in the week and established as a must-have for all of her bridesmaid events. Loaded with spare clothes, makeup, hair products, tissues, first aid supplies, and more, it had everything she could imagine needing in a wedding emergency. And after the back-to-back caketastrophes at Christina's and Regi's weddings, she'd prepared an emergency cake kit with offset spatulas, piping bags, cake supports, and buttercream ingredients for each event featuring cake.

With her car loaded, Amy headed to her first stop, a bridal salon in the fashionable Utica Square outdoor shopping center. The bride, who wanted Amy at every possible event so she could fully enmesh herself into the bridal party, was planning a *Great Gatsby*–inspired wedding. Her vision included champagne in coupe glasses, feathers, fringe, pearls, and a vague "speakeasy feel." Although Amy hadn't read *The Great Gatsby* since high school, she was pretty sure it was meant to condemn excessive decadence rather than promote it. But as long as the wedding didn't end up with someone dead in a swimming pool, Amy was willing to play along.

Amy didn't really understand her role at the dress fitting but tried to do what all the best bridesmaids on *Say Yes to the Dress* did: watch for what the bride seemed to like and support whatever made her happy. Considering Baz Luhrmann's film adaptation of *The Great Gatsby* was still showing at the dollar theater across town, Amy thought the Roaring Twenties theme would be a breeze for the consultant to nail. But the appointment dragged on, and the bride grew increasingly dejected with each dress. Amy saw an opportunity to make herself worth the money the bride was paying. She could see the bride eyeing her hips and stomach uncomfortably in the thin, boxy, flapper-inspired dresses. How many brides had Amy seen light up on television with the right fit and statement accessories? Sure, the salon experience wasn't exactly like it was presented on reality TV, but it was worth a try. At Amy's gentle suggestion, the bride tried a dress with a mermaid fit to flatter her curves, and the consultant decked her out in pearls and a feathered flapper headband. With the look complete, the bride and her entire wedding party teared up, even Amy. But her joy was interrupted when she realized the appointment had gone fifteen minutes past when she needed to leave for her next bride's shower. As she rushed for the exit, the consultant caught Amy by the elbow and offered her the store owner's business card. "You'd be great at this, you know," the consultant whispered with a wink.

Amy made up a little time in her speedy drive to a sprawling suburban home for the baseball-themed bridal shower but still arrived ten minutes after the start of the event. The driveway was overflowing with guests' cars, leaving Amy having to park halfway down the cul-de-sac and lug the four boxes of cupcakes to the house. The combination of stress and exertion brought a sheen of sweat to her forehead, which was made worse when the mother of the bride chewed her out for arriving late and ruining her plans to welcome guests with a beautiful cupcake display. But the high quality of the cupcakes combined with Amy's efforts to convince the bride's and her mother's very opposite friend groups to socialize won the woman over in the end. She even seemed sad to see Amy go by the time she left for the dance class in Oklahoma City.

As she hit the highway, Amy grinned, pleased with how well she'd pulled off the first two events of the day. She could bake! She got bridal fashion! She was the life of the bridal party! And now she was running right on time for a dance class her college theater experience had prepared her for perfectly. What could go wrong?

As if on cue, the lights on the dashboard went dim, and the creaking sedan stopped accelerating. Amy let out a string of curses as she guided the car to the shoulder just outside the Tulsa city limits. "Come on. I just replaced your spark plugs! What more do you want from me?" she begged as she tried to restart the engine. When it was clear the car wouldn't be revived, she dropped her head onto the steering wheel, her eyes filling with tears.

The first person she thought of calling for help was Charley. It was tempting to have an excuse to see her again, plus she wasn't immune to the romance of being a damsel in distress, rescued by Charley on her shining SUV steed. But knowing Charley was always busy with work, even on Saturdays, and not wanting to look like a loser with a broken car, Amy forced herself to consider other options. The problem was, there weren't any. Her mother was at dinner with Max and Greg in Claremore, forty-five minutes away. Joel and Zee were both working at Ruby Red's, and Damian was out of town for the weekend. Jae was DJing at the local gay dance club. Tala was photographing some Little League game in the suburbs.

When Amy finally gave in, she found out that the stars had seemingly aligned. Charley had just left her place for a big work dinner in Oklahoma City, and Amy was stranded along the way.

"Thank you again," Amy said about fifteen minutes later, climbing into Charley's car along with an armful of bags from her trunk. "I'm so sorry about this."

"I'm impressed by your dedication," Charley said, checking her rearview mirror with a hint of a smile on her lips as she pulled back onto the highway.

"Huh?"

"I'm just saying, I've never had a woman purposefully break her car just to have an excuse to call me. It's flattering. You must *really* like me."

Amy burst out laughing. "That's not even the half of it." It was a relief to smile again after the anxiety she'd felt. "I had to do some serious research to figure out how to get it to break down at this exact spot. Plus, now we have a built-in next date: You drive me back to my car and fix it while I stand nearby, fanning myself."

"I think I recognize that one from a 1950s lesbian pulp novel," Charley said.

"I'm impressed by your dedication too," Amy teased. "Inventing a last-minute work dinner in Oklahoma City just so you could be my hero? Not bad."

"I *wish* this was invented," Charley said, shaking her head. "I'd much rather watch you do your bridesmaid thing than watch all the members of the Oklahoma Energy Resource Board debate public relations strategy over steaks."

"This was pretty serendipitous." Amy reached her hand up and ran a finger down Charley's jawline.

Charley shivered at her touch. "See? The universe is on our side. Like I said, all we have to do is want this to work."

Amy texted her client that she was running about fifteen minutes behind schedule. Although it was looking more like thirty if Charley insisted on driving the speed limit. Which it appeared she did. Amy anxiously drummed her fingers on her knee as cars rushed past them in the left lane.

Charley glanced at Amy as she checked her watch. "You

know what takes longer than driving the speed limit? Getting pulled over for speeding. Or, God forbid, an accident."

Amy sighed. "Sorry. I got chewed out for being late to something earlier today, and getting yelled at again doesn't sound terribly fun."

"So what exactly is this thing in Oklahoma City you're rushing to?" Charley asked.

"The bride, Wendy, is an aspiring YouTube star, and she wants the bridal party to do a flash-mob-style performance during the reception in the hopes of going viral, so she scheduled a dance class for all of us to learn the choreography. The wedding isn't until late January, but she wants us to have plenty of time to practice."

Charley arched an eyebrow. "Are you a good dancer?"

"Good enough." Amy straightened the hem of her dress across her knees. "I'm no Baryshnikov, but I can triple-time step with the best of them."

"I have no idea what any of that means, but I assume you can keep up with a flash mob."

"I hope so." Amy stared out the window, imagining a worst-case scenario where she ran into dance class late, couldn't keep up with the choreography, and was fired in front of everyone. At least she would only be shamed in front of strangers.

Amy's anxious daydreaming was interrupted by a ringing projected through the car's speakers. "Sorry, I have to take this," Charley said before pressing a button on the steering wheel. "Hey, Rick."

"Hey, Charley," replied a deep voice. Amy's eyes widened. She knew Bluetooth technology existed in cars, but her old Toyota Corolla had been chugging along since before anyone had even heard of it.

"I hope you're calling with an update on the Ponca City site.

I was up all night working on their environmental management program, and I think I'm finally getting somewhere," Charley said.

As the conversation went on, Amy was struck by the sense of purpose and authority in Charley's voice. She had known Charley cared about her work, but hearing her in action was different. Although she hardly understood the acronyms and technical terms Charley tossed around on the call, Amy could tell how much this work meant to her—and that she was good at it. Sometimes Amy felt like Charley was using her job as an excuse, but maybe she really was just lost in her work. And if Amy was being honest, hearing Charley's passion for her work was pretty sexy. She was strategic, determined, and thoughtful, and absolutely wouldn't allow her colleague to talk over her. Not to mention how amazing Charley looked in the navy suit she was wearing for her work dinner.

"All right, I'll follow up with you after dinner with Jim to let you know what kind of deal we work out. Thanks, Rick." Charley ended the call by again pressing a button on her steering wheel. "Sorry about that, Amy. Some time-sensitive issues have come up, and . . . Why are you looking at me like that?"

Amy blushed as she looked back toward the road. "Like what? Anyway, no big. I'm the interloper here. Do whatever you need to do."

Charley took her up on the offer and made one more call. Meanwhile, Amy scrolled through her phone, trying not to get hot and bothered every time Charley said "drilling," "fracking," or "lubricant." But the sexiest part, Amy decided, was when she heard Charley argue heatedly against expanding operations into Native American reservations.

"So your job actually *isn't* evil," Amy said after Charley ended the call.

Charley laughed. "It's not the first thing people assume when I tell them I work in the oil industry, but there's a lot of room for meaningful change."

"That's really cool that you have so much passion for what you do. I wish I felt like that."

"Come on. I've tasted your food. I know there's passion in it."

Amy looked out the passenger window as signs for Oklahoma City exits began to appear. "Yeah, but cake doesn't change the world."

"Sure it does! Those muffins you gave me that first time I saw you at Daily Bread sure changed my world." Charley turned to check her blind spot before changing lanes. "Why did you quit anyway?"

Amy stiffened. It felt like she and Charley were so much closer after their heart-to-heart the previous weekend. And by her own admission, Charley knew what it was like not to bring something up at the first opportunity and then feel like you didn't know when or how to course correct. Amy tried to summon the words to explain what had happened, but a familiar feeling of shame crept over her. She couldn't bear to confess that she'd knowingly taken a job from homophobes with a plan to stay closeted. Her stomach roiled at the thought of admitting such a stupid choice to Charley, who took huge risks to fight for what she believed in at work. No, Amy definitely couldn't have this conversation right before meeting with a client. It would have to wait for later. "I just, uh, wasn't feeling it."

"So you've got more passion for this bridesmaid thing than you do for cooking?" Charley asked, sounding more curious than judgmental, but Amy flinched.

"I guess so. Hey, I think that's my exit up there."

Charley pulled up next to the dance studio door only twelve

minutes late, much to Amy's surprise. She leaned across the console and kissed Charley, lingering longer than she'd planned, reveling in the feeling of their lips pressed together. For once, her gratefulness outweighed her instinct to check first for passersby. Finally, she pulled back. "Thanks for the ride. I owe you one. Let me know when you're done with dinner?"

"Sure thing," Charley said, her voice hoarse and her cheeks flushed. She cleared her throat. "See you later."

Luckily, Amy had no trouble catching up on the choreography she'd missed. Wendy and her husband-to-be were apparently experienced flash mobbers. But unfortunately, their friends and family weren't all so gifted. During Amy's initial communication with the bride, they'd agreed to tell wedding guests that they were friends from dance class, so Amy was happy to make up for her tardiness by not only learning the choreography quickly but also helping a handful of the wedding party in the back row master the box step.

After the dance rehearsal, the bridal party walked to a nearby ice cream shop to cool down. Amy spent some time getting to know the bride, the groom, and their friends and discovered that they were actually a pretty enjoyable group. The way they poked fun at one another reminded Amy of her own friends, and although Wendy's friends seemed 100 percent straighter, Amy really did feel like she could fit in with them. So far, the hardest part of bridesmaiding had been managing the personalities of the rest of the bridal parties and guests. But it turned out that meeting people on the dance floor had a way of breaking down barriers, helping everyone bond over missed steps and tricky rhythms.

An hour later, Amy and Charley were on the way back to Tulsa. Now that both of their work commitments were successfully completed, they were considerably more relaxed than they'd been on their journey to Oklahoma City. Amy slipped off her shoes and crossed her legs in the passenger seat. "So I was thinking about earlier."

"About that goodbye kiss you gave me when I dropped you off? I've been ready to continue that kiss this whole evening, but we should probably wait until I'm not driving."

Amy's lips tingled at the thought. She reached out to run her fingers through Charley's short hair. "I can hardly wait to get home then. But no, I meant about me being passionate about bridesmaiding. I was thinking about it while I was helping everyone with the choreography and getting to know the bride and groom. I've been to three events with three different brides today, and I'm exhausted and can't wait to take off these shoes, but yeah, I love it." It wasn't until she heard herself say it out loud that Amy realized how much she meant it. Almost every wedding event she'd attended had been stressful, but they'd also required Amy to think on her feet, improvise, jump into the role of whoever the bride needed her to be. Witnessing wedding magic, saving the day, and getting free meals at the receptions? That spoke directly to Amy's heart.

"I'm glad." Charley placed a hand on Amy's knee. "I'm glad you found something that makes you happy."

"It really does! I know loving weddings is, I don't know, sappy and girly and whatever. But I love love. And being able to make the most important day of someone's life easier is really satisfying."

"Just because something is 'sappy and girly' doesn't mean it's bad," Charley said.

"Sure, of course," Amy added quickly. "That's not what I meant."

"I know I'm a little"—Charley gestured broadly at her suit and short hair—"masc of center. And you're . . ." Her eyes shifted toward Amy, with her ruffled teal dress and long curls.

"Femme of center, sure," Amy said.

Charley nodded once, her eyes back on the road. "Anyway, society spends enough time shitting on whatever is perceived as 'women's interests' and trying to figure out which lesbian 'wears the pants' in a relationship. We've got to take every opportunity in our queer lives to say fuck that patriarchal bullshit. Like what you like even if it's sappy and girly. There should be no shame around loving weddings! What's not to like? With the dancing, and the food, and the . . . um . . . ceremony . . ." She trailed off.

Amy stared at Charley for a moment. "You hate weddings, don't you?"

"What? No! I mean, well, 'hate' is a strong word."

"Oh my God, you completely hate weddings."

"They're just so self-congratulatory!" Charley said. "And unnecessarily expensive, and boring, and straight. And expensive. And did I mention straight?" Her voice softened. "But it's not because it's a girly thing."

"Maybe you just haven't been to any good weddings." Amy shifted in her seat. "You should have seen the first wedding where I was a bridesmaid, with Regi and Jared. It was so beautiful, and everyone was so happy. Anything but stuffy and boring. And soon same-sex marriage will be legal."

"First off, that's pretty optimistic. And second, just because gay people can get married doesn't make the whole wedding industry less heteronormative."

"Sure it does! Weddings are supposed to be about the couple getting married. It doesn't have to be all heteronormative." That was one of Amy's favorite things about weddings, how different they looked depending on the couple tying the knot.

Charley smirked. "We'll have to agree to disagree on this one. But just because I don't love weddings doesn't mean you shouldn't love weddings. And you *definitely* shouldn't feel weird about loving weddings because the patriarchy tells you to."

Although Amy was disappointed by Charley's antiwedding stance, her last comment struck a chord in Amy's chest. She tried the idea on for size: that it didn't matter what anyone else thought about weddings or Amy's new business as long as it made her and the brides happy. After all, Amy didn't love the oil and gas industry, but that didn't make her respect Charley any less. After years spent trying to do whatever other people wanted her to do, be whoever other people wanted her to be, didn't Amy deserve a job that made her happy and to forget about what people thought? But then again, wasn't the whole business of bridesmaiding just being whoever the brides wanted her to be?

Realizing she'd been lost in thought for too long, Amy broke the silence. "How about some music?" She turned a dial on Charley's audio system and, as a Kesha song sounded through the speakers, slowly felt the stress of the day fade away. Before long, the two were belting along together as they rode down the dark highway. And by the time they reached Amy's apartment, lips finally meeting again, heat rising, their clothes scattering across the floor, work was the last thing on her mind.

17

Amy's first bachelorette party ever—in her life, not just for her new business—was set for Thursday. The event was for one of the first brides who'd responded to Amy's Craigslist post, a DIY enthusiast named Olivia whose winter wonderland–themed wedding would take place on Saturday. It had been almost a month since she'd first made her Craigslist post, and Amy was proud of how quickly she'd adjusted to so many different situations. But she felt her most anxious yet at the prospect of a night that, to her understanding, was designed for drinking, sexual exploits, and general messiness. Amy's beloved rom-coms had prepared her so well for many of her bridesmaid tasks: *27 Dresses* for the perfect facial expressions during the ceremony, *My Big Fat Greek Wedding* for tricky family dynamics, and *The Wedding Planner* for keeping a cool head under fire, to name a few. But movie representations of a bride's final hurrah were more anxiety inducing than useful. So as she prepared for her first night of prenuptial mayhem, she called in the best reinforcements she could think of: Damian and Joel.

Damian turned up Lady Gaga on Amy's speakers and yelled, "All right, show us what you've got!"

Amy emerged from her room in dark-wash skinny jeans, a white V-necked shirt, a black blazer, and boots. "Too gay. Way too gay. Try again," Joel said, waving away her outfit.

She'd warned Joel and Damian that she wanted to blend in with the other bridesmaids instead of having her outfit come out for her. Unfortunately, "straight-girl club chic" was a category not well represented in her wardrobe. "Is it the boots?" Amy said nervously while examining the outfit in a full-length mirror.

"It's everything," Damian said. "You can't wear a blazer to a bachelorette party. This isn't a job interview! Wear a dress."

"But it's freezing outside!" Amy whined. "Can I at least wear leggings under it?"

"*No!*" Joel and Damian said immediately.

Amy rolled her eyes and returned to her closet, which had a stark divide between her queerer, more casual Ruby Red's outfits on the left and the chaste, cheerful clothes she'd once worn to Daily Bread on the right. Amy dug through the right side until she found a flowy fuchsia off-the-shoulder dress with a bow at the waist. Definitely more feminine. She pulled off her first outfit and replaced it with the dress. Although it was a thin material, Amy was pleased that it hit below the knee. Maybe she could wear warm shorts underneath.

She stepped into the living room and twirled.

"Definitely not," Damian said.

Amy's shoulders dropped dejectedly. "But it's shiny and girly! You can't tell me this one's too gay."

Damian shook his head. "It's girly, not sexy. Too *Little Mary Sunshine.*"

Joel placed his wineglass on the coffee table and stood from the couch. "Step aside, babe. You need my help more than I thought." He led Amy back to her room, where he began riffling through her closet. "Do you not have anything with sequins or glitter?"

"I have those rainbow-sequined overalls from Pride last year?"

"I mean, I'd love for you to wear those, but for what you're trying to do, absolutely not. Okay, let me think." Joel pulled a couple of black dresses from the back and examined them. "Which of these shows more cleavage?"

"The one on the left with the flared skirt."

Joel assessed the two options. "But the other is more fitted. Interesting. Well, let's go with boobs." He pushed the flared dress toward Amy. "Try this one."

She sighed and shoved him out of the room. This one required a bra change. Once she had wrestled herself into the dress and zipped it, she emerged into the living room.

"Better," Damian said, smoothing his short beard. "I think we can make this one work." Joel smiled smugly and gave Amy an I-told-you-so look.

Amy looked down. "I'll freeze if I wear this out tonight!"

"Amy, you need to channel your inner party girl. They never get cold. And if you show up to this bachelorette party without at least half of your skin showing, you'll stick out like a sore thumb." Joel circled Amy, dancing to the beat. "Now, what jewelry and shoes are you wearing?"

Knowing her everyday accessories wouldn't work, Amy dug through a box of old Halloween costumes for sparkly jewelry from a *Breakfast at Tiffany's* getup and red heels from the year she'd dressed as Cruella de Vil. When she stomped out of her bedroom with the final look completed, Joel squealed in delight, and Damian gave a bright smile of approval.

"You *have* to wear this next time you see Charley. She won't be able to keep her hands off of you. Maybe dressed like this, you can finally DTR," Joel said as he shimmied around the living room.

Damian looked from Joel to Amy. "DTR?"

"Define the relationship," Amy and Joel said in unison.

"Right, of course." Damian rolled his eyes. "Because everyone knows that."

"We must have said it at least a hundred times back when Joel was trying to figure out how to ask you to be exclusive." Amy wiggled her eyebrows.

"And little did Joel know that I was all in from our first date." Damian blew a kiss in Joel's direction.

Joel grabbed Damian's hands and pulled him up to join in his dancing. "Maybe Charley feels the same way about Amy. Just because Amy is too nervous to take things to the next level doesn't mean Charley's not into it. You know?"

"I'm not too nervous!" Amy said defensively. "I just, like, want to make sure we're on the same page. Sometimes work gets busy, and she just disappears off the face of the earth for a while, which doesn't really seem like the behavior of someone who wants to DTR."

"So perhaps you could say you're *nervous* she'll say no," Joel said.

Damian did a dramatic twirl as the key changed. "It's okay to be nervous, Amy. Maybe Charley's just taking things slow. Maybe she's trying to figure you out too."

"Hmm, I wish there was an easy way to find out what Charley's intentions for the relationship are. Like, I don't know, maybe *asking* her," Joel said.

"All right, that's enough analyzing my relationship, or flirtation, or fling, or whatever it is," Amy grumbled as she stuffed her clutch with Band-Aids and loose change, unsure what she might need in a bachelorette party emergency.

Damian looked at his watch. "We have to get to Ruby Red's for open mic night. We'll drop you off on the way, Amy. Where's this shindig?"

Amy directed Damian to the maid of honor's place several miles south of Cherry Street. The party was planned to start at the house and later move to a club. Amy's experience at straight clubs was severely limited, but she wasn't sure whether she'd prefer to trade the unknown for a more familiar queer bar in this circumstance. Rampage, the gay dance club downtown, was one of the most happening spots for bachelorette parties in Tulsa, but Ruby Red's was no stranger to groups of drunken bridesmaids behaving badly either. Although Amy understood the urge to let loose somewhere without straight men hitting on you, having groups of bridesmaids at Ruby Red's often made it feel like she and the other queer patrons were animals at the zoo.

Upon arrival, Amy helped Olivia and her sister, Rebecca, maid of honor and host of the party, set up the bar and lay out snacks. They had just enough time before the party started to remind Amy of the other bridesmaids' names and relationships to the bride, as well as review her backstory as a distant cousin from Florida, a great excuse for having missed the prior bridesmaid and wedding events. Amy had met Olivia and Rebecca twice already to help craft some of the wedding décor and party favors. But she hadn't yet met the other seven bridesmaids, who had apparently staged a bit of a coup after one too many DIY nights. This would be the biggest wedding party Amy had participated in yet. Despite her nerves, Amy knew it was important to Olivia that she build rapport with the other bridesmaids before Saturday.

Once Olivia's bridesmaids and a few additional friends

arrived, Amy put her bartender skills to work. It was the perfect opportunity to make herself useful while also breaking the ice with the other women. Although Amy had worried her outfit was too campy, she fit right in. If anything, it was severely lacking in the glitter, sparkle, and sequin department, and what she'd thought to be a bold smoky eye withered in comparison to the thick layers of makeup on the other party attendees.

When everyone had a drink in hand, Rebecca orchestrated a drinking game based on trivia about the bride. Amy surprised herself with how much she'd learned from their crafting sessions together; with the help of some lucky guesses, she managed to stay out of last place. But her penalty drinks for wrong answers led her to empty three glasses in a short period of time. At least the drinks helped with her nerves about taking their bachelorette party out on the town.

And the most important thing was that Olivia seemed to be having a great time. After a couple of cocktails, she was more relaxed than Amy had ever seen her. All of the prewedding projects were completed, she was surrounded by friends, and everyone was in a lighthearted mood.

Rebecca lowered the music and clinked a knife against the side of her glass. "Gather around, everyone! I have a few announcements!" The bridesmaids and friends tottered into the living room in their heels, everyone a little less steady than when they'd first arrived. "In about an hour, we're going to call taxis to take us to Gray Wolf." Drunken cheers went up from the group. Amy had never been to the club mentioned, but she had heard of it, primarily from jokes made about its clientele, a mix of bougie young professionals and postcollege frat boys looking to get wasted for cheap. Mostly, she was just grateful it wasn't a gay bar. "And when we get there, we're going to have a special bachelorette scavenger hunt!"

The assorted women chattered excitedly while Rebecca passed around scavenger hunt lists printed on cardstock. Amy skimmed the list:

- Get someone to buy you a drink.
- Get a stranger's number.
- Shotgun a beer.
- Take a picture with a bouncer.
- Kiss a stranger.

Amy stopped reading before she got to the end of the list. She'd seen enough bridesmaids embarrass themselves at Rampage and Ruby Red's to know she didn't want any part of this. She could be a good sport in other ways, but there was no way she would participate in a bachelorette scavenger hunt.

"Honeys, I'm home!" Joel announced as he burst through Amy's apartment door several hours later, a large pizza box and a grocery bag in hand. After placing the pizza on the coffee table, he shrugged off his coat and assessed the room. Amy was rubbing small circles on her temples, slumped into the couch, while Damian adjusted an ice pack on her ankle. "Is she going to make it, Doctor? Please tell me I at least have time to say my goodbyes."

Damian rolled his eyes. "She's going to live. Just a twisted ankle."

"I told you the heels were a bad idea," Amy said.

"You'll be fine in a day or two," Damian said. "The hangover will probably be worse than the sprain."

Joel unpacked the grocery bag that was hanging on his arm. "Well, I brought medicine for that." He waved two enormous bottles of Gatorade at Amy. "Glacier Cherry or Riptide Rush?"

"Cherry." Amy held out a hand, and Joel obliged. "And please tell me the pizza has pineapple."

Damian frowned. "Please tell me the pizza doesn't have pineapple."

Joel lifted the lid of the pizza box. "Half-pineapple, half-pepperoni, because I love you both."

Amy and Damian cheered. Once they each had a slice in hand, Joel gently lifted Amy's ankle and squeezed onto the couch, placing her foot in his lap and repositioning the ice pack. "Okay, tell me what happened."

"Well, my two best friends convinced me to wear this ridiculous outfit with shoes I couldn't walk in," Amy said.

Damian, who'd moved to the floor for better access to the pizza, placed his hands on his hips and gave Amy a strict look. "Excuse you. Tell him what really happened."

"Do I have to?" she asked.

Damian nodded firmly, a smile beginning to crack across his face.

"Fine. I twisted my ankle dancing on the bar," Amy said in a rush.

"You *what*?" Joel yelled, making Amy cringe.

"Shh, please, no yelling," she said. "I have a headache coming on. Can you get me a couple ibuprofen from the shelf above the bathroom sink?"

Damian walked to the bathroom while Joel cornered Amy. "How exactly did this go down?"

"Well, the dancing on the bar definitely wasn't my idea. There was this ridiculous bachelorette scavenger hunt, and I wasn't going to participate—"

"But then you got tipsy and competitive," Joel interrupted.

Amy scoffed. "I do not get tipsy and competitive."

"Except that time you tried to get everyone to race to Whataburger and sprinted while we all walked, and you had to sit there alone for, like, fifteen minutes," Joel reminded her.

"And that time you started a beer bottle–stacking competition, and we had to spend an hour cleaning up broken glass," Damian said, returning from the bathroom with ibuprofen in hand.

"And then there was that time you tried to make karaoke a competition and gave that drag queen a lap dance to try to win," Joel added.

Amy flapped her hands at her two friends. "Okay, okay. I maybe get competitive sometimes. But hey, it's my job to participate in this stuff, right? So it was really more of a professional obligation."

Joel giggled. "Yes, your professional duty to dance on the bar."

"With the bride! I danced with the bride, my *client* . . . on the bar." Amy joined her friends in a fit of laughter. "Fine, hand me another slice, and I'll tell you everything."

Amy regaled her eager audience with tales of flirting for free drinks, kissing strangers, and falling from the bar into the arms of an angry bouncer. Before long, all three were crying from laughter.

"And then I called Damian, my hero, who picked me up and brought me here and wrapped my ankle. Thanks again, Damian," Amy said.

"That's when I called you to pick up the goods on the way over from Ruby Red's," Damian finished, batting his eyes at Joel.

"So is this where you saw your career taking you?" Joel asked, resting his chin on his fist and putting on the serious voice of an NPR interviewer. "A professional bachelorette partyer?"

"Not exactly. I think my bachelorette-party skills could use some work. But the wedding part is great. And the crafting part! I made, like, a hundred paper snowflakes and a bunch of felt evergreen trees earlier this week for the wedding on Saturday. Apparently all the other bridesmaids almost quit after all the DIY stuff, but it was a total stress reliever for me. And when I told the bride I could sew the faux fur muffs she wants for the bridesmaids, she was so happy she almost cried." Amy felt a rush thinking about how much fun she'd had. "And did I tell you I have a couple of brides who hired me to bake for their weddings and bridal showers?"

"Dang, you're totally killing this business. An entrepreneurial legend. Oh, you can count all of those hours watching Julia Roberts and Katherine Heigl movies as professional development!" Damian said. "Can you expense Netflix?"

"But isn't it kind of shitty?" Joel asked in an uncharacteristically somber tone. "Watching all of these straight weddings when most of Oklahoma is fighting to keep gay weddings illegal? I mean, probably some of the brides you're working for would vote against marriage equality given the chance."

Amy adjusted the ice pack on her ankle as she considered the question. "Honestly, I've just been so grateful for the money that I haven't spent much time thinking about the politics of it. But yeah, it sucks. Especially when I think about how unfair it is that I can celebrate the weddings of these total strangers as part of their bridal party, but I couldn't do the same for you two, or Zee and Arnelle, or Max and Greg." Amy wasn't sure if it was the conversation or the pain in her ankle or the lingering effects of alcohol and embarrassment from earlier in the evening, but she felt her eyes filling with tears. She quickly tried to wipe them away. "Sorry, it's stupid that I'm crying about this."

Joel leaned over with a hug. "Babe! I'm sorry I brought it up. Don't apologize for crying. It's legitimately super shitty."

"Yeah, let it out, Amy," Damian said, wrapping his arms around her from the other side. "You don't have to hold it in around us like you do with your clients."

"Thanks," Amy sniffled, tears falling in earnest as she relaxed into the warmth of the best friend hug sandwich. "Sometimes I feel like this job is a perfect fit for me. But other times, doing all of this bridesmaiding just makes me feel complicit, you know? Like, I was so nervous we would end up at a gay bar tonight and I would be super uncomfortable trying to figure out if I should be a perky, fun bridesmaid there to party or if that would be a betrayal of the queer community. But on the other hand, do I have to reject everything I love about weddings just because Oklahoma sucks?" She shook her head. "I'm still trying to figure out how to love what I'm doing and hate how prejudiced and excluding the laws around it are at the same time."

Joel rubbed a hand along Amy's shoulder. "That's a lot of baggage for one lesbian bridesmaid to carry. But hey, eventually, Oklahoma will be dragged into the future, and we'll all need someone who knows their way around the wedding industry, right?"

Amy's face lit up with a teary smile. "Yes! Being the wedding whisperer for a bunch of gays? That would be like a dream come true."

"Oh my God, yes! I am so ready for you to take the queer wedding scene by storm," Damian said.

Joel quickly took up the idea. "Hire me! I am super into this new life plan."

"Of course! The three of us will be rich!" Amy said, trying to smile but not quite pulling it off. It could be years, decades, before anything changed. And even if same-sex marriage became legal, that wouldn't change the minds of the people who'd pushed against it. Still, it was fun to dream. And in the warmth of her friends' arms, she allowed herself, just for a moment, to imagine a day when they'd be standing behind her while she gazed at Charley smiling her crooked grin as she said *I do.*

18

Thankfully, Amy felt fully recovered from her bachelorette party injury by Olivia's rehearsal dinner the next evening. Amy was worried that Olivia and the bridesmaids would judge her for acting like a fool at the bachelorette party, but she quickly realized that most of them had been having too much fun themselves to think about her, and she wasn't the only person who'd crossed something off the scavenger list that hadn't been there to begin with. Relieved, she joined in as they reminisced about the wild night.

Olivia got her winter wonderland wedding wish, as Saturday dawned with a powdery dusting of snow on the ground. Amy braved the cold long enough to make a tiny snowman and sent a picture to Charley. They'd been looking forward to experiencing Tulsa's first snow of the winter together, especially since Charley had never lived anywhere it snowed much before, but an industry summit in Orlando had taken her out of town. Charley texted back a photo of her own tiny "snowman" made of oranges, toothpicks, and googly eyes, along with her wishes that they could snuggle in front of her rental home's fireplace. Amy's heart skipped a beat imagining the ways they could pass a quiet snowy Saturday if Charley were home.

Luckily, Amy had Olivia's long wedding day ahead of her to keep her busy. She bundled up and drove cautiously along the icy streets to the event space, an Instagram-worthy barn half an hour outside of downtown. She expected to find Olivia thrilled by Mother Nature's contribution to her theme but instead found the bride pacing, gesturing frantically while talking on the phone.

"I can't tell them to drive! It's six hours in snow and ice. They'll never make it!" She waved distractedly to Amy and continued her conversation. "You don't handle officiants at all? Then why are you a wedding coordinator?"

Unsure how to insert herself in whatever was going on with Olivia but anxious to do something to help, Amy looked for another way to make herself useful. She noticed the decorations they'd crafted that week were lying just inside the door of the barn and took the initiative to begin unpacking. Several other bridesmaids showed up shortly after and joined Amy in filling the barn with paper snowflakes, tissue paper poinsettias, silver-painted pine cones, and felt evergreen trees.

Not long after, Olivia jogged over. "Amy, thank God you're here. I'm freaking out and my wedding coordinator is useless. My uncle is supposed to officiate, but he and my aunt are flying in from St. Louis this morning, and their flight is delayed because of the snow, and I don't know if they're going to make it at all. My coordinator says she won't help with finding an officiant, because I only got the day-of-wedding package instead of the full planning package. How am I supposed to figure this out on my own at the last minute when I'm supposed to be getting ready? Oh God, this is a disaster."

Amy felt the increasingly familiar rush of bridesmaid adrenaline kick in. She hated to see a bride so stressed on her wedding day, but Amy loved nothing more than having a problem to solve while on duty. And she also felt a little responsible since she now realized Olivia might have hired her to pick up her wedding coordinator's slack. "You're not going to figure this out alone, because I'm right here with you. Let's take a breath," Amy said in a calm, measured tone. She pulled a chair from a nearby table and gently guided Olivia into it. "You're still going to get married today. Everything is going to be fine. Breathe in and out with me." Once Olivia had regulated her breathing, Amy continued. "So your uncle's flight is delayed, yes? How delayed?"

"By three hours, which means he won't make it until after the ceremony is over." Amy checked her watch. Olivia was right; the wedding was scheduled to start at noon, and it was already after 10:00 A.M. Olivia's face teetered on the edge of panic, her eyes wide and lip trembling.

Think, Amy told herself. What did she do at the bakery or bar when facing a customer on the edge of a meltdown? The answer was simple—solve the problem as quickly as possible and get them out the door—but in this case, not helpful at all. "Okay, so it sounds like we need a backup officiant," she said, thinking on her feet. "That will take some pressure off of your uncle and aunt so they can just focus on getting here safely."

Olivia's eyes filled with tears. "But we already have the vows and the ceremony all scripted and planned. And it's all about family and how he's known me since I was born! How can we find someone to replace him? And on such short notice?"

Amy pulled a tissue from her purse and handed it to Olivia. "How about we save the family stuff he wrote for toasts during the reception? Nothing a few edits can't fix. Do you have a copy of the ceremony script and vows?"

"I . . . I think so. In my car."

"Good, that's good. Have one of the other bridesmaids go grab those for you. I'm going to make some phone calls and see if we can find someone to officiate. Do you prefer a religious person? A preacher or a pastor?"

"I don't care," Olivia said with a sniff. "Anyone who can get here."

"Great," Amy said. "I'm sure we can find someone. Now, why don't you take a few more breaths and then take a look at how the decorations are shaping up. You focus on that, and I'll figure something out."

Olivia nodded. Amy smiled reassuringly and then stepped outside into the cold, snowy air, instantly losing her cool. "Shit. Shit. Shit. Okay, an officiant. Okay." She pressed her eyes closed and thought back to the recent weddings she'd attended. Regi and Jared had used a family friend who'd flown in from out of town. There was no way the Southern Baptist minister from Christina's ceremony would conduct a wedding outside of his own church. Amy quickly googled the First Presbyterian Church where Corinne had gotten married and called the main line, but no one picked up, and Amy was pretty sure Corinne was still on her honeymoon. Amy made a mental note to get ordained in case of future officiant emergencies, but it was too late for the wedding at hand. She could look up nearby churches and call until she found someone. Even in her desperation, she had to admit that seemed dicey, especially on a Saturday. After racking her brain for another minute and coming up with no new ideas, she did what she always did in a pinch. She called her mom.

Teresa picked up after only one ring. "Hey, honey. You building snowmen? Want to come over for hot cocoa?" Amy heard the sound of canned laughter emanating from a sitcom in the background.

"No, actually I'm bridesmaiding today," Amy said in a rush. "This is weird, but do you happen to know anyone who's ordained and might be available to officiate a wedding on short notice?"

"Like, today short notice?" Teresa asked, suddenly alert. Much like Amy, she loved a challenge.

"In-two-hours short notice."

Without skipping a beat, Teresa said, "Do you remember Dr. Douglas, from the TU theater department?"

"Yes, of course." A rosy-cheeked, Santa Claus–type gentleman with a white beard and deep laugh whom Amy remembered fondly from her college days, Dr. Douglas had been known to do voiceover work in the Tulsa area. His booming baritone was frequently heard on local radio stations advertising law offices or department store sales.

"I think I remember him saying that he officiated his nephew's wedding recently."

Amy pumped her fist. "You're a genius, Mom. Is there any way you can track down his number in the TU database? Would you feel comfortable calling and asking him if he'd be free to officiate a wedding today at noon?"

"Sure, I can do that. He owes me a favor anyway. I'll let you know what he says."

Amy thanked her profusely, hung up, and did a quick happy dance, which ended when she slipped and narrowly avoided falling on the ice underfoot. As Amy reentered the barn, Olivia whipped her head around and gave Amy a desperate, questioning look. Amy put on her most reassuring smile, strode over to Olivia, and whispered, "No promises yet, but I've got a good lead. So just relax and enjoy your day, okay? No matter what, at the end of the day, you'll be married." *Hopefully,* Amy added to herself.

The barn came together quickly as the rest of the bridal party arrived to help. The irritated-looking wedding coordinator showed up an hour before the ceremony and informed the room at large that decorating wasn't part of her contract. By then, though, the barn was ready, and Amy and the other bridesmaids escaped to the farmhouse next door to prepare for the ceremony. Amy felt her phone buzz with a text from her mother only a few minutes later.

Dr. Douglas can do it. Text him location and details. 918-555-3217

Thank you thank you thank you!!

After she'd texted Dr. Douglas the address and he'd written back to say he was on his way, Amy pulled Olivia aside to share the good news. Not only was she relieved; she was also thrilled to learn a Tulsa radio personality would be the voice of her big day. With that problem solved, Amy and Olivia rejoined the rest of the bridal party to style their hair and makeup. The large number of bridesmaids crammed into a small space made for chaos: hairspray clouding the air, dresses hanging from curtain rods, makeup covering every available surface, and a cacophony of voices vying for the bride's attention.

After a while, Olivia's mother joined the group, quietly perching in the corner of the room and watching the activity around her nervously. Amy didn't know the full details, but she'd gathered from the way Olivia and Rebecca talked about their mother during crafting sessions that she tended to be more of a hassle than a help. This impression quickly proved true when Olivia asked her mother to pin up the back of her hair and the woman burst into tears. Amy stepped in to help as Olivia's mother backed away, accidentally breaking a mirror in the process and then going on a tangent about bad luck. Some people just weren't cut out for the intensity of a wedding day. Olivia was handling her nerves relatively well, considering that was her model for how to handle stress.

Once Amy had donned her floor-length frosty-blue gown and matching cape with fur trim, she heard a knock at the door and answered it to find Dr. Douglas. He greeted her with a friendly laugh and firm handshake. "Amy! Good to see you outside of the classroom. I hear there are a couple of folks around in need of a minister. Or in this case, the next best thing—someone who once played one on TV."

"You're a lifesaver, Dr. Douglas!" Amy led him to an empty hallway past the bridal suite to talk through the plans for the ceremony and provide him the script she'd doctored with a marker to remove references specific to the relationship between Olivia and her uncle. After showing him to the barn and making sure he was ready to go, she paused to appreciate how well he fit the wedding's winter wonderland theme. With his cheeks rosy from the cold December air and his reading glasses perched on his nose so he could inspect the script, he really did look like Santa Claus. All he needed was to trade his black tuxedo for a red-and-white suit.

Amy didn't have long to bask in her success, as the wedding coordinator soon pulled her back to the farmhouse, where the rest of the bridal party was beginning to line up for their big entrance. Amy watched from a window as the groom and his groomsmen entered the barn. The bridesmaids around her tittered nervously, fixing flyaway hairs and adjusting their faux fur muffs.

Olivia's mother entered the farmhouse, letting in a blast of cold air. Olivia looked surprised. "Mom, aren't you supposed to be in the audience?"

Her mother's eyes were watery, her lips pulled tightly together. "I can't believe my baby is getting married. This is it. The most important moment of your whole life. Everything changes after this. Nothing will ever be the same. I hope you're ready." She sniffled, then burst into a fresh round of tears.

A strange look crossed Olivia's face, one that at first looked like terror but quickly shifted to what Amy recognized as nausea. "Not on the dress!" Amy yelled, grabbing a nearby decorative bowl and holding it next to Olivia's face just as she heaved. Amy balanced the bowl with one hand and pushed Olivia's mother back with the other. "Can you give her some space, please? Ma'am," Amy added, trying to counter her irritation with a reminder to herself that she didn't know much about the family's dynamic. "Maybe you should go find your seat inside."

Rebecca appeared and pulled her mother away by the elbow. "Mom, what the hell are you doing here? Go back to your seat and leave Olivia alone!"

Rebecca pushed a tissue into her mother's hands as they exited the farmhouse, leaving Amy alone with the puking bride. The other bridesmaids looked on nervously from the end of the hallway as Amy escorted Olivia into the restroom.

After Olivia emptied the contents of her stomach into a toilet, she collapsed onto a bench by the mirrors. "She's right. I'm not ready."

Amy blotted at Olivia's makeup with a moistened towel, praying that one of the bride's actual friends would join them. "That's not true. You've spent hours preparing for today. I've seen it."

"Why did I think I could plan a wedding? Everything is falling apart. The decorations are a mess. I'm a mess."

"You're not a mess. You're a bride. You look beautiful, and so does the barn. It may feel a little chaotic, but that's just how weddings go," Amy said, drawing on all the wisdom she'd gained from . . . had it really been only two weddings so far?

"What if this is a sign?" Olivia asked, her voice rising with panic. "What if my mom's right? What if everything changes and nothing is ever the same again and this is a mistake?"

Fitting, Amy thought. *The winter wonderland bride is the one to get cold feet.*

Talking Olivia through this was a job better performed by a real friend than a fake bridesmaid, but all of Olivia's friends seemed to be avoiding the bathroom. The encounter with the mother of the bride must have shaken them. At least Rebecca was handling the other side of that situation.

Truth be told, since her post-bachelorette-party cry with Joel and Damian, Amy was feeling less starry-eyed about weddings herself. It wasn't just the uncertainty about whether or not her bridesmaid business was selling out the queer community. With her and Charley seemingly cursed with conflicting work schedules, Amy was feeling a bit grumpy about romance in general.

Olivia blew her nose, looking at Amy with desperation. What was it about love and marriage that had made Amy want this job again? And what was the point of a wedding? Just spending a bunch of money to brag about your relationship to your friends? That sounded more like something Charley would say.

Amy smoothed Olivia's hair. She needed to channel herself from the weekend before, when she'd defended her rosy view of the wedding industry to Charley on their drive back from Oklahoma City. If only she could have bottled some of that magic she'd loved so much at Regi's and Corinne's weddings, maybe she could pop open the bottle now and give the perfect rousing pep talk. That had always been Joel's specialty, though, not hers.

That was it! She needed to think of what she'd say to Joel or Damian in a moment like this, how happy she would be to see her two best friends celebrate a lifetime commitment to each other, how gently she'd rub Joel's back if he were stress-puking on his special day. She took a deep breath. "This isn't a sign, Olivia. This is a wedding. They're always stressful, since everyone has always told you that it should be the most important day of your life. But it isn't the decorations or the officiant or the cake or the pictures that really matters. What matters is you and Mike, choosing a life together. You love Mike, and Mike loves you. I saw it on both of your faces at the rehearsal dinner last night. You're going to keep loving each other. That isn't going to change. This wedding is just one photo op on the long road of your relationship. You've been together for . . ."

"Two years," Olivia said with a sniffle.

"Two years! That's already a lot of road behind you. And you got engaged because you want to keep walking that road together. Now you're just saying that in front of your friends and family, but the two of you—you already know your path. Maybe some paperwork will come out of this, but fundamentally, your love for each other isn't changing. Right?"

Olivia took a deep, shaking breath. "Yeah."

"And sure, some things might change down the road. But even if things change, you'll get through it. That's how marriage works. You love each other, and everything else, well, you figure it out as you go along, just like we're doing with this wedding today." Amy wiped a bit of running mascara from Olivia's cheek. "So what do you say you go out there and promise Mike that you'll keep on walking together?"

Olivia took several slow breaths. "Let me just fix my makeup." The bride straightened up, gathered the skirt of her gown, and stepped toward the mirror.

Amy smiled kindly at Olivia's reflection, but deep down, she felt a pang. That love she'd described, the kind where two people could grow together, where you had someone to walk with you as you figured out the path you wanted your life to take . . . she wanted it so badly she could taste it. Damian and Joel had it. She'd seen their relationship from the beginning, and she could tell they had the kind of love that was more of a marathon than a sprint. Max and Greg had it too. They'd been walking their path together for almost thirty years, supporting each other even when the road got rocky. Both Max and Greg were HIV positive, and they'd had their share of health scares when their compromised immune systems had turned common colds into pneumonia or worse. But they'd chosen to take care of each other at every potential fork in the road.

As Amy helped Olivia adjust her hair and makeup, she kept thinking about the metaphor of relationships being a road. Her time with Autumn had been anything but smooth, and thanks to Autumn's playboy tendencies, it had more often felt like she was creating the obstacles in Amy's way rather than helping her navigate them. Amy needed someone who would reliably walk by her side, someone who made her feel more capable of conquering rocky terrain instead of leaving her to figure it out on her own, someone who could commit to the long journey ahead. They could have different opinions about which route to take as long as they were headed to the same place.

Could that person be Charley? Amy really wanted it to be. They were different in many ways, but being with Charley made her feel stronger, more herself somehow. Charley had made Amy feel confident in her passion for weddings, even if Charley herself didn't share that passion. In plenty of situations in Amy's life—at Daily Bread, with extended family, dating Autumn, even bridesmaiding—she'd found it easiest to change herself to suit the needs of everyone around her. But Charley seemed like she wanted to know the real Amy. Like she didn't expect Amy to be anyone but herself. A person like that seemed like the kind of person Amy wanted walking beside her, whether the road was smooth or bumpy.

"Um, do you think there are mints anywhere around?" Olivia said, interrupting Amy's wandering thoughts. "I don't want my first kiss as a married woman to be all pukey."

"Good thinking!" Amy said, encouraged that Olivia was recommitting to the wedding ahead of her. "I have some in my bag. I'll just grab that and your lipstick, and then we can get this show on the road."

Grateful for another bridesmaid task to pull her back down to earth, Amy resolved to focus on the love being celebrated that day. And once the wedding ceremony began, Amy felt the emotional rush of that exhilarating wedding magic tingle inside her again. This time, with her own pep talk echoing in her head, it was stronger than ever before.

19

Amy found that the afterglow of Olivia's winter wonderland wedding, which had turned out lovely despite all the last-minute hitches, was a perfect transition into the Christmas spirit. Charley flew back to Tulsa the day after the wedding, and Amy was elated to accept her invitation to go Christmas shopping that very afternoon before her shift at Ruby Red's. Charley had a long string of brothers, sisters, nieces, and nephews to wow with gifts, and Amy thoroughly enjoyed knowing the right spots in Tulsa to go for each item on Charley's list. When Charley confessed that she was terrible at wrapping, Amy volunteered to help in exchange for a last night with Charley before she left for Houston on Tuesday, which was Christmas Eve. Charley readily agreed, and this time they stayed at Charley's place so that she could more easily make her early-morning flight. Amy could hardly believe that Charley had flown back to Tulsa just for half of Sunday and all day Monday.

She liked to think that Charley found her just that irresistible. The truth was that Charley had to work on Monday before the upcoming holiday, which gave Amy time to have her regular brunch with Teresa and discuss their cooking plan for the next day anyway.

On the morning of Christmas Eve, Charley dropped Amy back at her apartment on her way to the airport with a goodbye kiss hotter than chestnuts roasting on an open fire. Amy comforted herself by running through her game plan for the coming days. She had two bridesmaid commitments before the New Year—one wedding dress appointment with a Craigslist bride and a bridal shower for Kim—and in between planned to pick up extra shifts at the mistletoe-laden bar and get her busted car fixed yet again. Charley had graciously offered Amy her roadside assistance benefits to have the car towed off the side of the highway, but it was still sitting in the lot of a nearby repair shop waiting for Amy to sign off on the repairs.

Finally, it was time to focus on Christmas at Teresa's. It would have been more convenient for Charley to drop Amy off at her mom's house on her way to the airport, but Amy had asked her mom to come get her from her apartment, not ready to answer relationship questions just yet. She packed an overnight bag, excited for her second favorite holiday of the year.

While Thanksgiving was an opportunity for Teresa and Amy to show off their baking skills for the extended Fariner family, Christmas was all about cooking their favorite classic dishes together for their chosen family. For many years, Amy and her mother had celebrated the holiday with Max and Greg. And although it made for warm, love-filled memories, Amy had always longed for the big family Christmases she saw in movies, the kind she now imagined Charley had. As Amy grew older and started making queer friends with varying degrees of estrangement from their families, she and her mom had adopted them one by one into their Christmas celebrations. Now Amy and Teresa hosted quite the gay gala each December.

This year's delicious spread took a day and a half to prepare and included a traditional glazed ham, Tofurky for the vegetarians, freshly baked buttery rolls, smoked Gouda and caramelized onion mac and cheese, a variety of veggie side dishes, cookies of every kind, and a festively layered peppermint brownie trifle. By the time their guests began to arrive the afternoon of the twenty-fifth, Amy and Teresa were surprisingly calm and ready. The moments before Christmas dinner began were usually chaotic, marked by last-minute grocery runs and panicked cleaning. As she examined their beautiful dishes and clean kitchen, Amy thought perhaps they'd finally mastered the art of the Christmas dinner. Maybe Amy had learned something about preparation and timing from her bridesmaid duties.

Joel and Damian were the first to knock on the door, several bottles of wine in hand. Next up was Jae, along with their new significant other and a green bean casserole. Tala was right behind with a tabbouleh salad and her digital camera to capture the festivities. Amy greeted Max and Greg with big hugs not long after and happily accepted the charcuterie board they'd brought for the celebration. Zee strolled in next with Arnelle and a large pitcher of homemade eggnog. Last to arrive was McKenzie. When Amy overheard her telling a friend at the bar that her parents were on vacation overseas and she didn't have any Christmas plans, Amy had offered an invitation before she could think twice. Even if they hardly knew each other, Amy automatically felt a kinship with any member of the Autumn's Broken Hearts Club. McKenzie showed up with a plate of homemade fudge and an enormous heartfelt thank-you to Teresa and Amy for including her.

If only Charley were there, it would have been perfect, Amy thought. At the same time, picturing Charley in Houston surrounded by the family she loved so much brightened Amy's mood. Charley's excitement when they'd shopped together had been infectious. She'd looked a bit like a kid on Christmas herself as she tested the lights and sounds on various electronic toys. *What would it be like*, Amy wondered, *to sit next to Charley at her family's table on Christmas?*

But Amy didn't have much time to daydream about Charley. Joel asked how Olivia's wedding had gone, prompting Amy to catch Max and Greg up on her new business. Before long, she was passing around the picture of the penis cake from Christina's wedding and regaling everyone with tales of her bridesmaid adventures. But the conversation paused once dinner was served, replaced with satisfied "mmms" and compliments to the chefs. Everyone pitched in to clean up after dessert. Once leftovers were put away and the dishwasher was started, the group meandered into the living room to enjoy Zee's rich homemade eggnog. Damian entertained with a story of his wealthiest personal training client's luxurious holiday party earlier in the month while Tala snapped pictures of Papaya toying with an ornament dangling from a low branch of the Christmas tree.

After a while, Joel and Amy left the postdinner conversation to add an extra splash of bourbon to their eggnogs in the kitchen. With a surreptitious glance toward the living room, Joel asked, "Remember how we talked about me proposing to Damian?"

"Yes, of course," Amy said, a thrill rising in her chest.

"I haven't been able to get what you said out of my head, about not letting the homophobes stop us from being loudly and proudly in love, and"—Joel was blushing lightly from the alcohol, the warmth of the fire, and his secret—"well, I bought a ring! I'm going to propose on New Year's Eve."

Amy squealed as quietly as possible. "That's wonderful, Joel! I'm so excited for you! What's your plan?"

Joel told her he'd made a reservation for them to watch the New Year's Eve fireworks from a swanky penthouse bar at the top of the Mayo Hotel, a more exclusive spot in the same hotel where Corinne's wedding reception had been held. He planned to surprise Damian with the ring right at midnight. "And I was thinking we could have a surprise engagement party with our friends at Ruby Red's afterwards. You're working that night, right? Any chance you could help on that end?"

"Of course!" Amy said. "That sounds so wonderful. I would love to help! Let's get together this week to figure out the details. Can I make a cake? Please tell me I can make a cake."

Joel let out a relieved laugh. "For the party or the wedding? Hopefully both!"

They agreed to get together in the next couple of days to plan for the surprise party but were then interrupted by Max and Greg entering the kitchen. With a nod from Joel, Amy filled them in on his plan to propose to Damian. They quietly but enthusiastically congratulated Joel.

"You two got married in Boston, right?" Joel asked, eyeing the couple's matching gold wedding bands.

Greg smiled fondly at Max. "Yes, in 2005. A little after it was legalized in Massachusetts. It doesn't mean much legally here, but it matters to us."

Amy looped an arm through Greg's and leaned her head against his shoulder. "I can't believe it's been eight years already. I still remember Mom and me decorating your whole house like a tropical honeymoon to surprise you when you got back. But I still wish I could have been there on the day."

"Oh, there wasn't much to see," Max said. "It was more of an elopement than anything," he explained to Joel. "Just the two of us and a couple of witnesses at the courthouse. I'm trying to convince Greg to have a recommitment ceremony with all of our friends and family for our tenth wedding anniversary."

Amy's eyes lit up. "That sounds amazing! You know, if you need anything—help planning, working with vendors, cake, whatever—I would love to be a part of it."

Greg mussed Amy's curly hair. "You've got it. You're our first choice, kid." Amy's mind filled with images of centerpieces made of Max's favorite flowers and a brunch buffet, which Greg would adore. But her plans would have to wait for later. If they wanted to avoid Damian's getting suspicious about their extended absence from the festivities, it was time to rejoin the rest of the group.

As the evening wound down, the guests gradually made their exits. Amy and Teresa handed out mason jars of homemade hot cocoa mix and tins of their signature peppermint bark to each person on their way out. Before long, Teresa, Amy, and Papaya were left alone, all three of them tucked under a fluffy blanket in front of the flickering fireplace.

"Did you have a nice Christmas?" Teresa asked, sipping the last of the eggnog.

"I did," Amy said. "It was perfect. Great food, great company. Did you?"

Teresa nodded. "We know how to throw a good party."

"Did Joel tell you he's going to propose to Damian?"

"No!" Teresa's voice filled with joy. "That's wonderful! When?" Amy shared the details, including the plan for an engagement party on New Year's Eve. "So are they going to Massachusetts or Canada or somewhere to tie the knot?"

"He's not sure yet," Amy said. "They may just have a

commitment ceremony here, or maybe they'll travel somewhere else where it's legal. It doesn't really matter, right? It's about a commitment for them, not anyone else's expectations."

"You're right. That's the important part. But there's a lot of other legal stuff that goes into it too." She paused. "I actually wrote a letter about gay marriage to Governor Fallin."

Amy's eyes snapped from the fireplace to her mom's face. "You did?"

"Well, after our conversation about God and people behaving badly in his name, I got to thinking," Teresa said. "I can try to see the good in people's hearts, but what does that do to actually change anything? To fix the damage that's been done or stop it from happening again? When I saw Governor Fallin being all bitter about that gay marriage court case, I figured I better actually do something about it. So I wrote her a letter telling her what was on my heart. And I was pretty darn proud of that letter, so I sent it to our senators and my representative too, and then I figured, hell, why not send it to all the Oklahoma representatives? Then that kinda snowballed into sending it to every member of the state legislature. Anyway, I ended up spending a lot on postage, but I figure it was worth it."

"Mom! That's wonderful!" Amy said, stunned. Her mother had always had a big heart, but she often fell into the trap of valuing politeness over fighting for what's right. If Teresa could get out of her comfort zone enough to send over a hundred letters to lawmakers about marriage equality, maybe, just maybe, those lawmakers could get out of their comfort zones enough to consider her argument.

"Thanks, honey. I want the world for you, you know? And it makes me so mad that people would stand in the way of your happiness and blame it on God." Teresa paused and sipped her eggnog. "I fully intend to throw a big ol' party someday for your wedding no matter what Oklahoma law has to say. But I'm hoping they'll end up on the right side of it."

Amy could rarely talk about the debate over same-sex marriage without getting angry. But in this conversation, it felt like her mother had taken the righteous anger right off Amy's shoulders to carry it herself for a while. It gave Amy a kind of warm, fuzzy, cared-for feeling that she quite enjoyed. "I hope for that too, Mom."

Teresa looked from the flickering fireplace to Amy, a mischievous gleam in her eye. "Speaking of, any new girlfriends I should know about?"

Amy laughed. "Since you last asked at Thanksgiving?"

"Hey, I'm your mother. I gave you a life, so I get to pry into it whenever I want. Those are the rules." Teresa paused. "Besides, you seem . . . I don't know, different lately. Happier. More at peace. But I guess it's just the new business glow."

Amy shifted on the couch, weighing whether or not to leave it at that. But remembering the intimacy of Christmas shopping with Charley, of wrapping her gifts to her family, of their sweet goodbye kiss, Amy wondered what it mattered if they hadn't put a name on it yet. It *felt* real, and that "yet" felt like it couldn't last much longer. Amy took a deep breath. "Well, yeah, business has been going surprisingly well. You wouldn't believe how many people are willing to pay someone to be a bridesmaid. I hardly believe it. But . . . I've also been seeing someone."

Teresa wiggled in a small happy dance from her seat on the couch. "I knew it! Mother's intuition strikes again! Tell me everything. Where did you meet her?"

Amy cringed. "Daily Bread. Before I got fired obviously. She was a customer."

Chastened, Teresa placed a hand on Amy's knee. "Well, at least something good came out of that terrible place, besides all those leftover baked goods you used to bring me. What's her name?"

"Charley."

"Short for Charlotte?" Teresa asked.

Amy paused. Why hadn't she thought to ask Charley that yet? She suddenly felt silly telling her mother about a girl whose legal name she didn't even know. "Um, just Charley. Anyway, she's from Houston originally, smack dab in the middle of five siblings. She's there now with her family. Lived in Austin for a while but just moved to Tulsa a couple months ago for a job in oil and gas." Teresa's forehead creased, and Amy held out a warning hand. "Before you judge, she's on the good side of the industry. Environmental sustainability, bringing in safe practices to prevent spills, protecting Native American land, that kind of stuff."

Teresa leaned back, impressed. "Wow. She must be pretty smart."

"Mom, she's brilliant," Amy said, a little embarrassed but in a pleased way. She knew her mom could see how flushed with excitement she was just *describing* Charley. "When she talks about her job, I can hardly keep up, but I can just tell. And she's so thoughtful and observant and totally herself, even if that's not who Texas and Oklahoma want her to be."

"And hot?" Teresa said, raising an eyebrow.

"So hot! In, like, a Shane from *The L Word* but cleaner cut kind of way." Wanting to support Amy when she came out, Teresa had bought the first season on DVD and tried to watch it with Amy. She had given up quickly once watching the steamy sex scenes together became too awkward to handle.

"Cute! Do you have a picture of her?"

Amy pulled up her phone to search through recent photos. As it turned out, she hadn't taken many photos with Charley so far. Maybe there was some crossover between her nerves about asking Charley to DTR and her hesitation to ask to take a picture with her. Luckily, she had the selfie they'd taken on their first date with the Golden Driller looming behind them. She'd spent plenty of time staring at the photo, especially when Charley was out of town.

Amy handed the phone to her mom, who pulled her reading glasses from her shirt pocket to examine the photo. "Wow, y'all make quite the cute couple. What do Joel and Damian think of her?"

Amy cleared her throat. "They, uh, haven't met her yet."

"Your best friends haven't met your girlfriend in the, what, six weeks you've been together?" Teresa looked at Amy skeptically over the top of her glasses.

"She travels a lot for work! Between that and the holidays and, you know, life, the timing just hasn't worked out. But soon!" Amy felt a little defensive, although she knew Teresa wasn't judging her. It did feel a little strange that Charley hadn't yet met any of the most important people in her life. But if they wanted it to work, it would happen eventually. *Right?* Amy pulled her phone from her mother's hands and changed the subject. "Plus, I've also been super busy with the bridesmaiding thing, and it's not slowing down anytime soon. I have a dress-shopping appointment with a new bride this weekend and then a bridal shower for Kim who I met at that first wedding I was in."

"That's fantastic, honey! I knew you would find a way. Do you ever bake the cakes for any of these weddings?"

"No, I haven't really offered. I've done some smaller orders of cupcakes and petits fours and things for showers, but I don't have all the same space and supplies and help as I did back at Daily Bread. I don't know if I could handle a big wedding cake on my own."

"Sure you could!" Teresa said enthusiastically. "You're the best baker I know."

"You're just saying that because you're my mom," Amy said. "But I guess I could try it out. Maybe I'll add it to my services on my new website."

Teresa smiled, looking pleased that Amy was taking her advice. "This is going to be your year, Amy. I can feel it. Big things are coming for you."

Amy leaned back into the couch, feeling hope bubbling in her chest. "I hope so, Mom. I could use a good year."

20

Between bartending shifts, getting her car fixed, planning Joel and Damian's engagement party, dress shopping with her newest client, and Kim's bridal shower, the week between Christmas and New Year's Eve flew by. In what felt like no time at all, Amy found herself decorating Ruby Red's for New Year's Eve and the engagement party to follow. She had baked a stunning three-tier strawberry champagne cake topped with white-chocolate-dipped strawberries and two large chocolate engagement bands. It was stowed carefully behind the bar along with a case of champagne for the complimentary midnight toast and a few bottles Amy herself had contributed for the engagement toast.

Zee arrived early to help with setup and quickly got to work hanging silver and gold balloons and glittery tinsel around the bar. Amy draped a "CONGRATS, DAMIAN AND JOEL" banner across the largest wall and then strung a "HAPPY NEW YEAR" banner over the top to hide it. The couple were expected to arrive about half an hour after midnight, shortly after Joel proposed at the end of the countdown. Most of Tulsa's LGBTQ crowd spent New Year's Eve at Rampage, wanting a more energetic atmosphere. But between the regulars, out-of-town visitors, and the other friends Joel had invited to the party, they were still expecting a large turnout.

"I'm so excited, I can hardly stand it," Amy said to Zee. "Damian is going to be so surprised. He'll be surprised, right?"

Zee's impassive poker face stood in stark contrast to Amy's nervous enthusiasm, although Amy knew Zee was just as happy to celebrate the couple. "If you and Joel haven't given it away with all your whispering."

"I can't help it! I just want everything to be perfect." And not just for Joel and Damian: Charley was on her way back to town, and she'd promised to make it to Ruby Red's before midnight to be there for the celebration. Amy would finally be able to introduce Charley to her friends and the dive bar she loved more than any place in the world.

Zee pulled a full rack of glass champagne flutes from the dishwasher. "If I know Joel, it will be."

Before long, it was time for Amy to flip on the dim "R.R." sign and unlock the front door. The bar began to fill up with familiar faces, the anticipatory buzz of a coming new year palpable. The first few hours of the night flew by, and though Amy hadn't had any champagne yet, she felt as bubbly and light as if she had. Although New Year's Eve wasn't a holiday that revolved around food and baking, Amy still enjoyed the opportunity to reflect on the year behind. She loved the feeling of being just at the cusp of a new year, a clean slate, and the celebratory air that coursed through Ruby Red's. There was something inherently queer about putting wishes into the universe that next year things would get better.

She glanced at the wall to check the time on the Tin Man's ticking heart clock after serving a round of shots to a table of Damian's friends from the gym. It was already half past ten. Two hours until the New Year's Eve party transitioned to an engagement party. And then, just as she looked away from the clock, the front door opened, and she turned to see Charley standing inside the entrance, smoothing her hair and taking in the crowded room. Before she'd even formed a conscious thought, Amy felt herself running toward Charley as if she were starring in the pinnacle scene in one of her favorite movies, her hair flying around her face, the noise of the bar seeming to recede into the background, the crowd parting in front of her as if on cue, until at last, she threw herself into Charley's arms and kissed her hard and long. For once, there was no little voice in the back of her head asking if it was safe, no worrying who might see. She felt Charley relax into her body, returning her passionate embrace. When they finally pulled apart, claps and wolf whistles sounded throughout the bar.

Amy gave the room a mock bow before turning back to Charley and running a hand along her cold cheek. "Welcome to Ruby Red's!"

"Do you give all your customers that warm of a welcome?" Charley said with a grin, although she looked nervous.

"Only the cute ones. Here, give me your coat, and I'll introduce you to everyone."

Charley's eyes widened. "Everyone?"

"Just about. Can I get you a Diet Coke, maybe with a twist of lime?" Amy paused as Charley fumbled with the buttons on her camel coat, her eyes on the flying monkey statue by her feet. "Are you all right?"

"Yeah, sorry. I've been traveling for hours and am trying to remember how to human." Charley finally pulled off her coat and placed it in Amy's waiting hands. "Can you point me toward the bathroom?"

"Of course. I'm sure this is a lot to take in," Amy said. "Restroom is in the back right corner. I'll save a seat for you at the bar."

As Charley squeezed through the crowd, Amy returned to the bar and draped Charley's coat over the back of an open barstool next to Tala and Jae.

"She's super cute," Tala said as soon as Amy was within earshot.

"Definitely a babe, but looks aren't everything, Tal," Jae said. "We've got a lot of questions to ask to make sure she's good enough for our Amy."

"Too bad Joel and Damian aren't here yet to interrogate her. I guess we'll have to double down," Tala said with a mischievous smile.

McKenzie squeezed through the dance floor to join the group at the bar. "Was that hottie Charley? Do I get to meet her?"

Butterflies flapped in Amy's stomach. "Be gentle with her, y'all. This is the first time she's met any of my friends. Please don't scare her off."

By the time Amy had mixed a vodka cranberry for McKenzie and poured a Diet Coke, Charley had made her way back to the bar. "Charley, these are my friends Tala, Jae, Arnelle, and McKenzie. They use she/her, they/them, she/her, and she/her pronouns," Amy said, gesturing at each in turn as Charley sat down.

Zee passed behind the small group with a tray of drinks in hand and paused to introduce herself. "Hey, I'm Zee. She/her. We've all heard a lot about you. In, like, a good way, though."

Charley smiled tentatively toward the group. "Nice to meet—"

"If you could kill one person and get away with it, who would it be?" Jae said.

Charley looked askance toward Amy. "Uh . . ."

"You can go back in time, if that changes your answer," Jae added.

"Give her a second to breathe!" Amy said, trying to give her friends a warning look while simultaneously smiling as if everything was totally fine and not stressful at all. Why exactly had she decided to introduce Charley to all of her friends during one of her busiest shifts of the year, when she wouldn't be around to supervise?

"Don't stress," Arnelle said warmly to Charley, quick to pick up on the panic in Amy's eyes. "Jae's full of intense icebreakers. When I first met them, Jae asked me if I would sacrifice a family member for eternal life."

"Lucky for me, I have some practice with the questions game," Charley said, winking at Amy. She paused briefly, looking up toward the ceiling in thought. "Christopher Columbus. That guy was a real dick. And I'd feel some guilt about killing anyone, but at least with him, I'd know I'd prevented a lot of other deaths in the process."

"Damn, that's a good answer," Jae said, their eyebrows raised. The rest of the group nodded in agreement.

"Now it's my turn," Charley said. "What animal would you like to be reincarnated as in your next life?"

Hearing Zee shout her name over the noise of the crowd, Amy looked around to see her dropping off another tray of drinks at a table. Zee tilted her head at the other end of the bar at a growing crowd of people waiting to be served.

Amy turned back to the little group, unsure if she could leave Charley to fend for herself already. "Go!" Charley said, flashing her lopsided grin. "I know you're working. I'm good here. I still have plenty of questions for these four."

"I promise we won't embarrass you, Amy," Tala said. "Right, Jae?"

"Yes, we promise," Jae said with feigned disappointment.

"And we won't embarrass *you* either," McKenzie said to Charley. "We're just really excited to meet Amy's new partner." Charley raised an eyebrow in surprise and Amy inwardly cringed.

"Can I get a drink over here?" a customer called from the other end of the bar, waving in Amy's direction.

"Thanks for being such a good sport." Amy squeezed Charley's hand across the countertop.

"I'm happy to be here," Charley said, her voice just a tiny bit quieter, which created a momentary feeling that they were in their own little world. She squeezed Amy's hand in return. "See you at the countdown."

Over the next hour, Amy had a chance to stop by the group only a couple of times between fulfilling drink orders, digging through the storage closet for supplies, and trying to keep up with the flow of dirty glasses. Before she could blink, it was a quarter to midnight, time to prepare for the countdown. Amy and Zee popped open the bottles of champagne to general cheers, then got to work filling and distributing nearly eighty flutes. Zee unmuted the ball drop festivities on the TV with only minutes to spare before midnight, and Amy carried the last glasses over to Tala, Jae, Arnelle, and McKenzie.

Finally, Amy came around from behind the bar and pulled Charley up from her stool into a tight embrace. "I better find out you all were on your best behavior," Amy said to her friends in a mock stern voice. "But right now we've got a midnight kiss to attend to."

The group laughed and whistled as Amy led Charley just behind one end of the counter. Charley, looking much more relaxed than when she'd first arrived, tucked a curl behind Amy's ear. "Hey, you."

"Hey to you too." Amy pulled two hidden flutes from behind the bar. "Sparkling juice."

"Have I ever told you that you're wonderful?"

Amy sneaked a hand into Charley's back pocket. "I just like seeing you smile."

"You make it easy," Charley said. As they gazed into each other's eyes, a private energy seemed to crackle in the small space between their bodies. The crowd started counting down.

"*Ten. Nine. Eight.*"

Amy leaned into Charley's arms. "Have I told you how much I love New Year's Eve?"

"*Seven. Six. Five.*"

Charley pulled Amy closer, their lips only inches apart. "You just like kissing me."

"*Four. Three. Two.*"

Amy felt a rush of tenderness. She was in her favorite place, holding and being held by this wonderful woman, surrounded by some of the people she loved most in the world. With the New Year only a second away, the future felt dazzling.

"*One.*"

Their kiss released a surge of adrenaline in Amy. With her lips on Charley's, she felt giddy, like nothing could touch her, like 2014 *had* to be her best year yet. As they came up for air, clinking their glasses of sparkling juice, their eyes locked on each other, Amy's lips parted before she could think. "I love you."

Charley froze, her glass halfway to her mouth, her expression inscrutable.

Amy clapped a hand to her mouth, momentarily mortified by her declaration. But then she remembered one of the very first things Charley had said to her, about how Charley couldn't help being honest, and Amy remembered how charmed she was by that way of being. How freeing it felt when they were vulnerable with each other, not just in conversation, but also in bed, something she'd never experienced with another partner. She remembered the metaphor of relationships as roads people walked along together and realized how certain she was that she and Charley had so much road ahead of them. She didn't have to keep pretending she was someone she wasn't, that she didn't feel the way she felt. She didn't have to backtrack or turn what she'd said into a joke. Not with Charley. She gathered her courage and took her hand from her mouth, placing it determinedly on Charley's hip.

Amy took a deep breath and said, "I didn't plan to say that, but I mean it. I love you, Charley."

Charley looked down at her feet, and in a split second, Amy went from feeling like she was floating way up in the air to feeling like she had jumped off a bridge and was in free fall. "I . . . I really like you, Amy. I do. It's just . . ."

Amy's cheeks burned with embarrassment, but she squeezed Charley's hip in reassurance. "It's okay. You don't have to say it back. It just kind of popped out, and I know this is all pretty overwhelming for you. We can—"

"Amy, over here!" Zee called across the bar. "Joel just texted!"

Amy cursed under her breath at the timing. "Can we talk about this later?"

Charley swallowed and nodded before kissing Amy's cheek and heading back to her seat. Amy watched her go, then forced herself to look down at her own phone, where she saw a glowing text from Joel.

He said yes!!!!!! Be there in 15!

Amy jogged over to Zee, reminding herself of how much she'd looked forward to this celebration all week. Whatever had just happened with Charley would have to wait. "Game time," Amy said. "Can you uncover their banner? I'll get everyone ready."

Zee jumped into action. Amy tapped a knife against an empty highball glass, quieting the chatter in the bar. "If you're here for Joel and Damian's engagement party, get ready!" Amy said. "They'll be here in fifteen minutes. And if you're not here for the party, play along!"

Zee and Amy refilled the champagne flutes as quickly as they could and passed them out to the eager partygoers with help from McKenzie and Jae. With only a minute or so to go, Amy set the cake on a tall table beneath the banner with two full glasses and a couple of glittery party hats she'd picked up earlier in the day. Just as she returned to her position behind the bar, the doors opened and Joel and Damian entered, beaming. The crowd cheered, and, spotting the banner and celebratory table beneath, Damian put a hand to his chest. As he turned to Joel with tears in his eyes, Amy felt her own eyes fill up as well. After all the loving moments she had witnessed at weddings in the past few months, finally she could laugh and cry and jump with joy over the love of her real friends.

Joel turned to the crowd. "Thank you all for being here. I can't believe I'm saying this, but we're engaged!" Laughter, cheers, and clinking glasses sounded through the room, and everyone threw back the celebratory champagne. As a group gathered around the couple, Amy headed over to the table to begin cutting the cake.

She caught Joel and Damian for a moment behind the cake display once the tidal wave of well-wishers had slowed. "You're both glowing. I can't believe my best friends are engaged! This is the best New Year's Eve ever!"

Damian held up the ring, a silver band with a thin line of tiny diamonds down the center. "He did good, didn't he?" Amy said, tearing up again at the radiant look on Damian's face.

"Oh God, Amy," Damian said, his voice cracking with emotion. "Don't cry or you'll make me cry."

As the line for cake calmed down, Amy glanced over at Charley. She was still sitting at the bar, a faint smile on her lips as she took in the merriment. Amy plated another slice of cake and pulled Joel aside. "I know this is your party, but do you want to meet Charley?"

"Of course!" Joel said. "Damian, get over here. We're finally meeting Charley!"

They made their way across the room, and Amy placed the slice of cake in front of Charley. "Charley, these are my best friends, Joel and Damian, both he/him. Joel and Damian, this is Charley, she/her."

Damian reached out for a handshake with a warm smile. "So nice to finally meet you, Charley. Amy speaks very highly of you."

"Welcome to the family!" Joel yelled as he pulled Charley into a big hug, physically lifting her away from her barstool.

After Joel stepped back, Charley cleared her throat and smoothed her hair. "Nice to meet you both, and congrats on the engagement. That's a big step."

"Amy, can I get your help with this keg?" Zee called from the other end of the bar.

"Sorry, y'all, I'll be right back," Amy said with a sigh. Before turning to go, she paused, taking in the faces of three of her favorite people, in the same room for the first time. "It means so much to me that you're finally meeting each other."

Damian smiled warmly and placed a hand on Charley's shoulder. "Us too." Amy hurried away as Charley asked the new fiancés for details about the proposal.

Changing the tap line was messier than anticipated. Once Amy and Zee finished cleaning up, they turned to a lengthy line of customers that kept them busy all the way to last call. And by the time the night was finally coming to an end, Joel and Damian found Amy sitting glumly on the barstool where Charley had once sat, picking at a slice of cake with a plastic fork.

"What a party, babe. I feel like a rock star. Damian and I should get engaged more often," Joel said as he plopped down to Amy's right.

Damian pulled up a barstool on her other side. "Oh, I think once is plenty for me. Hey, where's Charley?"

"I don't know," Amy said. "She left without saying goodbye."

Joel and Damian exchanged a look. "It's really late," Damian said. "And didn't she have a long travel day? She was probably exhausted."

"Or maybe she's waiting for you at your apartment, naked in your bed," Joel said, wiggling his eyebrows.

Amy's eyes filled with tears. "She didn't even try the cake!"

"Oh, babe," Joel said soothingly as he and Damian wrapped her in a group hug. "I'm sure it's a misunderstanding. I can tell she really likes you."

Amy sniffled into Joel's shoulder. "I told her I loved her, and she didn't say it back."

The two men stiffened. "Oh shit," Damian said under his breath.

Amy pulled back, smearing mascara under her eyes as she wiped at them. "I'm such a moron. I can't believe I did that. Why can't I ever just play it cool?"

Joel placed a hand on Amy's shoulder. "Do you need to talk to some onion rings about this?"

Amy nodded, a pronounced pout on her face. "Whataburger. Come on. I'll drive."

21

Amy awoke the next morning to Truffle pawing at her hair and meowing insistently for breakfast. Even before she opened her eyes, all the joy and embarrassment and disappointment of the night before came flooding back.

With a deep sigh, Amy sat up, squinting in the sunlight streaming through her window, and lifted her phone from her nightstand to find two texts from Charley.

Hey Amy. Thanks for inviting me last night. Your friends were great and I enjoyed Ruby Red's, but I think we should pump the brakes. I need some time and space to think.

Oh, and happy new year.

Amy read the texts what felt like a hundred times, trying desperately to make sense of the words in front of her. Then, wondering how she could possibly respond, she read them another hundred times.

Pump the brakes.

Time and space to think.

And then the afterthought of the "happy new year" that felt so final.

Where could Amy even begin? Should she apologize? But even though part of her wished she'd never said those three words, she didn't want to take back how brave and honest she'd felt in that moment. Should she just act chill and understanding? Say goodbye? The mere idea made Amy's lip begin to quiver, which turned quickly into a hurricane of tears and snot and messy feelings.

Between all of the recent weddings and the previous night's party, Amy had felt like she was floating along in a sea of other people's love and happiness and commitment. Now she felt like she was drowning. Amy wanted that kind of love so badly that she could feel a physical ache in her ribs. And not just with anyone. She wanted that with Charley.

After putting her phone facedown on her bedside table, Amy turned over and pressed her wet face into her pillow. Now that Charley had called things off, Amy could at least be honest with herself about what she'd lost. Sometime after their late-night heart-to-heart chat after Corinne's wedding, she'd started picturing what a wedding with Charley could look like. Imagining herself in an A-line antique lace dress, standing across from Charley in any one of her dapper suits. She would make blueberry cake in honor of the muffin she'd offered Charley when they first met or, if blueberries weren't in season, maybe a tiramisu cake like the first dessert Amy had made for her. Maybe they'd have the ceremony at the Philbrook Museum's beautiful gardens, dance on the lit-up disco floor during the reception.

Truffle seemed immune to the fairy-tale wedding that was crumbling to pieces in Amy's mind, continuing to meow and paw at the back of her head. Amy forced herself up, stumbling to the kitchen to feed Truffle through blurred eyes. What had gone wrong? Had her desire for a happily ever after with Charley come across as neediness and pushed Charley away? Amy's stomach churned with embarrassment and regret at the memory of her midnight three-word confession. But at the same time, how could she regret being vulnerable and honest about her feelings? All of the couples she'd seen while bridesmaiding were proud to proclaim their love for each other in front of hundreds of people. Joel and Damian had the courage to make a big commitment even though the state of Oklahoma said their love wasn't legitimate enough for them to get married. Amy loved Charley. It was as simple as that. And if she could, she would have yelled it from the mountaintops. If Charley didn't feel the same way, maybe it was for the best that Amy found out now rather than two years down the line, like with Autumn. The thought wasn't comforting.

Amy started a pot of coffee, feeling like her body was on autopilot. Maybe her love of love had turned her desperate, rendered her unable to see the signs. Amy normally had such a knack for reading people and knowing exactly what they wanted from her. But her feelings for Charley seemed to fog up her brain and make it impossible to access that skill. Maybe it was the way Charley seemed to see the real Amy underneath her people-pleasing instincts. Then again, did Charley actually see the real Amy, the starry-eyed romantic with a bit of an impulsive streak, if she was so taken aback by Amy's declaration of love? Well, that truest form of Amy had come out the night before when she'd put her heart on the line, and Charley obviously hadn't liked what she'd seen.

Amy dragged herself to the shower, where she indulged her feelings with a long, weepy Adele sing-along. But as Amy got out and dried off, she reminded herself that moping wouldn't really make her feel any better. The only thing that ever helped her survive moments of true devastation was baking, and it was high time she whipped her troubles into some batter.

Before long, Amy was mixing the ingredients for homemade cinnamon rolls into a thick dough. While she was elbow deep in flour, it was impossible to think of anything but the task ahead of her—just how she wanted it. She kneaded the dough atop her small kitchen table, pressing the heels of her hands into the warm, elastic substance. Once she was satisfied with the texture, she put the dough into a bowl to rise. Another hour alone with her thoughts while the dough proved? That wouldn't do. She fished through her cabinet for ideas. Lots of sprinkles. Next up: Funfetti cupcakes for Damian and Joel.

By the time the cinnamon roll dough had doubled in size, two dozen Funfetti cupcakes were in the oven and vanilla buttercream was whipped and waiting on the counter. Amy rolled out the dough and spread a cinnamon-brown-sugar mixture across the top. She shaped the dough into a log and sliced it into perfectly spiraled buns, which then went into a pan to rise again. Cupcakes out of the oven, cinnamon rolls in. While the rolls baked, Amy whisked up a smooth, rich cream cheese frosting to top them and then piped the buttercream onto the cupcakes. Her despairing thoughts still threatening to overtake her, she dug through her cabinets, searching for something else to bake with the ingredients on hand. Her uncle Greg's favorite peanut butter cookies could work, although she'd have to swap the milk chocolate kiss she usually put on top for smaller chocolate chips.

Once everything was baked and the dishes were cleaned, Amy felt the contentment of a job well done. But the feeling was quickly crowded out by thoughts of Charley's texts. *"Pump the brakes." "Time and space to think."* Time alone to think was the last thing Amy wanted. She boxed her goodies and packed them into her car, along with a bottle of wine. Her first instinct was to go to Teresa's house for a little maternal comfort. But remembering how insecure she'd felt about her relationship with Charley during her mother's questioning, Amy knew she couldn't admit defeat so soon, couldn't bear to see the knowing look on Teresa's face peeking through her sympathetic frown.

Instead, Amy drove east toward Max and Greg's house. They would understand queer heartache. But driving to their renovated bungalow led Amy past the Tulsa Fairgrounds and the looming Golden Driller statue, which naturally brought back memories of her perfect first date with Charley. The memory of their smiling faces in the early-morning selfies taunted Amy, bringing a sting of tears to her eyes. She was still trying to collect herself when she pulled into Max and Greg's driveway to find them in the front yard surrounded by bags of soil.

After a centering breath, Amy hopped out of the car with a big smile on her face. "Happy New Year, y'all! What's going on here?"

Greg climbed over the bags of dirt toward Amy. "Happy New Year, honey! What a pleasant surprise. You'll have to excuse our dirt. We're installing raised flower beds around the porch here so they can settle a little before we plant bulbs in the spring."

"They look great!" Amy said, examining the new wooden structure surrounding the porch.

"Just wait until you see the one we built in the backyard for herbs and vegetables," Max added, wiping his hands on his faded jeans. "Help us plant in spring, and you can have as much of the produce as you want. You'll probably put it to better use anyway," he said with a wink.

"Sounds like a good deal to me!" Amy opened the back door of her sedan and reached for a box of goodies. "Got time for a break? I brought snacks."

Amy followed Max and Greg into the familiar warmth of their kitchen and sat at the round wooden table. As they scrubbed their hands at the kitchen sink, Max and Greg filled Amy in on everything they planned to grow come spring, stopping to bicker about whether or not tomatoes would draw too many bugs. They eventually settled down across from Amy and dug into the baked goods, Greg predictably grabbing a peanut butter cookie while Max opted for a cinnamon roll.

"So, how was your New Year's Eve?" Greg asked before biting into his cookie.

Max wiped a smear of frosting from the corner of his mouth. "Did you spend it with the new girlfriend your mom told us about?"

Although she'd come with the intention of laying her broken heart bare, her resolve had withered as she'd watched Max and Greg bustling about. Their decades-long comfort with each other showed in their every move, a gesture as simple as passing the hand towel feeling as intimate as finishing each other's sentences. Her friends often confused Max and Greg at family Christmases, unsure how to tell the two older white guys apart, with their similarly styled brown hair streaked with gray, chunky-framed glasses, and interchangeable wardrobes. But Amy had always kind of loved how similar they were, like two trees grown so close together that their branches and leaves had become intertwined, blurring the lines between where one ended and the other began. Thinking of trees brought to mind Charley's tattoo, the image of the geometric earth and twisting roots like a punch to Amy's stomach. If she told Max and Greg the truth then, seeing the best model of love she knew right in front of her, she'd dissolve into a pitiful puddle. Who knew how long it would take to pull herself together? And she had more baked goods to deliver. No, she'd save the waterworks for Joel and Damian, who already knew how she'd messed things up the night before.

Determined to keep her troublesome emotions under wraps, Amy gave Max and Greg her brightest dimpled smile. "Oh yeah, great night. Lots of fun. But tell me more about those flower beds. Are you putting in any hydrangeas? They would look so nice on either side of the steps."

After fifteen more minutes of gardening talk, Amy wished her uncles luck with their project and continued her journey toward Zee and Arnelle's apartment downtown. She hefted a box of cinnamon rolls, cupcakes, and cookies up the four flights of stairs and knocked on their door. A figure darkened the peephole before Amy heard the door unlock. Zee appeared, looking underslept in her rumpled sweatpants. "Surprise delivery!" Amy said, handing over the box.

Zee lifted the top as Arnelle shuffled up, peeking over Zee's shoulder. Why were all of Amy's friends in such cute, happy relationships?

"Amy!" Arnelle said. "How are you feeling? We hardly survived the fun last night."

"Based on the baked goods, I'd guess she's stressed about something," Zee said. "I liked Charley by the way. Glad she finally made it."

"Me too!" Arnelle chimed in. "She was so cute!"

Amy looked down, unsure if she was ready to go there during a quick drop-off.

"Oh shit, what happened?" Zee said.

Grateful for Zee's intuition, Amy opened up the tiniest bit. "She, um, needs some space."

Arnelle pushed past Zee to give Amy a big hug. "I'm sorry, Amy. What a shitty way to start a new year."

Amy leaned into the hug momentarily before pulling back. "Hey, at least she didn't cheat with half the lesbians in Tulsa like Autumn, right? That I know of, I guess."

Zee was quiet for a moment, eyeing Amy. "She'll be back."

"Zee's always right about these things," Arnelle said reassuringly. "She's got a sixth sense."

Amy tried to look skeptical, but her heart betrayed her by clinging to the crumb of hope. What if Zee was right? "We'll see, Zee. Anyway, happy New Year! And thanks again for closing last night and letting me sneak out a little early. Enjoy the sweets!" She blew Arnelle and Zee a kiss and jogged down the stairs of their building.

Once back in her car, she drove on to her final destination, Joel and Damian's Craftsman-style home in midtown. She parked behind Joel's old Jeep and knocked on the door, balancing the baked goods on one hand and holding the bottle of wine under her arm.

Joel answered the door with a grunt and gestured for Amy to come in before collapsing on the couch in a heap. Damian was already there, curled in a ball under a fleece blanket.

"How are you two lovebirds this afternoon?" Amy asked in an overly chipper voice.

"Hungover as fuck," Damian said, his voice muffled by the blanket pulled over his head.

"Well, I brought your favorite medicine. Funfetti cupcakes, peanut butter cookies, and cinnamon rolls!" She placed the box on the coffee table, and Joel immediately opened it and dug in.

Damian begrudgingly emerged from the blanket, holding out a hand for a cupcake.

Amy nudged Joel over and plopped onto the couch. HGTV was playing at a low, soothing volume. "Newlyweds in Baltimore," Joel said. "They're awful, but their budget is high, so that makes it acceptable."

"He needs a space for his antique sword collection. It's a deal breaker," Damian said, and all three groaned in unison.

They watched, silent but for the sound of chewing, until a commercial break came on. Damian reached for the remote and pressed Mute. "So," he said. "This is a concerning amount of baked goods."

"Oh, we'll get through them. I'm not too concerned," Joel said through a mouthful of cookie.

"I mean for Amy's emotional state, Joel," Damian said with an eye roll.

"Oh, right," Joel said. "Still down from Charley leaving early last night?"

Amy sighed. "I wish it was just that. She texted me this morning. She needs some space to think. Said we should 'pump the brakes,' whatever that means."

Joel and Damian exchanged a glance Amy couldn't interpret.

"Let me see the texts," Joel said, grabbing for Amy's phone. She pulled up the messages and passed the phone over to Joel while Damian read over his shoulder. " 'Your friends were great.' At least she liked us, Dames," Joel joked.

"Joel, you have to tell her," Damian said.

"Tell me what?" Amy said sharply.

"It's not that big of a deal, really. Probably didn't have anything to do with . . ." Joel's voice faded as Damian crossed his arms.

"Tell me what?" Amy said again, feeling a sickening mixture of apprehension and desperation.

Joel's face showed a rare look for him: sheepishness.

"I, uh," Joel began. "I might have told Charley it was time to DTR."

"You *what*?" Amy yelled.

"Whoa, calm down, babe!" Joel said. "It wasn't a big deal! I just told Charley you're super into her and it was time for her to lock it down. That's all."

Amy pulled the blanket over her head. "Oh my God, Joel, you didn't! This is so embarrassing."

"What? You're my best friend, and you're a perfect, beautiful, magical unicorn who deserves only the best! If Charley can't give you the best, then she doesn't deserve you."

"First she meets all of my friends in one night. Then I tell her I love her. Then you tell her to DTR. No wonder she ran in the opposite direction," Amy said from under the blanket. Damian rubbed her back consolingly.

Joel huffed. "Still, I can't believe she broke up with you via text because you're into her. I thought I liked her, but that's just rude. And all the hot-and-cold business? Blowing you off the first time she was supposed to come to Ruby Red's? I'm not standing for this. Maybe she was never good enough for you anyway."

Amy threw the blanket away from her head, her embarrassment morphing to defensiveness. "You don't know if she's good enough for me. You hardly know her at all. If you knew her, you wouldn't have scared her off like that!"

"Whoa, *I* scared her off?" Joel said, matching Amy's defensive tone. "You're the one who told her you love her when you haven't even DTRed, so maybe you shouldn't be putting this all on me."

"Maybe we should cool off for a second," Damian said cautiously.

"I was trying to be honest about my feelings," Amy spat

back, her voice rising. "I didn't ask you to DTR for me. I didn't ask you to insert yourself in the middle of my business. Because I didn't think I had to spell that out."

Joel's face twisted in anger. "You want to talk about being honest? You asked me not to bring up your old job or your new job. Sorry if I didn't get the full list of topics to avoid." He was yelling now too. "And after you spend two years going back and forth with Autumn, then another six months crying about the breakup we all saw coming, you're saying you want me to stay out of your love life? Excuse me for trying to help so I don't have to listen to you mope and cry and pout, 'Oh, I'll never find true love' again for another two years."

"Joel, give her a break," Damian said quietly, looking beyond uncomfortable.

Amy stood, her cheeks flushed. "I didn't realize you were such an expert on my life. Just because you've got the *perfect* relationship doesn't mean you can lecture me or Charley on how love works."

"Oh, you want to talk about my relationship now?" Joel said, rising from the couch as well. "Then let's talk about how Damian and I just took this huge, exciting step of getting engaged and you haven't even asked us anything about it. We should be here celebrating and rehashing all the details, but instead we're listening to you cry about some girl again, as we have for the entire time we've been together."

Amy felt as if Joel had slapped her. "Are you calling me selfish?"

"No!" Damian said quickly.

"Maybe I am!" Joel yelled.

Angry tears stung the corners of Amy's eyes. "So planning a whole engagement party and decorating the bar and baking that giant cake—that was selfish?"

"Thank you for all of that, Amy. We really appreciate it," Damian said, looking desperate to get the conversation back on normal ground.

"Of *course* I'm happy for the two of you," Amy said, her voice breaking. "You know I want nothing more than to help plan and celebrate your wedding with you. Hell, it was practically my idea!"

"Oh no, you don't get to take credit for our engagement just because you think you have some monopoly on anything to do with weddings," Joel said. "We already have to listen to you talk about them all the time, and you never ask if it's a painful topic for us, who really, really want to get married, are actually *ready* to get married, and can't."

There was no stopping Amy's tears now. Joel's words triggered a feeling of guilt somewhere in her gut, but her anger and hurt were too overpowering for her to slow down. "Well, maybe I really, really wanted to get married too, but now any hope I had of a future with Charley is gone because of you!"

Joel rolled his eyes theatrically. "Here we go again, back to Amy's problems because ours don't matter, right, Damian?"

"Can we just leave me out of this?" Damian said pleadingly.

"Damian won't take your side, because he knows I'm right! Right, Damian?" Amy glowered down at him.

"Damian *will* take my side because he's *my* fiancé, and he knows that you're overreacting. Right, Damian?" Joel's tone mocked Amy's. They were both glaring down at Damian now, whose eyes darted back and forth between them.

Damian hesitated, seeming to weigh whether or not he could get away with not responding. Finally, under the weight of Joel's and Amy's silent stares, he sighed. "I mean, maybe we wouldn't be screaming at each other right now if you'd started with *Tell me about the proposal* instead of *Charley wants a break*, Amy."

His voice was apologetic, but Amy stiffened with a deep sense of betrayal by her two best friends. The atmosphere in the room was frigid.

"All right, I can see when I'm not wanted," she said. "I'll just go."

Damian moved to stop Amy as she headed for the door. "No, Amy, let's just calm down and talk about this."

"Let her go, Dames," Joel said. "Amy, come back when you're ready to talk about someone other than yourself for once!"

22

It wasn't Amy and Joel's first fight. It wasn't even their loudest, longest, or most dramatic one. Having been best friends since the age of eighteen meant they'd gone through a lot of growing pains together. But there was something about this fight—maybe the tension of Joel being at one of the highest points in his life at the same moment Amy was at one of her lowest—that stuck, making it their first fight that wasn't resolved within a week. And after a few tense shifts at Ruby Red's with two bartenders refusing to speak to each other, it became even clearer that this fight wasn't going to resolve itself. Joel asked for fewer shifts at Ruby Red's and instead started working more and more at an Irish pub downtown where he usually just filled in a few times a month. His absence at the bar put additional pressure on Zee and on Amy, who was already spread thin on weekends, balancing bartending with bridesmaiding.

The energy of Ruby Red's changed without Amy and Joel's

friendly rapport. Jae, Tala, Arnelle, and the other regulars remained firmly neutral in the battle, but without Joel and Damian hanging around, the whole dynamic felt unbalanced. Amy spent her shifts bored and staring at the door, hoping Charley would rush through it, declaring her love for Amy after all. But no matter how hard Amy willed her to appear at Ruby Red's, no matter how many stylishly masculine of center lesbians waltzed in who at first glance might have been her, Charley remained absent.

Two weeks after Charley's disappearance and the fight with Joel, it was a quiet Tuesday evening at Ruby Red's, with only a few customers smoking on the back patio and Jae and Tala poking around the jukebox. Amy was engaged in the messy business of cleaning out the draft beer lines when Zee came bursting through the door out of breath with Arnelle close on her heels. "Turn on the news."

"Why? What happened?" Amy asked as she peeled off her rubber gloves. Thoughts of terrorism, wildfires, and other disasters began running through her head. Zee was always one to keep a cool head, so her high energy was a notable change.

Unable to wait, Zee all but jumped over the bar and pulled the remote from its hiding spot. She flipped to a local news station, where a blond reporter was standing in front of the Oklahoma State Capitol building. Along the bottom of the screen ran the headline: "Federal Judge Rules Oklahoma Ban on Gay Marriage Unconstitutional." Zee turned the volume up.

". . . less than a month after a district judge struck down a similar ban in Utah. Federal judge Terence Kern released a sixty-eight-page opinion along with today's decision, which states that the ban, and I quote, 'intentionally discriminates against same-sex couples desiring an Oklahoma marriage license without a legally sufficient justification.' Brian, tell us when this goes into effect."

The camera cut to a reporter sitting behind a desk in the

news studio, his glasses slightly askew as he shuffled through a pile of papers. "Thanks, Liz. Although this ruling is similar to the recent ruling in Utah, Judge Kern has issued a stay in the Oklahoma case based on the U.S. Supreme Court decision to hold same-sex marriages in Utah while appeals are pending. That means that while gay marriage is technically legal, same-sex couples will not be issued marriage licenses in Oklahoma until a decision is made at a higher-level court."

"I knew there would be a catch," Arnelle murmured.

The people watching inside Ruby Red's were alternating between gasps, cheers, and impassioned side conversations. Amy, too, felt a bit as if she were on a rumbling wooden roller coaster, jostled and elated and nervous. The minute she realized what the news was saying, her mind went to Damian and Joel. This was really happening! They could get married in Oklahoma, maybe be one of the first gay couples to do so. But her euphoria quickly deflated as she remembered that she wasn't currently talking to Joel or, by extension, Damian. She felt torn in two, wanting to call them to celebrate but also refusing to make the first move after what Joel had done and said. The clarification that Oklahoma wouldn't actually allow marriages sent Amy down a different spiral. The courts were toying with the hearts of the state's LGBTQ citizens as if this were a game of chess instead of something that affected actual lives.

Zee hushed the room, straining to hear the news anchors.

". . . just received a statement from Governor Mary Fallin on the ruling." A collective groan rose from the room as an image of the politician appeared in a box at the top corner of the screen. The bar quieted as the anchor squinted at the printed statement in front of him. "It says: 'In 2004, the people of Oklahoma voted to amend the state's constitution to define marriage as "the union of one man and one woman." That amendment passed with seventy-five percent support. The people of Oklahoma have spoken on this issue. I support the right of Oklahoma's voters to govern themselves on this and other policy matters. I am disappointed in the judge's ruling and troubled that the will of the people has once again been ignored by the federal government.'"

Amy felt fire in her veins, and based on the angry jeers of the other people in the room, she knew she wasn't alone. *"The people of Oklahoma,"* the statement said. So were straight people the only Oklahomans who mattered to Governor Fallin? Did being queer make Amy less deserving of a voice in her home state? Less deserving of happiness?

Over the next twenty or so minutes, as reporters rehashed the judge's decision, customers streamed into the bar. Amy knew this was what she'd have done, too, if she'd been home when the news came in: rush over to Ruby Red's to celebrate, grieve, and discuss with her people. An excited chatter grew in volume as everyone speculated about what this meant.

Arnelle grabbed the remote to mute the television and then yelled for the room's attention, holding up her phone. "Oklahomans for Equality is holding a rally to celebrate now. Should we go?" A huge cheer rang out, and everyone burst into action, donning their coats and debating which cars to take.

As the bar emptied, Amy turned to Zee. "What do you think? Can we go?" They'd never closed the bar in the middle of a shift before.

"This is big," Zee said. "It's Oklahoma history! Let's go. Customers will understand."

Amy smiled for what felt like the first time in days and moved to shut off the "R.R." sign. "I was hoping you'd say that. Hey, can you grab the rainbow flags from the storage closet?"

After leaving a sign on the door directing customers to the celebration downtown and with a promise to reopen later that evening, Zee and Amy followed the stream of cars to the Oklahomans for Equality center. They parked a few blocks away and walked over to join a gathering of a couple hundred people bundled in their winter coats but emanating enough joy to warm the evening. And even though Pride celebrations were still months away, everyone seemed to have easily tracked down their rainbow gear. Flags were waving throughout the crowd, glitter was beginning to cover the concrete, and people were cheering for someone in a rainbow tutu dancing in the middle of the street. When she was watching the news earlier, Amy's optimism had been tempered by the hold on the judge's decision and Governor Fallin's cold words. At the Equality Center, however, the feeling was of pure joy. Couples were kissing, people were crying, and the air was electric.

Across the street, Amy saw two familiar figures dancing and jumping along to the music. She immediately recognized Joel's favorite Pride outfit, a pink-sequined cape, twinkling under the glare of the streetlights and could almost hear Damian's laughter as she watched them twirl. She wanted nothing more than to run to them, join their dance, and forget the screaming match that had torn them apart two weeks before. But they seemed to be having a great time without her. Truth be told, she missed them, but it sure didn't look like they missed her.

And piling onto her pity party was the supreme loneliness of watching so many happy queer couples celebrating around her. She and Charley could have been dancing right then, sharing happy tears, feeling the warm glow of a better future ahead. But instead, Amy was alone. Again.

Unbidden, Joel's voice from their fight suddenly came into her head, saying he was sick of hearing her whine that she'd never find true love. A wave of shame washed over her. She was doing exactly what Joel had accused her of. This should have been a moment of immense joy and excitement for Amy. The court decision was what she'd wanted, wasn't it? She knew she was just spiraling, focusing on what she didn't have rather than celebrating what she and the rest of her community had won. Instead of this realization breaking her out of her misery, though, she only felt worse.

Just as Amy was considering leaving the street party to reopen Ruby Red's, she felt a tap on her shoulder and turned to find Jae. "Hey, Amy. Why so sad? Did Betty White die?"

"No, and you've got to stop asking that anytime someone looks sad, or it will curse her," Amy said.

Jae stepped forward to stand beside Amy, watching the lively crowd. "I figured you'd be thrilled, being the biggest wedding lover of anyone I know."

"I don't know, Jae." Amy sighed. "I'm happy it's happening. It just feels a little anticlimactic, I guess."

"Ah, so perhaps you've joined the ranks of us who think marriage equality may not be all it's cracked up to be."

"What? You think this isn't a good thing?"

Jae shrugged. "Sure, for some people. But what about people who are polyamorous or aromantic or people who don't want to get married? Now if queer people want to be socially acceptable, they have to do as the straights do: be in a monogamous relationship and get married. It's a very sophisticated scam to yet again make us change ourselves to fit their standards."

Amy blanched. She understood the argument many people made that marriage equality was all about fitting queer people into a heterosexual word, but she didn't see the long, happy marriage that she'd wished for all her life as a way she could assimilate better with straight people.

"Sure, it will make some people happy, and I don't mean to shit on that." Jae paused for a moment, watching all of the happy couples kissing and laughing. "But all this talk about gay men and lesbians getting their happily ever afters doesn't mean anything for my life. You know what would? Laws that protect me from racist, transphobic hate crimes. Or laws that would have protected you, the best goddamn baker in Tulsa, from getting fired from Daily Bread."

"I know, Jae," Amy said softly. "But doesn't it feel like once gay marriage is allowed, it'll start to, I don't know, make being queer less taboo?" Amy looked from Jae to the rainbow-and-glitter-covered crowd. "Like, I know it doesn't mean I can't get fired for being gay or let you choose a gender that's not 'male' or 'female' on your driver's license. But what if gay marriage gets our foot in the door? It's a more fun topic than, say, laws that keep queer people from adopting, so it gets everyone's attention, and then as we start getting married . . ." Her voice trailed off. "Oh my God, I'm doing that 'proving we're just like them' argument I *hate*. I'm just trying to say, any step forward is still a step forward."

"Yeah." Jae tucked their hands into their faux-leather jacket pockets. "Just as long as we don't stop fighting, because we've got a long way to go."

"I think the problem is when people talk about it like it's the end of the road," Amy said. "But what if it's just the beginning? The source of disagreement comes from who and how we love and our right to live as our authentic selves, right? So if we can legally marry whoever we want, that means the government recognizes our love on an equal playing field. And if our love is equal, then firing us, or denying us the right to adopt, or kicking us out of the military, or whatever they think of next to keep us down . . . We are more empowered to fight back."

Jae paused for a moment, seeming to chew over Amy's point. "It's a starting place. The first step on a long road."

Amy nodded, then looked out at a cluster of people dancing and singing along to "Born This Way" blasting through a nearby set of speakers. Perhaps legalizing gay marriage was something like the way she'd described weddings to Olivia a few weeks ago—a photo op, a moment to celebrate, but just the beginning of the long road ahead. "Maybe still worth celebrating then," Amy said.

Jae eyed the crowd silently for another moment, then let forth a huge screaming cheer, one that carried over to the people surrounding them, eventually creating a tidal wave of cheers. Once the crowd had returned to its previous volume, Jae turned to Amy. "All right, I think I've celebrated then. Shall we go back to the bar?"

23

An early spring breeze blew through Amy's apartment as she sorted through her planner and email inbox on the couch, Truffle curled into a tight ball by her side. When she'd first created her Craigslist ad back in November, she'd had no idea how much interest it would garner. Four months later, she had eight weddings under her belt, and her schedule was packed. She'd figured out a workable payment schedule: half of the flat wedding fee up front, payment for extra events or time planning and decorating paid within a week, and the final check or money transfer at the wedding itself. Bridesmaiding was starting to feel very real instead of like a bizarre career she'd dreamed up out of desperation. And the reality would set in even more in a couple of weeks, as Max had set up a time to help Amy file taxes after he'd realized she thought a W-9 was a type of airplane. Just a few months ago, she'd been stressed about making rent, but now her bank account was more than healthy. She'd even been able to make a sizable dent in her mother's medical debt.

The rest of her life, though, wasn't looking as good as her finances. After seeing Joel from afar at the marriage equality rally, she'd sent what she thought was a pretty good apology text. Amy had said that she was sorry for taking her frustrations with Charley out on him, that she wanted to put it behind her and get their friendship back to normal. But after a long wait, Joel had sent an uncharacteristically cold response:

As Damian and I plan our wedding, we're seeking to limit negativity and focus on the joy in our relationship. I hope you understand and can give us some space.

The text was even more heartbreaking than Charley's breakup text. Amy worked so hard to always be positive and helpful, to make the day a little brighter for everyone she encountered. Joel and Damian were some of the only people around whom she'd felt like she could drop the act. Did that mean the true Amy was negative and draining to her loved ones? Well, it would certainly explain why Charley had wanted to end things as soon as Amy started to feel comfortable.

Although Amy had drafted dozens of possible responses to Charley's request to "pump the brakes," their text history was eternally frozen with Charley's New Year's Day messages. In her free time, Amy frequented the short list of places she'd once visited with Charley, hoping to run into her. She'd spent hours in January at Mornings by Brookside, where they'd bought breakfast sandwiches on their first date, often driving by the Golden Driller statue or the Center of the Universe on the way. But eventually, the nostalgia had become too hard to bear. Her longing to see Charley again had morphed instead into frustration and embarrassment. If Charley wanted to reconnect, wouldn't she be looking for Amy too? Wouldn't she have shown up at the bar? Or at least texted? By late March, Amy knew she had to find a way to move on. And she was trying do it the only way she knew how: by throwing herself even more into work.

After spending January with the bar understaffed thanks to Joel canceling shifts that overlapped with Amy's, she and Zee had convinced the owner of Ruby Red's to hire a new bartender: McKenzie. She'd grown on Amy a lot since that first visit to the bar as Autumn's date. And although McKenzie was still a little green, Amy was impressed by how quickly she caught on to working behind the bar. Adding McKenzie to the schedule helped Amy free up more time for bridesmaiding. She'd learned to be a little more discerning when saying yes to events after that whirlwind of a Saturday in December, but Amy still kept her planner packed. Keeping busy helped distract from the loneliness of having lost Charley, Joel, and Damian in one twenty-four-hour period.

Armed with an array of colored pens, Amy set to writing out her schedule for the coming month. If she had felt busy since January, things were only going to get more intense in the popular wedding months of April, May, and June. Blue for weddings, pink for showers, red for bachelorette parties. Next, she wrote the baking jobs in orange, crafting and decorating times in green, dress and registry shopping appointments in purple, and miscellaneous in black. Finally, she filled in her shifts at Ruby Red's in teal and sat back to admire her beautiful rainbow of a schedule. Each new bride was a roller-coaster ride of new tastes, insecurities, tricky families, and eccentricities. And each wedding had its own particular flare, with various religious traditions, friend group dynamics, venues, food, and music keeping Amy on her toes.

As different as every bride could be, there were some things about weddings that always ended up the same, even beyond things like the groom kissing the bride, the exchanging of rings, and toasts. There was always that collective breath from the room when the bride first stepped into sight, always a moment of awkward tension when the officiant asked for any objections (although Amy had yet to see an objection made, despite what movies would have her believe). And for some inexplicable reason, every DJ found a way to slip in the "Cha-Cha Slide." In fact, at her most recent reception, Amy had excused herself to the restroom as soon as she heard the opening beat to avoid having to "get funky" yet again.

With her calendar in order, Amy set to restocking her bridesmaid emergency bag with bandages, makeup wipes, safety pins, and double-sided tape, the items that most frequently came in handy. She'd seen her share of meltdowns, although she was loath to think of anyone as a bridezilla. Amy had always hated that term and the reality TV shows that propagated it. The more weddings she'd attended, the more she thought about how women spent their whole lives being told to be polite, to put others first, to never want anything for themselves. Amy had certainly internalized those lessons growing up. Although Teresa was refreshingly feminist compared to the rest of the Fariner family, she still honored a certain brand of southern femininity, the kind that said a woman should always overfeed houseguests and tuck her own feelings under a veneer of obsequiousness. She'd taught Amy how to make sure she never rubbed anyone the wrong way, to always smooth over conflict instead of contributing to it. Yet society told women that their wedding was the one and only day in their entire lives that was about them, that could be whatever they wanted, and then mocked them for being assertive for once. Which was it? Were brides supposed to be easygoing and carefree, or were they supposed to pile all their anxieties and desires into one day? How could any bride navigate the contradictions?

With her wedding emergency kit prepared, Amy carried her caketastrophe bag to the kitchen to refill the powdered sugar and check the levels on the most popular flavorings and food colorings. She hadn't yet had another close call like at Regi's wedding, but Amy often found herself approached about imperfections on the cakes that she was happy to repair. No matter what went wrong behind the scenes or how she felt about the couples themselves, Amy always felt that warm glow of wedding magic that kept her coming back for more. She'd learned to associate it with authenticity. The moments that sparked that wonderful feeling were the ones that broke through the traditional pomp and circumstance, the ones where you saw the real people behind the big white dress and sleek tux. Sometimes it was a hiccup in the script, a joke that referenced the couple's past, or even a shared look when they thought no one was watching. Sometimes it was the pride on a parent's face or an heirloom decoration that brought a sense of history to the moment. Every wedding so far had awakened that feeling in Amy, reminding her why she had started her business in the first place.

But inevitably, along with that moment of joy came a feeling of cognitive dissonance, a sense of unease at the role she was playing in an institution that explicitly excluded queer people. Unsurprisingly, Amy felt less duplicitous at secular weddings like Olivia's than she did at more conservative religious weddings like Corinne's. As the months wore on, though, it was growing harder and harder to reconcile her love and support for something that wasn't available to her and so many of the people she loved. To understand how something that was all about joy and hope could inspire hate and fear in so many of her fellow

Oklahomans. Maybe even some of the brides she'd stood beside on their big days.

Later that day, Amy swept into Teresa's house with her arms full of ingredients and baking tools. It had taken a while for Amy's baking services to take off alongside her bridesmaiding business. But missing the feeling of flour on her hands, she'd started giving out a free box of cupcakes to new clients, and the orders had started coming in. Then had come rave reviews that she added to her website, and suddenly, she was back in the baking business. Tiered wedding cakes, cupcakes and petits fours for showers, even naughty fortune cookies for a bachelorette party, had been added to her to-do list. And when big orders were placed, like the three-tier, flower-topped cake she was making today, she needed to call in reinforcements.

At first, Teresa had refused to take a cut of Amy's payment for the baked goods she helped make. But after one particularly grueling evening spent making two hundred frosted sugar cookies, Amy had put her foot down and insisted on paying Teresa for her time. It was certainly worth it to Amy, who needed Teresa's help as well as her slightly larger kitchen.

Once the three cakes were out of the oven and set on racks to cool, Teresa fanned them with a few paper plates to speed the process. Amy whipped the buttercream, then handed a spoon of the frosting to her mother. "Tell me if this needs more vanilla."

Teresa smacked her lips and considered. "Vanilla is good, but maybe a dash of almond extract would really make it pop."

"Almond! Yes, you're right." Amy grabbed the bottle from the pantry and added a dash. She switched on the stand mixer and then tasted again, nodding her approval. "Thanks again for your help today, Mom. I know you have a lot of exams to grade."

Teresa waved away the comment. "I'll get to them when I get to them. You know I always have time for baking with you. Where is this cake going?"

"A wedding tomorrow in Jenks. Floral themed. Floral bridesmaid dresses, floral invitations, flowers everywhere. The bride is spending twelve thousand dollars on flowers alone. Can you believe it? Twelve thousand dollars for a bunch of flowers that will die in a week." Amy blew a gust of air out of the corner of her mouth to shift the loose curls from her forehead. "That's why we're keeping the cake pretty simple. I'm going to cover the whole thing with edible flowers once I arrive at the venue."

"Probably could have saved money by getting married in a florist shop," Teresa said. "Any other cake orders in the next few weeks? I can make sure to block out some time in my calendar."

Amy twisted the bowl of frosting away from the stand mixer and moved it to the refrigerator. "Nothing too big. Some petits fours for a shower next weekend, frosted sugar cookies for an engagement party, and cake pops for a baby shower."

"A baby shower?"

"Well, some of the other bridesmaids I've met along the way have started ordering baked goods from me after tasting my stuff. Not exactly what I intended when I started all this, but if I can make money from baking without having to do the whole bridesmaid thing, I won't complain."

Teresa watched Amy bustle around the kitchen. "Getting tired of the bridesmaid gig?"

"Not tired of it exactly," Amy said, considering. "It's more like I feel weird. Like I'm lying. Like there's this beautiful day that's supposed to be full of meaning for everyone involved, and me being there, pretending to be a friend, cheapens the whole thing."

Teresa set down the paper plates she'd been using to fan the cakes and stepped to the kitchen sink to start on dishes. "Well, they wouldn't pay you if you weren't making their day better. You're providing a service they need, whether it's decorating, organizing, or emotional support. The brides want you to be there. Doesn't that make it authentic?"

Amy grabbed a dish towel. "I guess so, but it still feels wrong somehow. The pretending was fun at first, even if it was risky. And I was good at it! I mean, I'm still good at it. Maybe it's the hiding my gayness thing that feels weird. I know they're my clients, not my friends, and I don't have to tell them my whole personal history, but it just feels strange." She sighed. "Maybe I'm overthinking it."

"I don't think so, honey. I may not know what it's like to be gay or decide who to tell and how to tell them, but I certainly know what it's like to feel like you're not welcome because of your life choices. It's painful, and I can imagine why you'd try to avoid that feeling." Teresa handed Amy a freshly rinsed cake pan to dry. "You can keep whatever information private you want, if it makes you feel better."

"But that's the thing. I don't think it makes me feel better. It feels more like I'm ashamed, like I don't like who I am, and that's not the case." Amy placed the dried cake pan on the counter and accepted the next one from her mother. "Sometimes I worry that I'm falling into the same patterns I have since I realized I was gay, first with our family, then at Daily Bread—hiding myself to make other people more comfortable."

"Isn't that the point of being a professional bridesmaid? To make people more comfortable? To put the focus on the bride?" Teresa asked.

Amy bit her lip, focusing on drying rather than answering the question. She knew her mom was trying to help, but her comment just made Amy feel even worse. Had she really fallen into the same trap again?

After a moment, Teresa said, "You know, the baking is really taking off. Have you thought about opening your own shop?"

"I've thought about it," Amy said, drying another pan. "You know I love baking. But the money it takes to start a shop and the time . . . It's intimidating. And so much of bakery life is making the same things over and over again, the same bread and cookies every day. At least the wedding stuff never gets boring."

"The cakes and cupcakes and things you've been making for them?"

Amy paused, trying to remember what it was that made weddings so satisfying. "That plus the rest of it too. The decorating and event planning, the big buildup and the satisfaction of a great wedding wrapping up. Feeling like I'm helping someone have a positive experience with this event that's really important to them. Making it feel more about the couple than about stuffy traditions. Creating lifelong memories. There's a lot to love there."

Teresa rinsed out the sink. "You know what would probably bring you a lot of joy?"

"What?"

"Helping Joel and Damian plan their wedding and create lifelong memories."

Amy threw down the dish towel. "Mom, I don't want to talk about it."

Teresa turned off the water and turned to look at Amy. "That's what you keep saying about that Charley too. Seems like that's the problem. Maybe if you talked to Joel, you two could finally work things out."

"I tried! He doesn't want to talk to me!"

"It just feels wrong, y'all not talking to each other when you used to be attached at the hip. Maybe he'd have some insights on your business and being closeted too, since I'm out of my depth."

Amy scoffed. "He made it pretty clear he doesn't want to help me with my problems anymore."

Teresa dried her hands slowly. "So you're just gonna give up on your friendship? Because of one fight?"

Amy turned away, busying herself with setting up a frosting station. "I don't want to talk about Joel right now, Mom. I need to focus on this cake."

"Okay, honey, I'll let it go. But I just think you should consider talking to someone besides me about this stuff sometime. About being gay and your business and all that. Maybe Max and Greg? I know a lot, but I don't know everything," Teresa said gently.

Amy frowned at the frosting in front of her. "Thanks, Mom, but I'll figure it out. Can you pass me that spatula?"

24

April announced itself by turning the Oklahoma landscape a bright, fresh green. The change in scenery reminded Amy that Kim's wedding was less than two weeks away, and the related activities and stress were mounting. After surviving the wedding dress and bridesmaids' dress fittings (where Kim had not-so-subtly suggested all the bridesmaids go on a juice cleanse before the big day), Amy had also helped package four hundred wedding favors and served as a test subject for the wedding stylist while Kim debated what makeup look had the most "fairy-tale charm" for her wedding party. Amy was exhausted, but her bank account was thrilled.

The weekend before the wedding, Amy found herself again donning her ridiculous bachelorette party outfit, this time with an embellished belt and sparkly jewelry she'd added to her wardrobe since her first bachelorette party in December. At least now it wasn't quite so chilly to wear such a revealing dress. Still, she felt a pang as she checked her reflection in the mirror on her way out, reminded of preparing for and recovering from her first bachelorette party with Damian and Joel.

Upon arrival at Kim's house for the bachelorette party, Amy immediately located the person she was most excited to see: Regi, this time also a bridesmaid instead of a bride.

"It's so good to see you!" Amy said with genuine joy. In the past few months, she'd learned that Regi had inadvertently given her unrealistic expectations for how fun and low-stress her clients would be. But she wouldn't be where she was without Regi's original offer, which, Amy realized, felt like it had been more like five years ago than five months ago.

Regi wrapped Amy in a hug. "So excited to be on this side of a wedding together! I hope we'll actually get a chance to hang out tonight." Amy and Regi had exchanged brief pleasantries at Kim's bridal shower and bridesmaid dress fitting, but both events had been too tightly scheduled to properly catch up. Regi scanned the rest of the bridal party to make sure no one was listening and leaned in to whisper in Amy's ear. "And at least we're in the homestretch with the Iron Bride. I'm sorry I got you into all of this."

Amy smiled and waved away Regi's apology. "Hey, at least I'm getting paid for it."

Regi high-fived Amy. "Between being your first client, connecting you with Kim, and the testimonial I wrote for your website, I feel like I can take some credit for your success. Don't forget me when you're making headlines!"

"I'll never forget my first," Amy said, grinning.

The evening began with a limo ride to a shockingly expensive dinner at a fancy steak house, one Amy was grateful she didn't have to pay for thanks to her contract with Kim. Afterward, the group headed to a trendy speakeasy, something Amy found to be quite the contradiction. The bar was downtown, not far from the Center of the Universe, down a dark alleyway and behind an unmarked door with a mustachioed bouncer. The maid of honor dropped the password—scissortail—and they were admitted into the bar's swank, velvety interior. As Kim's bridesmaids went back to the bar for round after round, Amy noticed their carefully maintained decorum beginning to crack. Their friendly jabs at one another got less friendly and more jabby; their laughs transformed from carefully controlled titters to raucous shrieking. Kim was going all in and growing more and more vocal about her disappointment that the pricey cocktails weren't being comped by the bartenders, considering it was her special day. Even Regi's words were becoming more slurred, her eyes less focused.

As the evening grew later, Heather, the maid of honor, gathered the group for an announcement. "Ladies! Are you ready for the night to really get wild?"

Oh no, Amy thought. *That never means anything good.* She laughed along nervously as the other women whooped.

Heather tossed her platinum-blond teased hair and put a hand on her waist. "Next stop is all about being dirty and dancy and fabulous. We're going to Rampage!"

Amy's stomach dropped.

Heather lowered her voice to a conspiratorial whisper. "It's a *gay* club downtown," she said, pronouncing the word "gay" as if it were bad luck. "I went once with my bestie in college and it was nuts. You girls are going to love it!"

The other women giggled and chattered excitedly while Amy inwardly panicked. She'd known this might happen at one of the bachelorette parties, but why, *why,* did it have to be Kim's? The idea of Kim and her friends finding out Amy was gay made her queasy. The group gave off an ultraconservative vibe, and Amy was sure to run into at least one person she knew. She hadn't forgotten Kim's limp-wrist mockery about Jared's floral suit.

But even worse, she dreaded the thought of running into Joel and Damian. Since they weren't hanging out at Ruby Red's these days, Amy assumed they were spending more time at Rampage. If she ever hoped to repair things with Joel, she definitely couldn't show up at the gay club pretending to be straight with a group of rowdy bridesmaids. It would be yet another reminder that marriage in Oklahoma still wasn't for Damian and Joel and that she was still cashing in on it. Selfish. Negative. Everything Joel hated about her.

Amy had to say something. "Um, are we, like, allowed to go there? Isn't it for gay people?"

Heather waved a hand dismissively. "Duh, we can for sure go there. We're women! Gay guys love straight women! And I'm practically a gay man in a woman's body. I've said that forever. Haven't I, Kim?"

"Yeah. And gay people can come to straight bars, so straight people can go to gay bars too. Otherwise it's discrimination," Kim said with the air of someone reaching an unassailable conclusion. "Don't be nervous, Amy!"

Amy turned to look at Regi, who shrugged good-naturedly. "I've been to Rampage for a bachelorette party before. It's fine!"

Amy smiled weakly. They were just a group of friends looking for a fun night, she reminded herself. They weren't monsters. And they'd probably spend a fair amount at the bar and hopefully tip pretty well too. For a moment, she pictured a different path, one where she told them she was a lesbian and could, in fact, be their big gay tour guide. *We're about to start our journey to Rampage. Have one-dollar bills on hand to tip the drag performers. Keep your hands to yourself even if you think the gay men are hot. Make sure your barstools are in the upright position, and enjoy the ride!* But then she thought of the way her cousin Christina's face had turned so sour when she'd come out, the way their relationship had evaporated almost immediately. Losing Kim as a client wouldn't have the same element of heartbreak, but it certainly wouldn't be fun.

Resigned, Amy came up with a plan B: Get the women drunker. That way they would be less likely to notice if she knew patrons at Rampage, and she hoped they would end the night earlier if their booze-infused energy ran lower. It was the only way to keep her cover, which in turn would keep her highest paying client happy.

Amy arranged her face in an expression that she thought screamed "fun" and turned to the rest of the group. "Well, if we're going to dance, I think we need a round of shots!"

After waiting in line for fifteen minutes that felt like an hour, Amy and the rest of her party paid their seven-dollar cover fees to the stocky middle-aged lesbian bouncer at the door. Amy worried her cover might be blown by the woman, who had flirtingly waived Amy's cover charge on previous nights when she was in a good mood. The bouncer squinted at Amy's ID and back at her sparkly "KISS THE BRIDESMAID" sash before admitting her, raising an eyebrow but graciously not saying a word.

The club was packed with a sea of dancing bodies on the ground floor and even more people lining the balcony. Pulsing, moving lights bathed the crowd in bright colors. Alma Peeples, Tulsa's most iconic drag queen and former Miss Gay Oklahoma winner, lip-synced on the stage, and male go-go dancers bumped to the music on elevated platforms around the club. Television screens around the perimeter of the space displayed trippy, colorful images moving in time to the music. Amy wished the screens still showed gay porn, which had served to deter straight interlopers more than to actually titillate any of the queer customers and had unfortunately been phased out several years prior.

"See?" Heather said to the group triumphantly once they were all inside. "I told you! It's wild, right?"

As Heather led the group to the bar, Amy hung back, ducking behind one of the go-go dancer platforms to scope out the crowd. A scan of the dance floor didn't reveal Joel and Damian, although she saw plenty of familiar faces. She glanced up toward the DJ booth in the top right corner of the balcony and was relieved to see Jae wasn't controlling the music that night. But before she had a chance to look any further, Amy felt a tap on her shoulder and turned to find Heather.

"There you are! Thought you got lost," Heather said. Eyeing Amy's hunched position behind the tall platform, Heather moved closer, putting a reassuring arm around Amy's shoulders. "It's okay," Heather said. "I was nervous the first time I came here too, but you'll be fine. It's way less scary than a straight club, honestly."

That was something they could agree on. But Amy's skin prickled with shame at the fact that Heather thought she was hiding in a corner because she felt anxious about being around a bunch of queers. "I'm fine," she said.

"Here, do you want my vodka soda?" Heather asked.

Amy looked at her, knowing she was trying to be kind. "You know what? Sure," Amy said, even though she didn't feel like drinking. "Thanks."

Heather beamed, then pulled Amy onto the dance floor, where they joined the rest of the bridal party. Amy pointedly avoided eye contact with everyone else in the crowd. At least the erratic flashing lights were helpful in evading detection.

After dancing to a few songs—or watching the rest of the bridesmaids dance while trying to make herself invisible—Amy started to relax. There were definitely people here she recognized but not whom she knew well, and they were all too busy enjoying themselves to notice her. Seeing Kim's glass was empty, Amy handed off Heather's still full vodka soda and went to get herself something less spirited. It was the perfect excuse for a brief respite from the bachelorette group. Amy squeezed through the crowd back to the bar, where she was greeted by an old bartending friend.

"Hey, girl!" he said. "Wow, this is a new look for you."

"Long story," she yelled over the noise of the club. "I'm straight tonight if anyone asks."

The bartender laughed and filled her drink order. "Your secret is safe with me," he said, sliding over a glass of tonic water.

As she turned back toward the dance floor, the strobe lights lit up the balcony stairs, and she momentarily froze: Autumn was climbing her way up. Even though Amy had been bracing herself to see someone who might know her well enough to approach and blow her cover, she felt a flash of panic, spilling tonic all over her shaking hands. Recovering herself, Amy ducked into a shadowy corner to wait out of view until Autumn disappeared. She closed her eyes and took a deep breath. The tables were turned from the last time she'd felt this bone-deep dread at Rampage, back when she and Autumn were still dating. She'd caught Autumn making out with another woman on the dance floor and confronted her, causing a bit of a scene and almost getting all three of them kicked out by the same lesbian bouncer who'd let her in tonight. Although the stakes were lower this time, and Amy was the one at risk of getting called out instead of Autumn, it still gave her an ominous sense of déjà vu.

Luckily, Autumn didn't seem to notice Amy. And by the time Amy returned to the bachelorette party, the bridesmaids had gone from tipsy to drunk. Being a bartender for almost four years had given Amy a master's course in levels of inebriation, though, and it didn't seem like any of the bridesmaids had crossed the line into dangerous territory. Kim, on the other hand, was swaying in place, firmly on the other side of that line. Seeing that Kim had already emptied the vodka soda, Amy passed her tonic water to the bride, who didn't seem to notice the lack of alcohol.

Amy filled the next couple of hours with trips to the bar whenever anyone needed anything, wincing as Kim and the bridesmaids yelled out things like "Fierce!" and "Go girl!" during the drag performances. After Amy had plied Kim with a couple rounds of water, the bride seemed to have slid precariously back over to the "fun" side of drunk, although that still meant having to pull Kim away from trying to climb on a platform with a go-go dancer.

A little after midnight, Alma Peeples invited anyone celebrating a birthday, anniversary, or other special occasion to come onstage. Amy knew exactly where this was headed: some jokes at their expense, a dance-off, and a free shot. It's how drag shows always ended at Rampage. And she knew with a deeply ingrained sense of inevitability that Kim would go onstage and make a fool of herself. It had been written in the stars from the moment Heather said the word "Rampage" back at the speakeasy.

The other bridesmaids shoved Kim in the direction of the stage. She tottered up the steps to join three other audience participants: a tiny wisp of a guy celebrating his twenty-second birthday, a thirtysomething man Amy recognized from around town who had just gotten a new job, and another birthday celebrant whom Amy recognized as one of Zee's exes from several years before.

"Let me guess," Alma said before handing the microphone to Kim. "Becky the bride-to-be." The audience laughed.

"I'm Kim and I'm getting *married*!" Kim slurred into the microphone, following the announcement with a high-pitched "Wooo!"

The bridesmaids around Amy cheered, and Alma squinted in their direction. Amy tried to shake her curls in front of her face, as if they were a curtain she could close over her entire sash-adorned body.

"And that's your entourage," Alma said. "Hi, ladies!" The women screamed even louder. Amy accidentally caught the eye of someone she knew, not well but who came often enough to Ruby Red's that they'd recognize each other. He gave her a confused smile and raised a hand in greeting. She waved back, nodding toward the stage and rolling her eyes, and silently prayed the earth would open up and swallow her.

"Well, I hope you ladies are enjoying this little show we put on just for you," Alma said sarcastically. "Is this your first time here?" Kim nodded. "Is this your first drag show?" She nodded again. "Ladies, we have a virgin here! Kim the bachelorette, can you dance?" Kim raised her arms and gave an exaggerated wiggle of her hips and shoulders. "I'll take that as a no," Alma Peeples said as the audience snickered. "But you're gonna compete anyway! All right, you four, the DJ is going to turn on the music, and we're going to see which one of you can get the lowest. The winner gets twenty dollars off their bar tab, and the losers get to live with the shame for the rest of their lives. DJ, hit it!"

Amy, and probably everyone watching except the other members of Kim's bridal party, knew the tiny twenty-two-year-old was a shoo-in before the music even started. When the opening notes of "Talk Dirty" by Jason Derulo blasted through the speakers, he immediately began spinning and body rolling, while the guy with the new job shook his ass toward the crowd and Zee's ex leaned back and forth just enough to pass as dancing.

Kim, meanwhile, was doing some strange and embarrassing hair-flipping and shimmying combo that looked like a bad impression of Bob Fosse choreography. On its own it was a questionable tactic, but her inebriation made it even more uncomfortable to watch. The twenty-two-year-old dropped into the splits, causing the crowd to explode with cheers, and Kim's face lit up in a way that made it clear she thought the applause was for a move she'd just done that was akin to a "sexy" version of the chicken dance. Amy shook her head, wishing that she could look away but also unable to avert her gaze from the train wreck onstage.

Regi grabbed Amy's arm and leaned toward her. "I keep thinking it can't get worse," she shouted over the music, seemingly unable to stop giggling. "I'm going to get a few glasses of water. I think Kim could use a little sobering up after this. We all could. You want one?" Amy nodded and Regi disappeared in the direction of the bar.

"Well, wasn't that something?" Alma Peeples said, returning to the stage as the song ended. "All right, I know who I think the winner is, but this is a dragmocracy, so we'll have a vote from the people. Who thinks the birthday girl should win?" She gestured first to the lesbian, who had stuck to the back of the stage. The audience offered polite applause. "Okay, how about our businessman?" She held a hand toward the man with the new job, and slightly louder clapping followed. "What about Becky the bride?" She waved toward Kim. The bridesmaids cheered aggressively, but the rest of the audience offered only a small smattering of applause. Kim looked outraged but in an unfocused, drunk way that Amy couldn't help but find amusing. "And finally, our birthday boy!" The crowd went wild, and the dancer dropped into the splits again. "We have a winner! But don't worry. You all get shots for making fools of yourselves in front of all these judgmental bitches. Franklin, five shots please!"

The bartender brought a tray of violently green shots onstage. The drag queen and dance contestants threw them back before the contestants returned to the crowd. Predictably, the small dancer was rushed by fans, while the audience parted dramatically to avoid Kim. "I should have won," she slurred when she reached the bridal party. "It was rigged."

As the bridesmaids rushed to assure Kim that she had been amazing, Amy glanced up at the balcony, desperate to make sure Autumn hadn't been watching. The balcony was mostly in shadow, but Amy was relieved to see Autumn's back was to the lower level, leaning lightly against the railing. It was body language Amy recognized: Autumn's casual flirting pose. A wave of relief flooded through Amy, since she knew that meant Autumn wouldn't have spared a glance for the dance contest below.

From her position on the dance floor, Amy saw Autumn lift a hand, seeming to run her fingers through the hair of whatever poor girl was her target that day. Amy shivered, imagining not Autumn's touch but Charley's. Charley tucking one of Amy's curls behind her ears. Amy shook her head at herself and was about to turn back around when the target of Autumn's flirting leaned forward, coming into the light for the first time.

Amy felt her heart drop like a brick. This couldn't be right. She'd just been thinking of her, that was all. A trick of the club's moving shadows. But then the strobe lights illuminated the front of the balcony, and Amy saw that familiar lopsided grin that she herself had fallen in love with, that she would have known anywhere, that she'd hoped to see every day for the past three-plus months, that broke through any remaining denial that it *wasn't* Charley up there. In the exact instant, Kim knocked heavily against Amy, throwing her into a couple of people dancing behind her. She steadied herself, apologizing profusely to the angry strangers for spilling their drinks, then turned back to find Kim with a hand pressed over her mouth and her eyes scrunched in an expression Amy knew all too well from her job at Ruby Red's: Kim was about to throw up.

25

They made it to the bathroom just in time. Kim burst into the farthest stall, which was doorless and disgusting but still had a toilet that could serve as a vomit receptacle. Numbly, Amy pulled back Kim's blond hair as she retched, using a hair tie from her own wrist to secure it. The scene felt oddly intimate, especially considering Amy's general discomfort around Kim. But hiding in the bathroom felt pretty appealing right about then. "It's okay. Let it all out," Amy said distractedly, rubbing the bride's back.

As Kim gasped for breath between heaves, Amy's mind was racing. Charley was here. *With Autumn.* On this night of all nights, when Amy was with this ridiculous group, wearing this humiliating outfit. Amy's personal life had been in shambles for the past few months, but this had to be rock bottom. Here she was at the best gay club in Tulsa, where she should have been dancing with her friends and her hot engineer girlfriend, but instead she was chaperoning a vomit session for someone she actively hoped to never see again after the next weekend.

Amy tried to prop Kim up while reaching behind them for toilet paper to wipe Kim's face. She felt only the stiff cardboard underneath her fingers; the roll was empty. Of course. Amy heaved a deep sigh, momentarily closing her eyes in frustration. Every choice she'd made since New Year's Eve, or maybe even since she first met Charley at the bakery, felt like a step on the cursed path to this night. Why had Amy put so much energy into these brides she hardly knew instead of trying harder to repair her relationship with Joel and Damian and win back Charley?

Amy's thoughts were interrupted by a light knock on the side of the doorless stall. One of the bridesmaids must have followed them in. "Can you grab some paper towels?" Amy asked without turning around. Kim seemed to be done puking for the time being; she made to lay her head on the toilet seat, and Amy guided her away just in time. She heard the bridesmaid pull out a handful of paper towels from the dispenser as she settled Kim on the floor, which was probably equally dirty but felt less gross.

"Here you go," Amy heard from behind her, and she snapped around so quickly she almost tripped over Kim's legs. She knew that voice, and it wasn't one of the bridesmaids'. Steadying herself, she looked up to see Charley standing there, holding out a fistful of paper towels and wearing a button-down shirt that was just a touch too formal for a club. Amy felt a surge of affection for her.

"I thought I saw you come in here," Charley said. "Looks like you're still doing the whole bridesmaid thing, huh?"

Butterflies had optimistically taken flight in Amy's stomach when she saw Charley, but they seemed to evaporate at those words. Charley's tone wasn't cold, but perhaps worse, she sounded indifferent, like she was talking to someone she barely knew. "The whole 'bridesmaid thing' pays my rent, so yes," Amy said tersely, snatching the paper towels out of Charley's hand. "What are *you* doing here? On a date?"

Charley looked surprised. And maybe a little guilty. Kim groaned behind them, the stall divider creaking as she leaned against it. Charley rubbed the back of her neck. "Amy, can we talk for a second?"

Amy wished she could disappear through the bathroom mirror to anywhere else. She'd spent the past few months imagining a thousand versions of her reunion with Charley, and none of them had involved vomit, a disgusting bathroom, Amy wearing straight drag, or Autumn. Were Autumn and Charley actually on a date? The image of the two of them together seemed laughable. Could flirtatious, unreliable Autumn really be Charley's type? Hell, could clearheaded, straight-shooting Charley be Autumn's? Well, clearly Amy wasn't what either of them wanted, so what did it matter to her anyway? She turned away.

"I'm a little busy at the moment," she said, bending down to wipe Kim's face as an excuse to avoid Charley's gaze. If only Charley could have found her when she was in the middle of heroically solving a caketastrophe or looking flawless in full hair and makeup before one of the weddings. Well, maybe it didn't matter. Charley obviously didn't think Amy's job was valuable either way.

"Please," Charley said. Her voice had lost its neutral tone and become soft, pleading. Amy took a deep breath, then straightened up and gave Kim a once-over. Her eyes were closed, but she wasn't passed out. She actually looked a little better and just seemed to be catching her breath.

"Fine," Amy said. She stepped out of the stall and leaned back against the counter, her arms crossed. "What is it?"

Charley took in Amy's full outfit for the first time, including the bachelorette party sash, the beginnings of a grin lifting the corners of her mouth. "This isn't exactly how I expected to see you again."

"Seems like you didn't expect to see me again at all," Amy said coldly.

Charley's face fell. "Yeah, about that. I've been thinking about you a lot. About us, really."

Amy glanced toward Kim's stall and lowered her voice. "Can we not do this here? I'm with a client."

"She seems pretty distracted to me."

"Whether or not this looks like work to *you,* this is my job," Amy whispered furiously. "And I want to keep my personal life out of it."

Charley furrowed her eyebrows. "Are you not out to her?"

"Well, Charley," Amy spat out defensively, her voice rising despite herself, "if *you'd* been brutally fired for being outed at your last job, perhaps you'd *also* be a little careful about coming out when your livelihood is involved." She'd said it without thinking, forgetting she'd gone along with Charley's assumption that she'd quit, but what did it matter now, on what was shaping up to be the worst night of her life?

"What do you—Wait. Are you talking about Daily Bread?" Amy didn't respond, choosing instead to cross her arms even more tightly. "Holy shit. Why didn't you tell me?"

"Cool, dateable lesbians aren't closeted at their jobs, and getting fired isn't a great getting-to-know-you look," Amy said. "You'd be a little slow to trust people too if you'd been anonymously outed. But maybe if you'd stuck around instead of choosing to play the field, I would have told you." The severity in Amy's voice was unnatural for her, but it also felt kind of good.

She'd spent so long pining for Charley, she hadn't realized how angry she really was.

"When were you fired?" Charley asked.

Amy was thrown. That wasn't what she'd thought Charley would focus on. "The day before our first . . ." Amy couldn't quite bring herself to say the word "date." "The day before we had breakfast."

"Oh my God," Charley said. For some reason, she looked stricken, almost ill. "Amy, I think . . . there's something I have to tell you." She cleared her throat as Amy met her eyes. "I think it was me."

"You what?"

"The day after we first met, I dropped by Daily Bread to bring you those flowers, but you weren't there. So I asked the manager to give them to you for me."

Amy stared blankly at Charley's pained face. "What flowers?"

"The bouquet of dahlias and the note to say I was looking forward to our date. You didn't get them?"

Amy's stomach turned. So that was why she'd gotten fired. That was how Donna had found out. Amy felt irrationally angry. She knew it had been unintentional, but she also would never forget how she'd felt during that conversation with Donna. Humiliated. Ashamed. Dirty. So Charley had not only taken a chance at love away from Amy; she'd also taken Amy's job, her financial security, her path to a future where she'd finally have enough experience to open her own bakery. And for what? It had all been for nothing.

"I'm so sorry," Charley said in an impassioned voice, looking scared by the look on Amy's face. "I had no idea you weren't out."

A groan emanated from Kim's stall, shaking Amy from her tunnel of rage and reminding her of her surroundings. "I can't do this. Not here. Not now. *Especially* not with Autumn out there waiting for you."

"Autumn?" Charley said, which only incensed Amy further. On top of everything, Charley was going to pretend she didn't know what Amy was talking about?

"Please go away," Amy said, feeling angry tears filling her eyes. She turned to the towel dispenser on the wall, desperate to hide her face.

"Can we meet up to talk things through?" Charley asked from behind her. "Maybe tomorrow?"

Amy didn't say anything, just started pulling paper towels out of the metal dispenser one by one.

"I'm really, really sorry, Amy. Please, if we could just talk—"

The rest of her sentence was cut off as the bathroom door opened, letting in a burst of loud music.

Amy turned, a fistful of paper towels clutched in her hand, surprised that Charley had left in the middle of speaking, only to see that Charley was still in the exact same spot, and Regi had entered the bathroom balancing three glasses of water in her hands. "Here you are! Sorry, the line at the bar was super long, and then the girls said you'd gone in here . . ." Her voice trailed off as she looked between Amy and Charley, taking in the tension in the room. "I'll, um, give this to Kim."

"I'll help," Amy said pointedly, ignoring Charley as she stepped forward to take one of the water cups from Regi. She could see that Kim was still slumped against the wall, her eyes closed. Thankfully, it didn't seem like she'd absorbed a word of Amy and Charley's conversation. Amy hoped she was too drunk to remember either way. Regi paused, glancing at Charley, then passed Amy one of the cups of water on her way into Kim's stall. Amy downed her water, placed the empty glass on the counter, then, refusing to look at Charley for fear that she would burst into tears if they made eye contact, turned away to help rouse the bride. After a moment, another beat of club music sounded behind them as Charley opened the bathroom door and left.

Eventually, Regi and Amy got Kim to stand and finally leave the stall, her tiara askew and mascara smudged down her cheeks. Amy handed Kim a paper towel from the crumpled wad in her fist. "How're you feeling? Do you want to clean your face up a bit?"

Kim staggered to the mirror and groaned as she wiped the towel across her lips, further smearing her red lipstick. "I want to go home."

Regi caught Amy's eye behind Kim's back. "Don't worry, Kim," Regi said. "We'll get you home. I'll call a cab right now." She gestured to her phone and Amy nodded. After Regi stepped outside to make the call, Amy encouraged Kim to drink her glass of water and then draped Kim's arm over her shoulders to walk her out of the club.

As they staggered to the exit, the eyes of what felt like all of queer Tulsa following their walk of shame, Amy realized all the anger and sadness had left her. She just felt numb. Why was she doing all of this for a woman she hardly knew? Whom she would never spend time with in real life? Was Kim another Donna? Another person Amy felt some inexplicable desire to mollify?

"I can do the splits too, you know," Kim slurred, apropos of nothing.

"Of course you can," Amy said dully, then pulled Kim out of Rampage to find Regi and the cab.

26

Forty-five minutes later, Kim was safely tucked into her bed. Regi and Amy locked the door behind them and stared out at the empty street, breathing a shared sigh of relief.

"Are you hungry?" Regi asked.

"Starving," Amy said. "What are your thoughts on Whataburger?"

"Oh my God, yes. I would kill for a bacon burger right now."

Amy dug in her clutch for her car keys. "I can drive. I'm parked right over there."

"Are you sure you're okay to drive?" Regi asked.

"Oh yeah, I've been drinking decoy tonic waters. I only had the one drink at that first bar. And that was"—she looked at her watch—"four hours ago. Come on, let's get you that bacon burger."

A short drive later, Amy and Regi sat in an orange booth

with a tray full of fast food between them, framed by an array of dipping sauces.

Regi swallowed a bite of her burger and closed her eyes, tilting her head back in delight. "I am so glad I'm not dieting to fit in a wedding dress anymore. I've gained back all the weight I lost for the wedding and more, and I have no regrets about it."

"We deserve every one of these calories after surviving tonight. What a clusterfuck," Amy said, dipping a fry in spicy ketchup.

"If only Kim had gotten sick and passed out *before* embarrassing herself in front of a whole club," Regi said. "If I know her from her sorority days, though, she won't remember that performance at all."

Amy snorted. "I'm happy *someone* won't have it burned in their brain for the rest of time. What I wouldn't give to forget that image of Kim doing the weird chicken dance move."

"Or the look on the drag queen's face," Regi added, laughing. "The secondhand embarrassment was all over the place." She adjusted the wrapper around her burger. "So who was that woman in the bathroom?"

Amy took a nervous gulp of her Sprite. "Wow, didn't think you'd forget your friend Kim so quickly," she joked.

Regi laughed. "Come on, you know who I mean. Were you getting hit on at the gay club?" She raised her eyebrows suggestively.

"Not exactly." Amy bit off a corner of her grilled cheese to buy time. For a moment she considered playing it off as something other than what it was, coming up with some lie to divert Regi's attention. But she was beyond burned out. And besides, Amy liked Regi. After all they'd been through together, maybe it was finally time to tell her the truth. "We, um, had a thing a few months ago. But she wanted to take a break."

Amy watched realization dawn on Regi's face. This was the

worst part, the thing Amy dreaded most: seeing that look on someone's face right after she came out to them, the way they measured her against the person they'd thought she was. That look had been the end of her friendship with Christina. It had been the look on the faces of her colleagues at Daily Bread when she'd first walked in on the day she got fired, although she hadn't recognized it at the time. Embarrassed, Amy buried her face in her arms. "Ugh, this is awkward. I'm sorry."

Regi placed a hand on Amy's forearm. "Hey, don't apologize! I should apologize. I shouldn't have assumed you were straight. I'm a jerk."

"No, you're not. I should have told you earlier. I made it weird." Amy sat up and brushed her hair out of her face.

"I'm glad you told me," Regi said firmly. "It's totally fine that you're gay. You are gay, right? Or was it a one-time thing? Here I go again making assumptions. I have to confess that I haven't really had many people come out to me before, so I'm not really sure how this goes. But I support you! I think it's great that you're gay or bisexual or—"

"I'm gay," Amy said. Two little words. Now that they were out of her mouth, she felt lighter. "Hey, don't mention it to Kim, okay? It's probably easier if she doesn't know."

It was Regi's turn to look embarrassed. "Has she said anything to you? I'm so sorry if she has. She's a good person, really, but she's got some old-fashioned views. It's her parents' fault."

"No, it's fine. I didn't mean it like that."

"I was pretty skeptical when I met her too," Regi confessed. "When she was assigned as my big on bid day, I thought, *Really? The only Black pledge had to end up with the rich, conservative, probably racist white girl?* But she's turned out to be one of my most loyal friends. And I've been trying to get her to leave the prejudiced shit she was raised with behind. I really have. She's trying."

Amy nodded sympathetically. She had been wondering about how lovable Regi and grating Kim had ended up so close. "I'm glad. But it's not that I have a problem telling Kim. It's just easier this way."

Regi looked skeptical. "Amy, are you sure? You don't have to hide anything from Kim or her friends. I hate that you feel like you have to."

Amy shrugged. "It's just business, right? It's not personal."

Regi paused a moment to examine Amy's face, then said, "Sure. If that's what you want, I won't say anything." She reached for a fry. "So back to this woman in the bathroom. Tell me everything."

Amy gave Regi an abbreviated version of their relationship saga, ending with the humiliating "I love you" and breakup text. For the past three and a half months, she'd only really talked about Charley to her mom, Max, and Greg. Thanks to the fight with Joel, she'd brushed off gentle questions from Tala, Jae, Zee, and Arnelle, not wanting another friend to accuse her of making everything about herself. Spilling the details to someone her own age was refreshing. "Anyway, I was finally coming to terms with the fact that it was over for real, and then she shows up at Rampage out of nowhere, with my ex of all people, trying to talk again, and I don't think I can handle another ride on the Charley merry-go-round. I had to draw the line. I spent so much time and energy waiting around for her to make room for me in her schedule without showing her I was annoyed, trying not to text too much between dates, to look amazing without looking like I'd tried too hard, to be funny and charming and happy-go-lucky, to be the kind of girl she could see herself with, could love . . ." Amy's voice broke, and she cleared her throat. "Bottom line is, clearly I'm not what she wants."

Regi sipped the last of her Dr Pepper and shook the ice at the bottom of the cup. "Did you try just being you?"

"Oh my God, you sound like an after-school special," Amy said, groaning. "Besides, that's what I finally *did* do on New Year's Eve, and it seemed to be the final nail in the coffin."

"Okay, hear me out here." Regi placed her elbows on the table and leaned forward. "When Jared and I first met, it was fireworks from the very beginning. I knew he was the one, and I was willing to do whatever it took to be his 'one.' I was worried that being an art history nerd wasn't very desirable, so I tried all these different outfits and hobbies to figure out what would make him most interested. I creeped on his ex-girlfriends on social media to figure out what he liked or had stopped liking. I even got my belly button pierced. Huge mistake by the way. It got caught on my clothes all the time and hurt like a bitch."

Amy laughed. "Noted, no belly button piercing."

"Anyway, little did I know I was totally freaking Jared out. He couldn't figure out who I was, what I liked. It made it hard for him to really trust me and open up. And when I was putting on a show all the time, there was no honesty, no vulnerability, no real closeness. Then my birthday came around, and he got me this designer bag that was super expensive but also, like, not me at all. He could have spent that money buying something from a local artist or painting supplies or even on videogames, and I would have liked it way more. It spawned this fight where I finally realized that I couldn't expect him to *know* the real me if I wasn't *showing* him the real me."

Amy used a fry to trace swirls in the ketchup, picturing a montage of her most awkward and ill-advised moments with Charley: her first-date outfit anxiety, her need to be the perfect tour guide, her riffling through the sex toy box, the way she'd focused so much on finding Christmas gifts for Charley's family that she'd run out of time to buy any of her own, how she'd invited Charley to Ruby Red's only on nights she knew it would seem the most impressive and fun. What Regi said sounded good. But a mean little voice in Amy's head said, *What if the real you isn't worth knowing?*

"When did you feel like things were easiest with Charley?" Regi went on. "When you weren't analyzing what she wanted, or worried about how you looked, or trying to hide your flaws?"

Amy immediately pictured their New Year's kiss, when she'd felt so safe in Charley's arms in the middle of the bar she called home. She remembered how she'd felt having so many of her friends nearby, dreaming of a bright year ahead, a relationship meant to last. When she'd felt safe and wanted and connected enough to tell Charley she loved her.

"Well, last time I felt like that, Charley ghosted me," Amy said shortly. "I guess I showed her my true self, and she didn't like what she saw." Charley didn't like the real Amy. Neither did Joel and Damian, it seemed. Amy looked down at her tray, trying to will away the tears threatening to fall.

But then a few other images popped into Amy's head: the fun they'd had playing the questions game, Charley's gentle reminder that girly things were worth liking, the way Charley's face had looked when she bit into Amy's homemade pasta, the nights they'd spent together where Amy had been so caught up in feeling good that she'd forgotten about her stretch marks or what angle her body looked best at.

Regi put one of her hands on Amy's and gave it a squeeze. "Hey, all I know is what I saw tonight. That was not the face of someone who has moved on. Charley had lovestruck written all over her, mixed with a touch of heartbreak. In fact, knowing what I know now, you had some heartbreak on your face too." Regi slid the tray away from Amy, interrupting her ketchup doodling. "If you see her again, maybe just give your real self a try, okay?"

Amy thought of Regi and Jared's beautiful wedding day, how their love for each other had filled the whole room. How desperately Amy wanted a love like that when she saw it from the outside.

She wasn't sure how far Regi's advice would take her, but Amy still felt a little lighter from telling her the truth. Regi had been her first bridesmaiding client, and now she was Amy's first bride turned actual friend. "I'll think about it," Amy said.

27

Amy found herself in the exact right situation to do some thinking only a day later: kneeling in the grass, her hands covered in dirt, fresh air and sunshine melting away the chaos of the previous night. She'd promised Greg and Max that she would help them fill their new raised flowerbeds now that spring was finally upon them. Although she had considered canceling after Kim's bachelorette party went so wrong, Amy had known a little gardening would be good for her. She'd compromised by sleeping in a couple of hours but had still arrived by midmorning in a pair of Teresa's faded old overalls, ready to work.

Greg and Max were planting bulbs of lilies and crocuses by the front porch when she arrived. They pointed her to the small flower bed in the backyard and provided a diagram of their vision for the herb and vegetable seedlings they'd picked up from a nursery that morning. Amy spent a few minutes orienting herself, connecting the notes on the diagram to the wispy green leaves organized into tiny cubes of dirt. Her first project was a German heirloom tomato plant, which she placed right in the center of the plot before securing a wire tomato cage around it to provide support. Next were two pepper plants on either side of the tomato plant, jalapeño on the right and peperoncino on the left. Then she moved on to the row of herbs along the front of the vegetable garden: basil, mint, rosemary, parsley, and cilantro.

Everything Amy knew about gardening, which was admittedly not a lot, she'd learned from Max and Greg. Most of her and her mother's various rental homes through the years hadn't had much of a yard, and when one did, there were strict limitations on what they could do with it. But Max and Greg had lived in the same midtown bungalow Amy's whole life, and they took great pride in their yard. Amy had assisted with plenty of gardening projects over the years, like when Amy was in high school and Max had designed a rainbow flower bed that was truly breathtaking in full bloom or a few years later when Greg had decided to make their whole backyard as bee friendly as possible. On this day, the activity proved especially meditative. With her hands covered in dirt and her brow covered in sweat, she focused on the simple task of giving each seedling a place to thrive. With each herb, the frenzy of self-doubt in her brain grew a little quieter, making room for her to mull over the wisdom in Regi's words.

Amy leaned back to admire the completed vegetable garden just as Max came through the back door onto the porch, two glasses of lemonade in hand. He set them down on a small patio table, then shaded his eyes with one hand to examine the finished raised bed. "Wow, Amy! Looks great out here. Good time for a break?"

Wiping her hands on her dirty overalls, Amy rose from the grass and joined Max on the porch. She took a long chug of lemonade, not realizing what a toll the sun had taken on her until she'd reached the shade. "Where's Uncle Greg?"

"Ran to the nursery to get a new garden hose. Ours sprung a leak." Max leaned back into his chair, stretching his neck. "But I'm tired of talking about yard stuff. What's up with you? How's life? How's the job?"

At once, the whir of stress and regret seemed to wake up again in Amy's brain.

Max laughed, reading the expression on Amy's face. "That bad, huh?"

"I mean, objectively, the job is going well. I have more interested customers than I can take on." Amy paused, taking another long drink of lemonade. "I just . . . I don't know. How are you supposed to know what to do with your life? When you're on the right track?"

"Ah, the quarter-life crisis." Max sighed theatrically. "You couldn't pay me to go back to my midtwenties. Well, professionally, I mean. I would take my midtwenties body back in a heartbeat. But what has you questioning the career track?"

"You know how you and Uncle Greg have always taught me to be cautious in uncertain company? Well, there's nothing that feels more uncertain than being gay in a high-stakes religious context with near strangers. So none of my clients or their family and friends know I'm gay, and it just feels like, *Is this what I'm still doing?* Even when I'm running my own business? I don't know. It's just starting to feel like I have to either have a job I like or be myself. One or the other."

"Whoa, back up for a second," Max said. "Greg and I always told you playing it safe was about avoiding and escaping dangerous situations. It wasn't about living your life in the closet."

"I know," Amy said, blushing. "Sorry. I didn't mean to sound like I was blaming it on you." She shook her head. "I just . . . I never know if the brides I'm working for are gay friendly or not, so I feel like, to play it safe, I have to start out assuming they're another Donna Young. But even if I do come out, I still feel like I'm betraying the entire queer community even more by being out and still choosing to support something we're not allowed to have. I thought that court decision on gay marriage would make me feel better, but it all just feels like a disappointment now. Like, not only are same-sex couples not actually allowed to get married yet, but it's also"—Amy dug for the words Jae had used to describe it—"having to act like straight people to be socially acceptable. Get married, have babies, blah blah blah. I know it's a starting place for all the other LGBTQ rights we need, but it's kind of a shitty one."

"That's a bit harsh," Max said, leaning forward in his chair. "You're right that there's still a long way to go for equality, but that doesn't mean marriage rights are all about assimilation. It was HIV activists who created the momentum for this moment in history all the way back in the eighties. Marriage rights would have let same-sex partners visit their spouses in the hospital or have a say in their medical decisions." He cleared his throat, Amy suspected to hide the growing emotion in his voice. "And to be honest, it would still mean a lot to me and Greg. We had to grant each other power of attorney after a particularly scary few weeks in 1998 when I wasn't allowed to visit Greg at Saint Francis, but it still doesn't give us all the same rights as marriage."

Picturing Greg in dire condition and Max unable to do anything about it, Amy felt a sting of regret for implying marriage equality was meaningless. "I guess I hadn't thought about it that way."

"You're lucky you haven't had to," Max said, delivering what Amy knew was a much-needed truth bomb. "Marriage equality matters, *really* matters, to a lot of people, including yours truly. Even if it doesn't solve all of our problems."

Amy nodded, chastened, and Max softened.

"Let's get back to your career problem, though. You don't have to stay closeted just to make other people comfortable. But you don't have to come out or quit your job to make other people comfortable either."

There it was again, that idea of making others comfortable. Amy furrowed her brow.

"And, honey," Max continued, "whatever you decide, you're not betraying anyone just by trying to make a living by doing something you like. Think about all the gay wedding coordinators, photographers, dress designers, and florists out there. I've done hair for dozens of bridal parties over the years. If anyone told me I was betraying the entire queer community, I think you'd be first in line to tell them off."

"More like put a homemade pie in their face," Amy said. She'd been so focused on beating herself up, on doubting herself, that she'd never thought about it that way before.

"One with expired whipped cream," Max added with a smile before continuing. "Daily Bread *was* a safety issue, financially. But now you're your own boss. There's no one who can fire you for being gay but you."

"And my clients," Amy countered.

"Didn't you just say you have more potential clients than you can take? So what if you lose one homophobe?"

"What if they're all secretly homophobes, though?" Amy asked.

"The good news is the homophobes aren't usually as quiet or secretive about their beliefs as they wish we would be with our identities." Max shook an ice cube from his lemonade glass into his mouth and chewed it. "Speaking of weddings, how are Joel and Damian's plans coming along?"

Amy looked away from Max to the fence along the back of the yard, disappointed in her own answer. "I don't know."

"You don't know? You and Joel aren't still fighting, are you? I told Teresa that would blow over real quick and y'all would be back to normal."

Amy's eyes filled with tears. "I wish it was that easy, but I don't think Joel wants things to go back to normal."

"Oh, honey." Max wrapped an arm around Amy's shoulders. "A friendship like yours can survive a fight. I promise you. Have either of you tried apologizing?"

"I did, and he didn't accept it! He said . . ." Amy dug in her overall pockets for her phone, then scrolled to find her text thread with Joel. "He said while they're planning their wedding, they're 'seeking to limit negativity and focus on the joy' in their relationship. He asked for space."

"Well, that's not a 'fuck off forever,' is it? Pardon my French. But he just asked for a little time." Max squinted at Amy's phone screen. "Wait, is that your apology? 'I'm sorry I blew up at you. I was going through a lot that night. Can we put it behind us?' "

Amy said nothing, smearing dirt across her cheeks as she wiped away tears.

"Do you want my advice on this? My real advice?" Max asked, pulling his arm back from Amy's shoulders.

Amy sniffled and nodded.

Max clasped his hands together on the table in front of him. "I find that in most fights, both people are a little bit right and a little bit wrong. The truth lies somewhere in the middle. That sound familiar to you, if you step back from the situation a bit?"

Amy firmly believed that Joel shouldn't have said what he'd said to Charley. But she also knew that Joel's arguments held water; she'd recognized it from the sting she felt when she first heard them. "Yeah, I guess so."

"And you do want Joel back in your life, right? You don't want this to be the end?"

The image of Joel dancing with Damian at the marriage equality rally appeared in Amy's head. She'd wanted to celebrate with them so badly. "I want him back," Amy said, her voice breaking.

"Then you've got to actually apologize, own up to those bits you know you got wrong. Saying you're sorry you blew up at him and asking to put it behind you doesn't actually address the problem. You're just asking him to forget whatever it was each of you were mad about, and that's a recipe for a lot of resentment and maybe even another fight down the line." Max crossed his legs and leaned back in his chair. "A real apology requires you to put yourself in Joel's shoes first. What was he mad about during the fight? What were his takeaways? What still hurts for him? Hopefully that will help him see what he got wrong too, and y'all can find that truth in the middle."

Amy stared out at the newly planted vegetable garden, remembering Joel's points in the fight—how Amy was selfish, always putting her own relationship drama above whatever was going on in Joel's and Damian's lives, always measuring her own happiness up against theirs in a way that wasn't fair to any of them.

Max watched her for a moment, sipping his lemonade. "It's all right. You don't have to tell me. But you've got to tell Joel you get it and you'll try to fix it. And a thoughtful dramatic gesture never hurt anybody either."

"But what if it doesn't work? What if I show up on his doorstep with a big apology and he just refuses and breaks my heart again?" Amy asked, her stomach reeling at the thought.

"Well, that's a real possibility that you have to accept. But if you really want Joel back in your life, it seems worth the risk. Joel and Damian are going to get married sometime, maybe soon depending on what happens with that circuit court case, and you're gonna kick yourself for the rest of your life if you're not a part of it," Max said gently. "You and Joel and Damian remind me a whole lot of me and Greg and Teresa, and that friendship has saved my life more than once. You don't give that kind of friendship up without a fight."

At that moment, Greg came stumbling through the door, his arms full with a giant new hose, a strange clay pot with holes around the outside, and a tray of seedlings. "Hey, y'all, can I get a hand here? Saw this strawberry planter and couldn't resist."

Amy rose to lighten Greg's load, wiping the remaining tears from her face.

As Amy joined her uncles to complete their work on the front yard, she thought more about Max's advice. The image of Charley's tree tattoo came to mind—and what she'd said about the roots being just as large and complex as the branches visible above ground. Maybe the fight with Joel was a big storm that had torn down some of the branches of their friendship. But the roots were still there. If she wanted to regrow what they'd lost, she needed to tend to the roots first.

"Another round?" Amy asked Jae and Tala after she finished unloading a case of beer bottles at Ruby Red's later that night.

"Please," Tala said.

"Sure thing." Amy handed their dirty glasses off to McKenzie, who was still learning to operate the high-powered commercial dishwasher.

"Hey, help us solve an argument," Jae said while Amy poured rum into two glasses over ice. "What gender is Yoshi?"

"Like, Nintendo Yoshi?"

Tala nodded.

"I guess I haven't thought much about it. But Yoshi doesn't

strike me as buying into the gender binary," Amy said, filling the glasses with Coke from the soda gun.

"Thank you!" Jae yelled. "Yoshi is gender nonconforming. I told you."

Tala rolled her eyes dramatically. "Look, I'm all for destroying the gender binary, but there are male pronouns in the game text."

"But did anyone ask Yoshi what their pronouns are? No," Jae said, pounding their fist on the bar.

Jae and Tala continued to bicker as the door opened, letting in a burst of fresh spring air. Amy looked up to see a new customer entering Ruby Red's, someone she didn't recognize and who looked suspiciously young. They walked with a too-slow gait that suggested an artificial sense of ease, and as hard as they tried to hide their surprise at the excessive *Wizard of Oz* decorations, they were betrayed by widened eyes. It had to be either their first time at Ruby Red's or their first time trying out a fake ID. Maybe both.

When the customer approached the bar, Amy smiled. "Hey there. What can I get for you?"

As the customer pulled their hat off, Amy examined the round, nervous-looking face hidden underneath chunky framed glasses. They looked vaguely familiar. Regardless, they were almost definitely still a teen. The newcomer's eyes cut to the chalkboard of specials over Amy's shoulder.

"A beer, please?" they said, as if asking for permission. *Ah, to be eighteen and sneaking into bars again.*

"Can I see some ID?" Amy asked.

"Sure, yeah," the teen murmured, producing a driver's license from their wallet. Amy looked at the picture on the ID—a midthirties woman with a blond bowl cut and no glasses—and then back up at the person in front of her. Long brown hair pulled into a ponytail, no makeup, a plaid fleece over a pair of overly large jeans. The classic look of a young queer trying to fit in at their first LGBTQ bar. And they were here alone. Amy's heart went out to them. Even if the customer wasn't underage, they were brave. Clearly, being there was important to them.

Amy gestured at the license. "It says here you're thirty-seven. Is that right?" The teenager nodded.

Amy looked at the license again. "What are your pronouns"—she squinted to read the card—"Helga?"

"March twenty-sixth, 1977," they said automatically, then froze, realizing their mistake. "I mean, she/her." The customer smiled nervously, revealing perfectly straight teeth and the line of a retainer running across the bottom of her mouth.

Suddenly Amy realized why she recognized this young woman. Hiding her surprise, Amy pocketed the fake driver's license. "Come with me."

The blood drained from the girl's face. "Hey, I don't want any trouble. I'll leave. I'm sorry."

"I'm not going to bust you," Amy said. "I just want to chat. Hey, McKenzie, can you cover the bar for a few? I'm taking a break." McKenzie nodded eagerly. She was still technically in training and not prepared to run the bar on her own, but business was slow. Jae and Tala were the only customers that evening besides a couple of people playing pool. McKenzie could handle things for a few minutes. Hell, Jae and Tala were around enough that they could probably run the bar themselves.

Reluctantly, the would-be customer followed Amy out the back door. Once outside, Amy sat down at one of the tables and gestured for the girl to take the seat across from her, which she did, looking apprehensive.

The teen spoke first. "Are you going to call the police?" she said. "Please don't. I'm begging you. My parents will kill me." She looked like she was about to cry.

"Yeah, I know. That's exactly why I'm *not* going to call the police," Amy said.

"What do you mean?" she said, taken aback.

"Is your name Gracie?" Amy asked.

The young woman stood in one quick movement, her cheeks turning an impressive shade of red. "How do you know my name?"

"I used to work for your mom," Amy said. "She has pictures of you all over Daily Bread."

"Are you going to tell her?" Gracie said, her voice frantic. "You can't! I'll do anything. Maybe that's not even who I am. You can't prove it."

"I'm not going to tell her," Amy said. "Please, have a seat. I just want to talk."

Gracie remained standing. She looked like she was considering whether or not to make a run for it.

"The first time I went to a lesbian bar was right after I came out to my cousin, when I was sixteen," Amy said. "It went horribly, coming out to her. So I drove all the way to Dallas by myself because I was scared of getting caught underage at a gay bar anywhere near here. I spent the entire day picking out my outfit. I got this fake ID from some friend of a friend and drove four hours just to be around people like me."

Gracie was quiet, listening.

"Even after all that planning, once I got there, I sat in my car for forty-five minutes before I worked up the courage to go inside." Amy saw a flash of recognition in Gracie's eyes and smiled at her, continuing. "As soon as I walked in, I panicked. It was packed and loud, everyone seemed to know everyone, and I felt completely out of place. I walked straight to the back and locked myself in the bathroom. Then when someone started banging on the door, I left and drove back home." Amy chuckled. "It was not exactly the glamorous experience I'd imagined."

A small smile played at the corner of Gracie's lips. "I've never been to a gay bar before tonight," she confessed.

"Well, you found a good one," Amy said. "But unfortunately, you'll have to wait a few more years before you can come in. It's not that I don't want you here. I know it took courage to come inside. But serving a minor is a misdemeanor. I could be fined or even go to jail for serving you."

Gracie looked at her feet. "I just didn't know where else to go."

Amy understood all too well. "Well, hang on," Amy said. "What are you, sixteen?"

"Eighteen," Gracie grumbled. She sat down in the chair across from Amy. "Wait. You worked at Daily Bread? For my *mom*? Are you not . . . Are you straight?"

"Definitely gay," Amy said. "When your mom found out I was gay, she fired me."

"Oh shit, you're Amelia."

Her eyebrows rose in surprise. "Amy. Amelia was my straight alter ego. Your mom told you about me?"

"Sort of. My mom came home one day towards the end of last year and was grilling me about if I knew an employee named Amelia, what I said to you, and making me swear I would never talk to you. I had no clue why she was bugging out. Now it all makes sense. She must have had some gay conspiracy theory in her head."

After months blocking it out, Amy tried to think back to her conversation with Donna. What had Amy said? Something about how gay people were everywhere? Donna must have thought Amy knew about Gracie.

"Wait, you came out to Donna Young?" Amy asked, incredulous. "You *are* brave. I can't imagine that went over well."

Gracie pulled a box of cigarettes from her pocket. "Definitely not the first time. She made me pray about it every day and even took me to this conversion camp in Norman a couple years ago. Want a smoke?"

"No thanks. Those things will kill you, you know," Amy warned.

"Yeah, yeah," Gracie said, lighting the cigarette. Once the flame caught, she continued. "Anyway, she brought me to this camp. I was supposed to be there for two weeks, but after one day, I called some friends in Oklahoma City, and they helped me bust out. I went home at the end of the two weeks and pretended it worked and I was straight or whatever to get her and my dad off my back. Then I spent the next year and a half working my ass off to graduate high school early so I could leave home and start college the minute I turned eighteen."

Gracie kicked up her legs to rest her boots on the edge of the table. She took a drag and tried to disguise a cough. "Anyway, my birthday was last month, but I started at TU for the spring semester a little early, and once I got my parents to sign off on the enrollment paperwork, I came out to them again. Told them I'd always been gay, always will be gay, and they could take me or leave me, then packed my shit and left before they could answer."

"How are things now?"

Gracie exhaled a cloud of smoke, which Amy attempted to wave away. "It's okay, I guess. Mom says they're working through it. They're not rushing off to join PFLAG or anything, but I think they got the point that they're not changing me."

Amy sighed. "I'm sorry you had to go through all of that, Gracie. But good for you for standing up to your parents. That takes some real nerve."

Gracie shifted her enormous boots and sucked on the end of her cigarette. But underneath her stylish glasses, Amy could see a little pain in Gracie's eyes. "Thanks."

"So you thought you could get away with coming into my bar with that incredibly fake ID?" Amy asked.

Gracie stared off toward a streetlight on the next block. "I guess it was pretty dumb, huh? I didn't want to get you in trouble. I just wanted to be somewhere that felt . . . right."

Amy's heart hurt for the girl in front of her. She remembered being eighteen, starting college in Oklahoma, self-conscious and lonely, still trying to recover from losing most of her friends and family after coming out. At least she'd had the support of Teresa and the queer wisdom of Max and Greg. And then she'd met Joel, who became one of the most important people in her young adult life, who hopefully would be forever if she could nail the apology. Amy couldn't imagine having to come out to a mom like Donna Young, then being left with no one on her side. "I went to TU too, and I know it has an LGBTQ student group. Have you been to any of their meetings?"

Gracie shook her head as she ashed her cigarette. "Isn't it just a bunch of weird kids waving rainbow flags and singing 'Kumbaya'?"

Amy laughed. "Number one, definitely not. I made some of my best friends there. Number two, even if it was, waving rainbow flags is pretty fun. You should give it a try. Have you checked out Oklahomans for Equality?"

Gracie shook her head again, although Amy noticed that she looked interested.

"They have a center downtown, and they have a lot of great events for meeting people, plus special events for LGBTQ youth and young adults. They also offer free counseling." Gracie grimaced, and Amy held up a hand. "Hey, don't make that face about counseling. It did a lot for me in college. Sometimes you need to talk to someone who isn't going to judge you. Just keep it in mind."

"Fine," Gracie said.

Amy eyed Gracie's tough exterior, still picturing the photo of the girl with braces and a softball uniform that hung next to the Daily Bread time clock. "And if you're looking to dance and have a night out legally, Fridays at Rampage are eighteen and up. It's a lot of fun and a great place to get to know queer Tulsa. But don't go near there with that fake ID, and don't try to sneak a drink. The lesbian bouncer there may look small, but she will literally throw you across her shoulders, carry you outside, and never let you in again."

Gracie nodded firmly. "Noted."

Her day with Max and Greg still fresh in her mind, Amy knew the importance of having queer elders on your side. She held out a hand. "Give me your phone."

Gracie hesitated but then placed her phone in Amy's palm.

Amy poked at the screen for a minute before handing it back. "There. I put my number in. Call me if you need anything or if you just need to talk to someone. But I don't want to see you back here until you're twenty-one. Do you hear me? I am not going to jail for serving you beer."

Gracie laughed, a giggle that gave Amy a glimpse of the young girl Gracie had so recently been. She stood and slipped her hands into the pockets of her jeans. "Thanks, Amy. For everything."

Amy stood as well and placed a hand on Gracie's shoulder. "Sure thing. See you around."

As Gracie loped off around the side of the building, Amy yelled, "And quit smoking! No girls will want to kiss you when you taste like an ashtray!" Gracie flipped Amy the middle finger, then pulled the box of cigarettes from her pocket and threw it in the bar's dumpster before disappearing from view.

After returning to the dingy comfort of Ruby Red's, Amy

picked her work behind the bar back up. "How'd it go bartending on your own for the first time, Kenz?"

McKenzie laughed. "Oh, my first ten minutes were everything I always dreamed of. I served one beer. Please, hold your applause."

"I knew you were destined for greatness," Amy said, patting McKenzie on the back.

"Hey," McKenzie said as she wiped down the bar. "Who was that girl you were talking to?"

"Oh, a friend of a friend."

"Do you think you could give her my number?" McKenzie asked.

Amy let out a surprised laugh. "She's eighteen!"

McKenzie considered this for a moment. "I'm twenty-one. Is three years apart weird?"

It was hard for Amy to imagine flirting with a teenager, but McKenzie had a point. Three years wasn't that much, all things considered. Amy shrugged. "I'll see what I can do. But only if you hire me when the two of you start planning your wedding. Don't worry. I offer a discount if I played matchmaker."

28

When Amy walked into the church to prepare for Kim's wedding the following Saturday, her first impression was that it looked ready for an actual royal wedding, fitting for the "fairy-tale magic" theme. The church, already stunningly ornate, was stuffed with fresh flowers, decorative centerpieces, and draped fabric. Countless caterers, photographers, event coordinators, musicians, and decorators were swarming through the building, all decked in tuxedos. The pews were adorned with new cushions fitting Kim's color scheme (navy and gold with hints of blush), and technicians were hanging colored lights to give the space a more fairy-tale feel. It was a little much for Amy's taste, but as she headed back to the makeshift bridal lounge in the back of the church, she reminded herself that what was important was whether or not the wedding fit Kim's style.

The problem was, Amy didn't really understand Kim's

style beyond that it was expensive. Amy had nothing against a fairy-tale wedding. Hell, she'd obviously bought into the wedding fairy-tale narrative herself, or she wouldn't have ended up a bridesmaid for hire in the first place. But behind the blooming flowers, lush fabrics, and dramatic lighting, the event seemed to lack something. Personality, heart, soul—Amy couldn't quite put her finger on it, but whatever was missing left her feeling cold and disconnected from the wedding. Determined to meet the challenge ahead of her, Amy decided on her mission for the day: look for the unique, endearing love underneath it all.

With so many hands on deck, Amy was needed solely in the bridal lounge rather than in setup. And although she was relieved that the event could run smoothly without her pulling everything together at the last minute like at some of her other weddings, she secretly wished she had a task that would take her out of the dressing room. At least the other times she had been a bridesmaid she had felt like she was earning her pay, but now she was just sitting around with the other presumably unpaid bridesmaids. Why had Kim hired her if not to get things done? What was the point of coming up with an elaborate lie about how they'd met taking golf classes together and became lifelong friends just to have Amy sit around on her hands? In early meetings, Kim had told Amy she was impressed by her ability to handle emergencies at Regi's wedding and wanted Amy to do the same for her own special day. But with so many hired professionals, surely the best of the best from what Amy knew of Kim, Amy couldn't fathom how she could possibly make herself helpful.

Based on the dress shopping, bridal showers, and rehearsal dinner she'd already completed with the bride, Amy thought the best way to support Kim was to pay attention to her, laugh at her jokes, ask her if she needed anything, and try to keep a high-energy, positive attitude going in the room. Even when the chatter was totally inane or revolved around people Amy had never met, she did her best to stay engaged and echo the attitudes of the other bridesmaids. Luckily, Regi was nearby for a shared eye roll when needed. But after coming out to Regi the weekend before, Amy felt like the charade she was putting on was harder to perform. She'd crossed the line from hired bridesmaid to real friend with Regi, and the contrast with her relationship with Kim made the whole thing taste a little sour.

Once a stylist applied a thick coat of makeup and straightened Amy's naturally curly hair into gentle waves, she hardly recognized herself. Looking around, she realized that under Kim's careful direction, all of the bridesmaids had been made to look as identical as possible in their strapless navy chiffon designer dresses and elbow-length silk gloves. Truthfully, the costume effect of the clothes, makeup, and hair made it easier for her to play the role of Kim's friend and bridesmaid. Easier to forget her complicated feelings about Kim and her polite brand of homophobia. Easier to survive this weird, stressful, painfully straight day. An image of Alma Peeples in her outrageous drag outfits filled Amy's head. The dress, hair, and makeup she'd donned for Kim's wedding felt just as much like a costume of glamorous femininity to her, although Alma wore hers to stand out, while Amy hoped hers would help her disappear.

After Amy had been locked away in the bridal lounge for what felt like days, Kim's wedding planner knocked on the door with a ten-minute warning. Amy stretched her legs before putting on her gold heels and picking up a bouquet of calla lilies. Then she followed Kim and the other bridesmaids into the hallway outside of the chapel. Kim and the wedding planner had made the five bridesmaids practice walking down the aisle eight times the day before, critiquing their speed, posture, and stride until each woman perfected the walk. Even the angle at which

Kim would turn once she reached her position at the altar had been meticulously planned. As the bridal party proceeded down the aisle one by one and began to line up, Amy had to admit that all the practice resulted in a unique effect, something akin to a carefully choreographed dance. If perfection was what Kim wanted, she'd achieved it.

Finally, the audience of five hundred rose as one with a whoosh and turned toward the church's entrance. The enormous wooden doors parted to reveal Kim wearing a beautiful enormous ball gown that stretched so wide it was unclear if it would fit down the aisle. She looked beautiful but also slightly reminiscent of a giant marshmallow. Atop her head sat a sparkling crown to complete the princess look. She took the arm of her father (with some difficulty due to how far away he had to stand to avoid trampling the dress) and began her walk down the aisle. The audience watched with bated breath to see if she could make it to the altar without her dress getting stuck on the end of a pew or stepped on by her father.

Once Kim reached the priest and her soon-to-be husband, Gary, at the end of the aisle, Amy settled in for a long, uncomfortable stand. This was her first Catholic wedding, and she'd learned from the rehearsal that it wouldn't be quick. She was conscious of the hundreds of eyes and multiple cameras aimed toward her and tried her best to look appropriately enthralled and misty-eyed.

From her position behind Kim, Amy had a clear view of Gary. The groom was wearing a black tuxedo along with a lush royal-blue cape and a silver crown atop his head. The sense of whimsy in that outfit brought a genuine smile to Amy's face. She didn't know much about him, even after attending so many of Kim's prewedding events, and she'd assumed he was a little boring. Yet Gary's face beamed with pure joy and affection as he gazed at Kim in her dreamy white gown. It warmed Amy to him. She realized that part of the reason she didn't know much about Gary was that she hadn't asked; she felt ashamed now to think of how many assumptions she'd made about who he was based on what she knew about Kim. And for that matter, how many assumptions she'd made about Kim. Maybe Gary was the missing puzzle piece to understanding Kim. If only Amy could see Kim's face instead of the back of her head, maybe she'd see that same enamored look mirrored back to her groom.

Through the opening hymn and reading after reading, Amy focused on Gary's face, trying to imagine an equally adoring look on Kim's in an effort to conjure up that magical wedding feeling. A call-and-response singing of psalms, with hundreds of voices raised to support the bride and groom, almost got Amy there. The echoing of the songs in the beautifully decorated church raised goosebumps along her arms. *See?* She could be moved even by Kim's wedding if she really tried.

A second priest appeared at the front of the altar and cleared his throat into the microphone. "I've had the pleasure of guiding Gary and Kim through wedding preparation sessions over the last few months."

Perfect, Amy thought, standing even straighter. *Exactly the personal moment I need to get into this. Come on, wedding magic. Hit me.*

"And I must say," the priest continued, "in these uncertain times when marriage is under attack, it has been a true joy to advise this couple that truly honors and respects the sacrament of marriage as God intended. Please rise for the reading of the Gospel."

Five hundred guests shuffled to their feet as fire arose in Amy's chest. She looked toward the pews, hoping to see someone equally outraged by the priest's coded language. But she didn't find anyone. Instead, she saw Kim's father looking proud enough to bust out of his suit jacket and her mother wiping away happy tears with a lace handkerchief. The language that felt so hateful to Amy hadn't caused anyone else to bat an eye. She breathed out quietly, reminding herself she was in the homestretch.

The priest's voice drew Amy's attention back toward the altar. "Jesus said: 'From the beginning of creation, God made them male and female. For this reason a man shall leave his father and mother and be joined to his wife, and the two shall become one flesh.'"

She tried to keep her expression controlled while the priest droned on, citing other Bible verses she knew were some of religious conservatives' favorite backups for their "defense" of marriage. Why was this necessary? Why did he have to denigrate queer love to celebrate Gary and Kim? This whole wedding, the lush decorations, the fancy clothes, the hair and makeup, the extravagant food she knew was to come—wasn't it enough without stomping on the gays along the way? Joel and Damian's love was the most pure and wonderful thing Amy had ever witnessed. It deserved just as formal and expensive a celebration if that was what they wanted. Joel's voice during their fight suddenly filled Amy's head. *"We already have to listen to you talk about weddings all the time, and you never ask if it's a painful topic for us, who really, really want to get married, are actually* ready *to get married, and can't."*

Joel's words and the priest's voice crashed into each other in Amy's brain, and she wished desperately that she were anywhere else. It was too much to process, especially standing in front of hundreds of strangers. The ceremony kept moving forward, Gary and Kim reciting their vows and the priest blessing their rings, but Amy felt like she was watching it from a mile away, her heart pounding in her ears. She was so focused on trying to control an eye twitch that she missed her cue to return down the aisle, throwing off the carefully coordinated bridal party exit for just a moment before she rushed to catch up.

Back in the bridal lounge ten minutes later, where the bridal party was meant to freshen up for pictures after the long ceremony, Kim burst in, frantic, cursing and wrestling wildly with her enormous dress. "This can't be happening," Kim said. "I was literally just walking down the hallway to get here, and the whole thing fell apart!" Amy could see that a seam along the back had torn, leaving a hole between the bodice and the skirt. "We'll be taking pictures any minute. If Gary sees me like this . . . I've worked so hard to make everything perfect, and this stupid fucking piece-of-shit dress is going to ruin my wedding."

"Kim, we're in a church!" one of the bridesmaids squeaked.

The bride continued her rant as Amy massaged her forehead, wishing this wedding would end. She'd barely survived that ceremony, and *now,* when she was in no mood to be the gentle, optimistic, supportive bridesmaid she sold herself as, she got the kind of wedding emergency she'd actually wished for earlier. Kim had gone from tearful "I do" to "everything is ruined" in seconds. This was where Amy thrived. She needed to pull herself together and do her thing.

After a deep breath, Amy put a steadying hand on Kim's shoulder. "Kim, everything was flawless. You look beautiful, and Gary couldn't take his eyes off you. We can patch this tear in no time. I have a sewing kit in my bag."

Kim turned on Amy with a snarl. "I'm not letting you take a needle and thread to my thirty-thousand-dollar Marchesa gown. This isn't some sort of DIY mess."

Regi and Amy exchanged looks as the rest of the bridesmaids seemed to back away slowly.

"Calm down, it's an easy fix—" Amy began, starting to lose patience, but Kim cut her off.

"Don't tell me to 'calm down.' I've been planning this day for my entire life. There's no way you could possibly understand. I've invested more in this day than you'll make in a lifetime. You should feel lucky just to be here."

The room went silent. Even Kim stopped talking, seeming to realize she'd gone too far and avoiding Amy's eyes by continuing to fuss with her dress. But it was too late. The anger and hurt Amy had suppressed during the ceremony seemed to flood her entire body. She heard a roaring in her ears, and her chest felt like it was about to explode.

"Kim's just upset," Regi jumped in hurriedly. "She didn't mean—"

"No, I think she did," Amy snapped, all of her rage rising to the surface. And not just anger at Kim and the priest, but also at Joel for being right, so right, about this whole bridesmaid thing; at pop culture for making her think weddings were magic instead of institutionalized misogyny and homophobia; at Donna for having that smug look on her face while firing her; at Daily Bread and her extended family and Oklahoma and the Catholic Church and everyone who had ever made her feel like she had to hide her love while straight people could throw extravagant public parties to celebrate theirs.

Kim had stopped fussing with the dress, eyes wide.

"And you know what?" Amy went on. "You're right. I *don't* understand. I don't understand what it's like to plan for your wedding your entire life and then actually be able to see that dream come true, because it's illegal for me to get married." She threw her bouquet of calla lilies on the floor. "I don't understand why I stood up there smiling through a ceremony that argued that my love is less than yours." She kicked her designer heels across the room, one crashing into a chair. "I don't understand what it's like to spend more money on one day than I'll 'make in a lifetime.'" She pulled off her silk gloves and flung them toward the bride's feet. "And I don't understand why I'm bending over backwards to act like a perfect straight bridesmaid for some stuck-up, spoiled bride who has everything anyone could ever possibly want and still can't be happy."

As soon as she stopped talking, Amy regretted her outburst. The bridesmaids and Kim all stared at her in stunned silence. Amy had felt a release at first, but now she only felt sick. Not because she'd come out or because she'd likely lost the remaining balance on Kim's bill but because she'd let herself be cruel. Kim's face had crumpled in anguish at Amy's final words; that last bit had really gotten to her. This wasn't who Amy was.

But then a worse thought came to her: Maybe this *was* who she was. The kind of person who'd hurt her best friend and possibly lost him forever. Who was too scared to give another chance to a person she was in love with. Who'd scream at a bride who, Amy knew, was just afraid, afraid that if she wasn't perfect, she wouldn't be worthy of love. If anyone could relate to that, it was Amy.

Amy walked across the room to her bridesmaid emergency bag, all of the bridesmaids' eyes trained on her. It felt like an odd re-creation of the moment when she'd walked out of Donna's office and her former co-workers had watched in silence as she left the bakery for the last time. But this time, once she'd rummaged through her bag, Amy walked back toward Kim, holding out her sewing kit as a kind of olive branch. If she was going to have to go on an apology tour after all of this, she might as well start now. "I'm sorry, Kim," she said, glad to find all the malice had left her tone. "That was over the line. It's pretty clear we're not cut out to be friends, and I'm planning to leave as soon as I get this dress off. But take this so someone can fix your dress. There are clamps and pins you can use if you don't want anyone to sew the rip, but they won't be as sturdy for the whole reception. And you deserve to have a good time tonight without worrying about the hole in your dress."

Kim stared down at the sewing kit between them without speaking. Amy mentally prepared herself to be slapped. She'd certainly deserve it.

Finally, Kim's eyes rose to meet Amy's. "You know how to sew?"

Amy nodded. "I took two years of theater costume craft in college. I made the wedding gown for our production of *The Sound of Music* by myself."

"Could you . . . Would you sew the rip before you leave? Please?" Kim said in a subdued voice that Amy hardly recognized.

Amy felt the last vestiges of anger fade away as she looked at the bride, who she knew was offering her own kind of olive branch in return. "Absolutely."

29

The day after Kim's wedding, Amy woke up with a plan. She had been mulling over a proper apology to Joel since her heart-to-heart with Uncle Max the previous weekend and hadn't yet found the right words. But the way she'd behaved at Kim's wedding, exploding at everyone around her when she was really angry at herself for straying so far from the person she wanted to be, made one thing abundantly clear: It was high time for Amy to patch things up with her best friend.

Luckily, Amy knew exactly where she'd be able to find Joel. It was a Sunday, and since their fight, Joel only worked at Ruby Red's on the weekends, when Amy was usually tied up with bridesmaid responsibilities. So that afternoon, a couple of hours before the bar opened, Amy let herself in and got to work bringing her plan to life.

Two hours later, when Joel unlocked and opened the front

door, Amy set off a perfectly timed confetti explosion and yelled, "*Surpise! I'm sorry! I love you!*"

Amy took a deep breath, readying herself to launch into her speech, which she'd nervously practiced all morning in the hopes she could get it all out without Joel telling her to fuck off and never talk to him again. But before she could begin, Joel burst out laughing, pointing at the bar's new decorations. A string of glittery letters spelled out "AMY IS SORRY" along the right wall in the same place where she'd hung the "CONGRATS, DAMIAN AND JOEL" banner the night of their engagement party. Rainbow streamers lined the walls and bar, along with a few clusters of balloons.

Joel walked past Amy to look closer at the walls. She had covered them with photos of her and Joel throughout their friendship: baby-faced college freshmen on the quad, high-fiving in matching graduation robes, their first photo with Damian at the Tulsa State Fair, their first shift together behind the bar at Ruby Red's, even a candid photo of them that past New Year's Eve.

As Joel turned back toward her, his eye was caught by the showstopper, which Amy had placed on the bar: a three-tier chocolate and peanut butter cake, a smaller replica of the strawberry champagne engagement party cake but with "I'm sorry" written in chocolate instead of the two rings.

Finally catching his breath, Joel quickly closed the gap between them and grabbed Amy in a big hug. "Oh, babe, I've missed you."

Amy was thrown but also relieved by Joel's warm greeting. "But don't you want to hear my apology speech?" she said, her voice muffled by Joel's chest.

"Not as much as I want to stuff that whole cake in my mouth." Joel released Amy from the hug and moved to inspect the cake.

"Oh. I guess I was expecting you to still be pretty mad at me."

Joel swiped a finger through the chocolate ganache and licked it. "I was. And it was easy to stay mad when all you'd done to apologize was send a lackluster text. But I can't resist a grand gesture."

Amy made a mental note to thank Max for that suggestion. "Well, can I give you the speech anyway? Or at least hit the highlights? I think it's kind of important to, you know, address some of the stuff I messed up."

"I should get the bar ready for opening first," Joel said, glancing at his watch.

"Oh, I already did everything for opening," Amy said. "We just need to turn on the sign in twenty minutes. But cake is a great idea." Amy cut a generous slice and handed it to Joel before settling down in an old ripped booth across from him.

After a deep breath, she began. "I've spent a lot of time thinking about our fight on New Year's Day and a lot more since that—how did you put it?—'lackluster' text. And you're right, it was totally lackluster. I want to do a better job of taking responsibility for what happened between us, and I want to make some promises to change from here on out. I'm really, really sorry for blaming you in any way for what went down with Charley. That's not what was really at the heart of our fight, but it's where it started, so that's where I want to start. Charley called it off because of me, because I was moving so fast and trying to make our relationship into something it wasn't. I had my head so full of weddings and engagements and romance that I was trying to force our relationship into the fast lane instead of just letting it happen in its own time. That's entirely on me."

Joel swallowed a bite of cake, listening.

"And part of why I was trying to rush things with Charley, and why I freaked out on you and started the whole fight, is because . . . yeah, I was jealous. You and Damian have this amazing, supportive, beautiful relationship. And whenever I've been frustrated with my own love life in the past, it's been easy to use your relationship as a measuring stick. But that's not fair to you. I can be happy for you and Damian without feeling sad for myself. I *am* happy for you and Damian. Watching your love develop has been amazing, and I was more excited about y'all getting engaged than I've been about pretty much anything else since my mom beat cancer. So I promise from here on out to be happy for you without making it about my own stuff. And I hope that you'll always call me out if I fail you in that way again."

Amy paused, and Joel put down his fork. "Is that it?"

Amy shook her head. She wanted to make sure the roots of their friendship were fully repaired. "The whole bridesmaid business has taught me a lot about myself and my priorities. Mostly how wrong my priorities have been. I've spent too much time trying to hide who I am and bending over backwards to be whoever these total strangers want me to be and then unloading all of my stress on you and Damian. It's not fair to you. I want to be myself, my real self, the one who takes care of her friends instead of strangers, the one who is positive and fun instead of a negative ball of stress, the one who fights for marriage equality instead of blathering on and on about straight weddings without thinking about how that makes you feel. I like myself the most when I'm hanging out at Ruby Red's with you and Damian and the whole crew. So I promise to work hard on being that Amy instead of bridesmaid Amy. And I've already made steps to keep that promise by"—Amy cleared her throat and looked down at her lap, trying to remind herself that this was the right choice—"by shutting down my website and taking down my ads. I'll finish up the weddings I've already signed contracts for, but then my bridesmaid business will be over."

"Wait, what?" Joel said, his eyebrows approaching his hairline.

"It's for the best. I had a bit of an epiphany at a particularly stressful wedding yesterday. At least for right now, I can't seem to figure out how to be my true optimistic gay self while I'm pretending to be the bride's straight cousin or sorority sister and listening to priests spout homophobia while I bat my eyelashes and cash a check."

Joel wiped the crumbs from his mouth and pushed away his plate. "Is *that* the end of the speech?"

"Um, pretty much," Amy said.

"All right then, my turn." *His* turn? Amy tensed, preparing herself to be hit with whatever airing of grievances Joel had written. If it meant they could be best friends again, she would sit through anything.

Joel pulled his wallet out of his back pocket and dug through it for a wrinkled piece of paper. "I didn't know you were coming, and I didn't have a chance to memorize it, but a draft version will have to do."

He unfolded the paper and licked his lips. "I've been thinking a lot about our fight since New Year's Day and a lot more since your text." He looked up at Amy with a grin. "Of course we haven't talked in months and we still start our apologies the same way." Returning to his notes, Joel continued. "I told you then that Damian and I were trying to cut out negativity as we plan our wedding. But the truth is we haven't been able to plan a single thing, because planning a wedding, or even picking a date, felt so wrong without having you there with us."

Joel had hardly begun, but Amy's heart was already soaring. It wasn't too late!

"I know you were in a bad place when we fought, and I wasn't the friend you needed in that moment. You only hurt me because you were hurting, and I should have seen that at the time. I called you selfish, but I was the one being selfish. I wanted to celebrate the good things in my life instead of acknowledging the hard things in yours. But look at how much celebration and happiness and excitement I've lost out on now by cutting you out of my life! You love me and Damian more than anyone else I know, and having your support and your friendship now is so much more important to me than some stupid fight."

As she had so often in the past months, Amy felt tears filling her eyes, but this time they were tears of joy and gratitude for Joel's love and forgiveness.

Joel paused, refolding the paper in his hands. "Well, that's as far as I got, so I guess I'll wing it from here. I accept your apology, but you weren't the only person who was off base that day. I'm really sorry I called you selfish. I'm sorry I blew you off when you texted me. And I'm sorry for what I said to Charley that night. You were right. It wasn't my place. And I love you and I'm so fucking tired of fighting. Can we be done now?"

"Yes, please." Amy moved from across the booth to sit next to Joel, who wrapped her in another hug. "Let's never fight again."

"Well, I have one more bone to pick," Joel said, leaning back but leaving one arm around Amy's shoulders. "You can't just give up the whole business you built after one bad day. You've worked so hard to build it, and you're so good at it! I know it's been rough on you, but you love parts of it, don't you?"

Amy felt an enormous sense of relief to hear Joel defend her work, something she thought had only served to tear them apart. "But do I really love what I do, or do I just love making people happy? Am I letting people-pleasing change who I am?"

"I think there's a difference between people-pleasing and enjoying being good at something," Joel said. "You're *good* at all the wedding stuff, the baking, the event coordinating, the crafting. And it makes sense that you'd enjoy being good at it. That doesn't change who you are."

"That's fair. But I can't do all that stuff without also pretending to be someone I'm not. How can I be my true gay self within the big conservative Oklahoma wedding machine?" Amy pinched off a bite of Joel's cake.

"Well, back when I was wondering if it was worth proposing to Damian when I can't legally marry him, a very wise best friend told me, 'What better way to stick it to the homophobes than being loudly and openly in love?' So what better way to stick it to the homophobes than to bring your whole queer self to help other people celebrate being loudly and openly in love?"

"I don't know if it's really that easy," Amy said skeptically.

"Well, you've got a big job ahead of you with my wedding, and you better bring every ounce of the fun, thoughtful, talented, gay-as-hell Amy I know and love," Joel said.

"Of course I will, babe. But that's just one wedding. How do I bring that same energy to my other clients who didn't sign up for all of this?" Amy said, gesturing to the rainbow-and-unicorn pattern on her short-sleeved button-down shirt.

Joel smiled fondly at the shirt, one he'd given Amy for her birthday a couple years prior. "Anybody who doesn't respect you doesn't deserve your help throwing a kick-ass wedding." He grabbed Amy's hand on the table. "We'll figure it out together, okay?"

Joel was interrupted by a knock on the door and a muffled voice yelling, "Joel! Open up. It's ten past four!"

Amy jumped to her feet, realizing they'd lost track of time. After flipping the switch to illuminate the "R.R." sign outside, she unlocked the front door and swung it open to find a sweaty postworkout Damian.

"Amy? I thought Joel was on the schedule," Damian said, looking at first excited to see Amy but then chastened as he remembered his side of the fight.

"He is. We finally made up," Amy said, watching nervously for Damian's response. Luckily, she didn't have to wait long, as his relief was immediate.

"Thank God! Did he give you the speech? He's been working on it for weeks, and I kept begging him to just apologize already." Damian stepped into the bar and froze, looking at the decorations. "Wait, I didn't know this was part of his plan."

"Oh, that part was me," Amy said, gesturing toward the "AMY IS SORRY" banner.

"Dames! Our apology speeches literally had the same opening sentences!" Joel said, joining Amy and Damian at the entrance.

"So the fight is over? Things are back to how they were before?" Damian asked.

"Better than before, I'd say," Joel said, looping his arm through Amy's.

"Oh, that's amazing!" Damian said.

Amy knew there was one more thing she needed to do. She swallowed, gathered her words, and looked directly into Damian's eyes. "I owe you an apology too."

Damian shook his head. "That's not necessary. I was just a bystander, really."

"No, it is necessary," Amy said. "I've been struggling to figure out how to be my authentic self at work, and it poisoned my time with you and Joel. From now on, I'm going to try to find more balance in my life so I can be the friend you deserve. I'm thrilled that you're getting married, and I really, really want to be a part of your wedding, if you'll have me."

"Of course we will!" Damian said with a smile that could light up the whole dingy bar. "I would hug you if I hadn't just come from a cardio class. I smell awful."

"Who cares!" Amy said, wrapping both Joel and Damian in their first group hug in far too long.

When Amy moved to take down her apology decorations, starting with the photos, before any other customers showed up for the evening, Joel stopped her.

"Love deserves to be celebrated, right? Even best friend love," Joel said. "I say we make tonight a friendship celebration."

Joel logged on to Ruby Red's Facebook account and posted an event for that evening: Joel and Amy's Friendship Night. It might have been a weird announcement for any other bar in town, but all of Ruby Red's regulars already knew that something had gone down between the two bartenders. And the customers' enthusiasm to celebrate Amy and Joel's reunion was apparent, as the Facebook post was flooded with likes and comments, and familiar faces soon arrived at the bar to join the party. With Amy and Joel slinging drinks together again, the bar finally felt like it did before: like a quirky, grungy, queer, wonderful home. And as the *Wizard of Oz* doormat was quick to remind anyone who passed through Ruby Red's door, there's no place like home.

30

With the heaviest wedding months of May and June still ahead, Amy had a schedule full of clients to carry her through summer, and she would follow through on her commitments. But after her conversation with Joel, she knew it was time she took a look at her business with fresh eyes.

A week later, Amy set aside Monday for what Damian and Joel had lovingly dubbed Makeover Montage Day. That morning, music blasting and Truffle purring next to her, she officially updated her website (calling Damian every so often for tech help) to offer event-planning services instead of professional bridesmaid services, knowing that posing as a close friend of her clients was holding her back from the authenticity she craved. And even though she knew it might mean losing some potential business, she redesigned the website to specifically market to LGBTQ clients, highlighting queer commitment ceremonies and anniversary parties on her list of specialties. She spent the rest of the day researching potential venues in Tulsa for Joel and Damian's wedding, along with a list of destination wedding options where same-sex marriage was already legal, while a marathon of her favorite rom-coms played on the TV in the background. Amy would happily talk them through a long list of options, but she secretly had her heart set on Hawaii.

Although Amy knew she still had a lot left to do to pivot her business, over the next few days, she was overjoyed to hear from a couple potential customers who were thrilled to have found a queer business to support. She even heard from a pair of fifteen-year-old twins who wanted to throw a coming-out party for their father.

By the next week, her revamped business already felt like it was becoming a reality. She was happy to spend all day that Tuesday filling a variety of orders for baked goods: petits fours for a new mother-in-law gift, cinnamon buns for a bridal shower brunch, and an order for two dozen strawberry champagne cupcakes for an anniversary celebration. With Tegan and Sara playing in the background and her favorite rainbow apron tied around her waist, Amy got to work.

As she prepared to frost the cupcakes, Amy dialed her mother, turned on speakerphone, and placed her cell on the counter. She couldn't wait any longer to tell her about the change in direction of her bridesmaiding business.

"Hello?" her mother said breathlessly, picking up after a couple of rings.

"Hey, Mom," Amy said as she filled a piping bag with frosting. "I'm making strawberry champagne cupcakes and thinking of you. And guess what? Now that Joel and Damian and I are all back on good terms, they're going to help me revamp my business!"

"That's wonderful, sweetie!" her mom said.

Amy could hear music, clinking dishes, and people talking in the background. "Sorry, did I catch you at a bad time?"

"No!" her mom said. "Well, kind of. I'm just at lunch with . . . someone."

Not once in Amy's life had she heard her mother say the word "someone" in a way that sounded so loaded. Amy could almost feel her mom blushing through the phone.

"Wait," Amy said, frosting threatening to spill from the piping bag as she squeezed it in her sudden mixture of disbelief and excitement. "Are you on a *date*?"

"Well, I guess you could call it a date. I mean—"

Teresa was cut off by a jolly laugh in the background—a laugh Amy recognized immediately from a certain winter wonderland wedding.

"Mom," Amy said, her eyes wide. "Is that Dr. Douglas? Mom, are you on a date with *Dr. Douglas*?"

"Maybe," her mom said. Amy could hear the smile in her mother's voice and couldn't keep one from spreading across her face too. "Anyway, Joel and Damian! Your business! Tell me everything!" She heard her mom say something muffled to Dr. Douglas about stepping away.

"Hang on, Mom," Amy said. "I definitely want to tell you everything—and hear everything from you, by the way—but right now, enjoy your date."

"Are you sure?" her mom asked.

"Yes," Amy said firmly. "We'll talk tomorrow. I love you, Mom."

"I love you too."

Amy hung up, trying not to smear her phone with frosting. She set down the piping bag, her brain turning as she absorbed this new development. Dr. Douglas had always seemed more of a grandfatherly type to Amy, with his white beard and merry demeanor. He'd also been a widower as long as Amy had known him. He was certainly older than Teresa, but Teresa was no spring chicken either. And so what if there was an age gap? From what Amy knew of him, Dr. Douglas was kind, funny, and reliable. If they wanted to make it work, it would work, Amy thought—then put her head in her hands. Those were Charley's words. Words, Amy found, that she still believed. She thought again of Charley's face before she'd left the bathroom at Rampage, what Regi had described as the face of someone who hadn't yet let go.

Amy shook her head to clear it, letting the remembered picture of Charley fade. The idea of her mother and Dr. Douglas together might take a little getting used to. But as long as her mom was happy, Amy was on board. Also, she reminded herself, for all she knew, it was their first date. It was certainly too soon to start planning her mom's wedding based solely on conjecture. For now, Amy had a batch of cupcakes to finish.

Half an hour later, Amy loaded the three orders into her car. She took a moment to pat the hood of the old Corolla, which finally seemed to be reliably roadworthy, and considered all the things she could do with her rare free evening: Look at marketing opportunities for her party-planning business? Drop in on one of Damian's group exercise classes? Watch a rom-com on the couch, maybe with Joel? What a relief it was to have hanging out with Joel as an option again.

The first two drop-offs were both southeast of Amy's apartment in Tulsa's largest suburb, Broken Arrow. The drive took Amy directly past Daily Bread. She'd stopped taking alternate routes to avoid going east of Ruby Red's on Cherry Street sometime after the New Year, when the fight with Joel and parting with Charley had become distracting enough to take the sting off seeing the bakery full of customers. But with a car full of baked goods ordered from her website, Amy felt a sense of freedom that was totally new as she cruised past Daily Bread. She'd once thought she couldn't be a baker without that job, but she'd proved Donna—and herself—wrong. After off-loading the cinnamon buns and petits fours, Amy headed back toward the city center with the cupcakes, driving against rush hour traffic of nine-to-fivers heading home for the day.

As Amy pulled off the Broken Arrow Expressway and into downtown, she turned on the radio. "The Story" was playing—the exact same song she and Charley had belted out together on their way to their date at the Philbrook. At first, Amy's jaw tensed, but as the ride went on, the smell of freshly baked cupcakes filling her nose, the late spring breeze ruffling her hair, she began to feel lighter. She'd figured out a way to be out and, she hoped, financially secure at the same time, to be fully herself in her personal and professional life, and she was well on the path to making it happen. *I'm brave,* Amy realized. Brave enough to keep putting herself out there after Donna Young had fired her, even brave enough to offer kindness and support to Donna's daughter. Brave enough to start a business and to reshape it when it was no longer healthy for her. Brave enough to confront her estranged best friend and make amends. Maybe she was brave enough to reach out to Charley too. Or maybe she'd be brave enough sometime soon.

Amy parked on East Archer Street, feeling more like herself than she had in months. It felt so right that one of her first deliveries under the auspices of her revamped business was for an anniversary. Despite all of the conflicted feelings she'd worked through about weddings, she was still a romantic at heart. And finally, she didn't feel ashamed about it. There was nothing weak about loving love. *Brave,* Amy reminded herself.

Amy pulled the cupcake boxes out of the back seat, realizing she was still wearing her favorite rainbow apron. The Amy of a few months earlier would have torn the apron off in panic, but that day she smoothed it out and held her head high. Once she reached the corner of Boston and East Archer, she balanced the boxes on one hand and checked her phone. She was a few minutes early. The wind was picking up, and her apron blew straight up into her face. When she finally succeeded in pulling it down without dropping or shifting the cupcakes, she looked up to see someone crossing the street toward her, a bouquet of pink flowers in hand. Not just any someone. Someone with short wavy hair that begged Amy to run her fingers through it. Someone with hazel eyes and dark, thick eyelashes that made Amy weak at the knees. Someone wearing a perfectly tailored navy suit that Amy had once seen carefully folded on a chair in her own bedroom. Someone with a relaxed gait and crooked grin whom Amy hadn't been expecting to see, but God, she'd wanted to see her so badly.

"Charley," Amy breathed.

Charley reached the corner, stopping a few feet in front of Amy. She cleared her throat and smiled nervously. "I, um, was hoping we might have that talk."

Amy's pulse quickened as she felt a thrill and terror at once. *Brave.* "I'd love to talk," she said. "I just have to drop off this order first."

Charley took the cupcakes from Amy's arms with a smile. "Consider them delivered."

"But I . . . Wait. You ordered two dozen cupcakes just so you could talk to me?"

A blush rose to Charley's cheeks. "Well, I never got to taste that strawberry champagne cake you made."

"And you needed twenty-four cupcakes to taste it?" Amy asked.

"Well, one dozen didn't seem like enough to justify an order, and three dozen was definitely too much. Have you considered selling half dozens? Eighteen cupcakes would have been perfect." Charley grinned. "Not that I gave it a lot of thought."

"Oh, the champagne in the cake mostly bakes out, but there is a touch in the frosting. Sorry, I didn't know they were—"

"For me? Don't worry about it. I'm excited to try them." Charley shifted the cupcake boxes in her arms and handed Amy the bouquet. "And these are for you. I wanted to get you dahlias to replace the ones you never received at Daily Bread, but apparently they're out of season, so peonies will have to do."

Amy buried her nose in the explosion of pink petals and breathed their sweet fragrance. "Peonies are my favorite."

"Do you mind if we take a walk? There are some benches over there where we can sit down." Charley nodded toward the pedestrian bridge a block away that Amy recognized immediately as home to the Center of the Universe.

As they began walking, Amy looked down at her outfit: a wrinkled apron so covered in flour and powdered sugar that you could hardly see the rainbow pattern underneath, over ripped jeans and an old Ruby Red's T-shirt. Her hair was in a frizzy, curly knot on top of her head, and her face was makeup-free. Next to Charley in her impeccable suit, Amy felt like quite the ragamuffin. She tried to brush off her apron with her free hand, releasing a cloud of sugar. "Sorry, I'm a mess."

Charley stopped and grabbed hold of Amy's wrist, balancing the cupcake boxes in one arm. "You're the most beautiful person I've ever seen, and no amount of flour will change that for me." She ran her hand down Amy's cheek. "Besides, the first time I met you, you looked a lot like this, and I fell for you hard."

Amy flushed with pleasure before biting her lip. "I wish we

could go back to that first day and try again. Before everything got so messed up."

"Me too," Charley said as they resumed their walk.

This was a great start for an open and honest conversation, right? Since Kim's bachelorette party, Amy had been obsessing over what she might say to Charley when given the opportunity. But now that the opportunity was in front of her, Amy couldn't find any of the words she'd planned. She wished she'd had the same amount of time and energy to prepare her apology as she'd spent on Joel's. At least she'd spent some time reflecting on her own regrets. As they crossed the street, she said, "I, uh, want to apologize for that night at Rampage."

"Apologize?" Charley said, sounding surprised. "Why?"

"I wasn't myself that night. I wasn't being honest with myself, or with you," Amy said. Once she'd started talking, the words came easier. "But I'm trying this new true-to-myself-honesty thing where I'm going to be up front about my feelings. And the truth is that I was hurt that you disappeared on New Year's Eve. I really liked you. Actually, present tense like. I really like you now, and that scares me. And when I didn't hear from you for weeks, I thought it meant there was something wrong with me. So when I saw you at Rampage on a date with my ex, it brought up a lot of that insecurity. And I'm sorry—"

"On a date? With your ex? Are we talking about the same night?" Charley said, almost dropping a cupcake box as she turned to Amy.

Amy adjusted the cupcakes atop Charley's arms. "Autumn?"

"Autumn is your ex?" Charley said, looking stunned. "I had no idea. No wonder you were so upset when I tried to talk to you. I met Autumn while I was there to watch the drag show. She did flirt with me, but she's not my type."

"She's not?"

"I'm less into the flirtatious lesbian-Casanova type and more into the charming, down-to-earth, beautiful baker type." Charley shook her head. "I left the club after I saw you in the bathroom, and I haven't seen Autumn since. And you don't have to apologize. I want to apologize. That's why I ordered these cupcakes and tricked you into meeting me here, so I could try again. Sorry about that by the way. I'd like to get on board this true-to-yourself-honesty idea with you, if you'll let me."

Amy bumped her hip against Charley's as they walked. "Remember how easy it was in elementary school to be honest? You could just pass a note that said, 'I like you. Do you like me? Check box yes or no.'"

"I would check yes," Charley said.

Amy blushed. She wanted nothing more than to kiss Charley again, to feel the fireworks she knew would come from that, but she knew the honesty part needed to come first this time. "Then why did you end things?"

Reaching the wooden benches, Charley and Amy sat down with the boxes of cupcakes between them. "I didn't mean to end things," Charley said. "Really, I just needed some time to process. I'm an engineer. I'm methodical. I like to take my time considering things. After moving to Tulsa, I was feeling adventurous, like maybe being in a new city and a new job meant I could be a more daring person. And everything with you when we first met felt so right. Like fate, if I believed in that kind of thing."

"We did have a perfect first date," Amy said.

"We did." Charley looked at her lap as she twisted her hands together. "I liked you so much that I was scared. I just moved to this new city for a new job that I love, but it's time consuming and stressful and has a steep learning curve. Then there's this beautiful, charming woman who I can't get out of my head, and I like her so much that I'm losing focus at work. And besides, you were so sure, so ready to go all in, and I was still wrapping my head around the idea of you." She paused, looking up at Amy. "Does that make sense?"

Amy nodded.

"And then it's New Year's Eve," Charley went on. "I'm still trying to figure out what I'm doing in Tulsa, if I'm ready for a relationship. And then I meet all of your friends at once, you tell me you love me, everyone's all excited about Joel and Damian's engagement, and Joel tells me that I've got to get serious or get out." Charley buried her face in her hands for a moment, then reemerged. "I panicked. My brain needs time to process all of that. Especially you saying you loved me."

"That was my fault," Amy said. "I was so wrapped up in the moment and had all of those weddings and engagements on the brain. I realize now that I was going way too fast because I thought that was what I wanted too, that love had to happen fast. I'm sorry that I—"

Charley held up a hand. "Please, don't apologize! You didn't ask me to marry you; you said what you were feeling in the moment. And that's something I actually really like about you."

Amy felt a rush of relief. Charley was right. It *was* what she had felt in the moment, and she shouldn't regret being honest about it. "That's true. But I didn't mean to put you in a weird position."

"But maybe I needed to be put in that position, even if I handled it poorly," Charley said. "I wanted to say it back. I really did. But I've never said that to someone I've dated before. So I ran. And then I sent you those texts asking for some time."

Amy looked away, trying to hide the tears forming in her

eyes. All the pain she'd felt that day returned as a faint memory, less sharp than before but still there.

Charley continued. "And then I took some time to figure myself out, to think about why I'd reacted like that, why I couldn't just let a good thing be good instead of analyzing every possible way it could go wrong. I took inventory of what I want, what I like, who I want to be with, and everything kept pointing back to you. I was finally working up the nerve to talk to you again, to ask for your forgiveness, when I saw you at Rampage. And realized that I was the reason you got fired from Daily Bread. I felt terrible. I still feel terrible, Amy."

"You weren't the reason," Amy said, turning back to Charley with tears rolling down her cheeks. "Homophobia is the reason. I knew I was living a lie at the bakery, and I knew the risks that came with that. I wish I'd never . . ." She sniffled. "I wish I hadn't put myself in that position, hadn't gambled with my own identity. But I don't blame you for that."

"You don't deserve that pain." Charley cupped Amy's face in her hands and wiped her tears away with her thumbs. "I wish I could take it all back."

"I don't," Amy said, smiling through her tears. "I learned so much from that messed-up situation. I learned what I'm capable of, and I learned that I deserve better, even if I'm still figuring out what that looks like. I shouldn't have to hide or change myself to make other people more comfortable." She reached out a hand to caress Charley's neck. "And I met you."

"Here, come with me." Charley stood, pulling Amy up with her, then led them to the center point of the bridge, stopping at the circular pattern on the ground.

As they entered the circle, the sounds of downtown traffic, chirping birds, and other Tulsans enjoying the spring weather disappeared. Charley took Amy's hands in hers. "I'm sorry."

Sorry. Sorry. "I want to try again." *Again. Again.* "And . . . I love you." *Love you. Love you.*

Amy felt a smile stretch across her cheeks, her joy as wide as the bridge on which they stood. She wrapped her arms around Charley. "I love you too."

Amy's words echoed as their bodies met in a long-overdue kiss. And unlike after the last time they'd kissed in the exact same spot, Amy didn't worry about who might see them. The longer they held each other, the more the confusion and ache of the past several months shifted into something that felt even stronger for having healed. Something that felt right.

After a few minutes, Charley shifted their embrace out of the circle. "Do you remember what occasion I placed the cupcakes order for?"

Amy furrowed her brow. "An anniversary?"

Charley nodded. "I was hoping this could be ours."

Amy's heart melted like warm ganache. "I did say I'd like to go back to our first date and start again, didn't I?"

"Does that make this our . . . zero anniversary?"

"Happy zero anniversary." Amy kissed Charley again.

Charley led them back toward the cupcakes and flowers waiting on the bench. After sitting down, Charley pulled a box to her lap and took out two strawberry champagne cupcakes, handing one to Amy. "You know, the second greatest tragedy of New Year's Eve is that I never got to try this cake."

"True," Amy said with a sideways glance.

Charley peeled back the paper and took a bite. Her eyes lit up as she licked a spot of stray frosting from her lip. "Amy, this is the best cake I've ever eaten." She took another bite, her face a picture of pure pleasure. "The frosting is so light, and the fresh strawberry in the cupcake? Perfection. I can't believe I missed out on this."

Amy grinned, delighted. She leaned forward to kiss Charley,

this time tasting the flavor of strawberries and vanilla on her lips. “Wait till you try my butterscotch cake. And my blueberry-lemon muffins. And my caramel cheesecake. And my—”

Charley stopped Amy’s words with another kiss. “I want to try it all. But take your time. I’m not going anywhere.”

Epilogue

TULSA WEDDING FAIR
Saturday, April 29, 2023

Two couples approached Amy's booth, where a third was flipping through a book of photos on display.

"Hi!" Amy said. "Queerly Beloved Weddings is a full-service LGBTQ-wedding-planning business with in-house event coordinators, photographers, bakers, DJs, bartenders, and more. We also offer an endorsed list of queer-friendly vendors, wedding locations, dress and suit boutiques, bands, and officiants."

"Do you help coordinate destination weddings as well?" asked one of the new arrivals, who was wearing a tank top that read "TWO GROOMS ARE BETTER THAN ONE" across the chest. "My fiancé and I are talking about having a beach wedding."

"Yes, we do," Amy said. "Hey, Joel!"

Joel turned from his place a few yards away, where he was handing out minicupcake samples. "What's up?"

Amy gestured for him to join them. "Joel, my co-founder, was also one of our first clients. His wedding was in Hawaii back in 2015. Since then, he's headed up our destination-wedding planning, including researching queer and queer-friendly vendors across the globe."

Joel gave the potential client a charming smile. "I also travel to coordinate the big day, if you want someone onsite. Where are you thinking?"

As Joel detailed their services, someone else approached Amy. "Excuse me. You said you have DJs, right? Can I hire a DJ without using the full suite of services?"

Amy pulled a business card from behind the table. "Certainly! We can help with any part of your wedding, no matter how big or small. Our DJ, Jae King, recently won a Best of Tulsa Award. Here's their card. They should be here later this afternoon as well if you want to learn more." The person accepted the card and took a cupcake with a promise to get in touch.

Damian and Zee arrived at the side of the booth, pulling Amy's attention away from the eager potential clients. She'd tasked them with spreading the word about the Queerly Beloved Weddings booth throughout the convention center. Even after she'd been participating in the Tulsa Wedding Fair for seven years, the organizers still tucked Amy's booth into a dark back corner. But the Queerly Beloved Weddings team always found a way to get the word out to potential clients. And over the years, Amy had become the premier LGBTQ wedding planner in the region. "We're out of flyers," Damian said. "There are so many queer couples here, they're practically flying out of our hands. Do you have extras?"

Amy dug beneath the table and emerged with a stack of

papers advertising their services plus two water bottles. "Here you go. Don't forget to stay hydrated!" Zee gratefully took the flyers and water, and the two of them disappeared into the crowd again.

McKenzie appeared at Amy's side with an empty tray. "The cupcakes are a hit. I've already talked to at least a dozen couples who want to learn more about our pricing."

After McKenzie had become Amy's protégé at the bar, Amy had started training her in the art of baking. Now she'd become a crucial part of the Queerly Beloved Weddings team, dreaming up beautiful cake designs and creating unique craft cocktails to fit each couple's theme.

Amy smiled. "It's definitely your limoncello cake that has them coming back for more. Nice work."

McKenzie pursed her lips in concern. "I think Gracie was right about the frosting, though. Swiss meringue buttercream would be better. I'll workshop it."

The couple flipping through the book of photos paused on a full-page spread of first kiss pictures, and one of them looked up to say, "These are beautiful. Were they taken by your in-house photographer?"

"Yes, Tala Hemady. She's fantastic," Amy said, looking down to see that the couple had paused on one of her favorites: an image of her mother and Dr. Douglas just after their "I Dos." Max and Greg, Teresa's men of honor, were visible behind her in matching seersucker suits, wiping away happy tears.

"Does she do engagement photos too?" The potential client smiled and extended their left hand. "We just got engaged on Valentine's Day."

Amy grabbed their hand and examined the diamond ring. "It's beautiful! Congratulations to you both! And yes, Tala takes wonderful engagement photos. She would be here today, but she actually had a conflicting photo shoot. There are some examples in here, though. She books up fast, but I bet she could squeeze you in next month." Amy flipped to the back of the album, where the engagement photos began.

"Wow, I love her use of light." The couple looked through a few more pages. "Wait, is that you? With the pearl ring?"

Amy fidgeted with the same ring on her left hand and smiled. "Yes, it is."

"When were these taken?" asked the other potential customer.

"A few years back," Amy said. "Our wedding was perfect, thanks to our team. And I'm not saying that just because I'm the founder and CEO."

As if on cue, Charley appeared behind her with a full tray of cupcakes. "You're in good hands with my wife." She kissed Amy on the cheek before stepping aside to arrange the samples on the tiered display.

The couple returned to the photo album, and Amy pulled away from the booth for a moment, snaking an arm around Charley's hip. "Thanks again for your help today, Char. I know we should be celebrating our anniversary, but I'll make it up to you tomorrow."

"It's always a good anniversary as long as I'm spending it with you," Charley said. "And as long as I get cupcakes."

"Oh my God," another customer exclaimed as they stepped forward. "You're Amy Fariner! My fiancée and I drove all the way from Arkansas to visit your booth. We saw the article about you in *Out* magazine last year, and I've been obsessed ever since."

"I'm honored!" Amy held out a hand. "I'm Amy. What's your name?"

"Lily, she/her." The woman grasped Amy's hand, her eyes wide. "And this is my fiancée, Winona, she/her. I'm so excited to meet you. Your photo spread in *Real Weddings,* like, completely inspired my wedding vision. The cake that shot rainbow sugar bubbles into the air? Mind-blowing! How did you do it?"

"A little inspiration, a lot of sugar, and an engineer wife," Amy said with a wink. She looked around at her friends-turned-colleagues running the booth, overwhelmed with gratitude for the twisting path that had brought her here. She turned back to the couple in front of her. "But that's enough about me. Let's talk about your special day."

Amy's Strawberry Champagne Cupcakes

Perfect for any occasion but especially when celebrating love of all kinds.

Yield: About 30 cupcakes

Cupcake Ingredients:

½ cup champagne
1½ cups all-purpose flour, plus a few additional tablespoons
2 cups cake flour
1 tablespoon baking powder
1 teaspoon salt
1 cup (2 sticks) unsalted butter, room temperature
1¾ cups sugar
4 eggs
2 teaspoons vanilla extract
¾ cup whole milk
10 ounces fresh strawberries, hulled and finely chopped

Cupcake Instructions:

1. Preheat oven to 350 degrees. Pour the champagne into a measuring cup and set aside to allow the carbonation to release. Line cupcake pan(s) with cupcake papers and set aside.

2. Sift together 1½ cups all-purpose flour and all of the cake flour, baking powder, and salt in a medium bowl.

3. In a stand mixer with paddle attachment, cream butter on low to medium speed until light and fluffy, about 2–3 minutes, scraping down the sides of the bowl as needed. Add sugar and beat for another minute. Beat in eggs one at a time. Beat in vanilla.

4. With the mixer on low speed, add the following ingredients in this order and mix after each addition until just combined:

⅓ of flour mixture, milk, another ⅓ of flour mixture, champagne, final ⅓ of flour mixture.

5. Toss chopped strawberries with a few tablespoons of all-purpose flour. (This will help them stay evenly suspended in batter instead of sinking.) Fold strawberries into batter.

6. Divide batter among cupcake papers, filling each ¾ full. Bake until cupcakes are beginning to brown and cake bounces back when lightly pressed, about 18 minutes. Transfer pan to cooling rack and cool for 5 minutes, then remove cupcakes from pan to cool completely.

Buttercream Ingredients:

1 cup (2 sticks) unsalted butter, room temperature
¼ teaspoon salt
1 teaspoon vanilla extract
1 pound (approx. 2 cups) powdered sugar
¼ cup champagne
4–6 fresh strawberries, hulled and finely chopped
A few tablespoons milk (any variety, optional)

Buttercream Instructions:

1. In a stand mixer with paddle attachment, cream butter on low to medium speed until light and fluffy, about 2–3 minutes. Add salt and vanilla.

2. With the mixer on low, gradually add the pound of powdered sugar, alternating with a tablespoon of champagne at a time if the mixture becomes too dry. Add chopped strawberries.

3. Test for flavor and texture. If too thick, add remaining champagne or a few tablespoons of milk. Pipe or spread frosting on cooled cupcakes.

Notes:

- To make nonalcoholic, use sparkling cider or ginger ale in place of champagne.
- If you want an added kick of champagne flavor, brush cupcakes with a small amount of champagne as soon as they come out of the oven.
- Top iced cupcakes with strawberry slices or chocolate-dipped strawberries if desired.

Acknowledgments

First, thank you to every reader who chose to pick up this book. It took me a long time to believe anyone could care about a flour-covered lesbian in "flyover country," and the fact that you gave Amy's story a chance means the world to me.

This book wouldn't exist without the brilliant mind and kind heart of my editor, Katy Nishimoto. I wrote the book I wanted to read, and Katy helped me transform it into a book that other people might want to read too. Katy, I'm so grateful our paths crossed at exactly the right moment.

A huge thank-you to my agent, Jamie Carr, who is the best cheerleader and publishing whisperer I could ever hope for. May you have a lifetime supply of perfectly flaky croissants.

I love working with the phenomenal team at the Dial Press and Random House, a home for *Queerly Beloved* that is beyond my wildest dreams. Special thanks to Whitney Frick, Andy Ward, Avideh Bashirrad, Debbie Aroff, Maria Braeckel, Madison

Dettlinger, Susan Turner, Donna Cheng, Sarah Horgan, Cara DuBois, Sarah Feightner, Liz Carbonell, Frieda Duggan, and Nicky Watkinson.

Thank you to everyone at Book Riot, my favorite corner of the internet. The book world is a better place with all of you in it.

My heart belongs to my beautiful queer family / quarantine pod, who laughed and cried and stressed and celebrated with me through every step of this process: Trey Johnston (my true love), André Sanabia, Rebecca Cásarez, and Ally Johnston. And thank you to the friends who supported me just as much but from slightly farther away: my bestie, Jordan Gates, Anne Jessup, Sinovia Mayfield, Catherine Roberts, Meredith Nelson, Megan Zorch, and Noura Hemady.

I wouldn't be the writer (or the person) I am today without my parents, April and Ralph Dumond, who fed my childhood hunger for books and love me unconditionally. Thank you to my grandmother Nila Dumond, who shares my lifelong love of reading. I'm grateful for the unwavering support of Diane Britton, along with that of all the other folks I counted as family long before they officially became my in-laws.

A special thank-you and belly rub to Waffles, the best dog in the world, who never left my side during the writing and editing process. Thank you to Maple, the best cat in the world, who pushed me to be a better writer by staring at me judgmentally from the window like *Oh,* that's *the best you can do?*

And finally, thank you to my wife, Mary Jessup. Very early in my publishing journey, I said, "Wouldn't it be wild if I actually became a published author someday?" Mary said immediately, "I figured you would be from the beginning." Mary, thank you for believing in me way before I believed in myself. Our love story will always be my favorite.

Queerly Beloved

Susie Dumond

A BOOK CLUB GUIDE

Liz Parker, Author of *All Are Welcome*, Interviews Susie Dumond

Liz Parker: Let's start at the beginning. Tell me the backstory of writing *Queerly Beloved*.

Susie Dumond: I didn't really write *Queerly Beloved* expecting it to be published. I just wanted to see what happened if I put words on a page, and I wrote the story that I wanted to read. I've always loved rom-coms, and I want to see more queer rom-coms in the world. I am by no means Amy, but I love weddings and I'd never been a bridesmaid. I was frustrated because, for the second time, my wife was a bridesmaid and I was doing all the bridesmaid duties for her because she hates being a bridesmaid. I was like, "I would be an excellent bridesmaid. I'm crafty, I'm a good time, I can do whatever, I should put myself on Craigslist." This was a running joke for a while, that I should be a Craigslist bridesmaid. Thus Amy was born when I decided to try writing a book. So I had this idea, I had a blast writing it, I wasn't planning to do anything with it, and then I broke my leg pretty massively. I couldn't even stand up or put any weight on it for six months. So I was like, *What else am I doing? I might as well edit this book and see what happens.*

LP: That is awesome. So why set the book in 2013?

SD: I knew that it was going to have a wedding plot, and I thought there was this really interesting tension in the years leading up to marriage equality, this "will it happen, won't it happen?" It seemed like it would never happen, especially in a red state in the middle of the country. You can't foresee this ever happening, but on the other hand, there was so much momentum and so much was happening so fast. I really liked the tension of that moment, and I liked putting Amy in a situation where she had to grapple with it. And then I put her in these situations with her friends where she had nuanced conversations that I remember having with my friends in those years about what this does and doesn't do for queer liberation. It's not nothing, but there's so much more that needs to be done. Also, not as many queer stories were being published in 2013. The ones that were being published were often mainstream voices, so I think there's a dearth in queer history from this period of time in those "flyover" states.

LP: Charley is really sweet, but also subtly dynamic as a character. Talk to me about how she came to be on the page.

SD: I love Charley. I was putting myself into this mind frame of *Who is this dream lesbian who's going to walk into the bakery?* But in a lot of ways, she serves as a foil to Amy. Amy is a people pleaser; she often bends herself in uncomfortable ways to make other people happy, to hide herself if that's what it takes. Charley is like, "This is who I am. I have big goals, and I don't really care what you think about it." I think that's important for Amy to see on her journey and something she can learn from Charley. I also wanted to see a love interest who is a little masc of center. There are some really fantastic sapphic romance novels, but I feel like so often it's femme / femme situations, and that's great—there's definitely a need for that—but I wanted to see a little bit more of a butch love interest, and I wanted that person to be very sexy and desirable.

LP: What was your favorite wedding to write?

SD: The weddings were some of the more propulsive and fun parts for me to write, because I was just like, *What all can I make go wrong?* I definitely enjoyed writing the peacock cake scene. I giggled the whole time I wrote that scene. But the rest of that wedding is pretty uncomfortable and tortured, minus meeting Regi and Jared. I enjoyed the chaos of the winter wonderland wedding in a barn, which was very DIY. I wanted to see Amy in a place where everything is falling apart on her, and she's struggling to tie it all together and make it happen. All the weddings were fun in their own way and chaotic in their own way.

LP: Do you think Amy is ever going to be a bridesmaid again?

SD: She's definitely a bridesmaid for Damian and Joel. I believe she'll be a bridesmaid for all of her friend group from Ruby Red's. She's maid of honor for her mom's wedding. But she's never going to be a bridesmaid again for a stranger.

LP: We should talk about your decision to write Amy as someone who is semi-closeted in Tulsa. What drove you in that direction?

SD: Something that Amy grapples with in the book is this false idea that coming out is a one-time thing, that you come out once and you're permanently out to the world. In reality, it's so much more complicated than that. You're negotiating the boundaries of being out every day, every time you meet someone new. I wanted to show that, and that it's even more complicated in a place like Oklahoma, where the stakes are higher. The kind of rejection and even violence you can face tend to happen more frequently. You have less certainty that when you come out, people will be welcoming of that. Often, being out also means losing opportunities. Amy wanted to be a better baker, this is something she wanted for her career, and she had the choice: Do I get the job and the tools and the education I need if it means hiding who I am? Or do I give up on the thing that I really want to do? It was important to me to show how complicated coming out can be and also moving toward a place where she feels more comfortable being out in more contexts in her life.

LP: How do you feel a place like Tulsa has changed from 2013, when the book is set, to now?

SD: There are a lot of problems that are still present there, but I have to say that in the almost ten years since the book is set, Tulsa has changed. If people's opinions haven't changed, they've maybe learned that their opinions aren't necessarily popular, at least nationally. Amy's story of being fired from the bakery—that's still legal; that could still happen. But I have to hope that there would be more of an outcry from people in the community. I have to hope there would be some op-eds saying, "Don't go to this place, they fired someone for being gay." I hope that part of her story would be a little more complicated, but it's still technically something that could happen and there would be no legal recourse for Amy.

LP: When did you get married?

SD: I got married on Halloween 2020, our favorite holiday. My wife and I had been together for ten years at that point, six years before same-sex marriage was legalized across the country. We witnessed a lot of that history happening within our relationship.

LP: So what was it like getting married during a pandemic while writing a book full of weddings?

SD: It was a lot of weddings! When I started planning our wedding, it was going to be a big wedding in D.C. at the National Zoo. It was going to be a big costume party, a lot of fun. But going to vendors and bridal fairs even in the D.C. area, I was shocked at how heteronormative everything was. I brought my gay best man with me to these things and people assumed we were the couple, even though we were looking our gayest. I really wished for something like Amy's business while I was going through this process. But then the pandemic happened, and our plans changed. We ended up having a tiny pandemic wedding, and I think that highlighted that a marriage is more important than a wedding. It was still a lovely day; we were able to have a very small group of immediate family and a few friends to support us, but it wasn't at all the big shindig we were planning to throw. I do feel the difference between being married now, in a way we couldn't have been for the first six years we were together. The emotional resonance of marriage is really important and also the legal benefits of being married in a global health crisis, when we wouldn't have been able to visit each other in the hospital if one of us got sick. It made me appreciate the institution of marriage, if not the process of weddings.

LP: What was your favorite scene to write, and what was the hardest scene to write?

SD: The epilogue was a lot of fun, because when the whole situation of Amy being a bridesmaid for hire popped into my head, at the same time, the final business idea also popped into my head. I saw a happy ending for the characters, and it was so satisfying to have it all come together in the epilogue. For hardest scene . . . I have to be honest, and as a romance author this is embarrassing to say, but I struggled with the sex scenes. It felt very invasive to be in Charley and Amy's bedroom even though I created them. But I found what helped was thinking of it like songs in a musical. You can laugh at me for this if you want to. If a song is in a musical, it has to be furthering the characters' stories, building the characters in some way. What new thing are we going to learn about the characters through this sex scene / song? That's how I approached it and it helped a lot. I really like where they ended up.

LP: That leads me to a question that I think every reader is interested in, even if only tangentially. Tell us about your writing process.

SD: I basically had an idea and sat down to write it, beginning to end, with no plan besides knowing Amy would have this professional bridesmaid job pop up and she would end with this wedding business. That's literally all I had. My first draft had a lot of heart, and there are a lot of characters and moments that stayed the same, but there were also a lot of revisions with my agent, Jamie, and my editor, Katy, to get it where it is. It grew so much through that process. For my next book, which I'm already working on, my process is so different from when I went in without a plan.

LP: You have a plan for your next book?

SD: I do, yes. It's proving a lot easier to write when I have a little bit of a plan. It was a lot of fun sitting down with a blank page and being like, what do I feel like writing today? Do I feel like making a wedding? Do I feel like making a bar scene? That was an interesting process, but I'm not sure it's how I'll approach it in the future.

LP: Do you think you'll stay within the rom-com category?

SD: For a while. I have some ideas for rom-coms that I love, and I do, deep in my heart, love rom-coms. But I'm also a Gemini, which means I get bored if I do the same thing too much so I have to mix it up. I have a lot of ideas in other genres as well.

LP: I love it. Furthering the gay agenda within the romance genre is so critical. We like to read too!

SD: Yes! And I also have another genre that I'm obsessed with: historical fiction. I want to see a lot more queer historical fiction because queerness existed; we just don't hear about it because those aren't the stories that were recorded. I think being able to go back and show what queer lives looked like at different points in history is crucial.

LP: That's so true. What's your advice for aspiring LGBTQ+ novelists?

SD: There's still plenty for me to learn. But based on my experience, I would say, write the stories that you want to read. Partially because that just gives it so much more heart and makes it more dynamic than writing stories you think other people want to read. But also because you're going to end up reading it a lot throughout the editing process if you want to publish. If you don't like reading it, you're going to be in trouble.

LP: That's great advice. What are some of your favorite LGBTQ+ books?

SD: There are so many, and I'm really thrilled with how many amazing queer books are coming out these days. To name a few on the more recent side, anything by Akwaeke Emezi. *Dear Senthuran* is changing the form of memoir. I know they have a romance coming out soon that I can't wait to get my hands on. I loved *Cantoras* by Carolina De Robertis. It sticks with me. I think about it all the time. *Detransition, Baby* by Torrey Peters totally blew me away. I also love the essay / memoir space in queer literature. *The Groom Will Keep His Name* by Matt Ortile, *Here for It, or, How to Save Your Soul in America* by R. Eric Thomas, and anything by Samantha Irby makes me laugh out loud. And can I say your book, *All Are Welcome*? Is that cheating? I absolutely loved *All Are Welcome.* I think it's so fun to play with stereotypes around queerness, and I think your book does a great job of subverting those stereotypes, but bringing them in when they're fun.

LP: Thank you! I loved your book. I really loved it. And I'm glad we could do this.

SD: Thank you so much! This was a blast.

Questions and Topics for Discussion

1. How does Amy's family of origin, her mom and her extended family, inform who she is and what she believes? How do her chosen family—Uncle Max and Uncle Greg, Joel, and Damian—do the same?

2. Are there people in your life who have become your chosen family? Discuss how they have contributed to the person you are today.

3. Have you ever had an experience like Amy did at Daily Bread in which you felt you could not be your full, genuine self in the workplace or another setting? How did you navigate that?

4. Amy doesn't tell Charley about being fired from Daily Bread because she is ashamed to admit that she knowingly took a job working for homophobes and planned to keep quiet about her

sexual orientation. Do you agree with her decision to hide this information from Charley? If she had been honest, how might it have changed the development of their relationship?

5. Ruby Red's represents safety, home, community, and acceptance for so many of the characters in this novel. Do you have a place in your life that feels like your Ruby Red's?

6. How does Amy and Joel's friendship evolve over the course of the novel? How do you think their big fight contributed to their growing understanding of themselves and each other?

7. How does Amy's relationship with Charley evolve over the course of the novel? How do they complement each other as characters and romantic partners? What do they learn from each other? What qualities about each of them do you admire the most? The least?

8. Amy is hesitant to tell Charley about her new business as a professional bridesmaid. Why do you think Amy chooses not to share this with Charley?

9. Amy's former relationship with Autumn is highlighted throughout the novel. Why do you think the author chose to introduce Autumn to readers?

10. McKenzie is first introduced as Autumn's date at Ruby Red's shortly after her twenty-first birthday, and eventually Amy takes her under her wing. Why do you think Amy chooses to do this? What impact do McKenzie and Amy have on each other?

11. By the end of the novel, Amy becomes good friends with Regi, the first bride who employs her as a bridesmaid. How does this friendship impact Amy's life?

12. Amy meets her former manager's daughter, Gracie Young, at Ruby Red's. What does Gracie gain from this conversation? What does Amy gain? Why do you think the author chose to introduce this character?

13. Some of the LGBTQ+ characters in the book discuss the pros and cons of leaving Oklahoma. Why do you think they choose to stay? How does staying in Tulsa affect them and their community?

14. Amy turns to baking as a form of stress relief and self-care. What about baking comforts Amy? Do you have an activity or hobby like this that you turn to when you're feeling anxious?

15. If *Queerly Beloved* was turned into a movie or TV series, who would you cast in the lead roles?

16. How do Amy's beliefs about herself and the world around her change by the end of the novel?

PHOTO: MARY JESSUP

SUSIE DUMOND is a queer writer from Little Rock, Arkansas. She is a senior contributor at *Book Riot*, where she writes a monthly Horoscopes and Book Recommendations column as well as various quizzes, book lists, and bookish news pieces. Dumond received a bachelor of arts from the University of Tulsa and a master of arts in public policy and women's, gender, and sexuality studies from the George Washington University. Currently, she's probably making cupcakes at her home in Washington, D.C., with her wife, Mary, her dog, Waffles, and her cat, Maple.

susiedumond.com
Twitter: @SusieDoom
Instagram: @susiedoom

About the Type

This book was set in Baskerville, a typeface designed by John Baskerville (1706–75), an amateur printer and typefounder, and cut for him by John Handy in 1750. The type became popular again when the Lanston Monotype Corporation of London revived the classic roman face in 1923. The Mergenthaler Linotype Company in England and the United States cut a version of Baskerville in 1931, making it one of the most widely used typefaces today.

Random House Book Club
Because Stories Are Better Shared

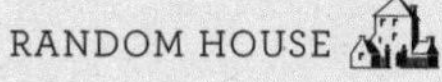

RANDOM HOUSE